FORCED ENTRY

I lunged across the console and punched the transmitter. "We've got four of MA's finest on our tail. Unless you want all five of us splattered across your field, let us in!"

But there was no response from Port.

Another volley of beam fire from the closing pickets sent a shudder through *Raptor*'s deck plates.

The hell with them, then! I decided abruptly. "Take us in. If they don't like it, let them lodge a protest." *Raptor* dipped in a sudden spiral as a beam of brilliant orange appeared off our starboard side.

"Return fire—high beams! Fry them all!" If we were caught—and there seemed no way we wouldn't be—I was damned if I'd go down without a fight.

PRISONER
OF
DREAMS

KAREN RIPLEY

A Del Rey Book
BALLANTINE BOOKS • NEW YORK

A Del Rey Book
Published by Ballantine Books

Library of Congress Catalog Card Number: 89-91659

ISBN 0-345-36162-8

Manufactured in the United States of America

First Edition: November 1989

Cover Art by Barclay Shaw

CHAPTER ONE

Anyone who knew me at all, as a freightman or as a woman, would have known that this was not the kind of thing I usually did. But I'd been bumped, outbid, skunked; what choice did I have?

This is how it happened. I was sitting in the food dispensary at Welles's at Port on New Cuba, barely three blocks from the scene of my royal screwing over by Transystems, drowning my sorrows in the biggest, greasiest chunk of formedsteak I could eat. While I was furiously chewing away, an oily-looking man in a skintight jumpsuit slid into the seat across from me. The autoserver promptly kicked in, its mechanical voice chirping, "Welcome to Welles's, the premier dining area in all of—"

"Gimme whatever she's got," the unctuous man interrupted as the autoserver droned blithely on. He leaned across the grease-streaked plastiplex table that separated us and said without preamble, "Heard you got skunked out of your load."

"Fine, thanks, and how are you, Rollo?" I replied, ruthlessly chucking a cube of steak half the size of my fist into my mouth.

"Hey," Rollo responded, raising his hands placatingly and flashing a practiced smile. "I don't make the news, sweetie, I just collect it."

The autoserver had finally come to the end of its recorded spiel. Its input circuits had already logged Rollo's premature order; now it emitted a cheery "Your request is being processed. Thank you for your patronage!"

"So," Rollo continued, leaning closer over the table, "what's the story?"

I glared up at him, still chewing viciously. It seemed that if you ordered an expensive enough formedsteak, you even got formedgristle in the damned thing. "What story?" I retorted. "I thought you knew everything?"

Rollo stroked his palms over his chest, smoothing the already wrinkleless fit of his trim maroon-and-navy jumpsuit. "I do," he acceded brightly. "But I thought I'd hear your version of it."

Rollo was an exasperating little creep, but you could never tell when you might need him. That thought alone kept me from decorating his expensively sculpted head of hair with the rest of my greasy solace dinner. Automatically, I glanced around the food dispensary. At that time of the day it was nearly deserted; most of the cramped and littered tables were empty. What few patrons there were, mostly Class Threes—Welles's was upport, after all—paid us scant attention. Most of them were either Port workers, distinctive in their tomato-red jumpsuits, or else Authority employees, garbed in Military Authority's cream and maroon or Civilian Authority's cream and navy. They were people used to minding their own business; it would probably take a minor riot to attract any interest. As the autoserver obligingly disgorged Rollo's order up through its table slot, I gave him a capsule version of my recent woes.

"I had contracted with Transystems for three priority-freight hauls," I explained reluctantly. "I'd already made two of them. Now they tell me I've been underbid on the last one."

"Ah hah," Rollo said, daintily slicing into his formedsteak. "Teamsters?"

I stabbed at the last ball of a substance that resembled a potato—it was best not to consider just what it might actually be composed of—and stuffed it fiercely into my mouth. "Yeah, Teamsters," I grunted, most of my old fury returning as I was forced to review the situation.

"Transystems is joinin' nuts letting Teamsters in!" I finished vehemently.

Rollo, fastidiously licking his lips, merely shrugged. "So they skunked you," he summarized dispassionately.

"Well, it wasn't the first time," I said gruffly, "but it sure as hell'll be the last!"

Rollo made a *tsk-tsk*ing sound, expertly spearing a strip of formedsteak. Dangling the meat before his lips, he remarked casually, "MA's got a priority run . . . if you're interested."

That little scab! The guy was a regular carrion bird, always hovering around waiting for some sudden death. I glared at him. "What the hell would the Military Authority have to haul that I could stow on *Raptor*—the collective pea-sized brains of all the Upper Council?"

"The Upper Council is half Civilian Authority," Rollo corrected automatically, impaling another strip of meat.

"Military Authority, Civilian Authority—what's the difference?" I retorted. I repeated a popular and scathing remark that called into question both the sexual preferences and the eating practices of both the MA and the CA. Rollo's perfectly arched eyebrows lifted slightly at the graphic comment, but he continued to calmly eat his steak.

"One run," he elaborated. "Advance fee." He named a figure that was hardly spectacular but nearly twice the fee of my trashed Transystems run.

"Advance fee?" I repeated reluctantly. The only thing worse than getting mixed up with MA or CA was getting mixed up with Rollo; here was my chance to go for the whole ball of wax. Rollo was a Class Three, an Authority liaison, playing both ends against the middle. He was slick, all right. Already, I knew I was in trouble.

"Maybe even a bonus if you beat the priority haul time," he said, dangling the bait without conscience. He knew where to hit.

"So what's the damned cargo?" I demanded.

Rollo finished chewing the piece of steak he had in his mouth, swallowed discreetly, and neatly wiped his lips with a napkin. "No cargo, just a passenger."

I leapt to my feet so quickly and so heatedly that I nearly sent my empty plastic tray sailing off the table. Several nearby diners started, caught sight of Rollo's maroon-and-navy colors, and then studiously ignored us. "Join that, Rollo!" I exclaimed. "I'm not running any damned slave—not for MA or anyone else!"

Rollo eyed my outburst distastefully, wincing at my use of the term "slave." He dabbed at his mouth again. "Indentured Servant, Jo, not slave," he corrected me quietly. "You know there's no such thing as slavery in the regulated worlds. Besides, he's going to Heinlein."

"You tell me what the difference is between an IS and a slave, then!" I snapped. "Forget it—I don't do meat runs!"

I stared furiously at Rollo, but the little man merely continued calmly devouring his meal. I'll give him this, he was a cool piece. No wonder both of the A's found him so useful. Finally I gave up and slowly sank down on my bench again. I figured by then that Rollo already knew he had me. I sure as hell knew it.

"Who the hell gets indentured to Heinlein, anyway?" I grumbled peevishly, toying with my plastic fork.

Rollo glanced up at me, much as if my outburst had never occurred. "It is unusual," he conceded, "but that's where this guy is assigned." He deftly sliced another strip of formedsteak and skewered it with the tip of his knife. "You've made runs to Heinlein before," he noted. "And MA trusts you."

"Wonderful!" I remarked with a sarcasm that was undoubtedly lost on Rollo. "That's what makes my life worth living!"

Rollo looked up at me again; beneath his perfectly drawn brows his round dark eyes were as opaque and oily as a lubricant dump. "So?" he said. "You want it?"

I snapped the stem of my plastic fork between my clenched fingers. "No, I don't 'want' it!" I told him grimly, mentally adding, You cod-swabbing little asshole! "But I *need* it and I'll take it!"

"Good." Rollo's manicured fingers dipped into the breast pocket of his immaculate jumpsuit. He extended a small plastic card. "Lewis, C. A. You can get him at the Authority Block anytime after oh-seven-thirty tomorrow."

I reached across the table and snatched the ID card from his fingers. I stuffed it into the hip pocket of my blue-and-gold flightsuit without even glancing at it and got to my feet. "I won't forget this, Rollo, old pal," I said.

"Oh, say, Jo?" Rollo piped up, as I turned to move away from the table. "Could you catch this for me?" He gestured at the remains of his formedsteak meal. "I seem to be a little overextended again in my credit accounts, and—"

I smiled very sweetly at him and saluted him with a certain graphically derogatory gesture that had lost neither its impact nor its popularity over the centuries. "Cram it, Rollo," I suggested succinctly.

Outside Welles's, on the crowded throughway, I took a deep breath of the rank, half-cycled air and felt my lungs burn. The greasy formedsteak was already making an unpleasant lump in the pit of my stomach. New Cuba's atmosphere was technically compatible with human requirements, but that was the planetary air in general; the air in the settlement always seemed unbreathable, thick with the effluence of recyclers, especially foul to those of us long used to ship's oxygen-rich mixture. For a CA-sponsored planet, New Cuba had some of the worst service utilities I'd ever seen. The natural atmosphere was humid and wretchedly hot. In a few more years pollution was going to make the place uninhabitable—not that it would be much of a loss. I headed up-port, nodding now and then to any passing freightmen I knew. There were no words exchanged; the throughway was simply not a social setting. Most of my fellow pedestrians seemed doggedly intent on getting somewhere else. They were dressed either in flightsuits or in some variation of the ubiquitous jumpsuit or coverall. The future of fashion was function, and post-War clothing tended to be prosaically utilitarian. Like most marginal commerce worlds, New Cuba's population was a highly transient one. Most

of the group I ran with had probably already sealed cargo
and lifted off the dump. All of them that hadn't gotten
skunked, anyway. All of them that hadn't met up with
that little twerp Rollo. Most of the people I knew there
didn't even live on-planet; they were, like me, merely
passing through the place in the process of trying to make
a living. Ironically, the very thing we had in common—
our presence in that port—was the one thing we were
least eager to acknowledge. And of the people who were
actually residents of New Cuba, I counted the ones I
knew—merchants, mechanics, dockmen, business con-
tacts—as just that: acquaintances, not friends.

I felt a hand land on my shoulder. I spun around,
confronting a big man in a flightsuit and face wraps,
carrying a beam rifle in a shoulder sling. His eyes, huge
and unblinking, peered out at me from behind the gray
wraps. It was Raydor, my second.

"Finished at that grease-pot so soon?" he inquired
mildly.

Raydor had a heavy-gravity-worlder's casual contempt
for eating meat—even pseudomeat. He, like most of his
kind, was a vegetarian. Their metabolism was slower,
ideally fueled by complex carbohydrates. But he tolerated my carnivorous ways, especially when he knew I
needed some comfort.

"I ran into that little rat's ass Rollo," I announced.
Raydor was silent, plodding along beside me without
comment as I continued to move up the throughway. Hell,
no one ever just "ran into" Rollo; Rollo intersected you,
like a remote going in for the kill, when and if he wanted
you. "We got a cargo," I continued.

"MA?" Raydor guessed.

I glanced over at him—over and up, really, since he
was nearly a half meter taller than me. "Yeah, an IS for
Heinlein."

I didn't expect much of a reaction, and Raydor didn't
disappoint me. His big eyes, all clear cornea with irises
as swimmingly dark as his pupils and no hint of white
sclera showing, betrayed no surprise. Raydor was Tachs,

a Class Five; behind his concealing face wraps, he was unfathomable.

Although the Class system had little to do with pedigree, it had a lot to do with heredity, and although it had nothing to do with a social register, it ultimately had everything to do with one's rank and privilege in life. The Classes were the most enduring legacy from the Old War—what they used to call the Nuclear War back on Earth. Ironically enough, as these things went, that had been so long ago that no one now living was even first-generation Altered. But the Classes seemed to be with us for good.

Supposedly, there were ten Classes, based on degrees of physical and genetic damage, but I had yet to see a Class One. Sometimes I thought they were just a fabrication, like the almost mythic Talents, something to keep the Class Twos in line. I was a Class Two. That meant that my phenotype was normal and that I was genotypically fit to be allowed to reproduce. Class Threes, like that worm Rollo, were phenotypically normal but genotypically Altered. Class Fours had mild, usually reparable physical abnormalities and Altered genotypes. Class Fives, like Raydor, had more severe physical deformities, although they were functionally sound. And so on down the line, worse and worse, until you got to the Class Tens, who, rumor had it, apparently approximated a platter of mixed veggies.

The Genetics and Reproduction Code enacted by the A's had brought some semblance of badly needed sanity and species survival to the disastrous postholocaust genetic upheaval. Other than the mysterious Ones, Twos were the only Class that the A's allowed to reproduce, although who—or what—you joined was your own prerogative. Of course, Twos were encouraged to join Twos for reproduction or, failing that, at least to make a donation at the nearest germination center if they were in too much of a hurry for natural reproduction. There was always a waiting list of surrogate Threes and Fours. I had never donated ova; I knew it would always gnaw at

me somehow if there were children somewhere half-mine
who would never know who or where I was.

Raydor was from Tachs stock, heavy-worlders. His
people were a closely knit, genetically stagnant sect of
agrarians who, centuries ago in the infancy of the Authorities, had defied the A's and their Code and had continued to reproduce naturally. Banished to a worthless
high-gravity planet—which they had patiently converted
into an agricultural paradise—the Tachs generally kept to
their own. All of them were Class Threes or less; most
were Fours or Fives. Raydor had the frame and form
typical of Earthheart's high gravity. His physical deformities were mainly facial; that's why he had to wear the
concealing face wraps off-ship on regulated worlds. The
A's never failed to repay the Tachs for the insubordination: They were one of the few ethnic groups who were
not considered Citizens unless and until they left their
home planet, and they were the only group subject to the
face-wrap law.

Neither the nature of our passenger nor his destination
appeared to disturb Raydor. He just looked calmly at me
and asked, "When do we get him?"

I fished into my flightsuit pocket for the plastic ID.
"Any time after oh-seven-thirty," I replied, fingering the
card.

"Want me to clear us with Port and confirm the Heinlein pass?" he asked me.

I rubbed the hard edge of the card with my thumb.
"Yeah, go ahead." I smiled up at him grimly. "I'm going to pop this guy into Handyman and see what I've
gotten us into!"

Port on New Cuba was immense; in fact, there really
wasn't much else to the settlement on New Cuba except
the port. The only kind of agriculture the planet was
suited for was the primitive kind of scruffy stuff they used
to make formedfood. No one grew realfood there. There
was a little mining, mostly the marginal, self-sufficiency
kind, and a quarry for poured-rock—most planets had
plenty of one thing: rocks. There weren't any ores plen-

tiful or valuable enough to excite any large-scale refining. New Cuba's main claim to fame was that it had been the first outpost established in that fairly unremarkable system. Although the planet had been CA-sponsored, both of the A's still had large installations there, and New Cuba's port was still the hub of most of the in-system trade.

Before the damned Teamsters had begun to worm their way in, New Cuba had been the kind of port where an independent freightman such as myself could be pretty well assured of sealing a cargo. It was starting to look as though all of that was changing, though. I was thinking that after this Heinlein business, we might jump system and try something farther out, somewhere near the Rim, where deregulated planets abounded. I knew Raydor wouldn't object. He was tired of the A's, tired of the damned face wraps.

I crossed the pedestrian gantry over the CA's port facility, nodding to the few Port workers I recognized on sight, and rode the pneumatic down to the ground level. Along the margins of the hangars, where crates and pallets piled with shipping containers were stacked, the dockmen maneuvered ground lifters in tedious trails amid the mountains of cargo. Most of the laborers in port were Altereds, Class Fives and Sixes, whose lower status made it difficult for them to receive the training needed to qualify for higher-paying jobs. But, surprisingly, they were probably the closest thing to a permanent population New Cuba had, and I knew several of them by name. My footsteps tapped hollowly over the speckled gray composite of the gigantic hangar's flooring, a surface that glistened with New Cuba's perpetual mist. The air there was curiously fresher than it had been on the throughways, smelling only of ejected exhaust and the hot ozone smell of overworked wiring. Puffs of vaporized fuel roiled along the floor of the bay, knee high. I felt like I was striding through the clouds.

She sat in bay 21-B, perched like a hawk among the chickens: my ship, *Raptor*. Named for a long-extinct class of predatory animal, she loomed like a great bird of prey. She crouched there on the scorched composite, her graceful keel arched, her long curved solar vanes bent back like sharp wings against the sleek silver lines of her body. I always felt a secret rush of pride whenever I saw her, no matter how briefly I'd been gone.

Raptor was officially registered as a short-haul freighter, licensed to seal priority cargo. She had been converted from a private-use passenger vessel, and so her cargo capacity was relatively small. But she was quick, efficient, and quite illegally armed. Most of the runs I made were short hops, freighting priority gadgets for the likes of those bozos at Transystems. But I occasionally made longer runs, even cross-system runs when the price was right, and I hadn't always been real fussy about cargo manifests. I had also hauled passengers a few times when all else had failed. But never for MA—and never an Indentured.

I palmed the landing lock, and *Raptor* dilated her hatch, welcoming me aboard. Inside the short access corridor I breathed with relief the cool, clean air of my own habitat. I strode up the passageway to the Main Integration room. The hatch had a palm panel access keyed only to Raydor and me. The hatch opened with a gentle hiss; inside, in Handy's domain, the room was warm and dry and bright. In direct contrast to the neutral whites and tans and steel-grays of the rest of the ship's interior, Handyman's bulkheads sparkled a cheery yellow-gold—his favorite color.

I sealed the hatch and pulled up a chair. "Hi, Handy," I said.

Handy's panel lights flickered to life. "Hi, Jo," he replied, his voice a rippling bass. Before me, the entire wall pulsed with the Integrator's massive circuitry. His red Access Open signal winked steadily. As I leaned forward, keying his Functions screen, I asked Handy, "Ready to leave this dirt-ball?"

"One dirt-ball is pretty much like another to me, Jo," he reminded me with a dry humor.

I think that a lot of people found it convenient to forget that Integrators weren't just machines; they were people, too. Actually, they were BMIs—Biological Matrix Integrators. Their function cores were built on a matrix of cells from a living brain: something that was once a human being, with all the experiences and emotions of a sentient creature. But in our way we had familiarized them. Even a miracle, when it becomes commonplace, is trivialized. Handyman was part of what had once been a man; he'd had a name, an identity, a life. When his natural life had been lost and he'd been Integrated, he'd lost all that. So I had given him back a name. No one needed to give him a personality; he already had that himself!

"What can I help you with, Jo?" Handy asked expansively.

I held up the plastic ID card. "We've got a passenger. He's an IS." I paused, but Handy didn't comment. "What can you tell me about him?" I asked, popping the card into the SCAN slot on Handy's console.

Handy's circuitry hummed softly. A few minutes passed. "It's deep," he finally announced. "They've buried this guy good."

"But can you get it?"

Handy made a snorting noise, a sound that was somewhat disconcerting when it came from an Integrator's speaker. "Of course I can get it," he asserted confidently, as if to believe anything less would be ridiculous. Even a BMI had his pride.

Behind me, I heard the hatch crack. I glanced back at Raydor; he had removed his face wraps, and the neck of his blue and gold flightsuit was unfastened, as if he were relieving himself of some near strangulation. New Cuba was starting to affect me in the same way. "We've got pull clearance," he told me, his eyes on Handy. He gestured. "He get it?"

"He will!" I grinned.

Unconsciously, Raydor rubbed one big callused hand across his now-exposed face. It was a little reflex gesture that I'm sure he wasn't even aware of. The face-wrap regulations were a crock; I couldn't imagine anyone being offended by the way Raydor looked. Even when the

relatively rare Class Three Tachs reproduced, they usually produced Fours or Fives. The Alterations had done
their work on Raydor, but he was hardly repulsive. His
scalp was hairless, and he had only rudimentary eyebrows and lashes. His eyes themselves were large, nearly
lidless; his gaze was unnervingly intense, and when he
did blink it was startling, like a snake striking. His nose
was flattened, with elongated slits for nostrils. His skin
was pleated and soft, like crepe, and very lightly pig-
mented.

I had shipped with Raydor for over eight years, since
after my mother died; I figured I knew him as well as I
had ever known anyone. In a lot of ways he was the only
family I had. Well, him and Handy.

"I've got something," Handy announced, a touch triumphantly. "Wait, I'll screen it."

Handy's Functions screen flickered, then lit. A chain
of bluish letters marched eerily across the viewer. Raydor leaned over my shoulder peering at the data flow.

LEWIS, CHARLES ALAN . . . T639/H0716/X138
ORIGIN: DNOF
DOB: DNOF

The stream of information bled on; most of it was MA
crap that made no sense to me: dates of hearings, com-
plaints on file, detention sites. Some of it might have
been CA's input; they could be expertly obscure in their
handling of civil law. I couldn't figure out what the hell
crime he'd been indentured for, but that lapse hardly surprised me.

Then the holo flashed onscreen, a blurry image of an
even blurrier man. He was young, barely my own age,
from what I could see. But there was one thing that puzzled me: He looked normal. I had expected a Class Five
or Six or at least an unrestructured Class Four. Who else
would get indentured? Nearly all criminal punishment
was levied as fines; only Class Fives or less were so low
in the economic strata that they would be unlikely to be
able to pay off their debt.

"Can you get any better definition on that?" I asked Handy.

The holo froze and shimmered. The dark, thin normal face wavered in and out of focus. "That's the way it's keyed," Handy finally conceded.

Raydor and I traded a quick glance. For some reason my palms were suddenly extraordinarily sweaty. I surreptitiously wiped my hands on the knees of my flightsuit. "I don't get it," I muttered, mainly to myself. "How the hell did this guy get indentured?"

The stream of data on Handy's screen was winding to a close. The blue figures slid on, a glowing trail:

    MA TERMINUS: UNALTERABLE
    DISPOSITION: INDENTURED
    DESTINATION: HEINLEIN
    CLASS: TEN

            —ENDIT—

The inexplicable feeling of dread that had been slowly building in me since I'd left Welles's suddenly burst, and I felt the sweat soaking through the back of my flightsuit. I stared numbly at the Functions screen and at the last bits of information caught there, the ghostly blue letters that spelled out our doom. I heard Raydor stir behind me, and I turned in my chair, locking eyes with him.

"Shit!" I said.

CHAPTER
TWO

At some time a little after oh-ten-hundred Raydor and I traveled the pneumatic to the Authority Block. I hadn't asked him to come with me, and he hadn't exactly offered; he was just there, his face wraps properly in place. Raydor knew how I felt about having to deal with MA. I was grateful for his company, because I knew how he felt about MA, too.

Although I was eager to get off-planet, I was determined not to show up too early. The hell with them; let them think I really didn't want the run. By that time, thanks to the data Handy had unearthed, I genuinely wasn't so sure I wanted the run anymore.

The Authority Block was one of the oldest buildings on New Cuba. That meant it was better constructed and had more conveniences than most of what came after, since it had been erected in that first flush of development when the planet had been settled. Things always seemed to go downhill after that, especially where the A's were concerned. Either A could sponsor a planet; MA obviously was interested in worlds with some strategic importance, while CA considered things like natural resources and trade routes. I doubt that New Cuba had been hotly contested. Although it had originally been sponsored by CA, there was a large MA garrison stationed there, and the upper levels of the Block were devoted to MA offices.

The Block was really more of a pyramid, a gigantic steel and extruded-concrete structure checkered with tiny square windows. It was just bizarre enough to not be totally ugly. I'd been there before, but I'd never managed to figure out the layout of the place. So when we popped out of the pneumatic and into the receiving area, I punched the schematic index on the Block Integrator to find out where to go.

"State name and business," the Integrator's speaker intoned solemnly.

"Jo-lac, of *Raptor*," I replied, adding to my name the formal suffix that denoted I had been carried and nursed by my biological mother. "I'm here to pick up a passenger for Heinlein."

The Integrator muttered electronically to itself. I imagined a giant bank of circuits permeating the Block, an endless living matrix, a glistening multitude of hypertrophied brain cells secreted behind those dull steel and plastiplex walls. How many BMIs served the Block? I wondered. There was more intelligence there than in any of the humans in MA, I was sure of that.

"Insert cargo ID," the Integrator instructed.

I dipped into my pocket, produced the card Rollo had given me, and fed it into the Integrator's input slot. The card disappeared with a soft hum.

I rocked back on my heels, glancing sideways at Raydor. His eyes, hooded beneath the face wraps, rolled expressively, nearly making me grin.

At last the Integrator's screen lit, flashing a schematic diagram of the Block's interior. "You are cleared for entry, Captain," it informed me, disgorging the ID card. "Please follow the directions indicated on the schematic."

"Thanks," I replied, pocketing the card again. The unexpected little pleasantry caused the lighted diagram to flutter briefly. I think the Integrator was actually abashed.

Raydor and I entered the lift and rode to the fifth level. Behind the gray wraps Raydor was silent but watchful. We came to the Block once a year, as required by law, to renew our freightman's permits for the sector, but all that was handled by CA on the lower level. We had never gone up into the gullet of the beast before. I found the acceleration in the lift distinctly unpleasant.

On the fifth level we followed the schematic's directions to an accessway marked with the MA logo and a sign reading EXPORTATION. I punched the buzzer, and the door cycled open. Inside, an expressionless woman in a cream and maroon jumpsuit turned from an Integrator console and inquired tersely, *"Raptor?"*

I nodded. She rose, gesturing for us to follow her, and led us across the anteroom. The next door was palm-accessed. As we stepped through, she stood aside, sealing the door behind us.

"Hey, Jo," a familiar voice greeted me. Rollo sat on the edge of a large platform desk in the center of the office, his legs dangling. The room was bright, barren, sterile. "I was starting to think you'd changed your mind," he continued cheerily.

I stared at him; the little jerk was everywhere, just like lint! "What's your joinin' hurry?" I retorted, being deliberately rude.

"We're in no hurry, Captain," a quiet voice responded. "Though it seems that most freightmen usually are."

I had been so surprised to find Rollo there, I had momentarily overlooked the man seated behind the big desk. He was trim, gray-haired, and erect, dressed neatly in MA's cream and maroon. He had lieutenant's braid on his sleeves and collar and the kind of fixed, bland expression that looked like it had been peeled out of a mold. A Class Four, I guessed, Restructured. His face was too tightly perfect, too symmetrical, to be normal. He rose snakelike to offer me one slender, boneless hand. "Jessup," he supplied.

I took his hand, touching it briefly. His skin was cool and dry, like the featureless office. He already knew who I was, so I didn't belabor the point. Behind me, I heard Raydor shift slightly. Jessup acted as if he didn't exist.

"If we can just get this guy and get going," I began tactlessly.

But Jessup cut me off with a wave of his hand. "A few formalities, Captain," he interjected.

I threw Rollo a sharp glance; he merely shrugged and spread his hands, absolving himself of all responsibility. If the little bastard had set me up—I stared evenly at Jessup, forcing myself to remain calm. "What 'formalities'?" I asked levelly.

"Just your cards, Captain," Jessup said. "As soon as they clear Integration, you'll have your passenger."

Unreasonable panic lanced through me; it took all of my will to keep from taking an involuntary and automatic step backward. Hell, I'd been carded before: every year at permit renewal, if nothing else. Raydor and I were in order. What was making me sweat this time?

"Sure," I said smoothly, fishing for my plastic ID. From behind me, Raydor passed me his card, and I presented both of them to Jessup. He turned silently to his Integrator access panel. I looked to Rollo, but the little worm turned his head, casually studying his nails, avoiding me. Suddenly I was very glad for Raydor's familiar bulk behind me. I would have been even gladder for Raydor's equally familiar beam rifle, but that was back on *Raptor*. You couldn't carry weapons into the A Block. Right then, Raydor himself was the closest thing to a weapon that I had.

Now, why the hell was I thinking about weapons? Suns, I was jumpy! I breathed slowly and deeply, forcing myself to relax. Although my anxiety made the wait seem interminable, I'm sure it was only a few minutes before Jessup turned from his scan screen and extended our IDs to me.

"Captain," he said evenly, his Restructured face perfectly bland. Then he snapped his comm switch, leaning over its speaker. "Medical, this is Jessup," he announced. "Send me Lewis."

I stabbed a sharp glance at Rollo. "Medical?" I hissed, not caring if Jessup heard. "What the hell is this? Is this guy sick? Or drugged?"

Rollo automatically flinched away, avoiding my eyes, but Jessup calmly answered my question. "Just routine,

Captain; examination and immunizations. MA regulations.''

MA regulations—as if that would explain everything! This time I glared directly at Jessup. ''What about my fee?'' I demanded. Now that my ID was safely back in my pocket, I didn't care if I was being rude.

''Disbursements has already keyed half of your fee to your credit account,'' Jessup explained smoothly. ''The other half will be keyed when your transfer is made at Heinlein.''

''Wait a minute!'' I wheeled on Rollo, who shied away from me like a spooked horse. ''You told me advance fee, you slime-joining little—!''

''Captain,'' Jessup intoned reasoningly, ''it's standard MA procedure: half fee in advance, half on delivery.''

I still glared at Rollo, whose eyes rolled convincingly. The Classless bastard; he *knew* the rules—and he'd known that I wouldn't. I turned to Jessup. ''What's to keep you from skunking me on this once Heinlein's got your boy?'' I grumbled.

Jessup's face was coolly placid. ''You've dealt with MA before,'' he reminded me. ''We've got no reason to cheat you. You do your job, we may do business again.''

Not joinin' likely! I thought fiercely, but I bit back the words. ''Who's my contact on Heinlein?'' I asked instead, still feeling more than a little belligerent.

Jessup tapped a plastisealed packet on the desk before him. ''It's all here, in your manifest,'' he explained. ''All you need to do is deliver the passenger and your job is finished. Then we key the second half of your fee.''

The door behind us hissed softly open, and a green-suited medtech entered. She was of indeterminate age—another Restructured Class Four if I had my guess—with closely cropped dun-colored hair and arms like a dock-worker. One of her powerful hands gripped the forearm of our passenger. The medtech stood him to one side of Jessup's desk. Then she nodded respectfully and said, ''Sir.''

Jessup returned the nod, a curt dismissal. The woman set something on Jessup's desk, something plastisealed, like the manifest. Then she disappeared back through the doorway, and I got my first good look at C. A. Lewis.

Jessup gestured. "Sit down, Mr. Lewis." It was more command than pleasantry, but Lewis merely stood there, his stare unblinking.

He was the man in the fuzzy holo that had fluttered on Handy's viewer screen, but nothing I had seen there had prepared me for the reality of him. The holo hadn't captured him any more than had the meaningless march of the mumbo-jumbo data on Handy's screen. None of that had anything to do with this beautiful, wretched man.

He was fairly tall, nearly my height—and I wasn't used to finding unAltereds anywhere close to my own size— and slightly built, a fact that was only exaggerated by the baggy, ill-fitting green med tunic and trousers they had clothed him in. His shaggy hair was so black that it looked almost blue against the sickly pallor of his skin. More startlingly, his eyes were a brilliant sky-blue—a color rarely seen anymore, since the gene for blue eyes seemed to have had the misfortune of sharing the same sinking ship of a chromosome with several other physical traits that had been neatly sabotaged by the Alterations. His brows and eyelashes were heavy, nearly sooty. His nose was just a little too long and narrow, pleasantly imperfect, and his full mouth was just slightly crooked, like the promise of a wry smile. His entire appearance, his delightful irregularity, was so much more than Normal. He was normal—a damned Class Ten, and he was *normal*.

I was standing there, bluntly staring. Lewis returned the scrutiny, his eyes direct but lifeless. If Jessup had told me the truth—and I had no reason to believe that he had—and Lewis wasn't drugged, then there was something else radically wrong with him. His gaze was vacant, like there was nothing alive behind those amazingly blue eyes. Either MA had rearranged his brain for him or he had the intelligence of a turnip. I wasn't sure which idea was more appalling, more disappointing to me.

I snapped my eyes back, sweeping my gaze over Jessup and Rollo in one continuous, contemptuous roll. "Let's get at it, then," I said abruptly, reaching for the manifest.

"Just one more thing, Captain," Jessup said quietly, pinning the manifest packet to his desk with one hand. He picked up the second plastisealed packet.

I rocked back slightly on my heels, furiously willing my racing pulse to slow. "Now what?" I asked suspiciously with a sense of exasperation I didn't try to conceal.

Jessup cracked the plastic seal on the second packet and disgorged its contents across the desk top toward me. It was a narrow metal circlet: a detention cuff. Its mate must have already been fitted to Lewis's wrist, unnoticed beneath the baggy sleeve of his ugly green tunic. The cuffs were MA's cheap insurance policy. Once activated, they functioned as a pair. If the two devices were separated by more than a quarter kilometer or if either of the pulses they were attuned to were to cease, the explosive charge planted in each circlet would detonate. It would be a very messy way to break off a close relationship.

I glared furiously at Jessup's imperturbable face. There was no point bothering to glare at Rollo; the little cockroach had practically crawled back into the woodwork by that time. "What the hell's the idea, Jessup?" I demanded indignantly.

That MA toady just spread his hands, smoothing down the edges of the torn plastiseal wrapper. "Standard procedure, Captain," he replied calmly.

I leaned over the desk, my teeth nearly bared, adrenaline burning in my veins. " 'Standard procedure,' my ass! Since when does MA use a detention cuff on an IS?"

Jessup gazed up evenly at me. "It's standard procedure for deregulated worlds like Heinlein, Captain," he reiterated. One neatly drawn brow arched. "If MA's procedures aren't satisfactory to you, perhaps you'd prefer not to make this run . . ."

Void take him! I glowered at Jessup, my hands tightening into fists, too angry to feel any sense of fear. He knew I couldn't afford to back out. If it ever got around that I'd agreed to a run for MA and then didn't seal the cargo, my already anemic chances of picking up any more hauls in the system would be royally shot to hell. Not that the system was looking so joining attractive to me anymore, but you had to be practical—and MA was everywhere. The cod-sucking bastard had me, and he knew it.

I felt the breath go out of me with a muted hiss. "All right, damn you," I said tightly, extending my left wrist.

"No!"

The hoarse cry froze me, and I suddenly felt the powerful grip of Raydor's fingers on my shoulder. It took me a few seconds more to realize it was not Raydor who had spoken. It had come from Lewis.

I glanced back to Raydor, then over at Lewis. I locked eyes with Lewis, both excited and frightened by the outburst and by whatever had prompted it. But those brilliantly blue eyes had gone dead again, and there was nothing there.

Jessup, his arms braced over the desk, looked merely annoyed at the interruption. I felt Raydor's big hand slide slowly from my shoulder, releasing me. He would never interfere. Perspiration crawled inside my suit liner, dampening my armpits and belly with an unpleasant clamminess. Quickly, with a false casualness I hardly felt, I extended my arm again.

Jessup snapped the narrow metal band around my wrist and keyed it. "Your contact on the other end has the code," he informed me brusquely, his impatience obvious, as if all the MA-bred greasy civility had worn off him at once. He shoved the sealed manifest at me from across the desk, eager to be done.

The cuff seemed to burn where it touched my skin; its unaccustomed weight dragged at my arm. I pushed it up under the sleeve of my flightsuit. "So what the hell's the idea?" I persisted. "You think I'd dump him somewhere—or space him? Just fly out with half my fee and never make the damned run?"

Jessup's brows flattened, his voice a hard rasp. "It's been done," he noted cynically.

"Yeah? Well, not by *me*!" I retorted angrily, seizing

the manifest. I wheeled on Lewis. "Come on!" I headed for the door, not waiting for a response. I don't know whether Lewis would have moved on his own, because Raydor was instantly at his side, guiding him after me. We were, after all, quite literally inseparable now.

I never paused to look back, not at Jessup, that bureaucratic ass, or at that slimy little Rollo. I marched out through the barren little anteroom, past that automaton in cream-and-maroon, and out into the maze of the Block's featureless corridors. I was halfway to the lift before I glanced back to find Raydor right at my heels, his hand locked around Lewis's elbow.

Waiting for the lift car, I eyed Lewis skeptically. Almost without will, my gaze drifted to his arm, dangling limply at his side. The too-short sleeve of the baggy green med tunic no longer concealed the deadly mate to my detention cuff. Lewis's wide-set eyes stared back unnervingly at me, his gaze vacant and direct.

Several things about all this were already bothering me—above and beyond the fact that I was now the second member of a two-man walking bomb. I punched the lift button, and Raydor herded Lewis in. Somehow my stomach managed to drop faster than the car did.

In the Block's cheerless lobby I strode across the polished floor. "Jo-lac of *Raptor*!" I growled irritably at the Integrator before the standard inquiry was even out of its speaker. To my surprise, the Integrator remembered my earlier courtesy to it. "Have a nice flight, Captain," it responded, sincerely, I was sure.

Out on the throughway, I found myself suddenly gasping for breath in the stinging air. I motioned Raydor toward the nearest pneumatic. We rode in silence, Lewis leaning helplessly against Raydor's bulk when the car suddenly changed directions and dipped into curves without any warning. The pneumatics were mass transit designed by sadists; the damned things were like a roller coaster ride, but they were efficient and they were free. As we stumbled out at the Port exit, I reached for Lewis's unresisting arm.

"Go square our docking fee," I briskly instructed Raydor. "We're lifting."

Raydor nodded and cut off across the concourse. I began to haul Lewis after me. He could be manipulated like a mechanical; he seemed to have only one expression, and it was not one of interest or opposition. His cheap med-issue shoes clacked obediently across the tarmac of the mist-capped hangar bay as I led him to *Raptor*. Once we were inside, I stowed him in the small cabin just off of Control.

"You're not a prisoner," I explained to him—uselessly, I thought, and downright falsely as well if the detention cuffs were taken into account. "I just want you out of the way until we're ready to lift." I pushed him onto the padded acceleration couch, where he promptly collapsed like a folded tent. His blank eyes watched me without a trace of reproach as I grimly sealed the hatch.

Up in Control I sank into my familiar pilot's chair with a grunt. "Handy?" I said.

On Console, the Integrator's lights winked to life. "Ready, Jo," came the easy rumble.

I ripped open the plastic seal on our manifest. "I'm going to feed you our coordinates," I told him. "Please give me the plot and our ETA."

"Of course, Jo," Handy replied agreeably.

I pushed the oblong course-card into the Navigation access slot. While Handy's hypertrophied neurons mulled over the preset course, I leaned back and let my own merely mortal neurons chew over something just as crucial.

Just why the hell was Lewis so important to MA that they would go to all that trouble? And if he *was* so important, why was he on his way to Heinlein as an IS? Why was he wearing a detention cuff, a device usually reserved for Terminals, those rare criminals whose Citizenship had been revoked, and not Indentureds—who were, after all, still Citizens and not normally subject to arbitrary disintegration? Why an IS to Heinlein at all, for that matter? They took immigrants, but damned few of them, and the occasional odd Volunteer, but I'd never heard of an IS being sent to Heinlein.

And if Lewis was so damned important, this unique IS to Heinlein, why was he going out on *Raptor* and not on some MA carrier? Why was he going with *me*?

And just who—or what—was he, anyway?

CHAPTER THREE

Say what you will about thermonuclear devastation, but if it hadn't been for the War, we'd probably all still be sitting around on Earth with our thumbs up our asses instead of out frantically colonizing every rockpile planet in the known systems. It was the red-hot push of radioactive contamination that had catapulted my ancestors out into space, forcing them to scramble, to learn more about interstellar travel and survival in a few short decades than man had managed to learn in thousands of years of civilization. Nuclear war had ravaged Earth, of course, and for decades it was uninhabitable. But maybe that wasn't such a bad trade-off: We got space. Then again, we also got things like the Alterations, the Classes, and the A's. Even war isn't perfect.

The two Authorities were the system of government that had evolved after the Old War, forged out of chaos, from the remnants of the pre-War civilization. Certain nations—what they had once patronizingly called the "Third World"—had initiated the conflict, and ultimately it had decimated their populations. The Civilian Authority had been formed from the pacifist survivors of the neutral nations, the Military Authority from what had remained of the martial forces of the combatant nations. But MA was literally "people-poor"—there was almost no one left. They had the technology and still much of the hardware to head spaceward, but they needed bodies. So MA was forced to accommodate CA, because that was where most of the trained people were. The two A's

entered into an uneasy alliance, forming the Upper
Council to coordinate the push to the stars. Ostensibly,
the two Authorities were equal, but the CA had always
been careful to maintain the upper hand in the things that
mattered. No one wanted to try a second round after the
Old War. The most valuable asset in the universe wasn't
material wealth or military strength; it was Citizenship.
And only the CA had the power to confer or revoke Citizenship. For all their flaws, the A's basically worked,
and we had never had interplanetary factions or war.

I wasn't waxing quite that philosophical as I ran the
prelift checklist through Handy's Control input. Philosophical matters ended where that detention cuff began
as far as I was concerned, and all I was feeling was a
bad taste in my mouth from all of New Cuba and a
powerful desire to finish the run and be somewhere
else.

The schematics for our pull trajectory spread across
my Navigation screen. Handy tinkered with the image,
pulsing the key figures for my benefit. Navigational
mathematics had never been my strong point. As I studied the screen, I heard the hatch unseal behind me. Without turning, I said to Raydor, "We clear?"

"Yeah," Raydor replied, dropping into the copilot's
chair beside me. He had come directly from the Port
Authority and still wore his face wraps.

"Then let's get the hell out of here. Handy?"

"Ready, Jo," came the prompt reply. The schematic
was shifting, stripped to its essentials, rotating into a
more graphic representation.

"Get us up," I told him.

Raptor had independent manual ground-lift capacity,
but she was still far from maneuverable. Planetary gravity tended to make her wallow. I usually let Handy take
her up because wriggling out of those damned hangar
bays was a tedious and nerve-racking job, requiring a
cool patience I didn't feel capable of at the moment. The
lifters engaged with a rumble, and *Raptor*'s nose dipped
slightly. The deck plates shivered beneath my feet. Then
the ship began to pivot, creeping forward across the tar-

mac, sending the hanging layer of perpetual vapor shooting away beneath her belly like the parting of the Red Sea.

Port's amber lights winked at us as *Raptor* edged past the lip of the bay. Once we cleared the structure, the lights switched to green. I leaned back in my contoured seat, bracing for the acceleration of lift. Handy took her up gently so that the force was moderated and predictable—my usual manual lift was more like an old-fashioned rocket ride. I relaxed, letting the G-force flatten me agreeably into the chair. I didn't mind that part. Gradually the pressure released me, and I leaned forward again as *Raptor*'s artificial gravity stabilized. The Navigation screen was displaying a climbing series of altitude figures.

"Assuming coordinates for potential entry into the magnetic pull," Handy announced calmly, "pending Port's release."

I turned to Raydor, who was bent over the comm board. "Go get Lewis," I instructed him. "I want him up here where I can keep an eye on him when we go to pull."

Raydor got to his feet and disappeared through the hatch. I leaned over the console, running the prepull checklist through Internals.

Strangely enough, as such things are wont to go, the secret to hyperlight travel had shown up where no one had theorized or anticipated it would. It had been just a lucky discovery, the accidental by-product of some obscure metallurgical research. But the utilization of the magnetic acceleration pull had revolutionized space travel and made the kind of work I did not only feasible but commonplace.

I'm no physicist, and I'm not going to attempt to explain the mechanical principles of the pull. To greatly oversimplify—which is the only way it made any sense to me—we were able to exceed the limits of light speed by artificially accelerating the effects of the natural magnetic pull that exists in space between even the farthest-flung planets. Somewhat of a disappointment, I'll admit, since I'd always thought that something like dilithium crystals or hyperdrive had a little more romance to it than something as prosaic as two large metal-bearing bodies calling to each other.

Tapping into the pull required a very precise initial centrifugal force and a very specific trajectory; otherwise you'd end up Powers knew where—even, theoretically, right back where you started from. For that reason, Integrators always performed the calculations and executed the actual pullout. And around regulated planets like New Cuba, Port always controlled the pull traffic so that no one got fried.

Pulling out wasn't exactly the most pleasant sensation known to man, but generally it was only mildly stressful. Still, I wanted Lewis where I could see him. If whatever drugs those vipers at MA had plugged him full of could affect his ability to withstand the pull, I wanted to be the first to know. I had more than a casual or humanitarian interest in his survival.

When Raydor returned to Control with Lewis, I motioned absently toward one of the ancillary chairs at the rear of the compartment. My primary attention was still on the Navigation screen, where Handy was negotiating with Port for our slot in the pull spiral. Raydor gently pushed Lewis down into the padded contour chair and strapped the network of the body harness over his pliant body. I spared Lewis a glance then, enough to see that he was almost languorously calm. He slumped will-lessly in the chair, his blue eyes inanimate and disinterested.

"We're starting our circle into holding," Handy informed me, "waiting on Port."

"Thanks, Handy," I replied. I reached for my own harness, fastening the catches with practiced dexterity. Being put into the holding circle usually meant a variable wait, but I decided to be optimistic. Maybe after my little display back at the Block, MA would be so happy to get rid of us that they'd expedite our departure a little.

Raydor slid into his chair, adjusting his outsized harness. His big hands danced over the comm board. He hooked the small cordless pickup over his head, keying in on the muted chatter that crackled endlessly between Port and the other ships approaching pull. On the Navigation screen the stylized schematic of the pull point twirled like a gaudy whirlpool. Handy, responding to some query from Port, began to feed them the coordinates from our manifest.

Then Handy remarked, "Good. We're up next."

I stretched slightly, surprised at the tension that was cramping my muscles. I pressed back into my chair until I felt my spine pop. I always felt a little jumpy going into pull, but this time that antsyness was tempered by a healthy dose of eagerness. Out of the corner of my eye I could see Lewis's green-garbed figure slumped spiritlessly in the ancillary chair. I found myself hoping they'd give him some decent clothes when he got to Heinlein; that med outfit looked ghastly on him.

Beside me, Raydor suddenly straightened up in his chair. His large head cocked quizzically to one side. Then he flipped a switch on the comm board, and the audio burst over the speaker with a snarl of static:

"—Heading oh-seven-oh to your five-five-nine. Repeat: This is Redding of *Nimbus; Raptor,* respond."

I exchanged a rapid look with Raydor but held up a restraining hand as the incoming message repeated.

"*Raptor,* this is *Nimbus.* We have the stats on a navigational hazard heading oh-seven-oh to your five-five-nine. Please respond, *Raptor.*"

Behind the hooded hollows of his face wraps, Raydor's dark eyes widened, but I dropped my hand to his thick forearm, thinking furiously. I knew Redding only slightly, more by reputation than by personal experience. We'd hit the same ports at the same time on a few occasions over the years. *Nimbus* was a distance freighter, a huge amalgamation of cargo pods that plied the fringe routes like a gypsy queen. Redding had a reputation for shunning the A's and working only free-lance, something I had always found suspicious, given the size of *Nimbus,* but something that still seemed vaguely admirable to me.

"Handy—" I began, but the Integrator's soft growl interrupted me. "Negative, Jo," he avowed, having anticipated my query. "I get nothing."

I leaned forward in my harness, reaching in front of Raydor to punch the transmit button on comm. "*Nimbus*, this is Jo-lac on *Raptor*. Our screen is clear, and we're up next for pull."

Static exploded again. Then Redding's voice returned, his tone more intense. "Negative, *Raptor*! You have a hazard in your blind spot—heading oh-seven-oh."

One of the many disadvantages in starting to pull out was that damned blind spot, an area beyond your entry spiral where the magnetic flux could mask something the size of a small space station. If another object was present on the edge of your spiral, it had the unfortunate tendency to distort your arc. If the object was large enough—say, a ship—your acceleration would abruptly be cut, and your ship would fly apart. That was the reason for Port's proprietary interest in regulating pullouts. They were supposed to keep "navigational hazards" off the edge of your spiral. Which is why I was overtly skeptical of Redding's report, since Port was on the verge of clearing our pullout.

I glanced over at Raydor, who shrugged stoically. Leaning over the transmitter, I demanded, "*Nimbus*, what have you got? I repeat: Our screen is clear, and Port has us up next."

There was a moment's hesitation, filled only with comm's empty hum. It occurred to me that Redding was definitely sticking his neck out for us. Port was surely monitoring the exchange, and word would get back to MA: CA ran Port, CA was in bed with MA, and MA had their nose in everything—especially, it seemed, Mr. C. A. Lewis. I couldn't fathom his reason for it, either. It certainly wasn't for old time's sake.

"*Raptor*, what is your heading for pull?" came Redding's delayed response, an oblique inquiry if ever I'd heard one.

"*Nimbus*, we have heading five-five-nine, up next for

pull," I reiterated, playing along. "What is your hazard?"

Again there was a hesitation, punctuated by a grumble of static. When Redding came over again, his tone of voice was subtly altered. "*Raptor*, we suggest aborting pull. Repeat: Abort pull."

Before I could respond to that startling idea, Port gave us clearance to go to pull. The transmission flitted stolidly across Handy's screen. "We're up," Handy informed me, nonplussed. "Do we go?"

Do we, indeed! I thought wryly. I was aware of Lewis at the periphery of my vision, shifting in his harness, his dark head lifting. But then comm was demanding my attention again.

"*Raptor*," came Redding's voice again, tenaciously, grimly, "if you cannot abort, we suggest substituting heading five-seven-five. Repeat: Substitute heading five-seven-five." There was a brief pause, then Redding's final pronouncement. "Or you're going to spin out and fry, *Raptor*."

Adrenaline began to leapfrog through my veins. As I squirmed in my chair, Handy's screen displayed another message from Port.

"Port is rather eager for us to get started," Handy explained serenely.

Join Port! I thought fervently. I punched the transmit button again. "*Nimbus*, what the hell have you got?" I demanded bluntly. Let MA get an earful!

In the brief lag that followed I saw Handy's screen flash with more imperative Port inquiries. We were being given unholy hell for not moving out at once. "What do you want me to tell them, Jo?" Handy asked me evenly.

"Nothing!" I retorted. "Nothing until we find out just what the hell is going on here." I attacked the transmit button again. "*Nimbus*, this is *Raptor*. Respond!"

At last Redding came over comm, his voice terse and clipped. "*Raptor*, we have *Herod*. Substitute heading five-seven-five, or you can kiss your ass good-bye!"

Herod? Suns, someone wasn't kidding! *Herod* was one

of the MA's big military cruisers, a troopship. What the
hell was it doing lurking around that close to a commercial port like New Cuba? One thing was for sure. If it
was indeed on the edge of our spiral, it was no surprise
to Port. And Port was sending us straight into her.

With one eye following the dizzying blur of transmis-
sions on Handy's screen, I hunched over the transmitter
on Raydor's comm console. I could feel the perspiration
clinging under my arms and breasts. My hands shook as
I hit the button. "*Nimbus*, can you confirm? We can't
screen *Herod*, we can't raise *Herod*, and Port is pushing
us out of here with both feet!"

"Substitute heading five-seven-five," was Redding's
obstinate reply. Then the comm went dead.

Adrenaline burned through me, making my heart hammer and my suit liner clammy with sweat. Beside me,
Raydor continued to grimly punch out a persistent signal
over the transmitter: inquiry to the phantom *Herod*. On
Handy's screen, Port was threatening to blow us out of
space if we didn't move out immediately.

There was a sudden sound behind me. I twisted to see
Lewis, free of his harness, staggering toward the console. It was like seeing the dead walk—the only living
thing about the man was an abrupt manic flash in those
rare blue eyes. I was so startled that for a moment I
couldn't move. I was still frozen in shock as Lewis fell
across the console beside me, his fist targeting Handy's
input, his voice rising in a harsh croak:

"*Go!*"

Raydor reacted more quickly than I was able to. He
released his harness snaps and lunged forward, throwing
himself at Lewis. One of his huge fists caught Lewis
squarely on the chin, and the smaller man went down,
colliding with the ancillary chair. Blood began to stream
from Lewis's mouth.

"No!" I cried, for I was afraid that Raydor was not
yet finished. But Raydor straightened up, pulling back.

Lewis, on the floor behind us, forced his wobbling head
up. Blood was collecting at his lips, and his eyes were

bright with terror. "Go!" he rasped again, his voice raw with effort.

I glanced at Handy's input, which was keyed only to Raydor's or my voice. I was still stunned by Lewis's sudden, lucid, but ineffectual intervention. Port was giving us its final ultimatum. Raydor's hand gripped the back of my padded chair, his big eyes dilated to nearly black.

"Can't you see what they're doing?" Lewis hissed.

I don't know what terrified me more at that moment: the idea that Lewis was crazy—or the possibility that he just might be sane. I wheeled on Handy, punching his override, shooting all his carefully preset pullout calculations all to hell. "Five-seven-five!" I shouted into his input. "Hit it!"

In the few seconds it took Raydor to plunge back into his chair and grapple with his harness, Handy recalibrated for the pull. *Raptor* leapt forward like a soaring bird, diving into the acceleration spiral. I set my spine against the base of my chair as the G-force hit me. On our Visuals screen the dark mass of *Herod* suddenly loomed, then vanished.

Those mother-joining bastards! I thought furiously, flattening as the pull overtook us and the G-force bloomed. The straps of my harness cut into my shoulders; my stomach dropped down to somewhere in the vicinity of my kneecaps. I grimly hung on, knowing that that part of the pullout, weirdly distorted in time, would be mercifully brief. I went limp and unresisting, swallowing down the wave of nausea that climbed in my throat.

When the force of acceleration began to ease, *Raptor*'s Internals automatically readjusted ship's gravity. As soon as I could pull myself up in my chair, I fumbled free of my harness and pounced on the console. "We okay?" I demanded of Handy.

"Fine, Jo; no problems," Handy reported cheerfully. Then he added, "That was a close one!"

No shit! I turned to Raydor, who was calmly shedding his harness. "Okay?" I asked him. He nodded, automatically beginning to run a check on his console functions. I turned back to Handy's input. "How far out?" I asked the Integrator.

As wonderful as magnetic acceleration pull was, it wasn't totally precise. In order to avoid the potentially messy business of careening at hyperlight speed into things like planets and orbital stations, ships always exited the pull at some unpredictably variable distance from their ultimate destination. You might find yourself hours out, you might be days out. You hoped for hours, but truthfully, that time I didn't much care.

Handy made some rapid calculations. He produced a schematic of Heinlein and the major spaceways attending it on his view screen. Then he pinpointed our present coordinates with a flashdot. You are here, I thought sardonically. "Approximately thirty-six hours to port, ship's present speed," he reported.

I slumped in my chair. Raydor was already releasing Internals from its pullout constraints: my job. All my muscles ached exquisitely, and I stank of my own sweat. I was suddenly abysmally sick of Control.

I got to my feet, turned, and nearly fell over Lewis. He lay motionless—possibly unconscious, I realized ruefully—rolled up against the base of the ancillary chair. Going through the pull without benefit of the restraints hadn't done him any good, either; he had a black eye as well as a bloodied lip. Without thinking, I fingered the metal cuff that dangled from my wrist.

"Get him out of here," I directed Raydor gruffly. Then I pushed the hatch release and left Control.

In my cabin, a small but homey cubical tucked into *Raptor*'s steadier stern section, I stripped off my sodden flightsuit and suit liner and stepped into the shower stall. I permitted myself the reward of a thorough drenching, keying the water temperature as hot as I could tolerate it. It was hardly an extravagance; water on freighters lasted forever. It couldn't be worn out or used up; it was just recycled over and over again. Finally, when even my fingertips began to go pruney, I stepped out and stood under the air gun. Then, warm and dry, I pulled on clean sleepers and crawled into my bunk

But damned if I could sleep. I just sat there, scrunched up against the headboard of my bunk, the cabin lighting turned to twilight dimness. The agitation I felt over everything that had happened was greater than my fatigue, and I had a monster headache gnawing behind my eyes. Just as I was thinking the hell with it, I might as well just get dressed again and go forward to Control, my cabin's hatch release clicked and the hatch hissed open. For a moment Raydor's bulk filled the doorway, silhouetted in the light of the corridor. Then the portal sealed behind him.

Raydor approached my bunk, his wrapless head lowered, squinting in the gloom. He looked down at me with wide, solemn, unblinking eyes. "Thought you might need something," he said quietly.

I moved my legs aside, gesturing to him. The bunk's springs creaked as Raydor lowered himself beside me. For a long moment neither of us spoke. Then, with my back braced against the headboard, I cradled Raydor's big head in my lap. My fingers trailed gently over his face. His Altered skin was soft, like well-cured chamois, wrinkled like crepe. I felt some indefinable, familiar comfort in touching him. What he felt, I never knew for sure. People from Class Five on down were not only sterilized, they were desexed—oh, not surgically; even the A's weren't that crude. They were HTA—hypothalamically altered—which presumably negated any possible response to sexual stimulus. But because Raydor was a Tachs, born free from the A's and that nasty little price of Citzenship until he'd left Earthheart, he had endured the process as an adult. How it had affected him I was never completely certain, but touch still seemed capable of giving him pleasure. I know that it had always given me pleasure to touch his soft Altered skin. Now, as always, it helped me to clear my mind, to relax and think more coherently. Gently, I ran my fingertips around the rims of his dark eyes, across the broad bridge of his nose. He stretched out contentedly on my bunk, crossing his long legs with a sigh. When I finally wanted to speak

I was direct; with Raydor there was no need for any preamble.

"He going to be all right?" I asked him.

"Yeah." After a moment he added, "It was mostly
from the drugs."

What Raydor meant was Lewis's reaction to the pullout, not his bizarre behavior in Control—which is what
both of us were thinking about, even if we didn't admit
it aloud.

Slowly, I framed Raydor's cheekbones with my hands,
stroking them. "Who the hell *is* this guy?" I posed—
rhetorically, Raydor knew. "And why is Heinlein taking
an IS?"

Raydor shrugged gently. "Heinlein's Heinlein," he responded, a marvel of logic that was perfectly apt.

My fingers paused, hooked at Raydor's ears. "Somebody tried to fry us," I said quietly, finally giving voice
to what was really eating me.

"Port?" Raydor offered.

But I shook my head. "No. Either it was MA, or MA
knew about it. No one even farts at Port without MA
smelling it." I caressed the soft fold of skin where his
ears joined his head. "I just don't understand *why*," I
continued. "Why go through all this trouble—" I shook
the detention cuff "—to see Lewis delivered and then try
to fry us?"

If the mystery was worrisome to Raydor, he didn't
express much concern. He stirred beneath my hands,
pulling himself up. His big hands found the front of
my sleepers. "Nothing to be done now," he opined
calmly.

I caught hold of his wrists. "When Lewis has come
around, I want you to clean him up a little," I told
him. "See to his face. Maybe find him some decent
clothes—those med greens are awful. Then I want to talk
to him."

"When you wake up," Raydor agreed placidly, his big
head moving lower.

"Hah! I doubt that I'll sleep," I replied.

But Raydor's hands were still there, moving softly and

knowingly and insistently. I relented then, releasing his wrists and falling back onto my bunk with a satisfied sigh. Raydor knew the secret things about me that I had never let anyone else learn; he could touch what no one else had ever been able to reach in me.

And once again he was right: Afterward, I did sleep.

CHAPTER FOUR

As far as my own family history goes, there really isn't that much to tell. My mother was a freightman and a ship owner. I grew up on *Raptor* and never spent much time planetside. The largest block of time I'd spent off-ship was when I'd reached eighteen and had Volunteered for Commercial Regulation. As a Class Two I was exempt from the Service Law that required all young Citizens Class Three and lower to devote at least two years of Service to either CA or MA programs. Volunteering was an alternative to Service. Volunteers served for four years, but they could pick their areas of interest, and they even had some choice about where they were sent.

My mother had encouraged me to Volunteer, even though for me it was optional. She had told me she wanted me to learn the things I couldn't learn on-ship. It was only years later that I realized that what I was supposed to have learned had nothing to do with Commerce Law or even freighting. She had wanted me to develop a sense of suspicion about the universe and a healthy dose of skepticism—things I never would have acquired in *Raptor*'s sheltered environment. And during my three-plus years with Regulation I certainly was exposed to enough greed and sleaze and corruption to do the trick. My education had only continued after my somewhat premature return to *Raptor*, after my mother's sudden death, when I found myself literally battling CA for possession of *my* ship.

My mother always told me that she wasn't sure who

38

my father was. But I think that she knew and that her evasion had just been something she used to protect herself from something even more painful. There were the usual genetic records, of course, but only a maternal affidavit, and no father had ever come forward for a chromosomal match.

Now, some twenty hours out of Heinlein, I sat in Handy's bright gold Integrator room and amused myself by randomly inserting scurrilous information about Rollo into his supposedly secret MA profile via a pirated access code Handy had stumbled across in his many wanderings through the Block's MA Integrators. It was childish but deliciously satisfying. It was also all lies, but I hoped it would cause him no end of problems, the unClassed little twerp! I held him personally responsible for nearly getting us fried.

"Jo?" Handy's rumbling voice interrupted me.

I looked up from my view screen. "What is it, Handy?"

"Slight malfunction in Generation." He sounded mildly apologetic. "I was running my regular Internals status check, and this popped up." His Systems screen flickered to life; ship's schematics flew by as he searched for the pertinent diagram. "There," he announced, enlarging a particularly complex-looking schematic.

"What's going on?" I leaned forward, the defaming of Rollo's reputation temporarily forgotten.

"We're down to less than half capacity in that generation rotor," Handy explained. "Might be spontaneous, or it might have been damaged when we pulled out at New Cuba."

I peered at what was to me a nearly incomprehensible diagram. "Why didn't the regular postpull Internals check spot this?" I asked him.

Handy made a *scritch*ing sound like a verbal shrug. "I'm not sure, Jo. Maybe the rotor hadn't started to fail yet then. Or Internals may have disregarded it if the diminished capacity was slight enough that it didn't endanger ship's function. We still have the other two rotors. We can get by on one if we have to."

"Reassuring thought," I commented dryly.

"I ran it through Internals' repair mode," Handy continued, "but it's no good. It's still failing."

I thought about it for a moment. The generation system was the main guts of *Raptor*'s Internals and propulsion systems. Magnetic acceleration pull might have gotten you between planets, but generation power still got you everywhere else and ran the artificial gravity and life support. "How serious is this?" I asked him, rubbing my chin. "Can it wait until Heinlein?"

Handy made a decidedly human-sounding noise, a sort of speculative grunt. "If the rotor retains at least partial capacity, yes. But if the whole rotor goes, I'd advise in-transit repairs."

Handy didn't take a lot of risks, no more than what I forced him to, at least. He had been a part of *Raptor* since she'd been built; I had complete trust in his judgment. "Okay," I agreed, "if it blows, we fix it."

The images on Handy's screen began to flicker again, a tumbling montage of schematics. He was searching for the repair specifics on the troublesome rotor, muttering obscure Integrator phrases to himself as he worked. I was just about to return to my self-imposed mission of sabotaging Rollo's MA profile when the in-ship speaker at my knee sputtered to life.

"Jo?" came Raydor's calm voice. "I think you'd better get in here."

I pressed the transmit button. "Where are you?" I asked him, puzzled by the atypical obtuseness of Raydor's request.

"With Lewis," Raydor replied. "You should see this."

Great. I had sent Raydor to clean Lewis up and get him into some decent clothes—a cast-off flightsuit of mine that I was sure would fit him better than the baggy greens. That seemed simple enough to me, so why the mysterious summons? When I left Handy, he was busy communing with Internals on the subtleties of generation rotor repairs.

In the little cabin off Control, Raydor stood patiently beside an impassive Lewis. He had cleaned the blood off

Lewis's face, but Lewis's left eye was now swollen half-shut. Lewis was also still dressed in the med greens; the flightsuit hung over the acceleration chair. I stared at Raydor, feeling a little annoyed. "What the hell is it?" I asked him.

Lewis shifted slightly, swaying. It was one of the few independent motions I'd seen him initiate, and with it I realized that there was something different about his expression, a level of awareness that had not been there before. Not rationality, I was sure, but at least some sign of sentience. Raydor answered me by speaking directly to Lewis, tugging at the loose bloused top of the med tunic. "Come on," he said quietly to Lewis. "Take them off."

Lewis rocked back a little, folding his arms protectively across his chest. It was a surprisingly intentional act from a man who had displayed very little will up to that point. The awareness in Lewis's blue eyes wavered. Raydor reached out and gently pulled free the neck of the tunic. Lewis twisted aside ineffectually but didn't step back. It was as if his newfound volition didn't yet extend to his feet.

I stepped forward, speechless with shock. Huge purple-blue bruises mottled the pale skin of Lewis's exposed neck. "Powers!" I exclaimed.

"It's worse," Raydor said grimly. He pulled again at the seam of the tunic, tugging until the garment fell free and even Lewis yielded, his arms dropping helplessly to his sides. As Raydor removed the tunic, I felt my mouth freeze in a rigid grimace. Lewis's chest and arms were covered with the same ugly bruises.

I exchanged a stunned glance with Raydor. "What the hell—" I began, appalled.

Raydor just shook his head and pulled at the drawstring closure of Lewis's baggy green trousers. Lewis's knees bent as, automatically, he clutched defensively at the waist of the loose pants. "Take them off," Raydor insisted softly.

Lewis's eyes, awash with tears and suddenly completely cogent, flew to my face: a wordless plea for what little dignity he still had left. Ruthlessly, ashamed of my bluntness but unwilling to temper it, I repeated Raydor's command. "Take them off."

Lewis's eyes fell, shining with the unshed tears. His hands trembled as his long pale fingers released the drawstring and let the pants fall free. I sucked in my breath with an audible grunt, my lower lip clamped between my teeth to hold in the first words that sprang to my mouth.

What the joining hells had they done to him? His entire body was a wretched maze of nearly contiguous bruises—even there, where I could not imagine anyone doing such a thing to another human being, not even those bastards at MA. The sight made me cringe. No wonder they had drugged him, I realized tautly. How else could he have concealed the pain?

Almost involuntarily, I took a half step forward. I reached out and gently touched the discolored skin on Lewis's shoulder. He flinched away from me; his eyes, still downcast, squeezed desperately shut.

"Are you in pain?" I asked him quietly. Beneath my fingers his bruised skin shivered delicately, like a horse twitching off flies. I was unsure of his capacity. "Lewis, do you understand me?" I tried again. "Do you need—"

Those wide eyes, that all-too-rare blue, leapt to my face, gathering all of his fragile dignity and incomprehensible pain in that single look. "I understand," he replied in the same hoarse voice that had so startled me in Control with its urgent command.

"Is there anything you need?" I repeated, dropping my hand from his shoulder.

To my alarm and shame, huge tears glittered in Lewis's eyes. Then they spilled helplessly across his wan and stubbled cheeks. He made several attempts to speak, but the tears seemed to choke him, and his body shook. Finally he just gave up and stood there, miserably hunched, his hands crossing to hide his nakedness.

I felt like some damned MA thug. Gesturing to Raydor, I told him in a voice gone rough with shame, "Take him to your cabin. Help him bathe and shave. Get him something to eat and then let him sleep.''

Raydor nodded, tactfully failing to remind me of my previously expressed intention to interrogate Lewis. As I turned to leave the cabin, I saw Raydor stoop to help Lewis dress again. A volatile mixture of self-disgust and self-righteous anger roiled in me as I strode up the corridor to Control.

Things just seemed to be getting worse and worse. It wasn't bad enough that Lewis was a Class Ten, an IS, and linked to me by a detention cuff. Not even bad enough that MA had drugged him, lied about it, and then tried to fry us on pullout. Someone had beat the living shit out of the guy—and I couldn't think of one logical reason for it.

I was in the galley—which on *Raptor* wasn't really even a separate compartment, more like a widening of the corridor, an alcove between Control and the main rotor shaft—when Raydor found me. I had punched up soup from the synthesizer. Vegetable soup was all I could get, since Raydor had programmed the damned thing. I was munching away—the food synthesizer having never quite figured out that ''soup'' was, by definition, primarily a liquid form—listening to the audiochip I had popped into one ear, when Raydor pulled up the bench across from me and sat.

Audiochips were, in my somewhat jaundiced opinion, one of the few truly worthwhile contributions of modern technology to post-War society. With them, anyone could have a veritable library of music contained in tiny micro-circuited earpieces the size of peanuts. Because the chips fit right into the ear, they were unobtrusive to others— no small consideration in the confines of a spacecraft— and eminently portable. I had hundreds of audiochips, mostly old stuff, even some rerecordings of twentieth- and twenty-first-century music. Maybe I favored the golden oldies because they took me back to a happier, simpler time, maybe just because musical trends had changed and my tastes hadn't. Most of the current popular music was shit, all synthesized instrumentals and electronically distorted vocals. There hadn't been a really good group since the Toiling Clones split up.

"Handy says we just lost the rear generation rotor," Raydor announced, eyeing the fibrous mass in my bowl.

I looked up at him, popping the chip from my ear. "Terrific," I responded dourly, shoving the soup aside.

"He advises in-transit repairs," Raydor continued mildly.

I nodded. "Yeah, I know." I gnawed thoughtfully at my lower lip. "How far out are we?"

"About seven hours," Raydor replied. He shifted slightly on the bench. "There's something else."

"Lewis," I pronounced flatly, damning Rollo for the hundredth time.

Raydor's big childlike eyes calmly took in the tense lines of my body and the way my hands had unconsciously clenched into fists. "After I cleaned him up, I ran Internals' med scan on him," he continued evenly. "And there's something funny there."

Stars, didn't I know it! "And what's that?" I asked him, fatalistically thinking, What the hell could be any "funnier" than all of this has been so far?

Raydor leaned forward, resting his elbows on the little galley table. "All those bruises are just hemolytic pigmentation—skin-deep. There's no underlying pathology or trauma." I stared up into his dark eyes. "And they're starting to fade, to disappear," he concluded.

I shook my head irritably. "That doesn't make any sense," I complained. The words were already out of my mouth before I realized that *nothing* was making any sense, anyway, and why should this be any different? Without thought, my fingers touched the rim of my detention cuff. "Where is he now?" I asked.

Raydor straightened. "His cabin, probably asleep."

I got to my feet, abandoning the soup. "Well, I think it's time Mr. C. A. Lewis provided us with a few answers," I decided grimly.

Raydor stood as if to follow me, but I waved him off.

"No, you get back to Handy," I told him. "See what we need to do about that damned rotor."

Raydor's face was impassive, but I knew him well enough to read the reluctance in his big eyes. It had nothing to do with any anxiety about the rotor repairs, either; like most of his people, Raydor was a natural genius at mechanical tasks. He was concerned about me going after Lewis; concerned about Lewis's welfare, that is, not mine! I gave him a playful clap on the arm. "Go on," I said, "I'll take good care of your friend."

A quirky little smile, the most Raydor would reveal, pulled at his mouth. He shook his head, exhaling with a grunt, and then headed toward Integration.

Outside the little cabin I'd assigned Lewis, I punched the door buzzer. When there was no response, I pushed the hatch release and let myself in. Lewis had slept through the sound of the buzzer, but the hiss of the hatch releasing woke him. He had been curled up fetal-like on the bunk, still dressed in my old flightsuit, but he jerked up with a start when I entered the small cabin. It was hard to read just what expression was on that delightfully normal face; whatever had been there initially, unguarded, had been quickly replaced by a swiftly frozen mask of careful indifference when I had entered. Only his body still betrayed him. Bodies aren't good liars, and Lewis's body was telling me that he was both frightened and embarrassed to have the sudden pleasure of my company.

"Don't get up," I said casually as he began to scramble up on the bed. I pulled up the room's lone chair and sat. Eyeing me, Lewis pulled himself up to the headboard of the bunk and sat stiffly with his back literally to the wall. One hand, the cuffless one, plowed back through the tangle of his clean black hair. I think that one automatic gesture, more than any possible calculated action, convinced me that Lewis was rational: The man had a natural tweak of vanity.

My old blue and gold flightsuit fit him pretty well. Too bad we didn't have any deckboots to replace the ugly, clunky med-issue shoes he wore. As Lewis sat there, blinking the sleep from his eyes, it took an effort of will for me to concentrate on why I had come.

Without preamble I asked him, "What did they do to you at MA?"

Lewis blinked again, rapidly. I saw his eyes narrow, the pupils constricting. But he did not reply.

I leaned forward in my chair, an unconscious gesture of intimidation that somewhat chagrined me when I recognized it for what it was. "Let me see the bruises," I commanded.

Lewis's eyes widened, his pupils involuntarily dilating. His body was talking, at least, even if he wasn't. But his hesitation was brief. I think he feared that if he didn't obey me, I'd be all too willing to take matters into my own hands. And he probably was right. Slowly, he unfastened the front of his flightsuit and its liner, pulling the edges apart. By the time he got halfway down the front of his chest, his fumbling hands were hardly moving.

"That's enough," I said abruptly, for I could see what I needed to see. The bruising was nearly gone.

I jerked my eyes up, catching his. His trembling fingers meshed, holding together the front of the flightsuit. "What did they do to you?" I repeated quietly.

Lewis wet his lips with a quick swipe of his tongue. "Drugs," he said, his unused voice still hoarse. "Gave me drugs."

"Drugs don't do that—cause bruises like that," I retorted. "And drugs sure as hell don't make bruises disappear like that, either!" I paused, trying to stifle the inexplicable spiral of anger I felt rising in me.

Lewis dropped his eyes, his hands moving awkwardly to reseal the seam of the flightsuit. I let him fumble with it for a moment, then I changed tack.

"Why are you Indentured, Lewis?"

I could see that the use of his given name had startled him. I had almost begun to think that it wasn't his own, that it was some alias, as phony as all the other MA bullshit we'd been hit with so far on the run. But I saw that I was wrong. No man reacts that way to an alias. It was as if his name was the only thing of his that they hadn't denied him.

Lewis folded his thin hands on his lap and curled his bare ankles together. "State Crimes," he said softly.

"State Crimes," my ass! What the hell were State Crimes anyway? Every Indentured I'd ever seen, wallowing under some fine too huge to be paid off, was up on State Crimes, and no one had ever been able to explain to me just what the joining things were—or if State Crimes, like the phantom Class Ones, even existed. Lewis had to do better than that. "What did you do?" I persisted.

But Lewis just shook his head morosely, helplessly, as if that answer had eluded him as well.

"Why Heinlein?" I asked him. I decided to give him a little support this time. "Heinlein doesn't even take many immigrants, and I've never heard of them taking an IS. How did MA get you in?"

Again Lewis's tongue swept over his dry lips. Cleanshaven, his face was disturbingly attractive in spite of its pallor. With the spark of life in them, his stunning blue eyes were the clincher. Stars! Now what was I thinking of?

"MA," Lewis offered. "MA got me in."

"How? Why?" I leaned farther forward, intentionally this time. "What do you know about Heinlein? Do you know why they want you there, what they want your Indentureship for?"

Once more Lewis helplessly shook his head. "MA sent me," he repeated, shrugging. With MA, maybe that was explanation enough.

I could see that Lewis was perspiring; there was a fine sheen of moisture on his upper lip and across his forehead where the fringe of gleaming black hair hung. And I felt of two minds then, woman and captain: the woman, who would feel compassion for him, and the captain, who would press on, knowing her advantage.

"I'm not trying to hurt you, Lewis," I said, hybridizing what I felt. I shook my left wrist, making the detention cuff dance. "Light knows, I have a definite stake in your well-being."

That remark brought the unexpected: a sudden smile, dazzling and unguarded, that lit his face with a breathtaking incandescence. Damn him, he was a beauty, all right—him and those blue eyes and that normal face! But then he quickly recaptured his runaway expression, the daring extravagance of that stellar smile, and his face abruptly sobered again. "Sorry," he said softly, meaning the cuff.

"Business," I replied briskly, dropping my wrist so that the sleeve of my flightsuit concealed the damning cuff again. But I wondered if that statement sounded as false to his ears as it did to my own.

Lewis surprised me again, this time with a question of his own. "How far out?" he asked me.

"A little less than seven hours." I got to my feet. "You may as well sleep," I added.

Lewis looked up at me shyly, almost gratefully, I thought, dashing to hell all the questions I had yet to put to him. Considering my lack of success so far, I hardly needed to bother to go on. I guess I would never make it as an MA thug. "Thank you, Captain," Lewis said solemnly.

The words were on my tongue and out of my lips before I could censor them. "Sorry about before, Lewis," I said gruffly to hide the shame I still felt. "About the clothes and—"

But Lewis stopped me with a strange expression, not quite a smile but something shaped with a wry, self-deprecating humor nevertheless. "Shouldn't matter," he said easily. "I must've stripped a hundred times for them." Meaning MA, I guess, which hardly made me feel any better about it.

"It matters," I told him.

In the corridor outside the cabin I paused, wiping my suddenly wet palms on the thighs of my flightsuit. So much for interrogation! I thought ruefully. It had taken more out of me than anything I had gotten out of Lewis.

We were less than an hour out of Heinlein when Raydor joined me in Control. His flightsuit was creased and rumpled, but he triumphantly held out the limp coil of a spent cylinder seal from the defective generation rotor. He dropped into his contoured chair with a grunt.

"Seal was shot," he told me. The damned thing was a real bitch to replace; how he'd done it in six hours was beyond me. Why the seal had blown in the first place was even more of a mystery.

"I'm putting our ID out on comm," I said, keying the plastic card from our manifest into Handy's terminal. "We'll probably be picking up audio from Port at Heinlein pretty soon."

Raydor methodically arranged the cylinder seal into a neat roll, coiling it in his big, callused hands. He made a casual gesture with a jerk of his chin. "He okay?" he asked me.

"Yeah," I grunted. Raydor waited, but I didn't elaborate. As he sat there, silently winding the troublesome seal in his hands, I noticed two fresh, deep scratches across the base of his right thumb. I reached out and caught his hand. "What's this?" I asked.

He shrugged, gently but firmly pulling his hand away. Out of cabin, Raydor could be unexpectedly body-shy. "Caught it on a rough edge, I guess," he offered, curling his fingers over the wounds.

"Transmission from Port at Heinlein," Handy reported promptly. "Just technical data. They request our ETA and manifest code clearance." He paused. "I'll put it onscreen," he offered matter-of-factly. Lines of eerie green figures began filling his viewscreen.

Raydor leaned forward in his chair. His big dark eyes regarded me closely, unblinking. "What are you going to do about him?" he asked me evenly.

I stared back at him. "What do you mean, what am I going to do about him?" I retorted quickly. "I'm going to deliver him to Heinlein, that's what I'm going to do!"

"There's something wrong with that," Raydor stated quietly.

"Yeah?" I held up my left arm, the detention cuff dangling. "Well, there's something wrong with this, too, my friend! Lewis is an IS—tried fair and square and found guilty. He's just a job to us. He's going to Heinlein, where I'm going to hand him over to them, and then they're going to relieve me of this little bit of jewelry and key the rest of my Void-cursed fee—and then you and I are lifting off that joining planet and heading out of this forsaken system!''

If Raydor had a response to all that vitriol, Handy robbed him of the opportunity to make it. "I'm getting audio from Port, Jo." he reported. "You want it on speaker?''

"Go ahead," I said.

The ever-present static sputtered over the speaker. Then a voice, deep, precise, and hauntingly familiar, broke over the interference.

"*Raptor*, this is Mimosa at Port. We have you in our scopes." A pause, then, "Welcome home, Jo."

CHAPTER
FIVE

To me it had always seemed one of the most disappointing aspects of the exploration of space that mankind had never discovered any other sentient life-forms. A few of the planets we had colonized had had native life, mostly lower plants, even once or twice a primitive microscopic animal species, but nothing even approaching intelligence. In a way, I guess, we had made our own alien life-forms with the Alterations, and for all our travels, the weirdest thing we had ever found off-Earth was still man himself. It was as if the Creator—if indeed such a deity exists—had looked down upon humanity in all its mutations and decided not to add insult to injury by creating any other sentient species.

To the Creationists in our midst, this dearth of extraterrestrials served as proof that man was divinely unique. It probably drove the Evolutionists crazy. To me it just added yet another disappointment to the generally depressing nature of post-War existence. And every time we made port on another planet, it always occurred to me that this would all be a hell of a lot more fun if there were some native sentients there to greet us.

I don't know if I was getting that lazy or if my nerves were just permanently frazzled, but I let Handy take *Raptor* in on Heinlein, even though Port had a truly beautiful setup, so well conceived that even an Alter-brained child could have set down a tanker ship without crunching anything. Port was laid out in a clean, geometrically precise grid with broad, well-marked landing fields and

generous taxiways to the hangars. It would have been difficult to make a mistake. As Handy slickly maneuvered
the ship along our taxi lane to one of Heinlein's massive
hangar bays, I took over the comm board at Control.

"Go get Lewis," I told Raydor. "Be sure he looks
okay and then get him up here."

After Raydor had gone through the hatch, I sat there
for a few moments, my fingers resting on the console. I
half listened to Handy's muffled chatter with Port Integration as he inched *Raptor* into our assigned bay. Then
he began flashing Port's data across his screen: planetary
date, time, temperature, even the latest news capsule. I
forced my attention back to Raydor's board, punching
Internals' checklist through. At least all three generation
rotors showed full capacity now.

When Raydor returned with Lewis, I was already in
the corridor leading to the landing hatch. I was mildly
surprised to see that Raydor had donned his face wraps;
they were not required there. He also wasn't carrying his
beam rifle; that was permitted on Heinlein but essentially
useless to us. The kind of trouble we were likely to face
had nothing to do with energy weapons.

Lewis's sober face still looked somewhat drawn, as if
what rest he'd gotten had not been enough for him. In a
way I understood how he felt. Each of us, for our own
reasons, was not real happy to be there. I glanced down
the length of Lewis's secondhand flight suit and decided
he looked presentable enough.

"Okay," I said grimly, "let's go."

The hangar we were berthed in was huge and nearly
empty; its great arched ceiling was striped with the curving bands of skylights. On the glistening wet expanse of
the bay floor outside *Raptor*'s ramp, Mimosa's envoy
waited. He was a short, balding, slightly overweight man
with a receding crown of fluffy white hair and a round,
cherubic face. He immediately approached me, his hand
extended and his mouth crinkled in a smile. "Captain,"
he said warmly. "Welcome! My name is Garth. Mimosa
asked me to meet you—" His gaze swung to include

Raydor and Lewis as well. ''—and assist you to her office.''

I shook his soft, dry hand. ''Thanks,'' I said indifferently.

Garth wore the emerald-green jumpsuit of Heinlein's Port and Immigration Services. He looked like an overgrown pixie in it, but his pleasantness was genuine enough. Only my MA-induced paranoia kept me from returning his friendly smile. He glanced curiously around us. ''No luggage for the gentleman?'' he asked, meaning Lewis.

''He travels light,'' I replied dryly.

''Very well, then,'' Garth decided with equanimity. ''If you will come with me.''

As if we have any choice! I thought sourly, shepherding Lewis ahead of me as we followed Mimosa's aide across the huge hangar floor. We rode a lift from the hangar to the overhead walkway in silence, Garth eyeing us with politely obvious curiosity.

''Mimosa regrets she wasn't able to greet you personally,'' Garth offered as we stepped out onto the glassed-in walkway. ''But she's been tied up in Procedures all afternoon.'' His cheerfully conspiratorial shrug suggested that we all must have known just how that went.

The view from the walkway was spectacular. Behind and beneath us spread the geometrically perfect grid of the port; ahead of us was the glass and steel sweep of Heinlein's main settlement. Beyond that, fading into the low-lying clouds, lay the dazzling green and white hills of the Koerber Range. I felt an unexpected ache at the sight. If Heinlein's Port was a marvel of linear precision, the city itself was a monument to the celebration of free-form architecture. Glittering in the sunlight, that creation of reflected light and soaring structures and whimsical oases of growing things, hemmed by broad ribbons of farmland and forested hills, called me back to a simpler time in my life, a time when my trust in the world had been as pure and innate as the air in that magical place.

I noticed Lewis was gawking; I pushed his arm abruptly

to make him walk faster. He half stumbled, lowered his head, and dutifully hurried to catch up to Garth.

You might expect that on a planet like Heinlein all the architecture would be soft and aesthetic and essentially useless, like old Grecian sculpture. But with the exception of the few inevitably ugly original Authorities structures, leftovers from the colonization period, most of the buildings were crisp and soaring constructions of pure function. The effect was satisfying and far more beautiful than any deliberate attempt at architectural aestheticism. Much of the main settlement, which was usually just referred to generically as "Heinlein," like the whole planet, was filled with open spaces or glassed in, like the network of elevated walkways. The buildings were separated by wide green concourses and glittering steel fountains or free-form sculptures. Backdropped by the brilliantly green Koerbers, the city below us sparkled with a beauty that caught even me unaware.

Mollified by the unexpected emotional response Heinlein had evoked in me, I touched Lewis's arm to slow him. When I had his attention, I pointed across the towers of the farthest structures to the verdant rises beyond. "The Koerbers," I told Lewis. "They even have real trees here."

"Oh, yes, indeed," Garth added, slowing to turn to us. "We have a lot of things made of real wood here—even furniture. We have one of the largest Craft Guilds in the sector, and our wood products are renowned across the systems." He smiled in a friendly manner at Lewis. "The pleasure of beautiful things is very important to us."

We rode in another lift, dropping this time into the heart of the massive eliptically shaped building I recognized as Immigration Services. We began to encounter other people, mostly women, all clad in the ubiquitous emerald-green jumpsuits. Garth greeted each of them with a few words or a pleasant nod. All of them, however surreptitiously, eyed us curiously—especially Lewis.

Garth led us to a small receiving area, like an entrance hall, where there were comfortable benches and a low table with bowls of hard candy and a rack of news cassettes. "Would you please have a seat here," he asked us politely. "I'll tell Mimosa you've arrived." He disappeared through a large double doorway—not even a hatch but an actual set of doors made of real wood—at the head of the hallway.

I sank down on one padded bench, pulling Lewis down beside me. Raydor remained standing, his back to the double doors, facing the corridor we had entered. His posture was deliberately casual, but I knew him well enough to read the wariness in him. In the cross corridor down the hall a pair of green-suited women paused, peering at us. One of them smiled.

Beside me, Lewis squirmed. He tried to tuck his feet, with their ugly shoes, beneath the bench. He stared down at his knees. Then, suddenly, those big blue eyes lifted imploringly to my face.

The sense of angry frustration that had been building in me since we'd left the MA Block in New Cuba now wrenched at me so fiercely that I lost all control of it. Damn Lewis! And damn his pleading blue eyes! "Well, here you are, Mr. Lewis!" I said. "How do you like your new home?"

Raydor turned briefly and wordlessly at my outburst. Then he calmly resumed his vigil on the hallway. Next to me, Lewis's eyes quickly dropped. He wedged his hands under his thighs as if to somehow make himself as inconspicuous as possible.

"Didn't you know what kind of place this is?" I persisted, my voice a nasty whisper.

Lewis kept his eyes averted. He spoke a single word: "Women."

I made a rude little snorting sound. "That's right, women. Heinlein's full of them—eight or ten women for every man." I leaned closer to him; automatically, he recoiled. "And what do you suppose they'd want with an IS in a place like this, eh?"

"I d-don't know," Lewis stammered, betraying his lie with a florid blush that quickly climbed to the roots of his blue-black hair.

I straightened up again. "Well, you just think about it, then," I told him cruelly. "You're pretty, and you've got your wits about you; I'm sure it'll come to you!"

Lewis looked up at me again, his eyes wide and plaintive.

"You thought this would be a good place to go, didn't you?" I continued, somewhat less savagely. "A nice little break from all the shit MA's been putting you through. You thought you'd be *safe* here, didn't you?"

Ahead of us, Raydor shifted his weight, signaling his uneasiness. But he didn't turn to intervene.

Numbly, Lewis shrugged. I could see the tears barely held back behind his furiously blinking lids. He looked so lost, so defeated, that I felt all my seething anger abruptly evaporate in a rush of aching sympathy for him.

"This isn't a very safe place for a man like you," I whispered, my lips close to his ear. At the startled jerk of his head, I quickly amended my response. "Oh, no, they won't harm you," I explained, my hand reaching for his arm. "But they won't want to let you go, either." I gazed stolidly up the corridor, where a trio of emerald-clad women stared in frank admiration. "It's not so bad here," I concluded quietly. "Most people would like it. And you—" I shifted my gaze to his face, his eyes awash with fear. "—you are a very valuable thing to them, a luxury they'll cherish." I dropped my hand from his arm. "Maybe you'll even like it."

At that moment the wooden double doors swung open, and Garth reentered the hall. He gestured expansively at us. "I apologize for the delay, Captain," he said. "Mimosa can see you now."

Beside me, Lewis's body shuddered. I had to pull him to his feet. His fingers, filled with a sudden strength, dug into my wrist, and his eyes caught mine in one frantic lunge.

"Help me!" he implored in a hoarse whisper.

As I twisted my arm, trying to pry Lewis's fingers free, Raydor came up alongside us. He took Lewis's arm none too gently and jerked him away from me. Lewis's grip suddenly shifted to Raydor's big rough hand.

"Help you *what*?" I hissed back at Lewis, my eyes riveted to his and Raydor's clasped hands, where something incredible had just happened. Glancing hastily at Garth's back to be sure the aide had not seen what I was certain I had seen, I shoved both Lewis and Raydor forward in the direction of the double doors.

Forced to release Raydor, Lewis dropped his hand, the hand that now bore across the base of its thumb the two deep parallel scratches Raydor had acquired in *Raptor*'s rotor tunnel. "Please—get me out," Lewis beseeched me, his voice a harsh whisper.

Hurrying to catch up with Garth, I pushed Lewis roughly ahead of me. I exchanged glances with Raydor: Raydor, whose injured thumb was now—impossibly— unmarred. His big dark eyes widened with surprise behind the hood of his face wraps. I don't know what would have been more alarming to me at that moment: trying to force myself to believe that I had not seen it happen or admitting to myself that I had. But there was no time to confer. Garth stood aside and politely ushered us through a final doorway and into Mimosa's office.

Inside, the brightness of the room momentarily confused me, and the vastness of the chamber only added to my sense of disorientation. The room was more like living quarters than an office, all chrome and wood and carpeting, filled with clusters of fat, upholstered furniture and tasteful accoutrements. There wasn't even a regular desk, just an Integration access console flanked by two well-stuffed chairs. From one of those chairs a smiling woman rose and approached us.

"Jo," Mimosa said, squeezing my shoulders in a friendly embrace. "So good to see you again. You look well."

Mimosa wore her emerald-green like an empress. She was nearly my height, but she had the kind of trim and curving proportions that my rangy frame would never have. Her honey-colored skin was tight and glowing, and her normal face was framed by a mass of chocolate-brown hair. She flashed an engaging smile at Raydor. "And your second,'' she added. ''Raydor, you don't have to wrap here. You're among friends.''

Raydor merely grunted, ''Hello, Mimosa,'' and shook her proffered hand.

I had stepped past Lewis when Mimosa had greeted me; now she discovered him in my shadow. ''And this must be Mr. Lewis,'' she said enthusiastically, reaching out her hand to him.

Lewis hesitated, then awkwardly stuck out his hand— his left hand, with the two deep scratches still screaming out across his thumb. Mimosa, who missed nothing, gently turned his hand palm up in her own. She looked to me, her brows arched. ''He's hurt himself?''

''Mr. Lewis is a little . . . clumsy,'' I offered dryly.

Embarrassed, Lewis tugged his hand back. ''It's nothing,'' he mumbled.

Mimosa threw me a second, sharper glance, then she looked back to Lewis. ''Well, come,'' she said brightly. ''Come and sit.'' We followed her across the springy rust-colored carpet to a group of upholstered chairs. ''Is there anything I can get you?'' she inquired as the three of us sat, with Raydor and I flanking Lewis. ''Coffee? Tea? Or something stronger?''

I shook my head, although I ached for something to wet my throat, which had gone alarmingly dry and had constricted like a cramped muscle from the moment I had seen Lewis seize Raydor's hand. Raydor murmured a negative as well. Lewis just sat numbly, his head lowered, in a posture Mimosa could hardly fail to interpret as a refusal.

''Well, I believe I'll have a little coffee, then,'' Mimosa remarked, punching the code into an autoserver at the edge of a low end table. No one spoke during the brief interval before the autoserver's hatch disgorged the cup of steaming beverage. Mimosa's ginger-colored eyes glided casually over Lewis's hunched form as she lifted her cup and saucer. Her scrutiny was frank and inoffensively forthright. Was she the one who would get his IS contract? That thought suddenly chilled me, and I longed for my own cup of hot coffee to wrap my numb fingers around.

Lewis sat motionless, his right hand folded over the marked left one in his lap. Mimosa got to her feet and carried her coffee cup over to the Integrator access panel. "I expect you're eager to be free of that cuff, Jo," she remarked, punching up something on the console.

To my amazement I found myself replying, "Not really."

Beside me Lewis started, his eyes lifting hopefully. Even Raydor's hooded head turned sharply.

Mimosa eyed me curiously. "No? Is there a problem?"

"You might say that," I replied, fingering the hated cuff.

"Then let's remove the cuff," Mimosa offered reasonably.

But I folded the cuffed wrist across my belly and shook my head. "Not until we have everything settled here," I maintained calmly. Inside me a small voice of reason was telling me that I was making a terrible mistake, but on the outside a cool and dispassionate person had nonchalantly taken over.

Mimosa sipped at her coffee. Sadistically, the aroma tantalized me. "What is there to settle, Jo?" she asked me evenly.

My mind made a heroic leap of logic. "The money," I responded. "The fee's not nearly enough." Not a hard point to stretch, given the circumstances; *Herod* and the pullout from New Cuba came immediately to mind, as did the detention cuff and Rollo's treachery.

"I'm authorized to key the second half of your payment upon delivery," Mimosa reminded me. "But I can't even do that until you release Mr. Lewis to me."

Again I shook my head. "I want more money," I reiterated, leaning forward in my chair. "It's not enough."

Mimosa's sculpted brows rose slightly, and she peered at me over the rim of her coffee cup. "I can't make any adjustments there, Jo," she explained with genuine regret.

I had been counting on that. MA was absolutely watertight when it came to the matter of credit; they weren't about to cough up any more. "Then who does have the authority?" I persisted.

Mimosa set down the coffee cup. She spread her hands over her thighs. "Mahta, I should think," she replied.

"Then let me talk to her," I said.

Mimosa's gaze flitted over Raydor and rested briefly on Lewis. "She's in the country," she explained.

"When will she be back?"

Mimosa sighed delicately. "We expect her tomorrow morning."

"Fine. I can wait." I settled back in my chair, hoping against hope that I wasn't making a monumental mistake.

Mimosa's swift, appraising glance swept over Lewis again. Yes, he was to be hers, all right. She could afford to be tolerant of me while waiting for her little prize. "I'll see that you have quarters, then," she offered graciously.

"We'll quarter together," I directed promptly. Raydor and I quartering together wouldn't have raised any eyebrows there; Lewis and I—well, the cuffs changed all the rules as far as I was concerned. And Lewis had some answering to do; he wasn't leaving my sight until I found out what the hell was going on.

Mimosa's pink lips pursed thoughtfully, and I could almost see her reconsidering the value of any protest she might make in the light of what she intended to gain from me eventually. "Fine," she said. She punched her transmitter and instructed, "Garth, prepare quarters for our guests. Yes, that suite will do nicely. Thank you." She turned back to us, smiling again. "Now, you're sure you won't have some coffee?" she inquired.

Beside me, Lewis stirred. "I'd like some, please," he said, his voice hoarse with tension.

Our suite of rooms was a luxurious little apartment on an upper floor of the Central Services building. It was nearly as elegant as Mimosa's office, a quality I was not exactly in the right frame of mind to fully appreciate at the time. The moment the door closed behind us, I turned on Lewis like an angry dog, seizing his wrist with a ferocity that made him wince. I spun him forcefully into one of the overstuffed chairs. "Okay, Mr. Lewis," I said, glowering at him, "answer time!"

Rubbing his wrist, Lewis gazed up at me with wide, panicky eyes. The marks on his thumb were already beginning to fade, but they were still glaringly apparent to me. He glanced sideways at Raydor as if seeking support, but Raydor's stance was impassive, his hooded eyes unfathomable behind his wraps. Lewis swallowed, a dry little effort that made him wince again. "Thank you, Captain, for helping me back there."

I plunged into the chair opposite Lewis's, leaning aggressively forward. "Yeah, I helped you all right—and now you're going to tell me just *why* the hell I should keep helping you. Why the bloody Void should I be risking this fee, my ship, my *life*, all to pull your sorry ass out of the fire?"

Lewis lowered his head again, defensively, as if to ward off my attack. He murmured something so softly that I couldn't hear it clearly.

"What?" I demanded.

His eyes lifted, his hands gripping the plump arms of the chair. "I said, you know now what I am," he repeated quietly.

"Yeah, I know," I retorted. "You're some kind of *freak*!" I saw Lewis jerk back as if I'd struck him. Even Raydor shifted uneasily behind me.

Lewis seemed to shrink back into the depths of the overstuffed chair. He was like a cornered animal. "You've seen my ID," he said softly. "What does it say that I am?"

" 'Charles Alan Lewis,' " I replied tartly. " 'Origin: data not on file—Class: Ten.' "

Lewis's breathing had changed tempo; it was rapid but shallow. His fingertips burrowed deeply into the upholstery. "Am I what you expected?" he asked me tersely, his eyes locking with mine.

I stared at him hard and plainly for several moments.

"No," I finally admitted. "I thought Tens were all vegged out. You're normal—not even Restructured."

With an obvious effort Lewis slowed his respiration rate. "Have you ever seen a Class Ten before, Captain?" he asked quietly.

I shook my head.

"We're all normals, phenotypically." His fingers crept nervously through the plush fabric of the chair arms. "The so-called defects are cerebral."

I dropped my elbows onto my knees, relaxing my aggressive posture into one of simple intense scrutiny. Lewis looked down into his lap, suddenly abashed by my stare. "You're a touch-healer," I said after a moment.

Lewis nodded, not looking up. Behind me, I heard Raydor clear his throat.

"That's a State Crime?" I asked, bemused.

At the softened tone of my voice, Lewis's head lifted. Those eyes, so brilliantly blue and so achingly vulnerable, searched mine as if to gauge how far he could trust me. "It's a cerebral alteration," he recited tonelessly, as if by rote, "warranting segregation, reorganization, and even termination."

"Bullshit!" I said amiably, unusually aware of the nearness of his face to mine. "In MA, the biggest cerebral alteration is intelligence!"

Lewis's lips tugged crookedly, an involuntary hint of that devastatingly wry smile. But he was still a creature ruled by his fear. His eyes went to the detention cuff at his wrist, and he shifted his hands as if to conceal it. "Thank you for what you did, Captain," he reiterated softly. "I know that you're taking a big risk for me."

"Maybe," I replied evenly. "So prove to me you're worth it."

Confusion flitted across his face, pulling his mouth into a frown. "I don't know what I can do," he began carefully.

I leaned back in my chair, taking some of the pressure off him. "You can start by telling me the truth," I told him. "What the hell was MA doing with you?"

Lewis folded his hands in his lap, unconsciously covering what remained of the scratches he had taken from Raydor. "The bruises?" he asked needlessly. "I—they were experimenting with my Talent; seeing how much I could absorb. They had others, other—prisoners." He fumbled with that word, but there was no better term for it. "They beat them to see how much I could take from them." Sweat had sprung up on his upper lip; he brushed anxiously at the dangling forelock of his hair. He was nearly squirming in the overstuffed chair, but I made no move to rescue him, and ultimately he had to go on. "They would keep at it until I—until I would faint," he concluded, his eyes fixed on his knees. "Finally, I couldn't take it anymore; I began to—" He swallowed painfully. "—to scream—and scream and scream!" The fabric of his flightsuit had begun to darken at the throat and armpits. A shudder went through him. "So they drugged me," he said, his voice hardly above a whisper. His face lifted; his eyes, unfocused, met mine. "The drugs kept me from expending the effects of the healing. That's why I was still so bruised when you took me." His hands, limp now, lay uselessly in his lap. "It wasn't until the drugs began to wear off that I could expend the effects of what I'd taken." He shrugged slightly. "The expenditure is still sluggish; I'm not sure how long it'll take before the drugs are completely out of my system."

Suns! What had they done to him? I leaned even closer to Lewis, my elbows sliding from my knees so that my shoulders dropped, putting my face forward on a level with his. "That business at the pull?" I asked quietly.

Lewis glanced down, almost reflexively, at his passive hands. His fingers jerked into a tight knot. He met my gaze reluctantly. "I—I thought that they would try to kill me," he said huskily. "When I heard it—that captain—"

"Redding," I supplied.

"Captain Redding," Lewis repeated dutifully. "When I heard his warning, I knew what they were going to do." When I failed to respond to that, his hands twisted agonizingly in his lap. "I would have tried to warn you sooner, I swear it! If I could have—if I'd known—but the drugs—"

I reached out and squeezed his arm, stopping him. I found that I had to pull my face back then. Powers! He was *normal*! More than normal—he was a *Talent*—and they had nearly killed him. They had packed him off, Light knew why, ostensibly to Heinlein, and then they had tried to execute him on my ship—*my ship*, damn them all!—so he would conveniently disappear. Another pullout accident, a careless captain—I could see the news cassette now, those ball-less bastards! Two volatile emotions—my sympathy for what Lewis had suffered and my fury at MA for what had almost happened at New Cuba— suddenly solidified and became totally compatible in my mind. No one was going to try to fry me and get away with it.

Lewis was looking at me quizzically, warily, fearfully, but with his big blue eyes wide with hope. I gazed back evenly at him, masking the rush of unwanted emotion I felt. I patted his knee in a comradely fashion and told him, ''Don't worry; MA doesn't have you anymore.''

Lewis's tensed body slumped slightly, probably more from anxious fatigue than from any genuine sense of relief; I was unable to give him any real sense of reassurance yet. He looked so vulnerable, so spent, I hardly knew what it was that I felt for him at that moment. Covering my confusion, I got to my feet. ''There's good facilities here. Take a shower, get something to eat. Raydor?'' I half turned. ''See that he finds what he needs.''

Raydor followed me to the doorway. ''Where're you going?'' he asked me calmly.

I grinned, wagging the detention cuff at him. ''Not very far,'' I predicted ruefully. ''Just out for a bit. Keep an eye on him, huh?''

To my relief, I was able to move unrecognized along the throughways and walkways of the Portside business district of Heinlein. It had been a long time since I'd been there and even longer since I'd spent any amount of time. There had been the trips there each year when I was growing up for the mandatory qualifying educational-level exams. Mimosa had also been in the group I had tested through with. But the last time I had spent more than just a few days there had been after my mother's funeral. No one there would equate that gangly, solemn-eyed girl with the mud-brown hair with the tall, flight-suited freightman who now strode purposefully from building to building. They would see me as a captain, an off-worlder, nothing more.

The crisp beauty of Heinlein still jolted me and kept my brain churning. It was my mother's world, the place that first she and then I in turn had shunned for the root-less freedom of space. Now, gazing across the achingly green expanse of a wedge-shaped minipark where several obviously pregnant surrogates chatted, some with half an eye on their gaggle of colorfully clad toddlers, and jump-suited personnel from Port and other services exchanged casual greetings in front of the Maternity Center, I won-dered if I had been wrong. I thought of the last time I had ventured into that shop district; it had been to buy the first flightsuit that I would wear as *Raptor*'s captain. But my memories could be held at bay; it was the next twenty-four hours that mattered. I cut across the land-scaped delta and down a long paved walkway, stepping through the dancing rectangles of sunlight that were re-fracted from the windows of the soaring structures around me.

I chose one of the most expensive clothiers I knew. What the hell—no matter what happened tomorrow morning, my chances of ever collecting the rest of my fee were looking punier than Rollo's conscience. And by that point MA had probably wiped the first half of my fee from my credit account for my having the poor man-ners to have missed my little rendezvous with *Herod*. Luckily, MA could wipe only what MA had keyed, or I'd most likely find myself totally destitute. Not that there was very much in my account, anyway; I'd already been scraping bottom when I'd gotten mixed up with Transys-tems in the first place. It seemed as good a time as any to treat myself to a little extravagance.

It was easy to buy what I wanted and even easier to find out what I wanted to know. Using my credit chip

established my identity and my planet of origin, but that
was hardly worth remarking on even in a fairly tight port
like Heinlein. Being a freightman was still an honorable
profession, one that had been embraced by many Heinlein natives before me. And the items I purchased gave
me a sort of status, one that made it simple for me to
glean the information I sought from the saleswoman at
the counter.

She was middle-aged but trim and rosy with Heinlein's
perpetual glow of health. A Restructured Four or Five, I
guessed, but with that careful attention to individual facial detail that marked her as the product of Heinlein's
own superior surgeons. Probably a native, then. "Beautiful colors," she remarked to me as she folded and
wrapped my purchases.

I nodded, smiling slightly. It was just enough to en-
courage the woman's natural curiosity.

"Something special for a special person," she decided, giving me a conspiratorial wink as her hands
smoothed the folds of the paper wrapper.

I nodded, smiling again, more easily this time.

"Did you hear about Mimosa's special person?" the
saleswoman inquired discreetly but cheerfully.

"Someone new?" I asked casually, picking up my
package.

"Just in," she confided. "An IS—she's so lucky!" The
last was said without a trace of envy; that was not the
way on Heinlein. Gossip was not the way, either, but that
kind of information was pretty easy to get if you didn't
seem overly interested in getting it.

"I guess he's lucky, too, then," I responded, satisfied.
If Mimosa had let the information about Lewis's arrival
stand, that meant that she was confident Mahta would
back her and accede to my new demands. I strode back
across the outdoor triangular green, my parcel on my
hip, my spirits improved. If Mimosa had any real doubts,
she would have begun to dissociate herself from Lewis
already so as not to lose face if anything jeopardized her
chances of getting his IS contract.

Back at the suite Raydor and Lewis sat companionably

over the remains of their meal. I noted that Raydor's face wraps were gone, and Lewis looked calm and refreshed for the first time in our acquaintance. I tossed the parcel at Lewis, and he caught it awkwardly with a look of surprise that amused Raydor.

"New clothes," I told Lewis. "I had to guess at the sizes, so you'll have to try them on."

Lewis hesitated, clutching the package.

"Not *now*!" I laughed at him. "Not *right here*! Before you go to bed will be fine."

Chagrined by the clumsy presumption he had made, Lewis fumbled with the paper wrap, and trying to cover his embarrassment, he pulled out the new clothes: a flightsuit in *Raptor*'s blue and silver, its white liner, black deckboots, and a flame-red pair of sleepers.

"Nice," Raydor commented dryly, a suggestion of humor on his wrinkled face.

Lewis's gratitude was colored by his embarrassment. He looked up at me, clutching the clothing with some stammering words of thanks at his lips. But I cut him off, dropping into one of the chairs and waving disdainfully at the remnants of their meal.

"What the hell's this crap?" I snorted. "Can't you get any *meat* from this Alter-brained piece of junk?"

We had three beds, two bedrooms. I sent Lewis to the single room. I thought Raydor would share with me, but he was curiously formal about the arrangement. I think he would have come if I had asked; surely to my room, and even to my bed. But my mind was so preoccupied that by the time I considered sleeping arrangements, Raydor was already snugly bedded down, Tachs style, in a mound of cushions and blankets on the larger of the two sofas. Maybe that was for the best. I wasn't likely to be good company that night, not with my head filled with thoughts of Heinlein.

I had thought, however, that I'd be able to sleep, with my belly filled with Heinlein's real meat and a debt of fatigue dragging on me. But I wasn't even good company for myself. I tried listening to some audiochips for a while; there were some really good ones there, stuff I hadn't heard in years. But even the music failed to help me. I ended up swaddled in Mimosa's elegant silky sheets, staring wide-awake into the half darkness of the dim bedroom with only my own misgivings for company.

When I first heard the strange sounds, I thought that I had finally nodded off and that I had dreamed them. But when the noise continued, I realized it was coming from the adjacent bedroom. Safely garbed in the prim white of the suite's guest sleepers, I trotted across the carpeted floor, out the door, and past good old Raydor—who could, I think, have slept through an asteroid storm. I punched the release on Lewis's door, and it swept open. Inside, the room was black. I hit the dimmer panel at the door plate and squinted into the rising illumination.

Lewis lay motionless on the bed. I think his very passivity alarmed me more than any kind of thrashing nightmare could have, but he was babbling a blue streak. It was all agitated, unintelligible, a mishmash of words. His face was contorted in distress.

I crossed the room and touched his shoulder. In a single instant, his eyes snapped open and his one arm came across his body to seize my wrist in a grip so tight that I actually gave a small, involuntary cry of surprise and pain. Flustered, Lewis released me, blinking into the room's growing brightness.

I suddenly felt somewhat abashed. "You were talking in your sleep," I explained hastily, struck by just how inane that sounded. I took a step backward. "I'm sorry if I scared you by waking you up."

Lewis reached for the edge of his blanket, hurriedly covering most of the regal red of his new sleepers. "I—I'm sorry if I disturbed you, Captain," he offered automatically.

I shrugged, wiping my palms on the thighs of my sleepers. "I thought you were having a nightmare," I said.

Strangely, that seemed to disturb Lewis. He tugged his blanket up tighter. "Did I—do anything?" he asked cautiously.

I shook my head, taking a step closer to the bed again. "Just a lot of babbling," I assured him. "Nothing that made any sense."

Lewis relaxed then, so visibly that I had to wonder what he feared he might have revealed. His head sank back onto the big pillow. His hands—the left unmarked now, its scratches entirely erased the same way his dreadful bruises had completely disappeared on *Raptor*—loosened their furious grip on the hem of the blanket. I stared at his thumb, less sure than ever that the marks had ever even been there at all. He looked up at me, the tension flowing out of his face. "I'm sorry if I woke you, Captain," he repeated with more genuine concern.

"I wasn't asleep," I told him, surprised even as the admission slid from my mouth.

That concession brought an unexpected little grin tugging at his lips. "Too much real meat," he pronounced almost teasingly.

I stared at Lewis, perplexed all over again by nearly everything that had happened to me since I had first laid eyes on the man. Lewis met my gaze, obliquely at first, then more directly. Having relaxed, he looked almost comfortable on the big, wide bed. The diffuse light of the room's illuminators flattered the contours of his handsome face. He looked good—too damned good.

I hooked one of the nearby chairs with my bare foot and pulled it across the plush carpet to his bedside. With a deliberate casualness, I dropped into the chair. I leaned back, crossing my legs, and draped one arm over the edge of the padded backrest. "Too much Heinlein," I corrected him.

Curiosity picked at him; I saw it flicker, poorly concealed, in his shining eyes. "You know a lot about this place," he said cautiously, alert for any missteps he might inadvertently be taking.

"Yeah," I conceded. "I know enough, anyway."

Some thought caused him to squirm slightly on the bed. He dropped his eyes to the point where his covered knees tented the blanket; then he lifted them again, almost shyly, to my face. "I really didn't know what—what would happen to me here," he began awkwardly.

I stretched lazily, slouching nonchalantly in my chair. At some level I was aware that even the simplicity of the stark white sleepers implied a subtle intimacy that gave me control there. "You don't have to worry," I told him. "They love men here."

Lewis flushed slightly, right to the roots of that shining black hair, hair that reflected nearly blue in the room's light. I was amused at his embarrassment, safe with his discomfort. I had to be careful not to be cruel with my advantage.

"Most of the men who immigrate here are Volunteers," I explained. "It's considered a good place to do your Service. A lot of them stay on; it's a way of life that appeals to a lot of people. The environment's good, and they're well taken care of." I shrugged matter-of-factly. "And if they get tired of it, they can always leave."

Lewis's brows rose in a questioning arc. He seemed confused. "But I thought they—the men—belonged to—"

I laughed, genuinely delighted at his excessive caution, and I spontaneously clapped him on the arm. "Men don't 'belong' to anyone here—they just have to fulfill their Service. There aren't any slaves here, sexual or otherwise," I told him. "If any man on Heinlein gets tired of being kept in luxury, he can leave. Even an IS," I added, "once his contract expires."

From his ruddy blush and the bashful dip of his head, I could see I'd struck a sensitive chord. I leaned closer to him, my voice dropping, serious now. "You didn't realize that, did you?" I said, chagrined at my tactlessness. "Outside Mimosa's office, when I—" I broke off, ruefully shaking my head. "I'm sorry, Lewis. That was low of me. Here you were, envisioning a life of sexual servitude, and I really stuck it to you."

Lewis's discomfort was tangible, causing him to squirm between the sheets. "No matter," he started to say, staring determinedly at the hem of his blanket.

I reached out and gently touched his leg, all safely

swaddled in the bedcovers. "Yes, it matters," I corrected him quietly.

Lewis looked up then, a universe in those wide, guileless eyes that made my fingers ache with a longing I thought I had surely forgotten years ago. He sucked in his lower lip, worrying at it with his white, even teeth, until he could make the necessary words come. "Today you asked me to prove that I was—that I was worth the risk you were taking to help me," he began, his voice cracking tensely. "If—if you don't think that you can take that risk—if you decide to leave me here—I can understand."

Abruptly, I thrust myself back into the contoured chair, flipping my crossed leg impatiently. "Mimosa starting to look pretty good to you, is she?" I taunted with a cutting cruelty I found absolutely necessary that time. "Well, forget it!" I glared at him, feeling those fused emotions of sympathy and anger shift so that it was my rage at what had been done to me that drove my words. " 'Get me out,' you said. After all the shit I've been through on your account, I'm sure not leaving you here now!"

Lewis's composure bent but did not break under my attack. He eyed me warily, then wet his lips and took the only tack I had left open to him. "Thank you, Captain," he said gravely.

I got to my feet, shoving back the chair with a bunt from the backs of my thighs. "Keep that until tomorrow," I advised him dryly, "when we see how much good I've done you. For now, just get some sleep."

I had already started to turn away when he spoke again; his tone was different, shyer but deeper. "Captain?" I turned back. He had finally released the hem of the blanket, exposing a few more inches of the cheery red sleepers but little else. He made a little gesture. "Thank you for the clothes; they all fit."

An unwilled little smile overtook me, and with it the delicious memory of shopping for expensive men's sleepers in Heinlein's Portside stores—the look on the saleswoman's face alone had been priceless. I gave a deprecating shrug. "If I'm going to convince Mahta tomorrow that I've decided I want you for myself, you'd better be dressed like I mean business.''

Lewis's eyes dropped for an instant, abashed by my frankness. When he looked up again, his expression was mildly perplexed. "Who is this Mahta?" he asked me. "The governor?"

I shook my head, nearly smiling again. "Not hardly. This is Heinlein, remember? No governor." I was half-way to the door before I paused, turning to him a final time.

"She's my aunt."

CHAPTER
SIX

One of the more predictable outcomes of the Alterations was the decidedly lopsided ratio of women to men in the post-War world. As had long been suspected, female fetuses proved tougher than male fetuses. Even when donor ova were fertilized with donor sperm for implantation in surrogates, more viable female embryos resulted than male embryos. More females survived gestation, and there were fewer major Alterations and mutations in the resulting female children. But one of the less predictable outcomes of all that were planets like Heinlein.

Heinlein had been sponsored by CA over a century before; it became deregulated a scant two decades later. After deregulation, it had rapidly evolved into one of several so-called women's planets, worlds that were peopled and run primarily by women. The Alterations had neatly accomplished what years of self-anguished, soul-searching equal rights crusading had failed to produce: They had sabotaged the traditional sexual stereotypes forever. To colonize the emptiness of the tens of new worlds, the capabilities and the sheer physical numbers of women were needed. Ironically, there was also no longer any real use for all those women in their old roles. The Alterations had made marriage and the nuclear family worse than meaningless. A child might never meet his or her biological parents; a family was the group of people with whom one shared one's life. And the future belonged to—depended on—people who could *do* things:

pilot ships, erect buildings, perform surgery, manufacture components, operate machinery. If two-thirds of those people now had ovaries rather than testicles, then so be it. In space, the Alterations had made us equal. And on planets like Heinlein, perhaps somewhat more than equal.

MA had a small station on Heinlein, one of the few ugly structures on the whole planet. But MA's authority was strictly token, dependent on the goodwill of Heinlein's Citizens. Once a majority of a planet's Citizens had voted for deregulation, neither of the Authorities had any real power unless they were asked in for some specific cause, such as the facilitation of trade or protection from pirates. Even Heinlein's Port was not run by CA, as it was on many other deregulated worlds.

Lewis's confusion concerning Mahta was common and understandable enough. No one who hadn't lived on a planet like Heinlein could easily grasp the subtleties of its organization. Essentially, there was no government, a fact that confounded and eluded most visitors. There were people like Mimosa, who were heads of the various services, such as Immigration. But most of the substructure of the services was social, not political. People aligned themselves in an orderly fashion because that worked. I knew that seemed bizarre to off-worlders, accustomed to the A's and their elaborate pecking order. But on Heinlein even an IS would hardly be considered a second-rate Citizen, and State Crimes didn't exist, because the state didn't exist.

Even given all that, Mahta was still tough to explain. Heinlein had no formal elected ruler or leader, but if there had been one, no doubt it would have been Mahta. She was not only the sole surviving matriarch of what was left of my family but the ''mother'' of an entire planet as well. She was the acknowledged, if untitled, authority on-planet, again, because that worked. Her function was necessary; therefore, she assumed it. And her decisions were followed because that brought order, and order ensured a pleasant and productive life. Not bad for a bunch of women.

And so, at a little before oh-ten-hundred, a courier, sleek in the silver jumpsuit of Mahta's Central Services, arrived at our suite to escort us to Mahta's quarters. Her chambers were in the same complex as our guest suite, and the trip was a mere climb in the lift and a short walk down another broad, bright corridor. Our guide buzzed at the wide, real wood doors, announced us, and then excused herself with one last cheerful smile.

Mahta herself answered the door. She beamed at me with a genuine affection, a sentiment I had hardly expected—or deserved—and took me in her arms for a hearty hug.

"Jo!" she said happily. "When Mimosa said you'd come, I could hardly wait to see you again!"

"Yeah," I responded, nearly grunting from the force of her embrace, "I was hoping it wouldn't be a problem." Honest if not particularly sentimental.

Mahta turned to Raydor, reaching for his big calloused hands and squeezing them with a real fondness. She popped up on her tiptoes to plant a surprising kiss on his wrapless cheek. "Raydor, so good to see you. Are you taking good care of her?"

Raydor rose gracefully to the teasing, responding with the wry observation, "That's a full-time job, Mahta."

Lewis, who had hung back behind Raydor, stepped forward. For the first time on Heinlein, I think his own sense of curiosity was at least as great as the interest he had aroused. He stared with ill-concealed surprise at Mahta. Whatever he had expected, obviously she wasn't it.

Mahta was my mother's older sister. I knew for a fact that she had a good thirty years on me, but to see her, we could easily have been contemporaries. There was an ageless quality about her, a vitality unusually intense even for Heinlein. A good head shorter than me, she was slender and petite but far from fragile. Clad in a loose, belted tunic and casual baggy trousers, both of bone-colored homespun woven from the natural fibers grown in Heinlein's fields, she looked more like a farmer's daughter than the tacit head of a planet. But in her understated way

Mahta was a striking woman, with fine, evenly drawn features and a thick mane of pale gold hair. Her face was dominated by her eyes, huge and velvety, the color of wet earth. She stared back openly at Lewis, the hint of a smile working at her full lips.

"Mr. Lewis, I presume," she said.

Embarrassed by his own forwardness, Lewis dropped his gaze and extended an awkward hand to Mahta. To his alarm, Mahta bypassed his outstretched hand and reached up to plant a friendly kiss on his cheek instead.

Enjoying Lewis's surprise, Mahta gestured to us. "Come, join us," she invited. "We were just finishing breakfast."

Beyond us, in a plant-festooned little alcove, three people sat on floor cushions at a low oval table over the remains of their partially eaten meal. One of them was a robust-looking man with dark curly hair, a full beard, and a quick smile. I recognized him as Mahta's longtime male companion, Jim. The other two diners were Mimosa and her aide, Garth. All three of them greeted us with cheery hellos and good mornings.

For the first time I found myself wishing that I had sprung for some new clothes for myself as well. It was all very casual, but next to Mimosa's elegant rainbow-hued silk caftan—hell, even next to Lewis's trim new blue and silver flightsuit—I felt moderately dowdy. Thank Powers for Raydor, who always dressed like a working freightman, and Jim, who was still wearing a night robe. Even Mahta herself always seemed to dress with a rustic simplicity. And after all, I reminded myself ruefully, I was hardly there to impress them all with my wealth—only with my greed.

"Would you like something to eat?" Mahta offered when we all were seated.

Almost in unison, the three of us shook our heads.

"The quarters were satisfactory?" Mahta inquired, nibbling at the last fragment of a fruit roll.

"Fine," I said.

"Food was good, too," Raydor added with unexpected enthusiasm. Nothing impressed a Tachs more than fresh fruit and vegetables.

Mahta laughed with delight. "You're just like Jim, Raydor," she teased.

I leaned back in my chair, a softly contoured piece with deeply padded upholstery. Mahta eyed me with some bemusement. "On to business, then," she announced with a good-natured smile. "Jo, Mimosa tells me there's a problem with your fee."

"The problem is that there isn't enough of it," I replied, trying for the same casual tone.

Mahta laughed again. The laugh seemed to suggest that it wasn't that much of a problem. "I see," she said matter-of-factly. "And just how much more does there have to be?"

I never made the mistake of underestimating Mahta. Her humor and affection were genuine enough, but there was steel beneath them. One had to come on square with her. I named a figure that was high but not completely ridiculous.

Mahta's brows rose, her rich brown eyes widening. Across the low table from me I saw Mimosa's face pull into a frown; my demand threatened her acquisition of Lewis's contract. On the chair beside me Lewis stared studiously into his lap, where his pale hands lay clasped together in a knot.

"That's considerably more than MA's original offer," Mahta remarked calmly, toying with a piece of fruit. "Yet you took the run."

"The run was considerably more trouble than I expected," I responded flatly. "We had some problems at pullout." I lifted my left wrist. "And then there's the matter of this jewelry."

Mahta viewed the detention cuff with honest distaste. She shook back her pale hair with an impatient little toss of her head. "Yes, that's hardly a popular piece of adornment here, either, Jo," she reminded me. She glanced over to where Mimosa sat, silently cradling a coffee cup in her hands, and then looked back at me. "If we met your request for the fee increase, would you release Mr. Lewis to us?'' she asked quietly.

Beside me, Lewis froze. His blue eyes were like flash beams aimed at my heart. I didn't dare turn my head even fractionally for fear he would impale me with that look. He might not understand what I had to do. ''Yeah,'' I said, nodding stiffly, willing myself to look only at Mahta. ''You give me the credits and he's all yours.''

Mahta casually arranged her elbows on the armrests of her chair. ''I feel there's some room for negotiation, then,'' she said evenly. ''I'm sure we can come to an agreement on this, Jo.'' Her gaze swept around the low oval table, smiling at the others. ''Mimosa, why don't you and Garth show Raydor our arboretum?'' She turned to Raydor. ''It's on the upper level—really beautiful, especially mornings. You'll love it.'' She touched Jim fondly on the arm. ''Jim, why don't you go along?''

As the others dutifully got to their feet, Lewis, automatically obedient, began to rise as well. But Mahta leaned across the table and gestured to him. ''No, Mr. Lewis, please stay. This concerns you as well.''

For a brief moment Mimosa froze, her eyes darting from Lewis to my face. Then she smiled graciously and took Raydor's arm. ''The bougainvillea's in bloom,'' she told him. ''It's unbelievable.''

As he followed Mimosa from the room, Raydor gave me one fleeting, impassive look, a look that only I could have read. *Good luck!* it said. Then the four of them were gone.

Mahta settled herself in her chair again, her dark eyes regarding me placidly. ''All right, enough of this formal bullshit,'' she said pleasantly. ''Now I want the truth, Jo.''

Beside me, Lewis went stiff with alarm. I didn't have to turn to look at him to feel the anxiety his posture conveyed. In the space of seconds several tacks presented themselves to me, but I rejected all of them. With Mahta only the truth would succeed, and if I couldn't manage the truth, then at least my most winning lie.

I leaned back in my chair, subtly mimicking Mahta's

pose, crossed my legs, and looked directly into her unperturbable eyes. "I want his contract myself," I said.

Mahta gave a little snort, then chuckled. She gave Lewis a brief but all-encompassing glance and then looked back to me. "Well, well," she said, still smiling. "This is the first encouraging sign I've seen from you in some time, Jo!"

Lewis squirmed uncomfortably in his chair. Even though he'd been forewarned, the nature of the negotiations profoundly embarrassed him, and Mahta's good-humored amusement only exacerbated his sense of shame.

"And when did you discover this . . . overwhelming desire for Mr. Lewis?" Mahta was asking me in a bemused tone.

I shrugged noncommittally. "Take a look at him," I offered easily. "There aren't many like him around. And I didn't say I had any attachment for him, just that I want his IS contract for myself."

"Oh, I see," Mahta responded, still smiling. "So, you want me to remove the cuffs, sign him over to you, and send you on your way—is that it?"

Automatically, I leaned forward. "I'll pay you for your trouble if that's what you're getting at," I replied tersely.

Mahta laughed again, dismissing my gruff offer with a wave of her hand. Her attention shifted to Lewis again, a frank scrutiny that made his already taut nerves jump visibly. "And how do you feel about all this, Mr. Lewis?" she inquired sweetly. "Do you find the captain's concern touching?"

Lewis was gripping the arms of his chair with the desperation of a green freightman facing a rough pullout. A hot flush colored his face, and he had to wet his lips twice before he could speak. "I'm willing to go with her," he blurted out. "She's been very good to me."

Mahta's brows made an amused arch. "Oh? And just how good?" The question was mercifully rhetorical; Lewis was too flustered to have been able to answer, anyway. He darted a sideways glance at me, seeking reprieve, but the effect of that covert look was only to enhance the impression of intimacy between us that he had so unwittingly created, and so Mahta's humor was un-dampened.

"So, what do you say?" I asked her bluntly, hastily interrupting the bizarre interplay between them. "Do I get him or not?"

Mahta's expression suddenly sobered. Silently, she regarded Lewis for a moment. "Would you like to join the others at the arboretum, Mr. Lewis?" she asked him, not unkindly. "Anyone in the building would be glad to help direct you."

Lewis stumbled to his feet, pathetically eager for dismissal. But at the door he paused awkwardly and looked back at me. I gave him a minute nod, as if to release him, for I could not reassure him. Then he hurried from the room.

I figured that Mahta no longer had any reason for tact, and so I faced her squarely, the expression of my last query still fixed on my face. But I had nearly forgotten just who it was I was trying to bluff.

"Have you joined with him?" Mahta asked me matter-of-factly.

She had managed to startle even me. I was caught off balance by her bluntness, and my affected nonchalance was clumsy and obvious. "Joined?" I snorted. "He's a Class Ten, Mahta." I tried to use irony to conceal my surprise at the question. "Surely you've seen his MA profile."

Mahta rolled her head back as if in silent laughter. When she looked at me, the corners of her eyes hinted at some secret amusement, obviously at my expense. "Surely you don't believe everything you read in an MA profile," she responded wryly, "especially considering who compiles them!" At my expression of skepticism, she continued. "If you're as taken with Mr. Lewis as you indicate, I would think you would have checked these things out, Jo."

Realization nibbled at me then; things that had made no sense up to that point finally began to fall into place: Lewis's shyness, his almost boyish naïveté, even the way he blushed. It occurred to me that I had never seen an HTA like Raydor blush, even in situations that would seem to call for it.

"He's not HTA," Mahta went on as if reading my thought; her amusement was more open now if still as gentle. "Not even sterilized, I'll wager." She let that sink in for a moment, then gave me a wry but warm smile. "An even better find than you imagined, eh, Jo?"

I couldn't help it: The whole situation was deteriorating faster than a rotting codfish at high noon, yet I couldn't keep from grinning back conspiratorially at Mahta. I almost laughed out loud!

Then Mahta leaned forward in her chair, her expression wise with an age beyond the youthful sparkle in her eyes. "And now, my wayward niece, the *truth*," she said to me. "How did you get mixed up with this job for MA, and what happened at New Cuba?"

And so, outclassed and outmaneuvered, I told her. I began with the Transystems fiasco and my meeting with Rollo; I told her about Jessup, the terms of my contract with MA, and the detention cuff. By the time I got to our pullout from New Cuba, Redding's timely warning, and *Herod*, Mahta was actually fidgeting in her chair with unspoken questions.

When I had finished, her first word was, "Why?"

"He's a Talent," I explained. "He touch-heals—I don't know what else." I laced my fingers together and looked levelly at her. "If I don't get him off-planet, they'll kill him."

Mahta straightened abruptly. She got to her feet, paced a few steps, and then halted in front of me. "How do you know that?" she asked me quietly.

"How do I know that he's a Talent? Or how do I know that MA is trying to kill him?" I specified.

She dropped into the empty chair beside me. "Both," she said.

I clenched my hands. "The touch-healing I've seen, and he told me." I stared into Mahta's wet-earth eyes, so dewy, so depthless. "As for the rest, isn't it obvious?

They've already tried it once; what's to keep them from trying it again?''

That presumption disturbed Mahta; it was the first time I saw genuine distress on her face. ''Why do you think he's in danger here?'' she asked me. ''You know MA has no authority on Heinlein, Jo.''

''Yeah—they don't have the 'authority' to fry a freighter in pullout, either,'' I reminded her sardonically. ''But somebody tried it—and since when does MA need authority to cover their own ass?''

Mahta considered that silently, thoughtfully. For the first time I realized that she knew something, something she was not going to tell me. ''I promise you he'll be safe here, Jo,'' she said finally.

I shook my head. ''No. Even if you think Heinlein can protect him, it's clear to me he's scared shitless of being left here. He begged me to get him off-planet.'' I gazed calmly at Mahta, trying to gauge her part in all this. ''What kind of life would it be for him here even if you could protect him?'' I concluded. ''He'd have to live like a damned prisoner.''

Mahta stood again, her agitation so close to the surface that I think she literally could not sit still. She shook her long pale hair off her shoulders and stepped back to her own chair, opposite mine. She gave me a long, hard look. ''And if you take him—Do you think *you* can protect him, Jo?''

I felt my chin lift stubbornly. It was like arguing with my mother had been; there is no more immovable object than a woman who is convinced that she's doing the best thing. ''I can get him out-system,'' I maintained evenly. ''Turn him loose where they'll never find him.''

Mahta's brows rose in a dubious little arch. ''Turn him loose?'' she repeated. ''You think he'd be safe on his own?''

I wouldn't beg, and I'd done just about all the bargaining I had the capacity for. ''Are you going to give him to me, Mahta?'' I asked her bluntly.

Mahta lowered herself into her chair, folding her legs

beneath her. Her expression was fixed, unreadable. "That depends on what he's worth to you," she replied.

I held my breath. There was only one thing I had that Mahta could possibly want: an untouched treasure that was the hidden wealth of that world, an inheritance that I had always blithely ignored. I bit my lower lip, staring across the low, dish-strewn table at the tough little woman with the childlike eyes. I let out my breath. "All right," I said softly. "I'll donate ova."

Mahta spread her hands. "You've never offered to do that before, Jo," she remarked, an almost quizzical look on her face.

I felt my mouth tighten grimly. "Maybe because I've never had to before," I replied tersely.

Mahta's hands turned palms up. "Maybe you don't have to now," she countered.

I stared at her in confusion. If it was a game, she had exceeded my tolerance for it. "I don't understand," I told her frankly.

Some of the old gentle affection returned to Mahta's expression as she faced me across the table. It was a look I had seen often enough before, one that I was never sure I had earned from her. When my mother had died while I was still a Volunteer and still underage, it had been Mahta who had intervened, using her considerable influence to convince CA to release me from the terms of my Service and to bend the rules to give me title to *Raptor*. I realized then, as now, that Mahta had always hoped I would consider staying on Heinlein and I had never understood her apparent willingness to make it so possible for me not to do so.

"You're a lot like her, you know," she said fondly, meaning my mother.

Not really, I thought. I was not so much like her, that tough young freightman who had turned her back on the luxuries of Heinlein's Services, who had pushed out into space on *Raptor*, who had, somewhere, sometime, joined with some nameless man to create me. If anyone was like her, it was Mahta—Mahta, who was a recalcitrant romantic beneath that humble homespun. But that was

something I doubted even Mahta could see or would acknowledge. And so all I said was, "Maybe. At least I
know that I can't stay here, any more than she could."

Mahta stared at me a bit longer, her big dark eyes
calmly appraising. "All right, then," she said. "He's
yours."

I tried to keep the nervous relief from my voice. "We'll
have to lift right away," I explained in a hasty apology.
"The ova donation will have to wait, but I swear that—"

But Mahta lifted her hand, neatly cutting me off. "No—
no donation, Jo. I said he's yours." She shrugged. "I
requested his IS contract from MA as a favor to a friend,
but I'm sure she'll understand this change of circumstances. I'll sign his papers over to you, then you're responsible for him." She stood, smoothing her tunic.
"There's no other price for him."

My expression surely betrayed my surprise and con-
fusion, for Mahta gave a little laugh as she moved to her
Integrator console. "Nothing else?" I echoed stupidly.
"But you said—"

"I said it would depend on what he was worth to you,
Jo," she reminded me, bent over her console, her fingers
flying over the keyboard. She looked up abruptly with an
expression of gentle indulgence that suggested she knew
something about me that I hadn't quite figured out yet
for myself. "And now I know what you think he's
worth," she concluded.

The hell with it—let her think what she wanted! I just
wanted out. I got to my feet and approached the console,
watching over her shoulder as she keyed up Lewis's ID.
"Uh, what about Mimosa?" I finally asked, feeling
strangely awkward. Mimosa was more than just a
"friend" to Mahta; she was more like a daughter.

But Mahta just gave a small dismissive shrug. "Mimosa will understand. Something else will come along."
She glanced over at me, smiling crookedly. "Although
something else like Mr. Lewis might be too much to
hope for."

I was saved from having to comment on that likelihood
as Mahta's Integrator politely disgorged a plastic card,

Lewis's IS contract, and a small electronic key. Eagerly, I held out my left arm, and Mahta deftly unlocked the detested detention cuff from my wrist. Then she offered me the cards and the key.

"How soon can we lift?" I asked, half-consciously rubbing my bare wrist as I slipped the cards and the key into the breast pocket of my flightsuit.

"Whenever you like," Mahta replied. She leaned over the speaker and punched the transmit button. "Jeryl? We have guests with Mimosa in the arboretum. Would you please send them back down here?" She looked up at me, dangling the open and now-harmless cuff from her fingertips as if it were something unpleasantly fetid. "Do me a favor, though, will you, and take this thing with you."

As I took the cuff from her and pocketed it, the speaker on her console sputtered to life. "Mahta? We have a Priority Distress from Integration on *Raptor* for Captain Jolac."

Mahta punched the button. "Audio," she requested. "Patch it through."

In seconds Handy's familiar bass voice was emerging from Mahta's speaker. "Jo, we have a situation."

"A situation." Handy's code for real trouble. He was too cautious to say more than that, over unshielded circuits. My glance darted over to Mahta. What the hell, she was hardly likely to try to sabotage me after what had just happened between us—whatever *had* just happened between us. I leaned closer over her console and touched the transmit button. "It's okay, Handy, let's have it."

"MA," he rumbled, hardly to my surprise. "They've put a hold on *Raptor*. Looks like half a dozen of their goons here in the bay." He paused a moment, as if checking something. "And a detail's been dispatched to find you in Services," he finished.

Mahta stared at the speaker grill, then at me. "How does he—" she began, but I just waved her down with a grim little smile.

"He cut into their codes," I explained, amused in spite

of myself at her naïveté in such matters. Handy made it a principle to always keep at least one step ahead of MA wherever we set down. That was not a standard function of shipboard Integrators; but then, Handy was hardly a standard shipboard Integrator.

"They have no authority here," Mahta responded indignantly. "Not to hold ships, and certainly not to send troops into Services!"

I wished I'd had the time to fully enjoy her outrage, but I was too busy rapidly considering our options. I punched the transmit button again. "Cycle her up, Handy," I instructed him. "Stand by. This may be kind of a rushed lift!" Then I started for the door.

Hurrying behind me, Mahta caught my arm. "Jo! What makes you think—"

Forced to interrupt her again, I noted tersely, "They were just waiting for us to make a break. As soon as you transferred Lewis's IS contract over to me, they knew I'd be lifting with him." At her wide-eyed look of astonishment, I added, "Yeah, they're in your system—code or no code."

In the corridor outside Mahta's apartment I demanded, "Where the hell is this arboretum? If we don't get out of here before those MA goons get in, they'll have us cornered here!"

"This way," Mahta offered, rushing into the lead. After several turns through the maze of corridors we reached a lift station. "They have to come down this way," she assured me. "It's the only lift to the roof."

I stared impatiently at the blinking IN TRANSIT sign on the lift control panel. It had occurred to me—unworthily, perhaps—when Handy's warning had first come over the speaker that maybe Mahta was somehow mixed up with MA in all this. I was certain she was involved in some way that she had not revealed to me, but the genuine shock and indignation with which she'd greeted the news of MA's incursion into Heinlein's autonomy had convinced me her involvement was not on MA's behalf. Basically, I guess I just still mistrusted the altruistic grace with which Mahta had committed Lewis's fate to my hands. Despite her lifelong benevolence toward me, it had been totally unexpected and the first bit of good luck we'd had so far.

With a brisk efficiency that nearly made me jump out of my skin, the lift doors *whoosh*ed open and five people emerged. Mimosa took one look at the expressions on our faces and asked, "What is it?"

"Come on," I said to Raydor, grabbing automatically for Lewis's arm. "MA's holding *Raptor*, and they've got a squad on their way up here!"

Instantaneously Raydor had correlated all that and noted my possessive hold on Lewis. Mimosa hadn't missed that, either. She threw a look at Mahta—a hurt look, like a disappointed child—but she managed to quickly mask whatever she felt with an honest concern for us.

"They'll come up through Receiving," Mimosa figured briskly. "The walkway is the quickest way back to Port." She glanced over her shoulder at her aide. "Garth, take point. Be careful," she added.

Nodding wordlessly, the little white-haired man hurried down the corridor ahead of us. I began to follow, still gripping Lewis's arm. Lewis was stunned and confused and frightened, all understandable reactions, given the circumstances. I was glad to have Raydor at our backs, even without his beam rifle.

Mahta moved to follow us, but both Mimosa and Jim reached out to stop her. "No, it's too dangerous!" Mimosa insisted vehemently, seizing Mahta's forearm. Their eyes locked.

What did Mimosa know? I could understand her distress at losing Lewis's contract, but her steely-eyed duel with Mahta convinced me that Mimosa knew there was more at stake than the luxury of a handsome IS.

Mahta hesitated, clearly torn. "Jo!" she called out. As I slid to a halt, she smiled at me, an infectious smile from that ageless sprite. "Good luck, Jo," she said.

Whirling around, I collided with Lewis. My grasp on his arm was broken. As I clutched for him again, my fingers touched the metal band on his wrist. "Wait!" I commanded, fumbling in my pocket for the key. To my dismay, my hands were trembling so badly that at first I couldn't even fit the key into the slot on his cuff. Lewis had to use his free hand to steady me; he wasn't shaking at all despite the terror in his eyes. When the cuff parted, freeing him, I stuffed the device into my pocket. Then I seized his arm again and began to trot.

Mimosa brought up the rear as we fled for the exit to the glassed-in walkway. It seemed impossible to me that our leisurely arrival on that same walkway had occurred less than twenty-four hours earlier. So much had happened since then, it was like everything had turned 180 degrees on Heinlein.

"Handy picked up on it," I puffed to Raydor as we half ran down the glittering skywalk. "As soon as Mahta transferred Lewis's IS contract, they were on us like flies on a pile of shit!"

"What've they got at Port?" he asked me.

"Half a squad, at least," I responded, still huffing. I felt dishearteningly out of breath already and not at all like having an all-out battle in the hangar bay. I caught a glimpse of Garth's emerald-green jumpsuit, rounding a corner about fifty meters ahead of us. I slowed enough to catch Mimosa's attention. "What's MA got on-planet?" I panted.

"Oh, nothing, really," she responded breathlessly. "Two picket ships, I think."

"Ground artillery? Beam cannon?"

Mimosa's exquisite brows rose in a surprised arch. "On *Heinlein*?" she asked incredulously. I was strangely satisfied to note that she was puffing for breath as hard as I was. "Of course not!"

"What's on those pickets?" Raydor continued from behind us.

"Range beams, I think," Mimosa answered. "After all, they do patrol for MA." She had caught up to me. "But they can't fire any weapons in Port, or—"

I made a contemptuous snorting sound. How could those women be so naive? My derision was so obvious that even Mimosa didn't attempt to defend her point.

Port's grid spread below us, radiant in Heinlein's mid-morning sun. We entered the hangar on the upper level, crossing the vast structure on the elevated walkway that would take us to the ramp that led down to the bay floor. Beneath us six armored and helmeted MA security men grimly ringed *Raptor*. My ship crouched there menacingly on the tarmac, her swept-back vanes arched like an angry hawk's wings. My ship—*my ship*, and now *my IS*. No one was getting either one of them away from me without a fight.

From our vantage point on the enclosed overhead walkway we had a clear view of Garth's portly figure as he approached the security men. He waved animatedly at them, gesticulating like someone chastising a group of dense but harmless Altereds. I hoped to hell he knew what he was doing. MA security teams on deregulated worlds were randomly armed, and I wasn't real eager to discover whether that particular bunch was carrying weapons by having Garth get himself fried right there on the tarmac.

Trying uselessly to control my gasping respiration and just as uselessly to make Lewis disappear behind me, I descended the rampway to our bay. With as much casual assertiveness as I could muster, I strode up to the group of uniformed men. "What the hell's going on here?" I demanded loudly.

The squadron head, faceless behind the reflective faceplate of his helmet, turned from Garth to me. "Captain Jo-lac?" he inquired formally.

"Right!" I replied brusquely. "What's the problem here?"

As we spoke, Raydor moved up behind me, his back to my back, with Lewis trapped between us. I cast an involuntary and longing glance at *Raptor*'s loading ramp, which was retracted and sealed, as was usual in dock—and which was also guarded by one of the MA goons, which was not so usual.

"Your ship is under a temporary hold," the squadron head told me stiffly.

"By whose authority?" Mimosa demanded, stepping around me to a point between me and the leader.

"Military Authority, ma'am," he replied stoically.

"Which is *no* authority at all on this planet!" Mimosa retorted tartly.

There was a new sound from the walkway above us: the muffled thud of running feet. My breathing, which had finally begun to ease up a little, suddenly abandoned me altogether. It was the rest of the squad MA had sent to the Services Complex—exactly what we needed!

The squadron leader's helmet tilted slightly as he glanced up at the sound of his impending reinforcements, contemplating, no doubt, a speedy end to the increasingly unpleasant little confrontation. Then suddenly, inexplicably, his whole body jerked backward and he made a small, strangled sound. To my astonishment—and to his as well, I suspect—a smoking black gash appeared at the juncture of his helmet and his collar line. With a sickening lurch, his armored head separated from his body and landed with a thump on the hangar bay floor. Twisting, his decapitated body followed.

It was the kind of thing I'm sure the MA recruiters never mention. Reconstruction is a great thing; they can even regenerate amputated limbs—no small concern where beam-weapon wounds are concerned. But I had a feeling that particular soldier was out of luck.

Completely incredulous, I swung to face Mimosa. She stood there stiffly braced with a still-humming beam pistol leveled in her hands. "Go!" she hissed fiercely at me, giving me a push in the direction of *Raptor*'s ramp access. "He was the only armed member in this bunch, but I don't know about what's coming!"

Still stunned by her cool ferocity, I staggered forward, dragging Lewis after me. Raydor lunged ahead of us, directly at a totally confused security man who was standing between us and the ramp. Raydor's huge fist hit the side of the guard's head so hard that the man's helmet actually dented. The guard dropped like a dead ox. Raydor thrust his palm against the ramp access lock and then spun around as the remaining four security men broke into action.

MA training must be a wonderful thing; I can't explain why else four unarmed men would so fearlessly rush us, considering what Mimosa had just done to their squadron leader. Bizarrely enough, I was grateful that Raydor had managed to knock heads on two more of them before Mimosa had a chance at them. She ruthlessly cut into the remaining pair, her beam pistol sizzling.

I pushed Lewis onto *Raptor*'s descending ramp just as the first beam fire from the second group of security men began to hiss around the ship's belly. Damned if Garth—sweet, elfish Garth—wasn't flashing a beam pistol, too. This was *Heinlein*, for Power's sake, not some muddy-boot colony world! Since when did Immigration carry beam weapons? Mimosa spun around, dropping to one knee to return the security men's fire. Glass panes from the overhead walkway shattered, showering the tarmac below with a hail of glittering shards. Raydor had disappeared into the ship; moments later, *Raptor*'s concealed belly guns dropped, swiveling predatorily.

I shoved Lewis roughly up the ramp, ducking behind the loading strut as a beam blast blackened the pavement below us. Mimosa was flung sideways by the impact, landing several yards away. She struggled to her knees, her colorful caftan torn, blood streaming across her forehead. But the beam pistol was still tightly gripped in her hand. Garth wheeled, moving with amazing agility to place himself between Mimosa and the line of fire. By then Raydor was returning fire. *Raptor*'s quite-illegal high-intensity beam guns blasted a hole the size of a hangar door in the walkway superstructure. Glass and metal fragments danced across the bay floor, along with what appeared to be pieces of several bodies. *Raptor*'s engines rumbled with Handy's prelift ministrations.

"Jo! Come on!" Raydor growled over the ship's amplified speaker.

But I hesitated, torn by divided loyalties. Garth bent over Mimosa, who was trying to get to her feet. She didn't appear to be seriously injured, but the blast had stunned her. She threw me a furious look, made even more manic by the streak of gore on her face. *"Go!"* she shouted, gesturing vehemently. "Before there are more of them!"

At that moment Lewis slid past me, pulling free of my grasp. He sped across the smoking tarmac toward Mimosa. Before I could even react, he had reached out and taken a startled Mimosa's head between his hands.

"Lewis, you ball-less bastard!" I shouted at him, fear fueling my fury. But the rest of my useless threats died unspoken. Within seconds Lewis was back at my side, preceding me up the ramp, his hands stained with Mimosa's blood. The hydraulics hissed, and the ramp began to retract. In the rapidly closing slice of view that remained of the hangar bay floor I saw a shocked Garth supporting Mimosa—Mimosa, whose head was unmarked now. Queasy, I was almost afraid to turn and see the echo of the laceration decorating Lewis's temple.

"Jo!" Raydor bellowed again. Automatically now, I reacted, sprinting up the corridor to Control.

"Come on," I snarled to Lewis. "Get strapped in— this is going to be one hell of a quick lift!"

From his copilot's seat, Raydor, already in his harness, was punching the lift sequence through Handy's access. *Raptor* was turning with a haste that made her wobble clumsily across the smoking bay floor.

"Standard trajectory?" Handy inquired calmly.

"Standard trajectory, my ass!" I retorted, fumbling with my harness. "Just get us the joining hells *up!*"

"Ship's discretion," Handy decided mildly.

The arch of the huge bay doors disappeared behind us as *Raptor* cleared the hangar. I felt the visceral pull of acceleration as Handy nosed her up and out. I flattened in my chair, fighting a rising tide of nausea while my pulse hammered alarmingly.

I twisted my head, looking back to the ancillary chair where Lewis had strapped in. He looked like shit. His skin was the color of oatmeal, and the ugly, bloodless gash—Mimosa's legacy—stood out starkly on his left temple.

"You okay?" I grunted at him.

He nodded mutely, gripping the arms of his chair. He looked *worse* than shit. I hoped he wasn't going to throw up. Hell, I hoped *I* wasn't going to throw up, at least not until all this was over.

"Jo? Two ships on our tail," Handy reported calmly.

I forced myself forward in my chair, fighting the G-force of the lift, and punched the visual on Handy's screen. The image was fragmented, jumping wildly, like electronic chaff in a high wind.

"MA pickets," Handy added needlessly.

"I'm getting Port," Raydor announced from my right, his head cocked into his pickup. He pushed the speaker button.

"—have no authority to pursue or harass commercial ships in this sector!" cracked the angry voice. "I repeat: This is Heinlein Port, to *Argent* and *Corona*! Cease pursuit and return to dock! You have no authority to pursue or harass commercial ships in this sector!"

The picket ships' only response was to open fire on us. Brilliant orange beams of energy exploded off our starboard side, causing the speaker to squeal in a spasm of static. The ships were too far away to do us much damage, but they were a hell of a lot faster and more maneuverable than *Raptor* in those close quarters.

I punched Handy's input. "Return fire!" I barked.

High-intensity beam artillery was outlawed on private ships, permitted only on MA's military cruisers. If the picket ships had had high-intensity beams, we'd have been just so much space trash. Handy was programmed for effect, not to kill. The guns that hung below *Raptor*'s belly whined; flares of achingly bright blue fire danced around the pursuing pickets. On speaker, Port continued its impotent tirade against MA's attack. But the pickets just kept on inexorably coming.

"Handy, get us ready to pull out," I said grimly.

"Jo," Handy reminded me logically, "I need some coordinates for that, remember?"

As if on cue, another fusillade of fire came from the pickets, closer this time. *Raptor* rocked slightly; Handy muttered to Internals. On the speaker, Port had changed tacks.

"*Raptor*, this is Heinlein." Mimosa: So she had reached the Port building safely at least. "Give us your coordinates, Jo, so we can get you out of here!"

I did some rapid mental file shuffling, juggling the risks. Then I leaned over Handy's input and gave him the name to code and scramble to Port. "Draco," I told him. "Give us Draco."

Handy's screen blazed into life, figures flying across it in an eerie green blur as his neurons surged into action.

"*No!*"

The cry came from behind us, causing me to twist around with a jerk. Not Lewis again! Suns! The man was turning into the worst backseat driver I'd ever had.

"Draco's safest," I shot back at him, furious that he'd try to usurp my prerogative again. "It's out-system, it's deregulated, and there's no big MA installation nearby!"

Lewis's eyes were glazed, reflective, like the crazy blue of *Raptor*'s high-intensity beams. The gash on his forehead looked garishly unreal, an affected insanity. His whole body was rigid. "No!" he repeated, almost pleading. "Not Draco—Camelot! We have to go to Camelot!"

"You're joinin' *nuts*," I shot back with a noticeable lack of tact. "Camelot's crawling with MA—they've got one of their biggest research stations there! We might as well go back to New Cuba as go to Camelot!"

But Lewis hung forward desperately in his harness, his eyes cutting through me, his voice fallen to an urgent whisper. "Please, Captain—I have to go there! *Camelot!*"

Raptor shuddered, beam energy sizzling over her hull. The pickets nearly had us within range.

"Jo," Handy chimed in, "Port is getting a little hysterical."

Wonderful; *they* were getting hysterical? We were about to be shredded into just so many metal filings, I had a crazy man in my cockpit who suddenly wanted to visit one of MA's scenic strongholds—and *they* were worried? My jaw clenched, I locked eyes with Lewis. *Camelot!*

I slammed my hand onto Handy's input. "Camelot!" I snarled at him. "Camelot. Code it to Port—*now*!"

Luckily, hysteria was not part of Handy's repertoire; not a part of Raydor's, either. As the new pullout plot figures began their dizzying journey across the screen, Raydor began a calm search through Internals' damage-monitoring system, alert for anything that might compromise us in the pullout. I fiercely refrained from turning again to glare at Lewis. I hoped the idiot was satisfied; furthermore, I hoped he puked!

"*Raptor*, this is Heinlein." Mimosa's voice sounded more than a little shaken. "You are cleared for your coordinates. Jo, are you sure you want to do this?"

"Not sure at all," I replied fervently. "Take care, Mimosa. *Raptor* out."

"Approaching spiral for pull," Handy rumbled. "Uh oh . . ."

The last comment was for the picket ships, which, like a pair of sharks, had finally gotten us within their range and were firing a fusillade of beam shots that would have popped our hull like a soap bubble had not Handy just made a sharp banking maneuver to bring *Raptor* into position for the spiral. As it was, the wave of energy passed beneath us, buffeting the ship. There was no way we were going to outmaneuver them once they locked onto our spiral pattern. We would have been sitting ducks.

I hit Handy's input. "Fry those bastards, huh?" I instructed him calmly.

Raydor's big head lifted abruptly. He stared at me, but I didn't turn or acknowlege him. Handy never hesitated. He was programmed to save us and preserve *Raptor*, not to make moral decisions about frying a few MA jerks. With the ship rolling elegantly into a lazy curl, her hot belly guns whined again. There were two barely separate explosions, a brief scream of static, and then an effervescence of light. Suddenly our field was clear, at least for the moment we needed to pull out. Bye-bye, *Argent*; bye-bye, *Corona*.

"Pulling out," Handy informed us dispassionately.

What the hell. If the pickets had gone back to Port,

Mahta would have killed them, anyway, possibly with her bare hands. I dug my fingers into my chair's padded armrests, bracing my head as the powerful G-force began to overtake me.

"Well," Raydor remarked laconically just as we went into the pull, "I guess we can forget about doing any more business with MA."

CHAPTER SEVEN

We popped out of the pull about forty hours out from Camelot—plenty of time to regret the move. Clumsily, I unbuckled my chair harness, trying to conceal the fact that I was still shaking. I turned to Lewis: Damned if he hadn't thrown up, after all.

In the ancillary chair Lewis fumbled awkwardly with the catches of his harness. His new flightsuit was smudged with Mimosa's blood and spattered with his own vomit. He looked even worse than he had before we'd gone into the pull, if that was possible. All I could think was, I turned down MA's fee for *this*?

He brushed ineffectively at the mess on his flightsuit. Then his eyes met mine, in their expression a chasm of misery and pain.

"Go on," I said gruffly. "Go get cleaned up." As Lewis hesitated, glancing at the mess he'd made around the chair, I repeated more emphatically, "Just go! I'll clean it up."

He got up shakily to his feet, reaching for the frame of the hatchway to steady himself.

"I want to see you in an hour," I added brusquely, "in my cabin."

There was a flash of something in his eyes, suspicion or fear or maybe both. But as usual, he owed me an explanation.

Raydor was running through the systems check with Internals; his comm board was lit up like a Christmas tree. "At least the new rotor seal held," he remarked placidly, his eyes on the console. I felt a small pang of guilt; he was doing my job again. Then again, I was the one who had volunteered to swab the decks.

That was another thing I had always wondered about: Just where were all those robots and droids and automatons that were supposed to liberate us human beings from drudgery in this glorious future of ours? Mechanicals had never really replaced human labor; it was another one of the endless little disappointments of post-War life. No warp drive, no little green men, and now no Robby the Robot. No one to do the mopping up but me.

In spite of myself, I felt an unexpected surge of sympathy and respect for Lewis as I crawled around the base of the ancillary chair with vacuum mop bravely in hand. His spontaneous gesture of concern for Mimosa had moved me, more than I cared to admit. He had literally risked his life to reach her on the bay floor. And I knew all too well what it felt like to experience nausea in the pullout. I had tossed up a few times myself when I was first starting out.

I realized that Handy had just asked me something and that I didn't have the faintest idea of what he had said. "Again?" I asked, getting to my feet.

"I said, if you don't have any objections, Jo, I'm going to use some of this coast time to recalibrate the belly guns," Handy repeated patiently.

"Whatever you want," I replied. Suddenly I was mortally weary of ship's business. All I wanted was a shower and a change of clothes. I glanced over guiltily at Raydor, who was still hunched over the console.

"Listen," he said casually, not turning, "there's nothing here that needs you. Why don't you sack out for a while?"

I came up behind his chair and gently cupped my hands around the crown of his soft, hairless head. I didn't say anything; I just stood there, my fingers caressing the sides of his scalp.

Raydor turned slowly so as not to dislodge me. One of his big hands closed on my forearm. When he spoke, it was in that soft, lazy tone of voice I seldom heard him use outside of my cabin. "Later, I want to hear just how you managed to get Lewis away from Mimosa," he said with a smile.

"Later," I agreed, winking. It was the kind of story Raydor would appreciate. He dropped his hand from my arm, and I turned to leave Control.

In my cabin, I stripped off my flightsuit and its sweaty liner and stumbled into my shower. I ran warm water, then cool, then hot—as hot as I could tolerate it. I stepped out of the stall with my skin tingling, the last vestiges of the pullout purged from me.

It would have been only early evening, Heinlein time. My body made a halfhearted adjustment; it felt like the middle of the night to me, but I was still wide awake. I pulled on clean sleepers and crawled up to the headboard of my bed. There, swathed in the blankets, I leaned back with a golden-oldie audiochip and closed my eyes.

The abrupt *bizz* of my hatch call button startled me. Raydor never punched it . . . oh, shit: Lewis. I had completely forgotten my earlier command to him, and now that I was blissfully narcotized by the pervasive sound of the Clones, I wished that Lewis had forgotten it, too.

"Come," I said wearily, popping the chip from my ear.

The hatch hissed open. Lewis stepped hesitantly through, glancing around with the wary curiosity of a tourist in a war zone. He had somehow managed to clean the stains from the blue and silver flightsuit, and he had washed his face and combed his damp hair. There was a bit more color in his face, although he was still distressingly pale. The ugly laceration on his temple had begun to resolve itself, but it was still damningly evident. When he saw me on the bed, he halted awkwardly about ten feet from me. "Captain," he said, with a wooden little nod.

In the space of a few seconds several weirdly disjointed thoughts occurred to me: I wondered how Lewis had been able to get the blood off his flightsuit; I remembered that it was now the only set of clothing he had; and I realized, lamentably, that we had lost his gorgeous red sleepers back on Heinlein. And as I watched a kaleidoscope of emotions sweep over Lewis's face, I also realized that I probably presented a singularly discomforting picture to him. Being summoned to my cabin and finding me in my bed in my sleepers probably suggested something to him that I had not—consciously, at least—planned.

I tried to redeem the situation by being as businesslike as I could. "Mr. Lewis," I replied just as formally.

He stared down at his hands, the right hand reflexively rubbing his left wrist, where the detention cuff had hung. Despite his discomfort, it was obvious that there was something he felt compelled to say. His eyes lifted to my face. "You saved my life," he said with a simple eloquence.

"So it appears," I replied, forcing a gruff neutrality into my voice. I sat up a little straighter, bracing my shoulder blades against the headboard of the bunk. "And now that I have, maybe you can explain to me just why the hell you're so determined to throw it away again."

That startled Lewis a bit; I think he actually would have taken a step backward if that wouldn't have put him right against the hatch. He stared mutely at me, apprehension washing through his expression like a dye. "W-what do you mean?" he stammered.

I didn't want him to panic, which would have been useless. Okay, so I didn't want to hurt him, either. But I did have the right to know what was going on.

"Come here; sit down," I said, my voice several decibels lower. I gestured toward the room's lone chair, a short distance from my bunk. "Sit—please, Lewis. Don't make this so damned tough!"

That seemed to get through to him. He clumsily tugged the chair around so that it faced the bed and gingerly sat down. "I'm sorry," he said—automatically, as if apologizing for everything he did was something bred into him, like his blue eyes or his Talent.

I tossed my head, dismissing the apology. I pulled up one blanket-covered knee and hooked my arms around it. Then I gazed levelly at his wary face. "Why Camelot?" I asked him quietly.

Lewis's hands clenched nervously in his lap. He stared down diligently at the bright blue thighs of his flightsuit. "I can't tell you," he said, his voice nearly a whisper.

"Can't or won't?" My voice rose involuntarily but determinedly. "Listen, my friend, I have risked everything I own—including my Power-be-damned *life*—to pull your sorry ass out of the fire again. We went blasting out of Heinlein—a deregulated port—like our suit liners were on fire, and we fried a few of MA's finest in the process! I think you owe me some kind of explanation for all of that."

Lewis's head lifted, stung by my anger. His eyes— swimming with despair—latched onto mine. "I *can't*," he repeated, his voice nearly cracking.

He looked perilously close to tears; I didn't think I could have taken that right then. His genuine anguish ripped through me, as deeply visceral as the nausea of pulling out. If Lewis had been a little closer to me, I would have reached out and put my arms around him and tried to comfort him. As it was, he was just far enough away from the bunk that we both just sat there, Lewis rigid with misery in his chair and me slumped in frustration against the headboard of the bed.

I dropped my interrogating posture for a moment, staring blankly at the foot of the bed while Lewis quietly struggled to compose himself. When I looked over at him again, his gaze rose to meet mine. He looked shaken but collected. Taking a deep breath, I tried a different approach.

"Okay," I conceded calmly, "you want me to take you to Camelot." I smoothed out the blanket where it tented in folds over my raised knee. "Then what? I don't think we can even get into port at Camelot." I made a heroic effort to keep the rising irritation I felt from creeping into my tone. "There's one hell of a big MA complex there. Considering everything that's happened, somehow I don't think we're going to get a very warm welcome."

Lewis leaned forward slightly in the chair, his expression taking on a certain pained earnestness. "We can avoid the MA settlement, land at Nethersedge."

I leaned forward, too, my eyes narrowing suspiciously. "Nethersedge? Where the hell did you hear about that?"

Lewis colored a little, like a small boy called out for uttering an unexpected obscenity. He made a spontaneous dismissive gesture with his hands. "A lot of people know about Nethersedge," he offered awkwardly.

"Yeah?" I settled back again, a skeptical frown on my face. "Just what do you know about it, then?"

Lewis shrugged clumsily. "That it's an unregulated port, that MA doesn't control it."

"*Can't* control it," I amended. "And you know why they can't? Because Nethersedge is a pirate's nest, a trash can for every kind of cod-sucking thug and smuggler in the system, that's why! MA wouldn't waste bodies trying to patrol it. And you want me to set you down *there*?"

Lewis's gaze didn't drop, although some of its directness wavered. "If you could just set me down at Nethersedge," he said softly, "I wouldn't ask for anything more."

"Hah!" I snorted loudly, jerking up my other knee. I stared fiercely at Lewis for a moment, until he began to squirm under my scrutiny; then I gave another rude snort and threw back my head, as if in silent supplication to whatever obscure gods might have lurked in the cabin's bulkheads. Why *me*? The galaxy was a desolate place; the populated systems were few and far between, and even the colonized planets were sparsely settled. I had seldom felt more alone. I had just fled the last living remnants of any real blood family I had when I blasted so precipitately out of Heinlein. Now there was nowhere else I could turn. All I had left was my ship's family, Raydor and Handy. And all Lewis had left was me.

When I looked to him again, Lewis was fretfully smoothing the silver piping on the cobalt-blue thighs of his flightsuit. Stars! He looked so pathetic, so bereft, he could have convinced me to set him down at the MA headquarters itself had he asked me right then. He cleared his throat, then hesitated. With his eyes directed studiously at his knees, he said slowly, "On Heinlein you—you bought my IS contract." He cleared his throat again with greater effort, and suddenly his eyes lifted to my face. "I—I'm very grateful for everything you've done, Captain. I don't have any way to repay you now. They—MA took everything I had." A quick, self-deprecating smile tugged at his lips. "I don't think it was very much, anyway," he noted sardonically. "But I swear to you that when I can—"

"You didn't cost me anything," I interrupted calmly.

Lewis's brows rose, his head slightly cocking, as if to better comprehend what I had just said. "W-what?" he stuttered, confused.

I braced my elbows on my raised knees, slouching casually forward. "I said, I didn't pay Mahta anything for your IS contract," I reiterated evenly.

He just shook his head, befuddled and somehow inexplicably embarrassed at his own confusion. "I—I don't understand," he admitted awkwardly.

For some perverse reason I was relishing the moment, perhaps because it seemed like the first time I had ever had any control over what was happening between us. "She gave you to me," I told him casually.

"But why?" he stammered, too confused to try to be oblique about it.

"She thought we made a cute couple," I replied, and saw Lewis wince. Then I found I'd had enough of the game. Whichever facet of my twin-edged justification for helping him—anger or sympathy—I chose to cite, it was still my choice. He didn't deserve that kind of treatment from me for it. I pointed across the room. "Reach me my flightsuit, will you?" I requested.

Still perplexed, Lewis leaned forward and picked up my discarded flightsuit off the floor. As I took the garment from him, I reached into the breast pocket and pulled out the two plastic cards. I extended them to Lewis. "Your ID and your IS contract," I said matter-of-factly.

Lewis nearly dropped the cards in his nervousness.

Then he clutched them, staring in bafflement at the two pieces of plastic.

"They're yours," I prompted. "Your ID is clear, and I terminated your IS contract." At his stunned expression, I added, "It's all legal—by the book."

Luckily for both of us, MA couldn't alter IDs or penal contracts. That was Citizenship and CA's province, and I had indeed done it all legally, through Handy's Central Access. MA might still fry Lewis, but if they did, they would fry him as a free Citizen.

Still clutching the precious cards, Lewis stared at me with open surprise. "Y-you released me from the contract?"

"Of course," I replied, shrugging indifferently. "What the hell would I want with an IS?" I gave him a sharp look. "All I want to do is get rid of you—Nethersedge or wherever it takes!"

Abashed, Lewis slumped back in the chair. He carefully pocketed the two cards, then eyed me cautiously. He wore a funny sort of expression, wary but not quite like the apprehension he had displayed earlier. It was something else, something . . .

"So?" I said, dropping my elbows and locking my fingers around my knees. "Unless you're suddenly going to start explaining yourself to me, you might as well go."

Lewis's eyes lowered, his dark thick lashes dropping. Then, slowly, his gaze lifted again. I suddenly recognized the peculiar expression on his face.

"Do—do you want me to stay?" he asked me with such effort that his voice nearly cracked on the last word.

I'm sure my reaction was amply displayed on my face. As Lewis recognized my response, alarm shot through his expression. Fearing he had made some presumptuous error in judgment, he hastily added, "Or if you—if you want me to come back later?"

With a curious mixture of horror and outright amusement, I realized what Lewis had so automatically assumed. He thought he owed me a debt, but he was materially destitute. He thought that he had only one thing that I could have wanted. Everything that had happened, from the luxurious red sleepers to my performance with Mahta and his summons here, had fostered that conclusion. Now, from some dutiful sense of gratitude, he was offering himself to me. Part of me was appalled by it, but I still had to struggle to keep myself from grinning wickedly at him and cracking some risqué suggestion! Luckily I didn't; he was far too earnest to have recognized a joke.

"Lewis," I began slowly, suddenly realizing that it would have been a lot easier if I hadn't been sitting in bed in my sleepers, "I don't expect that from you." He looked so tense, so anxious, that I couldn't keep from leaning forward and spontaneously squeezing his knee in what I hoped was a gesture of reassurance.

Relief mixed with acute embarrassment at his gaffe flooded his face. He blushed furiously. There was something about his tendency to color that rivaled even his blue eyes as an irresistible feature.

"I—I'm sorry, Captain," he murmured, ducking his head. "I thought—"

"Forget it," I interceded, gently patting his knee. "Hell, I'm flattered!"

Lewis realized I was joshing him, but he still squirmed with embarrassment. At that moment I had an unexpected, unbidden, but totally vivid flashback of exactly what Lewis had looked like stripped, even with the ugly mottling of bruises on his—

I shook my head, withdrawing my hand from his knee. "Go on," I urged gently. "Go to the galley and get something to eat. Or get some rest."

Lewis stood awkwardly. There were words stuck somewhere behind his lips. But I knew that I wouldn't hear those words—not yet. The thought of their very existence filled me with both dread and longing.

"Go on," I repeated, smiling reassuringly at him.

Lewis nodded shyly, then popped the hatch and was gone.

Later, when I told my Heinlein story to Raydor, I also explained about my little encounter with Lewis and his determination to be set down at Nethersedge. I didn't say anything about Lewis's misguided offer to me, even though I knew Raydor would find it more touching and amusing than alarming. Reclining together on my bunk, Raydor and I discussed our situation.

Raydor was understandably unhappy about Camelot in general and the Nethersedge idea in particular. "Nethersedge isn't even listed as unregulated—it's listed as unpopulated," he reminded me glumly. He succinctly summarized our chances: "They might fry us quicker than MA would!"

I shrugged. "I know, but it's not like we'd be going in there defenseless," I told him.

But Raydor merely grunted. *Raptor*'s high-intensity beams, and the fate of *Argent* and *Corona*, were things the two of us didn't discuss. Raydor was Tachs; he had a farmer's morals.

Later, when he touched me, he tapped a furious surge of pent energy in me, something that even I hadn't realized existed. Even long afterward, when my breathing had fallen back to normal and I was curled in his huge arms, I clung tightly to him, strangely desperate for his comfort. He stayed with me then, when I slept. It was only hours later, when I woke up again, that I found he was gone.

The galley was deserted. I programmed the synthesizer for stew and hoped for the best. While I waited, I punched Handy's access button and asked him how far out we were.

"A little over twenty-nine hours, Jo," Handy reported.

"How'd your recalibrations go?" I teased him.

"Beats Internals' idea of a good time!" he responded wryly. "I have some specs on Nethersedge for you, if you want to see them."

I frowned, but before I could comment, Handy added, "Raydor asked me to punch them up for you. Do you want to see them now, Jo?"

"May as well," I decided morosely with a sigh of

resignation. I leaned forward to switch on the small screen set into the galley's wall. I didn't even bother to question where Handy could have gotten specs on a place that officially no longer even existed. A schematic flashed onscreen.

"I tried to condense all of this for you," Handy offered brightly. "Unless you want the full specs."

"Forget that!" I retorted, reaching absently for the plastic plate the autoserver had just disgorged onto the table. "I'm lucky if I can even figure out half of your 'condensed' version."

Handy ran the specs, patiently making comments and answering questions. Eventually I found myself abandoning the stew—although for once it wasn't half-bad—and concentrating totally on the data on the screen. It was even worse than I had anticipated. The place was a damned fortress. The landing fields were in the center of a huge square of hangars, storage sheds, warehouses, and bunkerlike living quarters. Everything was hemmed by artillery posts; even the port tower was equipped with beam cannon. No wonder MA had written it off. Let the vermin kill each other off was probably the way they looked at it. Faced with having to penetrate Nethersedge's defenses, I almost wished for MA as backup.

I tapped the screen with the tines of my plastic fork. "What about this?" I asked Handy. "These look like pod hangars."

"That's what they are, Jo."

"Pods? Come on, you can't tell me freighters of that size and class traffic with those cruds," I protested.

Handy made a rude sound. "They're set up for it," he reiterated. "I presume there's a reason for it."

I shook my head. "I find that hard to believe," I insisted.

"And I find it hard to believe that you want to go down there," Handy countered neatly.

Scowling, I studied the screen a moment longer. "This is *not* going to be easy," I finally conceded.

"No shit!" Handy mimicked me perfectly.

I switched him off. When you're ferrying a crazy Class

Ten into a certain death trap, who needs a wiseass Integrator?

Usually on a long run I used the coast time for self-indulgent things like sleeping and reading and listening to chips. But this time, with more than twenty hours left to go, my anxiety was getting the best of me, and I found myself tackling the kind of scut work I normally never would have considered doing out of port. I was in Control, reorganizing and updating my entire file of log tapes, when Raydor joined me. Equally restless, he began running Internals' maintainence list over Handy's screen.

We worked in companionable silence for a while. Then I reached the end of a log cassette and glanced over at him. "Where's Lewis?" I asked him. "Sleeping?"

"I don't think so," Raydor replied, not looking up from the screen. He literally could do two things at once, so I knew that despite appearances, I had his attention. "He was in the galley a little while after you came up here. Then he asked me if there was anything he could do to help."

"Jump ship!" I suggested sourly. But Raydor wasn't so easily baited.

"So I set him up running the parts inventory in storage," Raydor continued mildly.

A simple job; even an Alter-brained dolt could have done it. Apparently the wait was beginning to get to Lewis, too. I turned back to my log tapes, but my concentration had been breached.

"You think we've got any chance of sneaking into Nethersedge past MA?" I asked Raydor bluntly.

His broad shoulders shrugged. He tactfully refrained from pointing out to me that it was one hell of a time to ask him that. "If we stick to Nethersedge's side of the planet, maybe," he allowed. "Lots of traffic in and out of there and not many questions asked."

I made a deprecating sound. "All of the system's garbage!"

Raydor glanced up at that remark. "Well, then we'll

just have to blend in with the garbage,'' he concluded
stoically.

I bent over my console, muttering, ''If MA's remotes
don't get us, we'll probably get trashed by those goons
at Nethersedge!''

Unfortunately, Raydor couldn't disagree with that assessment. Discouragingly, he didn't even try to dispute
it.

Countless hours and tens of log tapes later, even Raydor had given it up and packed it in. I had Control to
myself again, but fatigue was finally starting to drag me
under. Before I left the console, I punched Handy.

''How long?'' I asked him.

''Twelve hours out, Jo,'' he responded promptly.

''Buzz me when we're two hours out,'' I told him, ''in
case I'm not up here.''

''Sure, Jo. And if you'll give me authorization, I can
file the new parts inventory now.''

So Lewis had finished it; I felt unexpectedly pleased at
that. I palmed Handy's input. Then I got up, stretching
stiffly, and trudged out into the corridor. My mind felt
blessedly numbed by the mundane repetitiveness of the
log entries. For the first time since we'd pulled out from
Heinlein, getting fried by someone was not the uppermost thought in my mind. The comfort of my bed was
the leading contender for that honor.

In my semistuporous state I nearly dismissed what I
heard. In the corridor outside Lewis's cabin I heard the
low mutter of his voice. At first I assumed he was talking
to Raydor. I was several steps past the hatch before I
realized that his tone was not conversational and that no
one else was speaking. Even then I almost just walked
on by. It was, I think, my basic and ungracious mistrust
of Lewis that made me turn back.

Outside the hatch I could hear that Lewis's voice had
become more strident, more urgent. I hit the door buzzer,
but his weird monologue continued, uninterrupted. By
that time I realized that he was probably having another
bad dream, like the nightmare he'd had on Heinlein.

Again, I considered just walking on down the corridor

and forgetting about it. That would have been the easiest thing. But Lewis's voice was broken now, frightened and filled with pain. Hearing it tore at me in a way I neither expected nor understood. I punched the hatch release and, hitting the lights, stepped into the room.

On the bunk, Lewis was sprawled out flat on his back. In spite of the agitation in his voice he lay nearly motionless; only his ragged breathing shook his body. His hands were clenched into fists, his face contorted almost beyond recognition. He was wearing only his suit liner, with the blanket bunched up uselessly at the foot of the bed, but his skin was sheened with perspiration. Nothing that he said made any sense; only the vehemence of his tone was completely clear.

I reached for his shoulders to shake him awake. But the moment I touched him, his body arced as if he'd contacted an electric current, and his hands, more powerful than I had imagined, seized my wrists in a crushing grip.

"Ow! Let me go, you bastard!" I yelped at him, struggling as his nails dug into my skin.

Lewis came awake with a start. He sat up with a jolt, freeing me so abruptly that I nearly fell over backward. I pulled back, rubbing my wrists and glaring furiously at him. "You bastard!" I repeated with feeling. "You were having another damned nightmare!"

Lewis stared up at me, his eyes wide with alarm. A pulse was beating wildly at his throat. It took nearly a full minute before he seemed really cognizant of what had just happened. Then his taut body slumped on the bunk.

"I—Captain, I'm sorry." Even as he spoke, he reached out automatically for my hands and circled my wrists. And where he touched me, the aching red dents from his fingernails suddenly vanished, only to reappear on his own wrists. It was a totally unconscious gesture, a reflex, like the simple spontaneous way you'd reach out and flick a bit of lint off someone else's flightsuit as you stood talking to him. I watched in stunned fascination even as the shallow marks he had transferred began to fade from his own skin.

It was one thing to have seen him do this with someone else, quite something else to have it done with me. It unsettled me more than I was willing to reveal. Gently, I pulled back from him, freeing my hands from his. Stars, his eyes were so blue! I forced myself to drop my gaze away from the dangerously magnetic hold of those beautiful eyes. Maybe that was my mistake, because shifting my gaze made me acutely aware of something else, something that Lewis's position and the thin fabric of his suit liner made relentlessly clear. He had a definite erection.

His own awareness of that fact followed mine by mere seconds. The blanket, twisted at the foot of the bed, was too distant to be gracefully reclaimed as any kind of cover. To make a move for it then would only have drawn more attention to his condition. Quickly, he drew up his knees.

I struggled to look away, but my eyes couldn't seem to stay anywhere else I put them. A healthy flush of color had risen from Lewis's neck, creeping up to the blue-black roots of his hairline. He crossed his arms on his chest. "Please excuse me, Captain," he said with an odd formality that deepened his voice by several octaves. That, coupled with the high blush on his face, sent an unbidden pang straight through me.

I gave a negating little shake of my head as if to indicate that it hardly mattered—as if such events were such a boringly common occurrence around there that I barely gave them a second thought anymore—even as my palms went slick with sweat and my pulse began to kick.

Lewis made a little clearing noise in his throat and then went on with a tenacious dignity. "I—sometimes the nightmares—the energy comes out in ways that I can't control." I had managed to meet his eyes again; they were overly bright, but composed. "Please excuse me," he repeated. "I hope I haven't—offended you."

I gazed into those rare eyes while his pupils dilated like the rippling wave of heat that was now coursing through my body. *Excuse* him? For what? For being so Void-cursed beautiful?

With a wrenching effort of will I broke the moment— broke it as I had to before I, too, reached out, reflexively, just as will-lessly as Lewis had when he had taken my hands. I *had* to end it; what he had was like a poison to me.

I bent and caught the edge of the errant blanket, bringing it up and flipping it over Lewis's raised knees. I expected him to be relieved and grateful for the covering, but his reaction, an even deeper blush, gave me the impression that my action had somehow only embarrassed him further. He fumbled with the hem of the blanket, drawing it up over his chest. His hands worked nervously over the edge of it. Then his gaze darted back up at me. "Thank you," he said quietly.

Damn him! Damn him and his innocence! I crushed down the maniacal urge to rip that damned blanket off him and wrap it around his miserable neck!

But what I did instead was force myself to take a deep, calming breath and exhale it slowly. Then I sat down on the edge of the bunk, at his feet. I looked straight at him, my expression carefully neutral.

"Tell me what you plan to do if we can get you down at Nethersedge," I said levelly. "Do you have any idea what that place is like? How are you going to survive down there?"

The balance between us had changed, subtly perhaps, but it had changed nonetheless. What had happened had lent a certain bizarre sense of intimacy to our relationship. There was another look to Lewis now, something that had replaced the constant wariness in his cerulean eyes. Maybe he didn't trust me yet, but at least I believed that he wanted to.

Lewis looked squarely at me. Only his fingers, still toying with the hem of the blanket, betrayed any apprehension. "There's someone on Camelot," he told me. "A man named Lillard. I—I have to find him."

I cocked my head quizzically, intrigued by this possible memory of an earlier point in his life. "Someone you know?"

Lewis hesitated a moment. "Not exactly," he admitted. "But I know about him."

I shifted slightly on the bunk, almost light-headed with the unfamiliar experience of getting any actual information out of this man. I struggled to keep a tone of interrogation out of my voice. "You know how to contact this man?"

He nodded, his fingers nervously dancing.

I knew enough not to push that tack any further. "And you think that this man, Lillard, can protect you from MA?"

For a long moment Lewis said nothing. His eyes dropped, falling almost automatically into his familiar posture of evasion. Then, as if catching himself, he forced his face to lift to mine again. He swallowed. "No," he said slowly and softly. "I have to protect *him* from them."

I stared wordlessly at him, affected in a way I had thought I could no longer be touched. My entrapment was complete, I knew; it would have been ludicrous to have pretended otherwise. I realized I was holding my breath. I exhaled slowly and evenly. "It sounds like you're going to need some help, then," I found myself saying matter-of-factly.

It was probably the last possible response Lewis had expected from me. Like an illumination beam, an expression of hope shot unguarded across his face, softening his eyes with a mixture of relief and gratitude. He gave a quick little nod, quite unable to speak.

I leaned a little nearer on the bunk, close to speechlessness myself. Hell, who was I trying to kid? It'd been happening right along, inevitably and inexorably, and I couldn't seem to keep myself from it, even though I knew what it was capable of doing to me. I didn't need that kind of thing—I had avoided it religiously all my life— and yet there it was, and I was really ready to get down and wallow in it.

"Even getting you down to that snake pit isn't going to be easy," I reminded him.

Again Lewis nodded, but there was a childlike trust in his eyes. I stared at him. "Are you afraid?" I asked.

He plucked at the hem of the blanket, glancing down at his fingers. Then he abruptly looked up to me. "Yes," he replied quietly. "Yes, I'm afraid."

This time I allowed myself to do what I hadn't permitted myself the last time, in my cabin, when I had longed to comfort him: I slid forward on the bunk—slowly, so he could resist it if he needed to—and put my arms around him. But Lewis didn't stiffen or pull back. His thin body was relaxed in my arms, firm and surprisingly warm beneath the light fabric of his suit liner. And what stirred in me then, embracing him, strangely enough had nothing to do with erections or even with that core of heat in my belly.

"You know what?" I whispered into his dark, tousled hair. "I'm more than a little afraid myself!"

And I *was* afraid, scared shitless. But not just of Nethersedge's thugs or even of MA. No, I was also afraid of an even greater danger, one with the power to destroy me even more certainly than all of MA's goon squads or Nethersedge's pirates. I was afraid of something with blue eyes and unnamed fears, something that I now held in my arms. I was afraid because caring this much for him was going to make me endanger not only him and myself but also the others who mattered to me.

I didn't want to give up the moment, but neither did I want Lewis to misunderstand or be uncomfortable with me. We had achieved a level of intimacy that gave me a great and unexpected sense of satisfaction, and I wanted to be able to keep that intact. I pulled gently back from him. He released me, but the expression on his face was still strangely troubled.

I sat on the edge of the bunk, one hand lingering on his shoulder. I smiled reassuringly at him, but he still seemed disturbed. "Okay?" I said softly. When he didn't reply, I squeezed his shoulder. "No point in worrying now," I teased him. "We've still got twelve hours before we've really got to worry."

That crack brought the desired wry quirk to his mouth. But when I started to stand up, Lewis suddenly reached out and gripped my arm. Puzzled, I hesitated.

"Captain," he said earnestly, "I don't want you to get hurt in this."

"Believe me, *I* don't want me to get hurt in this, either," I assured him. I took his hand, gently disengaging it from my arm. "You just let me worry about that part of it."

I started to rise again, but once more he stopped me, his hand touching my leg. It took a visible effort for him to get the necessary words out.

"Captain, would—would you stay?"

My expression must have easily conveyed my surprise; maybe it conveyed far more than that. Lewis shifted abruptly on the bed, uncomfortably, as if he had just discovered some part of his body giving him some distress. He began to flush again, subtly this time, but I still found that the phenomenon had the power to arouse me more than I could let myself reveal.

"Stay here—with you?" I repeated stupidly.

Lewis ducked his head in shame. "I—I'm sorry, Captain; I wasn't trying to—" He had to break off and begin again, forcing his voice an octave lower. "I didn't mean to suggest that you—" He had to swallow just to get the word out. "—join with me; I just—"

He just needed some comfort, that was all. How long had it been since anyone had just shared contact with the poor man?

I cut Lewis off without a word and without hesitation, silently pushing him back onto the bunk. Stretched out beside him, on top of the blanket, I put my arms around him in a gentle, friendly embrace. He was a little shy about it at first, but having been able to ask for what he needed seemed to have relieved his fear. Soon he was curled comfortably against me, the clean smell of his hair and skin in my nostrils, the rhythm of his pulse warm against my body.

I fought to stay awake at first, even though I was exhausted. My thoughts were so profuse, so tangled, that it seemed somehow crucial to decipher all of them right then. But it was useless. The time for thinking was gone. In a short time I had fallen asleep.

Handy's conscientiously precise two-hour warning call found me in my own cabin, the sweet throb of a Clones audiochip thudding in my ears. Some time later I was at the console, puttering with the navigation scan, when Raydor entered Control. I nodded to him and was about to make some remark about the screen before me, but before the words could leave my mouth, Handy popped in.

"Jo? We've got a shadow," he rumbled.

I cocked a quizzical brow at Raydor, who merely shrugged. "A what?" I asked Handy.

"Something's tailing us," Handy elaborated. "Something big." There was a pause during which Handy's input screen sprang to life, fluttering with eerie green lines of data. "I thought there might be something there earlier, about a half hour ago," he continued while the figures on the screen whizzed crazily past. "But whatever it is, it's hanging right on the edge, just beyond our sensors."

"MA?" Raydor wondered aloud.

I was staring at the blur of data. It was meaningless to me most of the time, even when it was at a slow crawl, and totally incomprehensible to me at that speed. "Why the hell would MA bother to tail us?" I responded. "If they knew where we were, they'd just fry us. It's got to be something else." I addressed Handy. "Can you identify it?"

"At this range?" Handy replied serenely. His flow of data was slowing, solidifying into position coordinates and mass estimates. "Whatever it is, it's holding steady just beyond the edge."

I glanced over at Raydor, who was studying the figure on-screen. "It's big, all right," he muttered.

"You want me to hail?" Handy inquired.

"No, let's keep quiet," I decided. "Just keep monitoring it and let me know if anything changes."

"Okay, Jo," Handy replied. His neurons set up a little huddle with the sensors, programming the monitoring.

Raydor leaned back in his contoured chair. His broad, velvety face was creased thoughtfully. Some people think that Tachs don't have much facial expression, but I had always been able to read Raydor like a book. I lifted an eyebrow at him, soliciting his comments.

"Any ideas on how we're going to pull this off?" he asked me mildly. "Going into a place like Nethersedge isn't exactly like making port at Draco."

I grinned at him. "Are you asking me if I have a story?"

Raydor gave a gruff snort. "It had better be a good one!"

I shrugged with elaborate nonchalance, leaning back in my chair. "I guess we'll try the truth—at least as much of the truth as we know."

Then I told Raydor what that partial truth was, pieced together from what Lewis had told me. I told him why Lewis wanted to go to Camelot, about the man named Lillard, and what Lewis had said about having to protect him from MA. I was half hoping that it would all somehow begin to make more sense in the retelling, but it didn't. It still sounded crazy.

I told Raydor the rest, too, about Lewis's nightmares and about sharing contact with him. I think that in a way Raydor was pleased. He had never seemed to have much capacity for jealousy. Maybe the HTA had done that to him, or maybe it was just a part of his nature, deeper than any hypothalamic hatchet job could go. I knew that Raydor had felt a great deal of genuine sympathy for Lewis all along, from that first moment in Jessup's office. I suspected now that he was relieved to find out that I wasn't browbeating Lewis anymore. By the time I had finished my story Raydor had an expression of almost secret satisfaction on his face—very much like Mahta's on Heinlein—as though he had long since discovered something about me that I myself was still quite ignorant of.

"So where is he now?" I asked casually.

"In his cabin, I guess," Raydor replied. "I gave him some cassettes for his viewer a few hours ago."

"Get him up here," I said. "If there's going to be any trouble, I want him somewhere where we can keep an eye on him."

If there was going to be any trouble. Who was I trying to kid? We'd had nothing *but* trouble ever since we'd first laid eyes on Lewis, and there was nothing to suggest that our luck was about to change.

"Coming up on Camelot," Handy informed me. "Estimate audio contact in about ten minutes."

"Just keep it cool and easy," I cautioned him.

Camelot was a temperate but arid world about four-fifths the mass of Old Earth. Approximately seventy percent of the planet's surface was land, a series of three basically contiguous continents, but most of it was uninhabited wilderness. Most of the terrain was desertlike, with a rocky, soil-poor surface and very little native vegetation. There was only one large legal settlement, and that was dominated by MA's research complex. I doubt that anyone lived on Camelot who didn't have to be there, because officially the MA installation was the only means of livelihood. The only other thing on Camelot was Nethersedge, a failed and supposedly deserted shipping center that squatted in the middle of nowhere, nearly half the planet's circumference away from the MA settlement. The two entities seemed unlikely bedfellows, but Camelot, for all its ecological poverty, was strategically located at the hub of a commercially lucrative system. It was a good location for thugs and thieves of any stripe, whether they wore MA's cream and maroon or the ragtag garb of pirates.

I didn't turn or acknowledge Lewis's presence in any way when Raydor led him into Control and seated him in the ancillary chair. Handy's screen was running Camelot's planetary schematic; the MA sentry buoys blinked, outlined in garish red. Data on the research complex and the settlement bled across the bottom of the screen in a steady stream of flickering letters and figures. Sometimes even I had to wonder where the hell Handy got all that stuff; he must have egressed into every security-coded access MA had. He was a regular pack rat when it came to coded data.

"I estimate audio contact," Handy announced smoothly.

"Yeah?" I muttered, "Well, let's hope no one down there has anything to say to us." I glanced over at Raydor. He was wearing his pickup, his big head cocked in that peculiarly intent manner he reserved for deciphering periorbital chatter.

"Coming around," Handy noted, his schematic shifting so that the stylized sphere of the planet below began to roll away from us.

"I'm not getting much here," Raydor reported tersely. "Mostly routine—in-port."

MA's sentry buoys were unmanned and remotely controlled. They swept the space above Camelot on a random and supposedly unpredictable pattern. The odds of evading all of them at once were presumably rather slim, yet obviously the pirate ships using Nethersedge had succeeded in eluding them for years. Handy had upped our chances considerably by tapping into the buoys' programming. He brought *Raptor* up in a graceful arc, skimming beyond the seeking beam of the nearest buoy. Then we dropped, dumping velocity, to dip below the intersecting line of the next sentry. It was like playing a huge game of three-dimensional chess, darting over, under, and between the security beams before they could detect us. Only in that particular game getting caught would mean more than forfeiting a credit chip or two; in that game getting caught would mean getting fried.

The final blinking red light of the last sentry buoy disappeared from Handy's screen. I let out my breath with a painful grunt and allowed myself the luxury of giving Lewis a glance. He sat erect in his chair, his body rigid, but he acknowledged my look with a wan nod.

"So far, so good," I ventured sardonically. "Handy, where the hell are we?"

The screen's schematic changed, altitude and relative velocity figures blitzing across it in a green pulse.

"At subsentry altitude," Handy responded. "Apparently with no one the wiser—" His deep bass voice broke off, paused, and then boomed. "Oh, shit!"

I lunged across the console, thrusting my face needlessly close to Handy's input. *"What?"* I demanded, dismayed to find the adrenaline already tearing through my veins, hollowing out my belly in one great icy sweep.

"Pickets. We've got three of them—no, make that four of them—right on our tail."

Handy dumped the planetary schematic in favor of a tracking mode: four brilliant blue wedges closing on us at an alarming rate of speed. His circuits whirred— Internals, Security, Artillery—all galvanized by the instantaneous command of his hypertrophied neurons.

"Where the flaming Void did they come from?" I exclaimed angrily.

"I'm not sure," Handy replied calmly. He had the specs on the picket ships now, reeling across the screen beneath the menacing blue glow of their markers.

"I'm getting Port Security," Raydor reported quietly. "We've been spotted, all right." His big dark eyes met mine, placidly unblinking. "Coincidence, I think. They seem as surprised as we are."

"Great!" I grunted. "That and thirty seconds'll still get us blown into scrap metal!" I punched Handy's input with unnecessary force. "How long until we come up on Nethersedge?"

"At top velocity, four-point-two-eight minutes," Handy calculated promptly. "We're almost into their audio range now."

Wonderful. I didn't think I had to remind Handy about our top velocity. We couldn't outrun MA picket ships, not in the short run, anyway. And we couldn't outgun them, either, unless we let them get into range, and then even our high-intensity beams were damned poor odds against four ships. The way I saw it, we really had only two choices: We could pull up our nose and run for altitude, where eventually *Raptor* would have the advantage, even before we could go to pull. That presumed, of course, that we could make the critical distance before the four pickets caught us and also presumed that there wouldn't be anything bigger sitting just out of our sensor range, waiting to fry us. Or we could just run for Nethersedge and hope like hell.

"Distance six-point-six-seven and closing." Handy announced calmly.

I threw Lewis one last furious look. Damn him! But I had freely offered to get him down, no matter what; there was no blaming him for this. And one look at him, his wide blue eyes dancing with terror but his jaw stubbornly set and his hands clenching the chair's padded armrests so tightly that his knuckles were white, reminded me just why I had made that promise to him. They had wronged him, they had wronged me; there was no way I could just let it go.

I wheeled on Raydor. "Start maydaying Nethersedge," I commanded.

"Jo?" Handy inquired, his voice maddeningly casual. "Remember that shadow?"

"What about it?" I demanded, one eye on Internals' throbbing red panic light and the other on that deadly quartet of pickets on the screen.

"Well, it's a ship—an awfully big ship. And it's starting to close."

"Suns! What else?" I snarled.

Just as I realized that I didn't really want an answer to that necessarily rhetorical question, Raydor reported, "I've got someone at Nethersedge; they've received our Mayday." His eyes narrowed. "We've just been told, in effect, to ram it up our rotors."

I lunged across the console, punching the transmitter so hard that the switch nearly snapped off. "Nethersedge, this is *Raptor*! Listen, you cod-swabbing shitheads! We've got four of MA's finest right on our tail. Unless you want to have all five of us splattered across your field, let us in!"

But there was nothing from Nethersedge, not even the satisfaction of a tart retort.

"One-point-two-five minutes to Nethersedge's space," Handy informed me dutifully. He paused. "And, Jo? There's something else."

I slumped; *of course* there was something else. "What?" I asked him hoarsely, my voice raw with despair.

"I'm picking up some ships over the port at Nethersedge, about seventeen or eighteen of them—maybe more. They've got the port pretty well ringed."

Raydor made a curious grunting noise. "Rogues," he said quietly. "Keeping guard."

I stared over at Raydor, at his impassive Altered face. His calmness was the only thing that kept me from lapsing into outright hopeless hysteria, and at that moment I think I was never so happy just to see his big graceless bulk sitting beside me in Control.

"See if you can raise any of them, huh?" I suggested wearily.

Handy had switched his screen to viewer. A shimmer of dazzling orange energy exploded along our aft hull.

"Distance two-point-five-five," Handy intoned evenly. The little bastards were closing in.

"Pop them back!" I snapped.

Raptor's regulation beam-gun turrets swiveled and locked. The energy of our returning beam fire sparkled harmlessly off the approaching ships.

"Anything?" I asked Raydor hopefully.

He shook his big head dolefully. "They're reading us down there, but no one's offering to stick their neck out."

"I'm getting some specs on our shadow, Jo," Handy offered helpfully. Simultaneously, *Raptor*'s guns exchanged fire with the pickets again. Multiple flares, more intense now, shot past us, buffeting the hull. "Shall I screen it?" the Integrator continued calmly.

Why not? I thought morosely. Anything was better than having to just sit there and watch our ass get kicked in by those four picket ships. "Yeah, go ahead," I muttered.

"Still nothing," Raydor reiterated, rapidly running the channels on his transmitter. "They're all acting like we don't even exist."

It wouldn't be long before they'd be right; the pickets nearly had us within range. The last fusillade of fire sent the panics fluttering all over the console.

"One-point-nine-oh," Handy remarked with infuriatingly calm precision. I spun toward Raydor, but he just shook his head helplessly: Nothing from the rogue ships. Another volley of beam fire from the closing pickets sent a shudder through *Raptor*'s deck plates. "Internals reports damage to the port vane," Handy relayed stoically.

The hell with them, then! I decided abruptly. The hell with them all! I slammed Handy's input. "Take us in. If the ball-less bastards don't like it, let them lodge a joining formal protest with the Port Authority!"

Raptor dipped in a sudden spiral; we ran for the cover of Nethersedge. As the picket ships scrambled to re-form behind us, a spray of brilliant orange energy appeared off our starboard side. Wonderful: Now the rogues were firing on us.

"Beam fire aft—heading oh-six-mark-six," Handy noted unnecessarily. "Internals reports—"

"*Sweet!*" I snarled, jabbing the input switch. "Return fire—high beams! The rogues, the pickets—fry them all!" If we were caught—and there seemed no way in hell that we wouldn't be—I was damned if I'd go down without a fight.

But to my astonishment, Handy hesitated on my order. On the screen, the image fragmented, dissolved, reformed; then it was replaced by a bewildering roll of data.

"Jo, I'm getting—"

"I said *hit it!*" I bellowed at Handy.

But beside me Raydor suddenly turned, seizing my arm. The speaker crackled to life, rattling with a voice nearly as bellicose as my own.

"*Tangent*, this is Redding! Repeat: This is Redding! Cease fire on *Raptor*—cease fire and let her in!"

I hung over the console, my knuckles white. We had

discovered the identity of our mysterious shadow: *Nimbus*. And if our old friend Redding had any pull with those outlaws, we still had a chance.

And if he didn't, we all were scrap.

CHAPTER
EIGHT

You might think that an extraatmospheric battle would be exciting, maybe even exhilarating. But mainly it's just nauseating. There's something about ship's gravity that seems to make centrifugal force even worse. I couldn't think of a scrap I'd been in where my sense of equilibrium hadn't been ignomiously assaulted, often repeatedly. Artificial gravity was useless when your eyes were telling you one thing and your inner ear was telling you something else. It's hard to feel exhilarated, even in victory, when your most pressing concern is whether you're going to vomit.

Over Nethersedge, dazzling red-gold flares raced along *Raptor*'s hull as the picket ships closed in. *Raptor* dropped, listing slightly. Swallowing with effort, I hauled myself forward in my chair and pulled myself up over the console. I palmed Handy's input. "Belay those high beams!" I ordered. "Just get us down—get us in before one of those goons gets lucky!"

We were caught between the four pickets, which were nearly on us, and the menacing ring of grimly silent freighters guarding Nethersedge. It was a position that allowed me scant comfort from Redding's precipitous and totally unexpected intervention. All it would take would be one good shot from one of those rogue ships or another direct hit on our remaining generation vanes from the pickets, and it would be over for us. Handy banked us on a trajectory so acute that I felt the deck plates shudder beneath my feet. Perspiration had glued my suit liner to my back and belly, and my pulse had fallen to a dull, steady drum.

Then, behind us, one of the closing picket ships suddenly exploded in a starburst of stunning yellow light: *Nimbus*, for sure, now within firing range. One of her own banks of high-intensity beam cannon had just cut one of the vultures off our tail. And ahead of us the ring of rogue ships was finally, however reluctantly, parting, giving us a clear shot into Nethersedge's atmosphere. *Nimbus*'s cannon fired again; another picket vaporized in a bloom of golden light.

The sickening pull of our abrupt entry began to push me back in my chair. From the view screen I had a clear look at our fiery descent. On our port side, flapping bits of *Raptor*'s ruptured skin, torn from the damaged vane, ignited, sheared off by the friction of the planetary atmosphere in a blinding spray of sparks. We were going in for better or worse; it was too late to change our minds.

The rogue ships began to fire again, this time at the two remaining pickets, not at us. But the logistics of the hostilities no longer concerned me; I was far more worried just how the hell we were going to limp into that unknown port on our crippled wing. Everything on the Internals board was lit up like a pyrotechnics display, the panics strobing wildly.

"Handy?" I queried tersely. My head was being driven back against the chair's padded headrest so hard that I could barely get the single word out.

"We're okay, Jo," Handy replied levelly, even as the deck plates pitched crazily beneath me. "We're doing fine."

From the corner of my eye I could see Raydor, hung tenaciously over the comm station on the console, still doggedly calling Port. "No response," he grunted at me, his broad face further flattened from the G-force. "We don't even have coordinates for a bay."

"No problem," Handy assured us. "We won't need a bay, anyway."

"What do you mean, we won't need a bay?" I demanded, a fresh stab of fear flushing a new wave of adrenaline through me.

"We've lost our hover stabilizers," Handy elaborated.

"We *what*?" I exploded. "I thought you said we were *fine*!"

"We are," Handy responded calmly. Just then the landing retros cut in with a hollow *whoosh*, and I felt my chair pushing up at the base of my spine. My stomach obligingly dropped down to meet it. "We don't need the hovers to land," Handy continued matter-of-factly, "just to maneuver on the ground. We can get down all right; we just won't be able to ambulate down there."

"Great!" I snarled. "We'll be one big fat sitting duck."

Belatedly, it occurred to me: What the hell was I worried about? The damned *landing* would probably kill us, anyway.

We skimmed in obliquely over the sprawling hodge-podge of buildings marking the border of Nethersedge's port facility. Rising like a ghost town out of the flat, grayish rock of the bleak desert plain, from the air Nethersedge looked like an abandoned ghetto, like the hulking wreckage of a once-thriving industrial shipping complex that had fallen into ruinous decay. The whining retros dulled our velocity with a nauseating lurch. I gripped the padded armrests of my chair and forced myself to take slow, deep breaths. On the view screen I saw a charred chunk of something—something larger than a piece of our skin—no longer aflame peel off the port vane and go tumbling past us. Then Handy switched the screen to the landing schematic, a vision only slightly less harrowing than the actual view might have been. I was beginning to wonder if it was possible to be too terrified to vomit, when a familiar voice crackled over our speaker.

"*Raptor*, this is Redding on *Nimbus*. Do you read me?"

Raydor shot a glance at me, his brow cocked inquiringly. I nodded stiffly. "This is *Raptor*," Raydor responded into the transmitter.

"Set it down, shut it up, and stay put!" Redding commanded brusquely. "Don't so much as crack a hatch unless you want trouble! Just sit tight until I get down there."

Anger roiled in me, but I forced it down. For whatever reason, the man had saved our collective ass, after all. I nodded again.

"We read you, *Nimbus*," Raydor replied evenly.

The gentle thump of our set-down caught me by surprise. It was as smooth as any touchdown I had experienced, hover stabilizers or not. Good old Handy—he had been right again. I leaned across the console, conscious of the dull ache in my guts, and punched Handy's input. "Good job, my friend," I told him quietly.

"You want the damage reports now, Jo?" Handy inquired. He was a hell of a pilot, but he had absolutely no sense of timing.

"May as well," I decided morosely. I glanced sideways at Raydor. He was already running Internals' checklist, which was relatively easy this time, since over half of Internals' functions seemed to be blitzed out. We were lucky to have the basics and life support. "Just give me the worst of it," I added.

I heard a movement behind me. Looking over my shoulder, I saw Lewis, free of his harness, get shakily to his feet. It was the first time I had spared him a thought since we'd started down. He looked decidedly queasy, but he hadn't chucked up again.

"Is there anything I can do?" he asked me.

I shook my head, waving him back toward his chair. "You heard Redding; just sit tight," I muttered.

Ship's schematics had begun to flutter across the screen. Huge areas were colored a garish orange, the code for functional damage. Numerous smaller areas were colored blue for major damage. Then there were the green areas: parts missing. Nearly half the port generation vanes were colored green.

I slumped in my chair, grimly silent, as the diagrams of *Raptor*'s injuries paraded past on the screen. *My* ship—damn MA! Damn Nethersedge, too, for that matter!

Damn me, and my foolish ideas, and my helpless sympathy for Lewis!

My glum introspection was interrupted by Handy's deep voice. "Jo, we've got company," he announced.

The image on the screen flickered, dissolved, and reformed, revealing a stretch of greasy tarmac. We had just set down in the middle of a large pockmarked landing field about a hundred meters from the nearest structures, a towering bank of dilapidated hangars. Beyond the hangars stretched rows of decaying warehouses and what appeared to be barrackslike living quarters. Two vehicles were approaching us from across the empty field: crawlers, scuttling along like giant cockroaches. Crawlers were the land tugs at ports; they had tractor beams to help maneuver ships or cargo containers on the ground. Those two crawlers also happened to have an impressive bristle of beam cannon. We had a welcoming committee.

Raydor shrugged at me. Not Redding; ships of *Nimbus*'s size couldn't land at that kind of facility. Their various cargo pods were brought in by sky tugs, and their personnel came down by shuttle. And a shuttle from *Nimbus* couldn't have gotten down that quickly. She had been too far behind us, and shuttles weren't that fast.

I felt fresh rivulets of sweat creeping through my hair. "Stand by on artillery," I instructed Handy tautly, my eyes locked on the screen.

Raydor hunched over the console, running the ground channels. In the heavy silence the crackle of static sounded like metal rending.

"Standing by," Handy relayed.

On the screen I watched the two armed crawlers circle us like weasels circling a crippled bird. Then the vehicles rattled to a halt, their multiple turrets swiveling, their cannon covering our hatch.

Raydor's head was cocked attentively, his pickup receiving his full concern. Almost languidly he reached out and flicked the switch on the speaker. A harsh command filled Control.

"*Raptor*, depressurize and prepare to be boarded. You have thirty seconds!"

Rage, acid like bile, burned in my already rebellious stomach. "Like hell!" I snorted. I hit Handy's input. "Stand by to drop high beams!" I barked.

Raydor's hairless brows rose, but he said nothing. I didn't give a damn what Redding had said; there was only one reason why anyone would be trying to board us. I hadn't come through all of that just to knuckle under to the first thug who tried to breach us.

"*Raptor*, your thirty seconds are up," the voice grated over the speaker. "Prepare to receive boarders!"

Even as he spoke, the beam cannon mounted on each crawler rotated, fanning across our damaged hull.

"Prepare to receive *this*, you ball-less bastards," I murmured softly. Then, to Handy, I instructed, "Let them have a taste!"

Once the slender, deadly barrels of the high beams dropped from their concealment beneath *Raptor*'s belly, the men in those crawlers had a negligible amount of time to react before Handy cut loose with the first volley. Because Handy was programmed—somewhat lamentably, I had always thought—to defend us, not to kill other people, he put his first line of shots across the tarmac at the crawlers' prows. The heat of the high-intensity beams exploded the pavement. The ground erupted like a miniature earthquake, heaving the two vehicles over backward like overturned turtles in a shower of dirt and shattered tarmac.

I leaned across Raydor's panel, pushing the transmitter switch, and announced sweetly, "What was that again? We seem to have had a slight weapons malfunction here . . . ."

Raydor struggled to suppress a rueful grin. "We're still a sitting duck here," he reminded me solemnly. "They've got a hell of a lot more hardware in this dump than two armed crawlers. What are we going to do, blast everything in port?"

"If necessary," I retorted. "No one's going to kick *Raptor* when she's down. I'll fry as many of them as I have to."

Behind me, I heard Lewis shift in his chair. He cleared his throat nervously, but I refused to acknowledge his presence. It was easier for me to justify what I was doing if I pretended it had nothing to do with him.

If there was such a thing as a port master in that rats' nest, he was going to be apoplectic by then. The stretch of tarmac where we sat looked like a land-mined war zone. The two upended crawlers were buzzing angrily, their cleated treads spinning uselessly in the air. Several dazed men had begun to wriggle out of the vehicles' hatches. Between the crawlers and *Raptor* stretched a smoking trench, nearly three meters deep, and beyond that a formidable mound of heaved earth. A second pair of crawlers had assembled at the bank of hangars, their engines whining ominously. What had Raydor said about blasting everything in port? Then our speaker exploded again with a familiar and furious voice.

"*Raptor*, this is Redding! Damn it, is this what you call sitting tight?"

I lunged over the console, hammering the transmitter with the heel of my hand. "Then keep those mother-joining crawlers off our back!" I bellowed back at Redding.

"Shuttle approaching, Jo," Handy interjected smoothly and needlessly. The view on our screen shifted from the stretch of devastated tarmac to the sky above the landing field, where one of *Nimbus*'s silver ellipse-shaped shuttles was gracefully descending.

"They had orders to keep clear," Redding retorted a trifle less belligerently.

"Great! That explains why they were just about to breach our hatch," I remarked.

Redding did not reply. I watched on the view screen as the shining, curved form of the shuttle set down a few dozen meters off our starboard vanes. The ship settled herself with the muted hiss of hover turbos. Next to *Raptor*'s violated hull, she looked achingly sleek and fit.

Redding's voice growled over our speaker. "Jo-lac! Pull up those belly guns and get over here!"

"*You* get over *here*!" I retorted stubbornly. "I'll pop the hatch if you come alone."

Aggravation was plain in the hard edge of Redding's

voice. "Meet me on the tarmac, then, but pull up those damned guns."

Raydor and I exchanged a brief but meaningful look. I would have preferred to confront Redding on my own turf, especially since we seemed to be surrounded by so much of his. But I didn't see any way around it at that point. For all practical purposes we were helpless on the ground. Redding was still all we had to protect us from the rest of Nethersedge. I shrugged, and Raydor spread his broad hands in a gesture of reluctant acquiescence.

"Okay," I grunted into the transmitter. "Outside, then." I palmed Handy's input. "Retract the high beams," I instructed him grimly. "You're on Security Prime. No one gets through that hatch again except us."

"You've got it, Jo," Handy responded brightly. "Be careful."

I had to grin. Handy could take a crisis of major proportions and turn it into a moment of hearty bonhomie. But just as Handy was more than a device to me, *Raptor* was more than just a ship to Handy. In a way she was a physical extension of himself. Although Integration had rendered him incorporeal, in a sense she had become his body. His programming to protect her was as intrinsic to him as his covenant to protect life.

Raydor stripped off his harness, got to his feet, and ducked out the hatch into the corridor. I released my own harness and turned to face Lewis. He was hunched forward in his chair, his hands locked together between his knees. His face lifted hopefully to mine.

"You okay?" I asked him.

Lewis nodded promptly, his expression a pained mixture of apprehension and trust. I had gotten him down at Nethersedge, all right, just as I had promised him. But just what had I gotten us all into?

I leaned closer to him, close enough to see that the collar of his flightsuit and the exposed edge of his liner were both dark with sweat, close enough to smell the tang of fear on him. And Lewis leaned toward me, his blue eyes earnest but grave.

"Listen to me, Lewis," I said quietly. "I don't know

what we're stepping into here. I can't even figure out why Redding—Suns light him!—keeps sticking out his neck for us, unless he wants something." Somehow, that thought had the potential to concern me even more than the proven threat of MA or the probable danger of those pirates at Nethersedge. It was beginning to seem like more than just fortuitous coincidence that Redding showed up whenever we needed our asses bailed out of some fire. I stared into Lewis's open, trusting face. "Just stay with me, huh? I won't let them separate us. Just follow my lead, even if what I say or do doesn't make any sense to you. Understand?"

Lewis nodded solemnly, his handsome face etched with anxiety, his blue eyes luminescent with fear. With a rush that was simultaneously exhilarating and despairing, I realized that the man was the only thing of real value I had, the only wild card I held with which to bargain for our fate. But that gave me an idea.

Shifting in my chair, I reached into my hip pocket and pulled out a forgotten bit of cargo: the detention cuffs. Lewis's eyes widened as I reached for his hand, pressing one of the metals bands into his fingers. He glanced down at the cuff and then, confused, looked back at my face.

"Put it on," I urged him, snapping its companion onto its old familiar place on my own wrist. At Lewis's stunned expression, I elaborated. "They're harmless now—just a set of transmitters; they'll lock, but they aren't keyed. Put it on."

Lewis turned the cuff in his hand, regarding it with a mixture of fear and loathing. But when I made an encouraging gesture at him, he obediently fumbled to fasten the device on his wrist. Then he looked across at me again, his eyes blinking with a sweep of those incredible soot-dark lashes.

I leaned forward in my chair and squeezed his knee. "Don't worry," I said gently, not because there was no reason to but because there was no use for it. "Just follow my lead."

I got to my feet, and Lewis followed me. In the corridor outside Control I paused and touched his arm. When his eyes met mine, I gazed into that clear and guileless face. "Just remember," I reminded him, "you're a free Citizen now, no matter what I might have to say out there."

"I understand," he said.

"I'll try not to compromise you, Lewis," I vowed. "But I'll tell you this right now: I'll say whatever it takes to get us out of this mess alive."

A small smile tugged at the corners of his mouth at the bluntness of my assessment. Standing close to him, I could see the glint of his even white teeth behind his slightly parted lips. "It wouldn't be the first time I've been compromised," he confided ruefully.

I smiled back at him briefly, buoyed by a sudden small bloom of optimism that was totally unfounded and completely welcome.

As we joined Raydor at the hatch, I noted that he had donned his face wraps. He, in turn, duly noted the cuffs on our wrists. He said nothing, but comprehension was evident in his impassive eyes.

Outside, a small knot of angry men milled around the two overturned crawlers on the other side of the trench we had so rudely carved in the tarmac. Ignoring them, the three of us negotiated the rubble of broken pavement at *Raptor*'s prow and crossed the clear stretch of field that lay between our ship and *Nimbus*'s shuttle. From the extended ramp of the shuttle a group of four people approached us.

Redding had said nothing about weapons. Raydor wore his beam rifle slung casually across his broad back. He was hardly overarmed; three of the four figures who met us on the oil-stained pavement were double- or even triple-armed with beam rifles in shoulder scabbards and beam pistols in belt holsters. One of the three, a red-haired woman, had a big pistol jutting from each hip. Only Redding himself was unarmed, or not visibly armed, at least; there was a difference, I had long ago found.

The four of them stopped a couple of paces short of us. For a moment no one spoke. Redding's three com-

panions eyed us with varying degrees of open mistrust.
Then Redding slowly shook his head.

"Nice work, Captain," he said, gesturing at the
crudely excavated tarmac and the overturned crawlers.
"I can see why you're so damned popular in all the systems' ports these days."

I glared furiously at him, struggling to throttle down
the anger I felt. Redding was tall, as tall as I was, which
was unusual for a man; I could meet his gaze eye to eye.
"We were being threatened with a forced boarding," I
explained tautly, acutely aware of the tense anticipation
displayed in the postures of his crew mates. "Or are you
saying that I should have let the bastards fire first?"

That hit Redding right where every freightman and
captain lived. His steely gray eyes, the color of tarnished
gunmetal, flickered momentarily to the plowed earth and
the disabled crawlers surrounded by their irate crews.

"If I'd wanted trouble, I wouldn't've hit the tarmac,"
I added. "And your buddies in those crawlers would have
had more than a few cracked skulls to worry about."

Redding stared gravely at me for a moment. He had
the level presence of a man who was used to being
obeyed, but he hadn't abandoned good sense for principle. Of indeterminate age, in the dusty green of *Nimbus*'s
flightsuit, he looked deceptively unremarkable, nearly indistinguishable from his crew members. His brown hair
was unfashionably shaggy, hanging over his ears in careless locks. His face was totally normal, with those slate-
colored eyes, a broad jaw, and a nose that was just
slightly too long and slightly too crooked to be anything
but natural. An old scar, nearly invisible, ran from the
left corner of his mouth to the middle of his cheek. When
he smiled, as he suddenly did, the scar came to light,
pulling his mouth into a pleasantly quirky shape. In that
era of ubiquitous plastic repair it was a totally unnecessary and completely agreeable affectation, just what one
would expect from a king of pirates.

"I suspect they wouldn't be worrying about much of
anything by now," Redding conceded wryly.

I felt myself relax minutely, but I still kept myself be-

tween the four of them and Lewis, and I was still glad
for Raydor at my back. Redding's crew mates shifted
slightly, adopting his somewhat less belligerent stance.

"You seem to be real popular with MA lately," Redding remarked evenly, giving both Raydor and Lewis a
deceptively cursory glance.

"The feeling is mutual," I replied. "That's because I
have something they want." I noted with secret satisfaction that the detention cuffs hadn't escaped Redding's
surreptitious glance. I wasn't the only one at odds with
MA. A lot of things, including the presence of pod hangars at Nethersedge, were beginning to make a little more
sense.

"Lots of people have things MA wants," Redding
countered matter-of-factly. He gave me a sharp, analyti-
cal look. There was no pretense about the man, I had to
give him that. "Why land here, then?" he continued
bluntly. "Camelot's crawling with MA. And you can see
that Nethersedge isn't exactly renowned for its hospital-
ity, either."

I shrugged indifferently. "There's something here that
I want," I replied calmly.

Redding gave a small snort, staring past me to where
Lewis stood silently at Raydor's side. "Want or need?"
he asked. His expression suggested that he knew exactly
which it was. "If you need something, this is hardly the
place to look for help," he informed me. "People here
tend to be more interested in looking out for themselves
than in helping their fellow man."

"So I've noticed," I remarked dryly, encompassing
the upended crawlers with one deprecating glance.

Redding's gray eyes narrowed, and his shaggy head
cocked slightly. I had piqued his curiosity at least. And
there was something else there as well, perhaps the same
something that had prompted him to stick his neck out
for us twice already. "What are you here for?" he asked
me bluntly.

"I'll explain that to whoever's in charge here," I countered.

Redding gave a little hoot of derision, his mouth pulling crookedly again. "In charge?" he echoed. He waved casually, inclusively, at the jumble of dilapidated buildings around us. "You think there's anyone in charge of *this*?"

I kept my expression completely unchanged. "Yeah, I do," I told him evenly. "No operation this size could last unless there was someone in charge of it."

Redding's face sobered. He studied both Lewis and Raydor again, overtly this time. I had the feeling this man's bluntness had saved his skin more than once. It was a natural thing, far more reliable than the cultivated obliqueness most men would have substituted for it. "What makes you think," he said at last, "that whoever's in charge here would be interested in seeing you?"

I shrugged nonchalantly, letting the detention cuff dangle blatantly. "I've got a crippled ship down on their field. If anyone tries to breach her, she'll take this whole place out in one hell of a big Prime explosion. But if she stays on the field—" I made a simple but evocative gesture. "—I just get the feeling that sooner or later MA is going to take an interest in her."

Redding smiled grimly; his teeth were large but even. "You have a point," he conceded.

"And," I continued, "there's the matter of the damage to the tarmac."

Redding laughed; it was a harsh but not unpleasant sound. "Okay, Captain, you've made your point." He glanced toward the rise of buildings beyond the landing field and the decrepit hangars to where whatever passed for the Port Authority apparently resided. "I'll see what I can do." He fixed me with a sharp eye. "Not that I have a hell of a lot of pull around here."

I merely shrugged; whatever his pull, it was bound to be greater than ours. Redding gestured to one of his crew members, advising me, "I'd suggest you and your friends wait on the shuttle."

But I shook my head. "We'll wait on *Raptor*," I told him firmly.

Redding paused, hands on hips, surveying the three of us like we were a trio of recalcitrant children. "No good," he explained. "You haven't exactly made any fans here with that little stunt, Captain. You stay with your ship, she's going to attract all kinds of trouble." He gestured at Raydor and Lewis. "Send them back if you're worried about her, but you're far safer off-ship."

I shook my head again, politely but resolutely. "Uh-uh," I responded, raising the wrist with the detention cuff. "We stay together."

Suppressing his exasperation—a maneuver that was almost a pleasure to watch in a man so controlled—Redding tossed his shaggy head. "You're a target here," he repeated patiently. "Don't tempt every hothead on this garbage heap to try out your high beams. Let her be."

I glanced over my shoulder at *Raptor*, my beautiful crippled bird. As I turned, I exchanged fleeting but significant looks with Raydor and Lewis. Then I met Redding's stoic gaze again. "All right. But we stay together—and not on your shuttle."

Redding frowned but spread his hands in a gesture of concession. "Have it your way. Follow me."

He turned to move away, but I stayed rooted. "What about my ship?" I demanded.

Masterfully summoning his patience, Redding motioned to one of his crew members, the redheaded woman with the impressive display of beam pistols. "Martz, stand their hatch," he instructed her calmly. As she moved off toward *Raptor*, he nodded to one of his men. "Call Dalton," he told him. "Get me more security down here." To the last man, Redding just gave a little wave. That man, a squat but powerfully built Normal with closely cropped gray hair, wordlessly accompanied us across the landing field.

We crossed the tarmac under the oppressive glare of Camelot's yellow primary sun. Heat shimmered up in waves from the stained pavement. Beyond the cracked field a creaking lift carried us up the outside of one of the buildings to a network of rusting metal walkways that spanned the sprawl of rotting hangars. As we crossed the rooftop thoroughfare, I saw that Lewis was glancing around with a dispirited air of disappointment, no doubt recalling the pristine geometry of port on Heinlein; there was no comparison. Everything here looked neglected, makeshift, worn out. The buildings were stripped down, falling apart, filthy. Their windows and skylights were pocked with holes and missing panes; their metal sheeting was pitted with corrosion and rust. Even the few men and women who peered out at us with varying degrees of curiosity and outright hostility from the other walkways and doorways of the battered buildings looked ill used and abraded. Most of them looked like renegade freightmen or outright thieves, Class Threes and Normal Class Fours, dressed in everything from ships' flightsuits to much-patched CA jumpsuits. It was as though something in that unforgiving place made everyone who stayed there become embittered and mean-spirited. Generations of pirates had laid waste to what could once have been a bustling and legitimate commercial hub; like a succession of rapists, they had quite literally used Nethersedge up.

We rode another ancient lift into the dusky bowels of some building; stepping out from behind Redding, I saw we were in a huge, cavernous warehouse at least three levels above ground. The part of the structure that I could see was nearly empty, but the lighting was so dim that the interior of the building stretched far beyond the range of my sight. I suspected that it had originally been designed for the storage of perishables, because there was an elaborate network of coolant pipes snaking up the wall next to the lift. Most of the pipes looked too corroded to be functional, but that was probably a moot point since there weren't many perishables anymore, anyway; that might have explained why the building looked so long abandoned.

Redding gestured to his stout crewman. "Take them down to the can," he instructed the man. "Don't let anyone near them." He looked over at me, his gray eyes grave. "Stay with Monk. Between him and your man, I don't think there'll be trouble. I'll see what I can do."

Before I could comment or question him, Redding turned and headed briskly off across the vast and empty warehouse, his boot heels tapping hollowly on the gritty floor.

The man called Monk nodded to us and pointed mutely to a door several meters down from the lift. As we filed into the room behind him, I realized with some amusement that our sanctuary was indeed an old rest room. It looked as unused and nonfunctional as the rest of the building, but all the old stainless-steel facilities were still in place. Raydor and Monk both took up casually vigilant stances at the small room's metal-plated door. With elaborate nonchalance, more assumed than felt, I leaned back against one of the old urinals and caught Lewis's eye.

Lewis gave me a small, almost embarrassed smile and leaned back against the wall beside me. His detention cuff clicked forlornly against the metal-bonded wall. Awkwardly, he folded that arm across his stomach. But I was the only one who seemed to have noticed the sound.

I found it singularly fitting that our first accommodations on that cesspool should be in an old toilet. It somehow gave me some small assurance that our old familiar gods of bizarre irony were still on our side. I glanced at Redding's Monk, stolid and silent, nearly shoulder to shoulder with Raydor at the door. I figured him for the kind who questioned little and said even less.

Just as I was about to make some wry, encouraging remark to Lewis, I heard the protesting screech of the lift. Too soon to be Redding returning; that same thought was echoed back to me in the grim expression on Monk's slablike face. Raydor's big eyes narrowed behind the hooded edge of his face wraps. Smoothly, instinctively, he scooped his beam rifle out of its scabbard. Monk raised one of his weapons, a particularly nasty-looking portable beam cannon. Leaning forward, he rested its muzzle against the rest room's door.

The lift squealed to a halt on our level. Footsteps boomed in the empty warehouse. Beside me, Lewis drew himself erect, his hands clasped in front of him. He darted a glance to me as the footfalls thudded outside our door. For some perverse reason the thought that we all could have been safely back at *Nimbus*'s shuttle kept intruding into my mind.

Something solid—a fist or perhaps even a booted foot—battered against the door. "Captain!" someone outside shouted. "Come on out of there!"

If they had beam cannon—and I suspected they very well might—or even a few good beam rifles, there was nothing about the little door that would keep them for long. Only the fact that they didn't know what we had on the inside was probably keeping them at bay so far. And so I saw no advantage in replying; keeping them guessing was the best we could do.

I caught Raydor's eye and mouthed the question, *How many*? His big head, swaddled in the wraps, cocked toward the door; he listened intently. One of Raydor's many talents was his almost preternatural sense of hearing; it was one of the many things that made him so skilled on comm. I swear he could hear hair grow—when he was awake, that is; asleep, he was as deaf as a stump. After a moment he turned back to me, gave an abbreviated shrug, and mouthed, *A dozen—maybe fifteen*.

Too many for us to hope to overpower, then. We were safer trying to hold them off. I nodded tightly to Raydor.

"Captain!" the voice outside the door bellowed again. "Come on—open up! Or we're coming in!"

Still we waited, not responding. I gave an unprofitable glance around the abandoned rest room, searching hopefully for something we could use to barricade the door or something I could use as a weapon if it came to that. But the place was barren, stripped of everything but the basic plumbing fixtures. Braining someone with a toilet might have been soul-satisfying, but it was hardly feasible. I leaned forward a little on the balls of my feet, tense and perspiring. My tongue felt like a sour rag.

What I had expected them to do was to try a little more haranguing or at the very least to fry the door off its hinges with a good blast of beam fire. But I guess they knew the decrepit old building better than I did, because what they did instead was just knock the door down: very quick and very effective. The impact pushed Raydor over backward and sent the beam cannon flying from Monk's hamlike hands. As the men outside lunged into the room, Lewis leapt in front of me, pressing me against the wall. My breath left me in a startled grunt.

In the chaos that followed events seemed curiously segmented, like a series of images, although in actuality everything happened nearly simultaneously. Rolling on the floor, Raydor brought up his beam rifle in a defensive sweep. But before he could fire, a heavily booted foot kicked the weapon from his hands. Monk, his fists balled like bludgeons, swung into the fray. He managed to flatten two of the intruders before they coldcocked him with the barrel of a beam rifle, and he went down like a bag of wet sand. Then all that stood between me and the thugs was Lewis: Lewis, pushing me protectively against the wall, confronting the angry mob alone.

"Stand away!" one of the men demanded of Lewis. The man was huge, as tall as Raydor and a good 150 kilos. He was dressed like a dockworker and had a beam cannon the size of a fence post in his hands. "Stand away!" he repeated with a menacing wave of the weapon. "*She's* the one we want!"

The man pressed against me was a Lewis I had never seen before. His brilliant blue eyes were cold, hard, glittering with a jewellike defiance I had not imagined him capable of. His jaw was doggedly set. *"No!"* he hissed, shielding me.

His foolhardy display filled me with a bizarre mixture of affection and irritation. I tried to push past him, but he literally had me pinned to the wall. Just when I was ungraciously considering kicking him in the shins to free myself, one of our attackers took the initiative away from me. The man, a muscular Normal in a much-patched red flightsuit, swept Lewis aside with one bearlike swipe of his arm, sending Lewis sprawling on the rest room's dirty concrete floor.

In the next few seconds, as I faced my antagonists alone, I was surprised and dismayed to find that a concern for Lewis's welfare was uppermost in my mind. A dangerous distraction at the very least, because in my consternation I nearly missed Raydor's covert counterattack. Suddenly the three men who had been crowded closest to the downed Tachs dropped like stunned oxen, felled by one furious chop of Raydor's legs. Then chaos returned to the room.

The huge dockman who had menaced us let out an unintelligible bellow of rage and swung his beam cannon at the most expendable target for his fury: Lewis. Automatically, I dove for the floor, throwing myself over Lewis. I don't know whether the enraged Goliath would have tried to fry me, too. Luckily, I never had the chance to find out, for at that moment a noisy scuffle erupted outside the doorway. The mob of men filling the rest room milled uncertainly. Then a loud and furious voice roared, "What the bloody Suns is going on in here?"

Nearly giddy with relief, I looked up from the floor to see the familiar dusty green of Redding's flightsuit. Behind him, a wedge of powerfully built men in Tachs tunics were pushing the dissident mob aside. And behind the Tachs, the possessor of that outraged voice strode imperiously into the room. And then I felt like we had all fallen into some kind of weird time warp.

She was a big, broad-shouldered woman with skin the dark, creased brown of well-cured leather. Her grizzled gray hair flew unfettered in a great frizzy mass. She was dressed in a crossed and belted tunic of coarse ochre weave and baggy Tachs trousers over calf-high boots. She was Normal, but even that modification gave her powerful features an alarming cast. I could not imagine what she would have looked like as a normal.

She swung her head commandingly with a contemptuous toss of her manic mane, and her ink-black eyes flashed. "Well?" she demanded. "Scum join you—what the starless Void do you think you're doing?"

Even the gargantuan dockman cringed under the woman's wrath. He gestured feebly with the barrel of his beam cannon. "She landed without clearance, shot at our crawlers—"

The big woman made a derisive snort and batted her hand at the man's weapon. " 'She landed without clearance,' " she mimicked. "*Clearance*! What the hell do you think this is, a damned MA base?" She snorted again even as the huge dockman winced away from her. The rest of his bully band were already shrinking toward the door. "I'll give you *clearance*, you bunghole! Get the hell back to your work!"

Like chastised children, without so much as a mutter or a backward glance, the mob of would-be vigilantes slithered out of the room. The cadre of Tachs—Altereds, but none wearing face wraps—formed a phalanx to the rear of the departing men.

Moving forward, Redding stooped to offer me a hand. But I declined it, getting slowly to my feet on my own, my eyes still riveted to the woman in the ochre tunic. Redding gave Monk a hand instead; other than a rather nasty bruise on the head, the big man seemed unharmed. I saw Raydor stand up. I reached down to Lewis without really seeing him and helped pull him up. A small smear of blood marred his pale cheek, squeezed from a shallow laceration where his face had connected with the concrete floor.

Redding had missed nothing in my reaction or in the big woman's subtle expression of wry amusement at my expense. Now he glanced from me, to the woman, to Raydor, and then back to me again. "You know each other?" he asked.

I stared at the woman. "Alexandria Moore," I said softly. I hesitated, then blurted out, "I thought you were dead!"

"Did you, now?" the woman responded with the suggestion of a smile. "Good! The more people who believe that, the longer I'm likely to live!"

The woman turned abruptly, clapping Raydor companionably on the arm. "How're you doing, Raydor?" she asked him. "Can't you keep this woman out of trouble?"

I could read both relief and surprise in Raydor's hooded eyes. "I'm glad to see you, Alexandria," he responded.

Moore laughed, a sound both abrasive and infectious. "Damned *surprised* to see me is more like it, eh?" she corrected, clapping his arm again. Then she wheeled on the Tachs who stood at the doorway. "Ennis! Manto!" she boomed to two of them. "Get in here."

Moore turned to me again, sparing Lewis a quick but penetrating look. "Redding's told me you've got business here, Jo," she commented. "Well, I've got some business, too—off-port, and I'm supposed to be on a shuttle right now. I'll be back tomorrow morning, Powers willing." She paused, shooting Lewis another less than casual look. "These two Tachs will see you quartered; you can wait for me if that suits you."

I just nodded mutely, still stunned by the mercurial turn of events. Alexandria Moore alive was shock enough; Alexandria Moore alive and running that rats' nest of pirates was totally incomprehensible to me.

Moore thumped my shoulder, nearly knocking me off my feet. "Good," she pronounced heartily. "Tomorrow, then." She grinned, showing big square teeth. "I suspect this'll be a good story, too!" She winked broadly at a startled Lewis. Then she spun around and strode briskly out the doorway.

Redding was eyeing the three of us with a certain grudging bemusement. "Old friends, right?" he remarked dryly. He motioned to the two Tachs Alexandria had denoted; the rest of them had left in her wake, like tugs around a big cruiser. "These two'll take you to Moore's compound," he explained.

"What about *Raptor*?" I interjected quickly. I hadn't been bluffing about MA's interest in my ship; we couldn't afford to just leave her on the tarmac.

"Moore gave me clearance—" And he stressed the word "clearance" with wry humor. "—to tow her into a hangar. To begin repairs, too, if that suits you."

I motioned to Raydor. "Go with him," I instructed him. "Take Handy off Prime but recode him."

Redding's one brow climbed as if my paranoia both amused and impressed him. But he shrugged indifferently.

"Stay with her," I continued, looking up into Raydor's dark, impassive eyes. My intent was implicit, at least to him. There was no one in that dump I trusted with my ship, including Redding.

Raydor just nodded and moved wordlessly toward the door. Redding followed him, the silent Monk at his heels like a large and agreeable dog. At the threshold, Redding paused for a final comment. "Despite the way the rest of this place may look, Moore's quarters are real nice, Captain. I think if I were you, I'd spend all my time there until she gets back."

It was only a suggestion, not a threat; Redding had demonstrated a repeated interest in our welfare and a willingness to involve himself personally in it. But something about the comment rankled me, and I felt an unexpected surge of resentment rise in me. "Thanks for the tip, Captain," I responded. "But I don't remember Alexandria saying anything about us being in custody."

The sarcasm seemed lost on Redding. He merely shrugged again and continued through the doorway. Moments later I heard the squealing grate of the lift. I glanced over at Lewis, noticing what I hoped no one else would have: The small laceration on his cheek was almost completely healed already.

I nodded to the two Tachs. "Let's go, guys," I said.

CHAPTER NINE

I suspect that if any of my ancestors on Old Earth had survived to see the exploration and settlement of space, they would have been as depressed as hell by the uniform lack of imagination in extraterrestrial architecture and design. With the possible exception of places like Heinlein—women's planets—the majority of what humankind had constructed off-Earth was singularly utilitarian and relentlessly grim. Most of Nethersedge typified the worst the future had to offer: a culturally sterile, derelict sprawl of truly ugly buildings and nearly deserted thoroughfares, all laid out with the mindless predictability of Integrator grids. Even the housing was endlessly drab, with barrackslike blocks of gray native stone and concrete.

That's why our quarters inside Moore's compound were such a pleasant surprise. Not only was the apartment tastefully decorated, it was downright rustic, employing such rare and unique details as real wood paneling, electric lamps instead of wall illuminators, and—best of all—not an Integrator access in sight. Moore's pair of taciturn Tachs deposited us at the quarters, merely grunting in response to my words of thanks. They left me standing in the doorway, somewhat bemused, with the door card key in my hand.

Lewis, his eyes wide, moved quickly through the apartment. His hands greedily skimmed the real wood furniture with its lush fabric upholstery like a hungry man sampling food. Completing his whirlwind tour, he rejoined me at the entry hall, his face a transparent mixture of excitement and confusion. He made an inquiring gesture with a slight sweep of his hand, his dark brows arched.

I just shrugged casually. "Moore has eclectic tastes," I offered. "Make the most of it."

Lewis suddenly grinned, a brief and unguarded bit of relief and delight. Then his expression sobered as if he had abruptly judged it inappropriate. He stood before me, his hands hanging limply at his sides, his gaze dropping in sudden chagrin. I knew what was coming then and almost moved to divert it, but Lewis was too quick for me.

"I—I'm sorry, Captain," he told me gravely. "I disobeyed you back there. I know you said I should just follow your lead and keep out of it but . . ."

A thousand thoughts hit me then, randomly, like blasts of chatter from comm, far too many reactions for me to make any sense of them. The little shit *had* disobeyed me! His heroics could have gotten us both killed. I could have told him that. I also could have told him that as long as we wore the detention cuffs, it was unlikely those bullies would have killed or even separated us—a fact that even I, in the heat of the moment, had neatly forgotten. But I didn't tell Lewis any of that. Another thought, a staggering thought, occupied me: I hadn't even *considered* dressing Lewis down for his conduct this time.

I hadn't considered it because—damn it!—I cared too much about him.

And so I just held up my hand to silence his abject apology and felt the words coming, almost will-lessly, from my mouth.

"Forget it," I said, my voice sticking roughly in my throat. "Things got a little hot, and you just reacted, that's all." Lewis's eyes, still round with remorse, clung to me. "Besides," I finished determinedly, "it didn't work out so badly. Maybe it bought us some time, till Redding got back with Moore."

Lewis's expression changed rapidly again, his brows rising and then knitting in a frown of intense concentration. "You know her," he said speculatively, cautiously.

I heaved an abrupt sigh and moved past him, sinking down into one of the heavily upholstered chairs in the living area. I leaned back into the thick cushions and hooked one ankle over the other knee. Then I waved at him to sit. Lewis came over quickly, like an obedient pet, and sunk down in a chair opposite mine.

I gazed calmly at him. "I used to know her," I corrected him. "I knew who she used to be." I shrugged almost helplessly. "Damned if I know who she is now!"

But Lewis just leaned forward in his chair, his hands clasped in his lap, waiting for me to go on. So I told him what I knew about Alexandria Moore.

Seeing her boldly stride into that crowded and dingy warehouse rest room had been like being unwillingly swept back more than twenty years in time to an age when I had known the big, gregarious woman only as my mother's good friend. But even then I had realized that my mother's ties to the woman must have long predated my memories of Alexandria, and I knew that her first career had not been the diplomatic one I had been witness to but a technological one. Alexandria Moore had once been an integral part of MA's Integration Research and Development team. While the science of Integration was nearly a century old, most of the real advances and refinements in technique had been made within my lifetime. Moore and another researcher, a woman named Hanlon, had shared the credit for perfecting creative cognitive function in Integrators. The technology had advanced BMIs from the category of merely extremely complex computers into the realm of thinking, reasoning beings. Handyman—my mother's own Integrator, now mine—was a part of that new generation of BMIs, the product and beneficiary of Moore and Hanlon's joint research. Not that Handy owed quite all of his impressive abilities to IRD, however; most of his encyclopedic knowledge came from his insatiable curiosity and the streak of petty larceny that kept him egressing into every Integrator access in the known systems. But it was creative cognitive function that made it possible for that curiosity and larceny to have survived Integration intact.

Then something happened between Moore and Hanlon—a falling out, burnout, something. Alexandria had left IRD for the Diplomatic Service; Hanlon seemed to have dropped out of the public eye as well. Alexandria became MA's liaison to the Tachs. There, the robust, compassionate woman devoted herself to finding off-world training and employment for the thousands of unlanded Tachs Altereds. When I was twelve years old, she had approached my mother about Raydor. He was fairly typical of Alexandria's protégés, a lower-Class, unskilled Altered who had shown some special gift and drive. On the basis of Alexandria's recommendation, my mother took Raydor on and never had reason to regret it. The big Tachs did more than justify his mentor's faith in him, he also became my best friend. And after my mother died, Raydor became the closest thing to a family I had.

After Raydor came on board, I had seen Alexandria only two or three times when we made port at Earthheart. Then she seemed to have vanished. Finally, there was an MA announcement: Alexandria Moore and a shipload of her cohorts had been killed in a freak accident at pullout. That was the official version, anyway; obviously, it was a lie. Perhaps it had even been an attempted execution; in light of the vicious tangle we seemed to be getting snarled in, that idea suddenly seemed all too plausible.

Lewis had listened to me gravely and thoughtfully. When I stopped speaking, he nodded half to himself and said, ''Then she gave Raydor his freedom.''

Oddly put—Tachs, even the Altereds, were Citizens once they left Earthheart—but strangely apt nonetheless. ''That's one way of looking at it,'' I conceded.

But something about the idea seemed to comfort Lewis, and he leaned back a little in his chair. He was silent a moment, staring at his knees. Then he looked up at me, his dark lashes lifting. ''Do you think she'll help us?'' he asked me.

I shrugged again. ''I don't know,'' I said. I still hadn't figured out just how she fit into all of this. ''Maybe—if she can.''

Lewis seemed momentarily discomforted. He shifted a little in the thickly upholstered chair. He was gazing at his hands, and this time when he spoke, he didn't look directly at me. "What are you going to tell her?"

"The truth," I said bluntly, not needing to add, *or as much of the truth as I know*! Only the truth would work with a woman like Alexandria. Maybe she would be able to do what I had been unable to accomplish and pry it out of Lewis.

Lewis was definitely fidgeting; his fingers unlaced and relaced in his lap like creatures acting on their own volition. "I think we can trust her," he offered, totally unsolicited.

"Hopefully better than you trust me," I had to add dryly.

That was cruel—useless and cruel. I saw that it wounded Lewis, and instantly I regretted having said it—even though it was true. He had tried to keep me clear of this, after all. I had been the one who had followed my heart rather than my head, who had volunteered to help him. There was no blaming him anymore.

I leaned forward, diminishing the sting of my cutting remark by slapping him playfully on the knee and suggesting, "Come on, let's see what kind of food we can scare up in this dump."

An uncertain smile flickered on his face. "Maybe real meat?" he offered hopefully.

I cocked an eyebrow at him and asked, with mock horror, "Am I making a *carnivore* out of you?"

Lewis grinned, obviously more at ease. "Only when Raydor's not here," he confided.

We adjourned to the food processor in the eating area to sample whatever Nethersedge had to offer. Real meat was not on the menu.

It was several hours later, long after the planetary dusk, when the door buzzer sounded. Lewis and I had both had a chance to eat and clean up; I had even begun to think of sleep. I knew that Ennis and Manto were still stationed in the corridor outside our quarters, so I assumed our visitor had their indulgence. I punched the release, and the door *whooshed* open. It was Redding.

"Captain," I said tersely, stepping back.

"Captain," Redding responded as he entered and punched the reseal button.

I studied him a moment, my appraisal quite overt. His dusty-green flightsuit was wrinkled and lightly soiled, and there were smudges of ingrained component lube on his hands. He must have come directly from the hangars. He returned my direct scrutiny, his mouth pulled into that crooked half smirk that seemed to indicate some amusement at my expense.

"What about *Raptor*?" I finally asked when he made no move to volunteer any information.

"She's good," he replied placidly, moving a few steps farther into the room. His cool gray eyes swept the living area, where Lewis had been seated on an overstuffed lounger. Lewis got quietly to his feet, wariness in his very posture.

Redding's gaze moved past Lewis, roving the rest of the room. He continued speaking, not looking directly at me again. "We're replacing the whole vane. Your man did the interior work."

I knew my voice betrayed my surprise; I suspect it was the reaction Redding had intended to provoke. "Replacing it? You have the facilities for that in—"

"In this dump?" Redding completed for me, his gun-metal eyes flickering with mild amusement over my face. "Of course," he went on, answering his own question. "Should be finished by morning." The corner of his mouth quirked wryly. "I told your man to close up and come back here; he's done all the inside repair and hookup, and the techs can do the rest of the external modular work. But he's a hardheaded one, even for a Tachs." Relishing my obvious disbelief, Redding concluded, "She'll be as good as new, maybe better."

"Well, good," I said awkwardly, fumbling ineffectually to conceal my surprise.

Redding just shrugged dismissively and turned back toward the doorway. "Oh, and don't worry about the

repair bill, Captain," he tossed off over his shoulder.
"I'm sure Moore'll square it with you."

I hesitated a moment, still caught off guard by his
breezy assurances. "Captain, wait," I called after him.
I caught up to him by the door.

Redding swung around, his face on a level with my
own, his stained thumbs hooked casually in the belt loops
of his flightsuit. His shaggy brows lifted in mild inquiry,
as if he couldn't possibly imagine what further questions
I might have. Oh, he was a cool one, all right. Looking
into those slate-colored eyes, gray pools pinpointed with
black, I nearly lost my resolve. Then the words tumbled
from my lips.

"Why did you stick your neck out for us?" I asked
him. "Here—and back at New Cuba?"

For a moment Redding was absolutely motionless, and
I was acutely aware of Lewis making some small motion
behind me. Then Redding's mouth pulled into an almost
feral grin, those metallic eyes narrowing. He made a
snorting sound of amusement. "Let's just say I had my
reasons, Captain." His intense scrutiny was like a leer.
"Maybe you've got something I want," he suggested sardonically.

I felt an unexpected flush of heat climb from my collar;
I had to drop my gaze. As I did so, Redding laughed, a
sharp raucous sound. "No, not *that*," he hooted. His
gaze slid over my shoulder, settling where Lewis stood,
and the corner of his mouth crinkled wolfishly.

I silently berated myself for the sense of startled shock
I felt; I shouldn't have been so naive. I wasn't exactly a
beautiful woman, and Lewis was a very beautiful man.
But my ill-concealed expression of chagrin only seemed
to further fuel Redding's amusement. He chuckled again,
but more gently this time. "No, not *that* either," he said.
"Though Powers know, he's easily the prettiest thing in
port."

I had to force myself not to turn then; Lewis's anxiety
was a palpable thing to me, but I couldn't turn and give
Redding the satisfaction that my reassuring Lewis would
have afforded him. I injected a tone of dry civility into

my voice and met Redding's gaze squarely. "Then I trust
that if I owe you some debt, Captain, I'll be allowed to
repay it?" I said levelly.

Redding looked mildly bemused. "In good time," he
remarked. He punched the door release. He glanced back
toward Lewis again and then to my face. "Anything else
I can get you?" he offered casually.

In the corridor behind Redding I could see the reassuring forms of Alexandria's two Tachs. Neither betrayed
even the slightest interest in what was happening.
"Yeah," I decided suddenly. "They got any audiochips
in this place?"

Redding's features momentarily froze. He peered at me
skeptically, as if he suspected I was taking some kind of
oblique cheap shot at him. When he seemed satisfied that
I was indeed serious, his face dissolved into one of those
crooked grins. "Audiochips?" he repeated somewhat incredulously.

"Yeah, the Clones, if they've got them. Otherwise,
Stressed Metal or Autasia," I said, absolutely straight-
faced.

Redding capitulated with a helpless shrug. "How can
you listen to that shit?" he asked me. "It all sounds like
a damned asteroid storm." He shook his head, his unruly
hair bouncing. Then he motioned to me. "Come on,
then; I'll show you where the library is."

I paused only long enough to throw Lewis a calm and
reassuring look. Then I followed Redding through the
doorway. One of the Tachs—Ennis or Manto, I was
ashamed to admit that I didn't know yet which was
which—fell automatically into step behind us as Redding
led me up the corridor. "Audiochips," Redding muttered again, but I suspect he was thoroughly enjoying
himself.

The library was at the far end of the corridor on our
level. Redding punched out the release code, and the door
cycled open. "There you go," he remarked. "Help
yourself." He began to turn away, saying, "Me, I've still
got half my cargo pods to get down."

I realized then, with a fresh infusion of bewilderment,

that Redding had just spent half a day seeing to *Raptor*'s
repairs while his own ship was in the process of unloading cargo. It was another confusing concession on his
part, and it troubled me that I could see no reason for
any of it. I caught hold of the sleeve of his flightsuit as
he turned away.

"Redding, wait."

He paused, turning back with that cool, detached look
of mild amusement on his lean, normal face.

"Redding, what I said to you earlier, in the warehouse—" I stammered to a halt, made clumsy by his
frank and bemused scrutiny. "I—uh, I'm sorry I was so
bitchy," I finished awkwardly. I couldn't bring myself to
say the other, obvious thing: thank you.

But Redding just shrugged his ubiquitous shrug, an indifferent gesture of dismissal that did not suggest that the
alleged bitchiness had not occurred, just that it was of
no importance to him. Then he nodded and moved away
back up the corridor.

I exchanged glances with the silent Tachs. Had it not
been for my years of close association with Raydor, I
wouldn't have been able to read the expression in those
unblinking dark eyes, an expression suspiciously like
amusement. I grinned ruefully and stepped through the
doorway, into the surprisingly large and well-stocked library.

They even had three Toiling Clone chips.

I was half drowsing in one of the big overstuffed chairs,
the mournful sounds of the Clones wailing softly in my
ear, when Raydor returned. Lewis went to the door when
the buzzer sounded. Raydor thumped him good-naturedly
on the arm and then dropped into a chair beside me.

I popped the chip from my ear and surveyed Raydor
with unconcealed relief. "You okay?" I asked him quietly.

He nodded. Somewhere during the course of the afternoon or evening his face wraps had been discarded: a
needless artifice in that place. His crepelike skin seemed
even more wrinkled than usual, and his big eyes were

rimmed with fatigue. But his expression was not distressed.

"Redding told me about the vane," I told him; I did not need to add that it had come as one hell of a surprise to me.

Raydor nodded again. "It's a good job," he confirmed with satisfaction. "Shipyard quality. This place may look like a junkyard, but they have some pretty sophisticated equipment in those hangars, better than you'd get in any MA port."

I grinned spontaneously. "Looks like our pirate friends must need a lot of repairs," I noted.

Raydor smiled in agreement. "A very efficient bunch."

I glanced up at Lewis, who was hovering uncertainly between the chairs and the door. I motioned for him to join us. As he settled himself into the chair across from me, I asked Raydor, "What's ship's status now?"

"Handy's on Security Prime," he told me. "They were just finishing up when I left. There's nothing they could do now without Handy catching it," he added needlessly.

I wasn't concerned about that; I was thinking that Raydor could have come back hours ago, but he wouldn't have. It wasn't his way to delegate anything where *Raptor* was concerned. "Well, I'm glad that's done," I admitted.

Raydor shifted in his chair. "What about tomorrow, Jo?" he asked.

I shook my head. "What do you make of Moore?" I countered.

I saw something stir in those deep, dark eyes, something that I suspected had to do with a part of Raydor's life that lay forever beyond my reckoning, that predated his association with me and the universe beyond Earthheart. I knew that on his homeworld he had, like most of his kind, been born a farmer. I also knew that on that population-dense planet, the inheritance of the Tachs' family land followed a complex system of hierarchy. Like so many others, Raydor had been forced to seek his livelihood off-planet. But Raydor had held an ace card, an advantage in that scramble for success: He'd had Alexandria Moore. When she had befriended him and facilitated his training, I think she had done more than just given him a career advancement. I think she had, much as Lewis had phrased it, set him free. Now his big hands spread evocatively in his lap. "Alexandria wouldn't change," he offered.

Wouldn't she? I could afford to assume nothing, least of all that. But I knew the depths of Raydor's loyalties; Powers know, I had plumbed them myself. He had always been my one absolute in a universe of sudden shifts of circumstance and tenuous social affiliations. So I just shrugged and remarked calmly, "Well, it doesn't matter what we think of her. What's going to matter is what *she* thinks of *us*."

Raydor rewarded me with another smile. Then he got to his feet. "I'm going to clean up, turn in."

While Raydor showered, I returned to my audiochips, but my heart was no longer in it. Surreptitiously, I watched Lewis as he restlessly prowled the apartment. His compulsive movements were more those of a man trying to avoid something than those of a man seeking something. Then I remembered his nightmares.

When Raydor came out of hygiene, I suggested, "Even with Alexandria's guys out there in the hall, I'd feel a hell of a lot better if we stood watch, too." I held up a couple of chips. "I've got some great stuff here; I'll take it first."

From the next room, Lewis watched me reflectively. Raydor merely shrugged agreeably. "Wake me up when your ears go numb," he advised me good-naturedly.

"Lewis," I called before he could protest, "how about you getting some sleep, too, huh?"

There was one bedroom, two beds. As Raydor began to move away, I caught his sleeve. I pitched my voice low so only he could hear it. "Stay close to him, will you?" I asked.

A flicker of understanding passed in those big, unblinking eyes. "Sure," he said softly.

Raydor closed the bedroom door against the flare of

light from my lamp. I sprawled out on the upholstered lounger and wriggled out of my boots. I felt a deep and boneless fatigue, but an obsessive uncertainty gnawed at me, an anxiety that would not let me rest. There were just too damned many variables. I fretted under the sense of helplessness I felt. I had lived most of my adult life as a captain; I ached to take charge and direct things, not to be forced to wonder and wait. I wasn't used to feeling that powerless, and I didn't enjoy the sensation at all.

At length, I switched to a Stressed Metal chip. The synthesized screeching made me recall Redding's disparaging remark about my musical tastes, and silently, briefly, I had to smile. Redding: another variable. Camelot and MA, Redding and Moore—the little litany of paradoxes danced through my brain. All of them were random factors, out of my control. But above it all the most persistent vision of danger, the most damning threat, was still the one thing I could not seem to find a way to defend myself against: Lewis. Because he was a threat that was sustained by something inside of myself. If I had lost control on that one, it was because I had given it up of my own volition.

An image of Lewis insinuated itself into my mind then; it was an image of a man I could hardly recognize or reconcile with the Lewis I had come to know. Lewis, that almost feral snarl on his handsome face, defying the huge dockhand in the dingy warehouse john. Lewis, wedging himself between me and the threat of danger. Lewis, fearless and foolhardy—or terrified and foolhardy—I was not sure which.

I shifted restlessly on the lounger, pulling up my knees and crossing my ankles. The comfortably archaic room was silent. The soft yellow glow of my lamp cast weird shadows that floated on the walls and then disappeared, swallowed by the dark grain of the real wood paneling. Somewhere, far off in the entrails of the complex, a lift ground dully.

No one was exactly what he seemed anymore, I decided fatalistically. Not Lewis, not Moore, not even Raydor. I knew Raydor as well as I knew any human being, yet that night I had been reminded that there were depths and layers and cul-de-sacs to the laconic Tachs that even I was not privy to. He had a past, experiences that I could not hope to share, and a quiet reservoir that even I, in all my intimacy with him, had never been allowed to penetrate. In that regard Alexandria Moore must still have known him better than I did.

And just how much had Moore changed? She'd had a brilliant career in Integration once; why had she given that up? Then she had worked for MA—in the Tachs' interest, to be sure, but for MA nevertheless. Now she headed up this rogue port, outside of the law. And she was on Camelot—still, by proximity, associated with MA. I was convinced they had once contrived to kill her; so what was she doing practically under their noses? And why was this woman, my mother's good friend, now an outlaw?

My head throbbed. I popped out the Stressed Metal chip and reached up to dim the lamp. All I needed was to start hashing over Redding in my mind and my monumental headache would be complete. I sank back into the padded lounger, my arms folded across my chest. Like a corpse, I thought glumly. I tried to doze, but lines from the Clones' songs kept looping through my brain.

Whether or not I would have been able to sleep was to be a moot point, anyway. Because as I lay there, trying to dampen the chorus out of my mind, I heard a loud, agonized groan from the other room. I scrambled to my feet, tripping over my discarded boots. Two clear and contradictory realizations dominated my thoughts as I sprinted toward the bedroom. My one reaction was a fatalistic lack of panic, because I knew the sound had come from Lewis. The other reaction was stark distress—for the very same reason.

I punched the bedroom door release and flung myself into the room. Raydor had turned on the bedside lamp, and in its muted glow I saw him and Lewis crouched together on the bed. Lewis was curled into a stiff fetal position in the center of the rumpled mass of sheets and blankets. Raydor hovered over him, his big hands holding on to Lewis's arms. I could hear the deep rumble of Raydor's voice murmuring some wordless comfort. But Lewis's eyes, wide in his colorless face, were blank and filled with terror.

Quietly, I crossed the room. With a certain sense of automatic detachment I noted the details of the scene before me. Both men had stripped down to their suit liners to sleep. Only the one bed had been slept in. Lewis clung frantically to Raydor's thick forearms, his thin liner soaked with perspiration and his alarmed eyes unfocused in his taut face. Raydor murmured something further, and Lewis's head fell back, his breath coming in hard sobs.

I sank silently onto the other bed. I leaned across the space between the two beds and touched Raydor on the back. He turned to me, still holding on to Lewis's arms. His normally impassive face betrayed him, his wrinkled brow furrowed deeply with concern and his big dark eyes alight with Lewis's pain.

"Another dream," he told me needlessly.

I nodded, then gestured. Gently but firmly, Raydor slipped free of Lewis's grip and stood. I moved across from the other bed and took up Raydor's place beside Lewis. Lewis stared up at me, his beautiful blue eyes blank. His fingers clutched at the front of my flightsuit like a frightened newborn seeking safety. His breath came in harsh, irregular gasps.

"Lewis?" I bent over him, pulled down by the desperate grasp of his hands. I reached out to touch the side of his pale face, where cold sweat was beaded like drops of dew. "You okay now?"

Lewis's eyes, eerily refractive in the soft glow of the lamp's light, tried to focus on me. He made a convulsive swallowing movement. Then he mumbled hoarsely, "Oh, my God!"

I reached out for Lewis's hands, prying them off the front of my flightsuit. Our detention cuffs clicked sharply together. Lewis grappled with me, then clung; the bite of his fingers was like steel bands. Wincing, I shifted on the bed. His sweat-soaked liner was plastered to his trembling body like a second skin. I noticed—only peripherally this time—that once again he had an erection.

I hadn't even realized that Raydor had left the room until he reappeared at the bedside. He carried a plastic drinking cup of water and a damp washcloth from hygiene. Crouching by the bed, he helped me draw Lewis gently up into a sitting position. And then, because Lewis was still clinging to my hands, Raydor held the cup to Lewis's lips. The gesture didn't surprise me any more than had the fact that Raydor had obviously offered to share contact with Lewis. It must have been an offer that even the shy and reserved Lewis had been grateful for in his desperation to keep his night terrors at bay. While the Tachs are not a physically demonstrative people, their emotions run deep. Raydor had the kind of deeply ingrained tenderness that only the very strong could afford to reveal.

Lewis drank the proffered water too rapidly; he sputtered, half choking, and then drank again, more slowly this time. His eyes began to regain some lucidity. He peered gratefully at us over the rim of the cup.

Raydor leaned back, setting the empty cup on the night table. He draped the damp washcloth over my forearm and then made a large and unspecific gesture with his shoulders. "I'm going to sit watch for a while," he said simply. Then he rose and left the room.

Lewis slowly sank back onto the bed again. Clumsily, he released his death grip on my hands. In the lamplight his damp hair gleamed blue-black against the pallor of his clammy skin. He looked like a man who had just survived a hard pullout with a bad hangover.

I bunched up the cool washcloth in one hand and gently touched it to Lewis's sweat-spangled forehead. He let out his breath in a thin, ragged sigh, and his eyes closed. Encouraged, I ran the cloth lightly across his face, pushing back the sweat-matted forelock of his hair. Then I lifted his hands one at a time and wiped them off, too. His hands were so slender; his long fingers felt like nothing but sinew and bone. He offered them to me silently and solemnly in a manner that was almost courtly in its shy reserve.

I watched Lewis's face. His eyes opened, but he met my gaze only obliquely. His initial agitation and fear had been assuaged, but there was still something tense about him, a palpable undercurrent of reservation that puzzled me. Was he that shy about being touched? Or was it the muzzy remainder of the nightmare that was pulling at him?

"Better?" I asked him, wiping his wrists, my voice pitched matter-of-factly.

Lewis nodded somewhat jerkily, his gaze moving almost will-lessly to my face.

"Powers, you're soaking wet," I told him, needlessly stating the obvious in a mock-scolding tone, as if I could reduce something of such oppressive gravity as his fear simply by making light of it. As I spoke, I casually freed the neck fastener of his suit liner and peeled down the top of it. "A hell of a good way to catch pneumonia," I continued calmly, running the damp cloth across his sweat-slicked throat and chest.

Lewis blinked, the shadows of his thick lashes sweeping his cheeks. He shuddered slightly, but I knew it wasn't from a chill. I was nonchalant about my ministrations and gave him little cause for alarm. I set the washcloth aside and smoothly pulled the edges of Lewis's liner together again. And then, to hide the sudden tremor in my own traitorous hands, I shifted on the bed.

The taut curve of Lewis's body relaxed into a weary sprawl. His hands spread on the rumpled expanse of sheets beneath him. He drew several deep breaths and shakily released them. Then he gazed up at me, his earnest expression so achingly familiar that I could almost hear his words before they left his lips.

"I—I'm sorry, Captain. I—"

I put my hand to his mouth, abruptly stifling him. "No!" I said, more fiercely than I had intended.

And then Lewis did a curious thing, something that frightened me even more than his congenital sense of remorse and rendered me helpless. He caught my hand, the hand that I had pressed to his mouth, and held it gently to his lips, kissing my palm, my fingertips, my—

Awkwardly and abruptly, I jerked my hand away, my heart lurching painfully.

I think we both were a little abashed then. Perhaps Lewis had frightened himself as well as frightening me. There was a tension in the air between us, crackling like stray voltage. In an attempt to dispel it, to deny its very existence, I noisily cleared my throat and sat up straighter on the bed. I stared evenly at him, compelling him to meet my eyes. "It's the same dream, isn't it," I said calmly. It was not a question.

Still embarrassed, Lewis shifted his legs and nodded silently.

My voice dropped, gaining intensity. I leaned closer to him, both my tone and my posture forcing Lewis to keep his eyes on mine. "What is it about the dream that scares you so much?" I asked him earnestly. "And what the hell does it have to do with this place?" Lewis stared up helplessly at me. His bright blue eyes seemed enormous in his pale face, filled with unspeakable pain. He literally squirmed, and in that movement I was acutely aware of the pressure of his bony hip against me. He shifted as if to relieve some ache, and his obvious, unspoken suffering cut through me like a beam weapon, laying me open in a way no less wounding, no less deadly.

Spontaneously, I reached out and clasped his hand again, squeezing it tightly. "Let me help you, Lewis. *Suns*! Help me get you through this," I whispered urgently. "Please tell me."

Tears bloomed in his eyes. He blinked just once, his pupils suddenly dilating. His eyes had gone midnight-black in his pallid face. "Lillard," he said hoarsely. "It's Lillard."

My brow furrowed; I was confused. "Lillard—the man you know here?" I asked him. "The dream is about Lillard?"

Lewis's eyes were depthless, like bottomless chasms rimmed in sapphire blue. He shook his head jerkily, reluctantly, with a little shudder. "No," he said, his voice a ragged whisper, "the dream *is* Lillard."

I stared wordlessly at him, frozen by those gleaming eyes. My pulse began to hammer wildly, driven by some instinctive fear, a horrible knowledge beyond any reason. My fingers, twined with his, were suddenly slick with perspiration. I felt Lewis's grasp tighten, his sinewy grip imprisoning me with his hand, just as his pleas had imprisoned me in the circumstances of his fate. "W-what?" I stammered in a voice that was scarcely audible.

Lewis's breathing was so slow, so measured, that I could hardly reconcile its cadence with the pulse that raced against my fingers. His tongue crept out timidly to wet his lips. "I'm not sure when the dreams started," he began, his voice a low rasp. "Before New Cuba, I think, but it's hard to be sure." His free hand, seemingly of a separate volition, fretted with a pleat in the tangled bed sheets. "I don't really remember anything that happened to me before New Cuba. There was something they did—the drugs, I think. I don't have any memory of anything before that time."

His voice was flat, a monotone, as if he were reciting the trivial details of someone else's life. But I felt my own breath catch painfully in my throat, and I knew that in my eyes, at least, the unguarded reaction of my horror and anger could hardly be concealed from him. Damn them! They had taken everything from him: his freedom, his dignity, even his past. They had left him with little but his life, and then they had even contrived to take that from him as well.

I leaned even closer, squeezing his hand reassuringly. "The dream?" I prompted; my voice came out like a croak from my tensed throat.

"When it began, or when I first remember it, I could tell that I was dreaming something that—someone else's experiences," Lewis continued quietly. "But I didn't know whose or why. Then, when we left New Cuba, when they tried to kill us—" The hand stroking the wrinkled sheet paused, clutching. "—then the experiences became sharper somehow, more vivid. And they were—"

He hesitated, groping for a word, his dusky lashes blinking rapidly. "—they were painful, horrible, like he was being *tortured* somehow."

My mouth worked soundlessly. My mind was filled with questions, all without a voice, but Lewis seemed able to hear those questions nonetheless.

"Lillard is another Class Ten. He's being held here, on Camelot—somewhere in MA's research complex. There's a woman—someone who controls him." Lewis wet his lips again, but his face had been transformed, suddenly calmly composed. "The dreams are a—a sending of some kind. He has to escape from her. He's calling me to help him." I could read the last words in Lewis's eyes even before he spoke them. "She's going to kill him."

"*Jesus!*" I said breathlessly—an archaic exclamation seldom uttered in the universe those days. I exhaled raggedly, suddenly aware that I was clutching Lewis's fingers with painful force. I had to make a conscious effort to ease my grip.

Lewis shifted his shoulders, his free hand rising to brush at the damp forelock of his tousled hair. His eyes dropped toward the foot of the bed. "The dreams keep getting worse now. This one—this one was almost unbearable . . ." His gaze darted back to my anxious face. "I don't know why this is happening! I didn't want to involve anyone else in this, Captain. I—" A sudden blush, unexpected and startlingly vivid, mottled his cheeks and throat. Something deep within me lurched, fighting for freedom, as Lewis's fingers tightened on mine. "I've used you, I know," he admitted miserably, his voice so low that it vibrated in his throat. "But he's gotten into my head somehow, and if she kills him—"

There was no way to finish the thought, no way and no need to. It took every bit of will I possessed to keep myself from falling forward across that last little space between us and embracing him. The desire was like an inexorable physical ache. But instead I forced my expression into one of sympathetic composure, throttling down the rush of blood that thundered through me, and

seized the tenuous thread of logic that I was counting on
to save me.

"Are you sure he's being held in the research complex?" I persisted, my voice unnaturally quiet and calm.

Lewis nodded.

"You think if we could get in there, you could find
him?" I continued.

Again Lewis nodded. "Yes, I know I could. It's like
he's a part of me."

The monumental absurdity of what I was willing to do
suddenly occurred to me, so I knew I wasn't completely
divorced from reality. But it merely occurred to me and
then was calmly dismissed, as if the wild impracticality
of it was only a small matter of logistics, to be neatly
calculated out of existence. Maybe I was crazy, after all.

I was silent for a moment, thinking furiously. Lewis
stirred again, gently flexing his fingers in the clasp of my
hand. That movement broke my concentration, and I
glanced at him. Shyly, he slipped his hand from mine.

"Well, Alexandria was right about one thing," I remarked, laying my hand deliberately over his again.
Lewis looked up at me, blinking owlishly. "She's going
to get one *hell* of a good story!"

A smile, furtive but sparkling, broke over Lewis's face,
and I poked teasingly at his arm and echoed his relief
with a crooked grin of my own.

When Lewis's expression became more sober, there
was an even core of composure to it that negated all the
old anxiety. He lifted both hands, reaching calmly for
mine. His eyes, clear now, like polished sapphires,
glowed warmly. "Thank you," he said simply. And on
his face, the stunningly beautiful normalcy of it, I could
see the new serenity he had gained by sharing his dreadful burden with me. And in that serenity I could easily
see the strength that had thrust Lewis between me and
that armed dockman in the warehouse.

I bent forward, clasping his hands, and pressed my mouth
against his. And when he responded heatedly, his lips and
tongue hot and seeking against mine, the buried fire I had
been stifling deep in my belly for so long roiled re-

belliously. The depth of his response startled him, I think, for after a few minutes of intensely escalating oral groping he pulled back from me. His breath was coming in little pants, and his fingers dug into mine. The hard prod in my side was no longer just his hip. His eyes, wide and dilated with desire, shimmered with a tearlike film of moisture as he gazed up at me.

I had never felt such compelling need. I took his question from him, answering it before he could ask me. "Yes, I'm sure," I whispered, my lips inches from his ear. "It's all right. Are you afraid?"

The last question was a sudden insight, a revelation that seemed to hit home, for I felt Lewis tremble against me. I gently traced the curve of his lips with the tip of my forefinger, overwhelmed by the tremendous impetus of a desire that was tied to emotions I had never before experienced. Lewis's dark lashes fluttered.

"You want to?" I asked him softly, needlessly.

Lewis nodded quickly and fervently, his cheeks hot and bright with color.

I smiled gently at him, brushing back his black hair. "It's all right," I repeated. "There's nothing you could do that would be wrong."

Embarrassment or desire—or some dizzying mixture of the two—flushed fresh color into his face. But when I tugged gently at the edge of his suit liner fastener, he fumbled eagerly to help me release it. As I pulled the garment down, he kicked free of it, and I felt a physically painful and desperately urgent wrench of longing at the sight of him. For a moment the feeling was so overwhelming that I wasn't sure I could go on. But Lewis's hands were suddenly there, strong, slender hands deftly helping me from my flightsuit. Their very touch seemed to burn me, firing me with both a ferocity and a tenderness that I had never before felt in the joining. I hardly gave Lewis a chance to be gentle. Driven, I pulled him over on top of me and, with a sharp grunt, deeply into me. And then our mutual urgency overtook both of us.

Afterward I cried. It was something I don't think I had ever done before, except maybe the first time. Hell, no—

who am I trying to kid? I hadn't even cried the first time. None of the other times had meant anything compared to this. I clung to Lewis, pulling his lean warmth against me, holding him tightly in me, and let the huge, alien tears roll across my face while my burning body shook with silent sobs.

When I was finally able to lift my head, Lewis was gently stroking my back. And I saw that he, too, was weeping.

CHAPTER
TEN

I woke up to the touch of Raydor's big hand on my bare arm. I stirred groggily, burrowing my face more deeply into the tangled bed sheets. Raydor squeezed my shoulder gently but insistently. "Moore's coming," he said gruffly.

My head jerked up. "Now?" I mumbled stupidly. I struggled to focus on my wrist chronometer, but since I had never bothered to synchronize it with planetary time, the figures I was squinting to see were useless, anyway. "What time is it?" I asked Raydor, my tongue thick with sleep, as I lurched into a sitting position.

Raydor stooped to retrieve my flightsuit and liner from the floor beside the bed where they so obviously had been quite unceremoniously discarded the night before. "Seven hundred," he replied, handing me the garments.

I glanced muzzily around the room. "Where's Lewis?"

"Hygiene," Raydor responded mildly. His usually inscrutable expression was colored with something that hinted at wry humor. "I'll go keep Alexandria entertained," he offered matter-of-factly, heading for the door.

I staggered to my feet and clumsily began to pull on my clothes. I didn't have time for a shower. I felt a persistent torpor, like an agreeable hangover, as I stumbled over to the bedroom's dressing console. My reflection in the full-length mirror caught me by surprise. I winced at the sight that greeted me there: a tall, somewhat raw boned woman in a rumpled blue and silver flightsuit with wildly tousled brown hair. Well, what the hell did you expect? I chided myself morosely. Think last night was going to turn you into a princess? I appropriated a brush from the console inset and began to tug it through my tangled mane.

I hadn't heard Lewis approach me but I sensed his presence even before I saw his reflection behind me in the mirror, even before I felt the touch of his hands as he gently took the hairbrush from my grasp. I stood motionless with surprise as he slowly and carefully ran the brush through my unruly hair. The gesture was totally unexpected, both tender and erotic, possessive yet selfless. It was entirely like the second time we had joined only a few hours before, initiated by Lewis, ripe with a gentle passion that had completely overwhelmed me. I let my head fall back as he deftly slid the brush over my ear and gave myself over completely to the moment. There would be, I realized with a morbid twinge, very little time for anything else.

When Lewis had finished his ministrations and my hair lay over my shoulders in gleaming waves, I slowly turned to face him. He had washed and shaved and looked at least as presentable as I did in his blue and silver flightsuit. His cerulean eyes met my gaze levelly, and in their guileless depths I saw all the things that still had the power to terrify me.

There were a hundred things I could have done then, I guess. I could have kissed Lewis or even embraced him. I could have given him one damned little smile, at the very least. But what I did instead was just calmly nod toward the bedroom door and say, "Come on, let's go."

As I turned, oh-so-coolly, Lewis caught me by the arm, gently but firmly spinning me around and pulling me toward him. My face was just inches from his. He did not speak; there was no need to. In his dazzling eyes I could see the truth I was trying to deny: I could not shut him out any longer. And he knew. Last night I had let him inside, given him access, and there was no way to reverse or negate what had been done in that wide, warm bed. I had revealed to him what I had never revealed to another human being and had taken him into all my secret places.

Oh, yes, Lewis—Lewis, with all his awkward gentleness and his fiercesome ardor.

I lifted my hand almost reflexively and lightly touched the curve of his upper lip. "Lewis," I whispered. And I knew from the warm glow in his eyes that it was all he had wanted to hear from me, the only acknowledgment he needed.

"Come on," he echoed. "Let's go."

I was a little surprised at the size of the gathering that greeted us in the apartment's living area. Alexandria Moore sat in one of the overstuffed chairs, Raydor at her side. A small contingent of her Tachs stood impassively near the open door. Beyond the door I could see Ennis and Manto, still guarding the corridor. And in the doorway Redding stood talking to a red-haired woman in *Nimbus*'s dusty green. I recognized her as the security officer he had assigned to watch my ship the previous day. All of them looked up as Lewis and I entered the room, but only Alexandria moved.

She stood, stepping around the low, real wood table. She was still dressed in the same ochre-colored Tachs tunic and trousers she had worn the previous day in the warehouse, but they were rumpled and pleated with wrinkles. There were bruised-looking dark circles under her formidable eyes. She looked like she'd had a hard night out with no sleep. In fact, I realized that no one in the entire room, with the possible exception of the implacable Tachs, looked particularly well rested. Redding still wore the same lube-stained coveralls he had worn the night before, and his lids half drooped over his slate-colored eyes. Even his crewwoman was propped wearily against the door frame, as if she heartily welcomed its support.

I glanced sideways at Lewis, and he met my eyes. Suddenly I no longer felt scruffy or out of place. Hell, Lewis and I had undoubtably spent the most pleasant night of anyone in the room.

Alexandria approached me, her great mass of grizzled hair bouncing. I started to hold my hand out to her—the wrist with the detention cuff, I realized belatedly—and said quietly, "Alexandria." But she stunned me by reaching for me and enfolding me in a great bear hug of an embrace. "Alexandria," I repeated, grunted into her engulfing bosom.

"Jo-Jo," she murmured in that deep, throaty voice. I don't know what surprised me more, the enthusiasm of her embrace or her unexpected use of that affectionate diminutive from my hazy past. I clung helplessly to the big woman, suddenly carried back dizzily to a time I had nearly forgotten. And I realized then, with an abrupt and reluctant stab of comprehension, why it was that having to deal again with Alexandria made me feel so uneasy. It wasn't just that she was so dynamic, so avuncular; it wasn't even that her very expression always seemed to hint that she knew more than she was letting on. No, it was because she had the unique ability to make me feel like a child again, helpless and plaintive, relinquishing control.

Abruptly, Alexandria released me. She turned to Lewis, her inimitable face splitting into an infectious grin. "Welcome back, Mr. Lewis," she said.

Stunned, Lewis just gaped at her for a moment. "Do I—do I know you?" he stammered clumsily.

Alexandria shook her head, her frizzy hair flying. "No, I doubt that you do," she replied. "But I know you."

Lewis still stared at her, blinking in confusion. Alexandria spared him any further awkwardness by directing her next comment to me. "So," she said, "I understand that you have some kind of problem, Jo."

Understatement of the decade! I thought, almost saying it aloud. But instead I just nodded, meeting her black eyes squarely. "Alexandria, we need to talk to you."

Her formidable face sobered. She made a minute gesture in the direction of the knot of Tachs at the doorway; wordlessly, they melted from the room. I didn't even see any such small signal pass between Redding and his crewwoman, but just as automatically, she turned and left the apartment. Redding closed the door on Ennis's and Manto's broad backs.

"Let's talk, then," Alexandria agreed, waving toward

the overstuffed chairs. I glanced over at Redding, but he remained standing at the doorway, apparently with Moore's tacit approval. I sat down in one of the big chairs as Alexandria reseated herself beside Raydor. Behind me, Lewis made a small movement, but he couldn't bring himself to sit. His anxiety, which was echoed in me, was just too great.

Alexandria leaned forward in her chair, her elbows resting on her thighs, her forearms crossed over her knees. She cocked one bushy brow at me in an expression of inquiry. "And so?" she prompted me.

I swallowed to clear my throat, which suddenly seemed alarmingly dry, but I didn't drop my gaze. At the periphery of my field of vision, I could see Raydor, nearly shoulder to shoulder with Alexandria. Seeing them together made me feel, abruptly and very unexpectedly, totally alone in all of this. "We need your help," I said levelly.

Alexandria made a small sound, more of a grunt than a snort. "If you think you're going to crack into that research complex, you'll need more help than *I* can give you," she observed.

I just gaped at her, dumbfounded. Although Raydor's expression was still typically controlled, I could see that he was as astonished as I was. It was useless to try to hide my surprise. "What makes you think we're going to try to do that?" I asked her lamely.

Alexandria shrugged, her frizzled mane bobbing. Her eyes shifted to Lewis. "Why else would you be here— with him?" she responded placidly.

Behind me, Lewis shifted uneasily. His fear was like a knife blade wedged between my ribs, slowly twisting. It seemed that from nearly the moment I had first met him, his emotions had been palpable to me; gradually, they had become so entrenched in my own feelings that I didn't even need to see his face to know what he was feeling. A small part of my mind wondered about that, but Lewis was a Talent; who knew what effect our new-found intimacy would have on either of us. Then Alexandria was continuing, her expression calm, even benign.

"I know who Mr. Lewis is," she said, "and I know what he is. I think I might even know why he's here. What I don't know is *how*. So why don't you just start from the beginning."

I hesitated, but only momentarily. I knew that if I turned to look at Lewis, I'd betray both of us, so I kept my eyes straight ahead on Alexandria's implacable face. And then I told her everything that had happened to us since Rollo had screwed me so royally on New Cuba.

It became easier to talk once I got started. It was, after all, a pretty good story. Raydor made no attempt to join in my narrative, but that didn't surprise me. Tachs are not particularly loquacious. When I reached the part concerning Redding, the gray-eyed captain made no comment. He didn't even move; he just lounged silently against the door frame, his eyes half-closed, like a man on the verge of sleep. I tried to stick to the objective facts and not add my own speculations, even though some parts of the story fairly begged for embellishment. And when I started to explain about Lewis's nightmares, Lewis himself began to participate in the narration. He was shy at first and spoke only a hesitant word or a halting phrase. But that much of it was his story, and by the time we'd gotten to the events of the last twenty-four hours, he was doing as much of the talking as I was.

I saw Alexandria react only once, and that was when I first mentioned Lillard as the man whose nightmare Lewis was certain he shared. Her dark eyes narrowed, and her broad chin lifted fractionally. She interrupted and asked me to repeat the name, then nodded for me to go on. As Lewis finished his description of his last dream, recounting the danger Lillard was in from the woman who was threatening his life and revealing his dreaded certainty that saving Lillard was the only way to save himself, Alexandria leaned back abruptly in her chair. There was a peculiar look on her face; her black eyes were distant and hard. I had the feeling she was remembering something that had nothing to do with those of us in the room, or at least something that went beyond our limited understanding of the desperate situation. Then a sudden bemused expression softened her face, and she leaned forward again with a loud, horselike laugh. She shook her head, making her corona of frazzled hair dance. Her gaze shifted from me to a very perplexed Lewis.

"The only thing that's more amazing than the fact that you're still alive, Mr. Lewis," she announced emphatically, "is that you'd come back here!"

Lewis's bewilderment became shot through with alarm. I felt his fingers dig into the lush upholstery of the back of my chair. There was a moment of utter silence, so absolute that in it I swear I could hear the sound of my own blood coursing through my veins. Then Lewis's ragged voice stammered, "I—I was *here*?"

Alexandria regarded him calmly, her large body poised but relaxed. "You were heavily drugged, so you don't remember it," she said.

Obviously, we were not the only ones there with a story to tell. Behind me, Lewis stirred, stumbling around my chair and sinking down into the one beside it. I glanced sideways at him, and the devastated look on his face made me want to reach out and clasp his hand. But I didn't—I couldn't.

Alexandria was smiling gently at me, as if she had read my mind. She gestured toward my wrist, the one with the detention cuff. "May as well take those off, Jo," she suggested. "I think they've outlived their usefulness."

Distractedly, hardly glancing down, I released the cuff from my wrist and stuffed it into my pocket. I was secretly pleased to see Redding jerk into temporary alertness at the casual way I dispensed with the device. Apparently we had succeeded in fooling him at least. Beside me, Lewis had to fumble several times with the catch on his cuff before he was able to free himself. He barely caught the band before it fell to the floor and then jammed it into the pocket of his flightsuit.

My eyes stayed on Alexandria's craggy face. "What do you have to do with all of this?" I asked her.

She leaned back in her chair again, this time more comfortably. She hooked one booted ankle up over her knee. Her lids were hooded with fatigue, but her eyes were bright—predator's eyes, missing nothing. "What do you know about the research complex?" she asked me.

Damn her! She was as oblique as Lewis. Were there no straightforward answers left in the universe?

"What do you mean, what do I know about it?" I responded tersely. Two could play that little game.

Implacably, she went on. "Do you know what they do here?"

"No," I admitted, then added glibly, "research?"

Alexandria gave a little snort, more at my annoyance with her question than at my lame joke. Her obsidian eyes snapped to Lewis's face and stayed there until he shifted uneasily in his chair. "You know, don't you?" she said softly to him.

Lewis's head dipped. He stared at his hands, which were clutched together in his lap. "Pain," he whispered, his voice hoarse.

Alexandria's eyes softened. "That's all you can remember because that's all you have left," she told him quietly. "Yes, pain; they hurt you there. They didn't leave you with anything of your own, anything from before, did they."

It was hardly a question; it asked for no reply.

I glanced over to where Redding stood, slouched in the doorway. His eyes were open now, but his face was an unfathomable mask. Across the low table from us, Raydor sat immobile and silent, like a piece of the overstuffed furniture.

"I'll tell you what's being done there," Alexandria resumed suddenly, her voice a harsh grumble. "Although it's illegal and no one in the Council knows about it, or will admit to it, they're experimenting on people, people like Lillard—people like you, Lewis." Her eyes jumped to me. "I'm sure you're wondering just what the bleeding Void I'm doing in a place like this," she said to me, gesturing as if to include all of Nethersedge.

"Not really," I replied, absolutely straight-faced. "I always suspected you were a pirate queen at heart."

Alexandria rewarded me with an abrupt, raucous laugh.

"It looks like you were right, Jo," she said heartily. At my side I felt Lewis begin to relax fractionally, and some of the lancing pain in my belly began to ease.

"There's only one reason why you'd be here," I said slowly and intently. It was a revelation to me as well, but I could see the truth in it even as I spoke. "And there's only one reason why you'd know Lewis. Somehow you got him out of that complex, and now you're trying to get the rest of them out."

Alexandria nodded, seemingly pleased with my deduction. Then she glanced over to Lewis, her mouth curling in amusement. "Of course, I'd kind of hoped that once I got him out, he'd *stay* out."

I stared at her, ignoring the irony of her remark. "But how did you know he was there if this is so secret? And how did you get him—"

Alexandria interrupted me with a wave of one big, broad-fingered hand. "There are a lot of advantages to being 'dead,' Jo," she told me blithely. "People have a tendency to get a little . . . careless with their secrets when they don't think you're around anymore to find them out."

I studied the calm, leathery face. "You found out someone was doing secret research on Class Tens," I concluded.

She spread her callused hands. "We'd been working on this for months," she told us, "just to set it up. We were able to infiltrate the underground facility; we had a man on the inside. He was finally able to locate one of their prisoners and get him out."

"Lewis," I said.

Lewis's hand, which had crept up almost of its own volition from his lap, clutched at the heavily padded arm of his chair. I reached across the small space between us and clasped his fingers with mine.

"Once we got him off-planet," Alexandria went on, "we tried to 'lose' him right under their noses, within the system, by forging his ID status and creating a false record that would list him as an IS." I didn't even bat an eye at that. Alexandria had practically rewritten the book on Integration; forging an ID and creating an IS would have posed no problems for a woman of her resources. "I saw to it that he would be indentured to Heinlein, because it was one place I had people I could trust. I thought he'd be safest there, at least until we could blow this whole thing open."

I blinked, still staring at her. "Then it was *you* who were the 'friend' that asked Mahta to—"

Alexandria nodded, her gray mane bobbing. "I asked her to keep him safe for me. Of course, we didn't realize that you'd get mixed up in all of this, Jo; it was just coincidence that you were the one MA contracted with to transport Lewis to Heinlein."

'Coincidence'? I thought acerbically. Just bad luck! I remembered Rollo's greasy nonchalance as he had reeled me in: 'You've made runs to Heinlein before . . . MA trusts you.' Then I was suddenly reminded of a very sore sticking point in all this. "If MA thought Lewis was a legitimate IS, then why the hell did they try to fry us— twice?" I demanded.

Alexandria's big hands meshed, her fingers lacing together over her knee. "Don't underestimate who we're dealing with here, Jo," she warned quietly. "You don't just appropriate the resources to start up your own little illicit research program like this unless you're well connected. When they discovered Lewis was missing, they must have torn the quadrant apart looking for him. They were able to trace him to New Cuba, because that's where his false record resurfaced." She shrugged with equanimity. "But by then it was too late; you already had him, and they had no way to get to him before you left Port. So they called in some markers and used someone in Port to try and stop you."

I just gaped at her, incredulity and anger twisting my face. I could understand corruption in MA, even in CA. What I could not accept was corruption in Port—the perversion of the brotherhood of those who made their lives in space.

"We're dealing with someone who has connections in both MA and CA," Alexandria continued. "If they couldn't get Lewis back, then they were perfectly willing to kill him—along with anyone else who may have gotten in the way—rather than let him live to reveal their secret.''

Bitterly, I digested that. If anything, it seemed even worse than I had originally believed. The system, as flawed as it was, was aggravating enough, but to subvert that system, to abuse it—that seemed to me to threaten Citizenship itself and all that I believed in. Furiously, I wrenched my mind back to the line of Alexandria's explanation. ''You said that you had someone on the inside.''

''And 'had' is the operative word,'' she replied tightly. ''He was eliminated after Lewis escaped; at least we have to assume that he was.'' Her lips thinned grimly. ''He missed the last rendezvous, and we haven't been able to make contact with him.''

''Eliminated?'' I repeated warily. ''You mean killed?''

''Or worse,'' Alexandria added gruffly. ''We believe there are still Class Tens being illegally held there, being subjected to Powers know what. Now that they know we're on to them, those Class Tens are in special jeopardy. So you see,'' she concluded, ''we want to get into the complex, too. The only question is how the hell to get to them.''

Lewis's breathing had become reduced to short, shallow rasps. He gazed almost will-lessly at Alexandria's brooding face, his eyes filled with both fear and anxiety, waiting for her to go on. His fingers, twined with mine, were trembling.

''Security access—'' I began into that taut silence.

But Alexandria interrupted me with the sweep of one powerful hand. Her thick mane bobbed emphatically. ''Accessing the complex isn't the problem,'' she explained. ''We did that months ago; that's how we got Bertram inside. Everything is security-coded, but we all know what that means.'' She grinned wickedly. ''Any Integrator worth his juice can breach MA's security codes.'' She shook her head again, even more vehemently. "No, what we need isn't even in the security access; what we need doesn't even officially exist."

I stared numbly at her, the rhythm of Lewis's pulse thudding against my fingers. "What do you mean?" I asked, confused.

Alexandria shifted in her chair. The room had become so preternaturally quiet that the creaking of the chair's wooden joints sounded like explosions. At her side Raydor hunched impassively, his face gravely set. Alexandria's dark eyes were narrowed to slits. "I mean," she said, "that the Class Ten project in that complex is completely unauthorized; it's housed in a labyrinth below the main structure, and no MA records of its existence are kept in any Integrator access."

Beside me, Lewis swallowed dryly. He silently mouthed a single word, "Lillard."

"Yeah, that's where Lillard is; that's where they all are," Alexandria concluded grimly. "But now we can't get to them, because the one man we had who was about to infiltrate their cadre has been neatly eliminated."

"Even if we could breach the complex—" I began.

Again Alexandria raised her hand in a negating motion. "It wouldn't help," she insisted doggedly. "It's a separate facility; there's no way in from there. The only way to get in is someone who's gone through, who knows the codes, and we don't have anyone like that anymore."

"Maybe we do."

I was startled by the sound of Redding's voice from the doorway; it was the first time he'd spoken. I twisted in my chair to face him, my fingers biting into Lewis's.

"What do you mean?" Alexandria asked him, puzzled.

But I knew what Redding meant.

Languidly, Redding straightened. His chin nudged in our direction. "Him," he said, indicating Lewis. "He's been inside."

Alexandria's expression was still perplexed. "But his memory of that time is lost; the drugs they gave him saw to that," she reminded Redding. "He doesn't remember anything specific."

Redding shrugged nonchalantly. "Not consciously," he corrected.

"What are you suggesting?" Alexandria pursued.

But I knew what Redding was suggesting, and I felt my spine stiffen like an angry cat's.

"Integration analysis," Redding supplied blandly.

"*No!*" I exclaimed, so loudly that Lewis's hand jerked in my grasp. I glared furiously at Redding. "*No*, that's out of the question!"

Alexandria touched her square chin comtemplatively. "It's been used," she mused.

"On *criminals*," I retorted. "And never on Class Tens. No way! It's much too dangerous!"

Beside me, Lewis writhed in his chair, the unwitting object of an unsought controversy. Alexandria's mouth quirked in a tired grin. "Class Tens *are* criminals for all practical purposes, Jo," she reminded me gently.

I threw Raydor a desperate glance, but the big Tachs was nervelessly silent. At the doorway Redding still slouched casually. Damn the man! I stared intently at Alexandria; it was her show, after all. "No," I repeated, my voice a low growl. "No way!"

"It may be the *only* way," Redding drawled.

I spun again in my chair, my face contorted with fury, several choice freightman's oaths on my lips. But it was Lewis who stopped me. His fingers squeezed mine tightly and urgently, and as I turned to face him, he caught me with those wide, clear blue eyes.

"Please, Jo," he said softly.

His unexpected use of my name completely disarmed me. I even forgot to be concerned about what such familiarity would suggest to the others. I just stared helplessly into that trusting, terrified face.

"Jo," he continued gently, insistently, "it *is* the only way. If they kill Lillard, it'll kill me."

Who the hell's side was he on, anyway? I couldn't imagine anyone being so willing to let an Integrator ream through his neurons—until I remembered Lillard and the terrifying dreams. For Lewis, perhaps there was no other way, then. And so I forced myself to capitulate, against all instincts and with as much grace as I could muster. Clutching Lewis's hand, I nodded stiffly. "Okay," I muttered. "But only if we do this my way."

Alexandria's bushy eyebrows lifted in a quizzical arch. "Your way?" she repeated.

I darted a scathing look at Redding, who appeared totally nonplussed. "First of all, we use my Integrator on *Raptor*," I announced firmly.

Alexandria looked skeptical. "This is going to require a hell of a lot of sophistication, Jo," she began. "We have some very special equipment here. I know that your Integrator is good, but I'm not sure that a shipboard Integrator is—"

She was interrupted by a sudden hoot of laughter from Redding. For the first time he moved from the doorway and came up behind my chair. "You need sophistication, eh?" he said to Alexandria, his mouth pulled into that crooked grin. "You got any idea what she's got on board?"

Alexandria shrugged casually. "I thought I did," she said.

Redding laughed again, showing white teeth. "If he hadn't been Integrated, this Integrator would have been intergalactic czar by now—and we'd all be working for him instead of risking our asses trying to rescue Class Tens from MA complexes!"

His cheerful hyperbole brought an unwilling smile to my face, which probably had been Redding's intention all along.

"All right, you use your Integrator," Alexandria ceded smoothly. "What else?"

My smile vanished. "Lewis and I do this alone," I asserted. "And we access all information—coded only to him."

Alexandria's brows rose to nudge each other like small, affectionate animals. I kept my gaze on her, determinedly ignoring Redding, Raydor, and even Lewis. After a moment's pause she nodded. "All right, if that's how it has to be."

"That's the very least of it," I muttered grimly. It was

a nasty, risky business, and I was determined to save what I could of it.

Once Alexandria Moore had decided on something, she didn't waste time. She stood abruptly and gestured to Redding. "Get your crew," she told him crisply. "Meet us at the red hangar at ten-hundred." She looked down at Raydor. "I can use you," she told him, her gravelly voice suddenly softening. "Unless," she added, with a glance over to me, "you'll need him."

I exchanged a look with Raydor, silently reestablishing in seconds what I once feared I had lost to Alexandria. "Lewis and I have to do this alone," I told him quietly. "If you want, you can help her."

Wordlessly, Raydor got to his feet and followed Alexandria to the door. She paused in the corridor, speaking in short, gruff bursts to Ennis and Manto. Then she and Raydor were gone.

Pointedly ignoring Redding, who was again lounging indolently at the threshold, I urged Lewis to his feet. My legs felt discouragingly stiff already, and the day was still young. I released Lewis's hand but moved shoulder to shoulder with him as we went through the door. In the corridor the two Tachs greeted us with the first words I had heard them utter.

"We'll take you to your ship," one of them said.

"And stand watch," the other concluded.

I nodded but added, "We won't need a watch."

Their broad Altered faces were unfathomable, immobile. "We'll stand watch," the one just repeated implacably.

I shrugged and began to follow them up the corridor, Lewis falling into step at my side. We had scarcely gone thirty feet when Redding's voice called out from behind us.

"Captain, wait."

I considered just not stopping; there was nothing I wanted to discuss with him. But Lewis had already hesitated, and I didn't want to cause him any more distress by creating a scene in the corridor. I squeezed his arm and glanced back, glowering, at Redding. "You go ahead," I said. "I'll catch up."

Lewis paused, reluctant to go on. His eyes swept anxiously over my face. I nodded encouragingly at him. "Go on," I repeated. Then I said firmly to the two Tachs, "I'll catch up."

As the three of them moved with varying degrees of unwillingness out of earshot, I turned on Redding. "What the joining hells did you think you were doing back there?" I demanded.

But my attack slid off Redding like lube off a hot manifold. He stood casually in the corridor, his posture a relaxed slouch. "Trying to save some lives," he said mildly. "His, too, by the way," he added.

I glared fiercely at him, knowing that from his own point of view the son of a bitch was right. He didn't waver under my angry scrutiny. "It's too dangerous," I finally muttered in frustration.

Redding shrugged noncommittally. "He doesn't have much choice," he reminded me.

"No, some of us don't," I retorted, my hands clenching into fists. "But *you* do, don't you, Captain? Just what *is* your interest in this little escapade? Certainly not charity, eh?" Aggressively, I moved a step closer to him and stared into those cool eyes. "Just how much is Alexandria paying you for all this?"

Redding returned my stare, nonplussed. Then that feral grin curled at his lips. "Barely enough," he announced sardonically.

Automatically, I swung at him. Redding was surprised enough that his tardy attempt to evade the punch merely caused my blow to land harmlessly on his shoulder rather than on that smug face. By then he had seized me by both wrists, but I furiously twisted free of his grasp. "Keep your joining hands off me!" I grunted angrily.

For a few moments we both just stood there, squared off like two barnyard roosters. Then Redding gave a casual shrug and continued as if the little altercation had never taken place.

"I just wanted to tell you," he said calmly, "that when we hit the complex, it'd be better if you didn't stick with

Lewis. Let Alexandria or some of her crew back him instead.''

I stared at Redding, frankly puzzled and still furious. ''Why?'' I asked suspiciously.

His voice was smooth, his expression bland. ''He's going to need to be able to concentrate on what he's doing, not be worrying about you.''

Warmth bloomed up from the collar of my flightsuit; I hoped the flush wasn't visible to Redding. ''We'll let *him* decide that,'' I asserted, trying to conceal my reaction. Was it so obvious to all of them, then?

''No,'' Redding repeated firmly. ''We can't take that kind of a risk in there.'' There was something in those slate-colored eyes that almost approached sympathy; at least he wasn't laughing at me. But I didn't allow myself to accept the idea of understanding from him.

I hesitated until the pause finally became awkward. ''Okay!'' I finally barked. The hell with him—the hell with them all. I turned on my heels and strode resolutely up the corridor after Lewis and the Tachs. I never looked back at Redding.

The two Tachs displayed no curiosity when I rejoined them, even though I was quite sure that my voice had carried far enough for them all to have been aware that I had been arguing with Redding. Lewis regarded me warily, longing to speak, but I hustled him briskly along, giving him no chance. It was only when we were in the lift, riding down to the lower level, that he was able to confront me with his concerns.

''What—what happened back there?'' he asked me, his anxiety overriding his natural reticence.

I glanced briefly up at him, then glared straight ahead at the lift's seamless walls. ''That son of a bitch,'' I muttered.

Lewis leaned closer; he smelled of soap. ''What happened?'' he reiterated, his voice rising.

''Nothing.'' I shook my head, managing a small smile for him. ''The guy's a jerk. Forget it.''

On the ground level we were only a short distance from the port. We crossed a wide courtyard cluttered with disabled vehicles and entered the high arched doorways of a row of ancient hangars. We wove between the silent hulks of derelict ships, over the stained and pitted floor, with the hot yellow light of Camelot's sun falling eerily in tinted fragments from the half-ruptured overhead skylights. Then I saw her before us, berthed in a spacious bay: *Raptor*. She crouched, waiting, on the greasy concourse, her newly repaired generator vane gleaming. I felt a stab of hope at seeing her again.

I turned to the Tachs. "Wait here," I said simply. Neither of them responded, but they both took up a stance of quiet vigilance at the periphery of our berth.

Approaching *Raptor*'s belly, I palmed the hatch access release. The hydraulics hummed into life, and the boarding ramp peeled down in a graceful arc. "Handy," I called out, leading Lewis up the ramp, "you're still on Security Prime?"

"Of course, Jo," came the deep bass answer. There was no tone of reproach in his voice.

As the hatch hissed shut behind us, I took Lewis's arm and aimed him up the corridor toward Integration. "Ship's status?" I demanded briskly as we went along.

"All systems optimal, Jo," Handy replied promptly. Then he added, "This dump has good hardware."

At Integration's hatch I palmed the access lock. As the door cycled open, I urged Lewis ahead of me into the cheery gold room. The door cycled shut with a soft thunk.

"I'm glad you're back, Jo," Handy remarked brightly as we entered the room.

"Miss me?" I teased automatically, swinging around one of the padded swivel chairs.

"What's happening?" Handy continued, a query that was bizarrely like Lewis's earlier question.

I plopped down into one of the chairs, offering the other to Lewis. I think the brightness of the room overwhelmed him; it was not what he had expected. He stared around in confusion, the imposing array of Handy's addenda only adding to his bewilderment. He glanced sideways at me, his expression expectant, but my attention was on Handy.

"We're going into the complex," I told Handy, flipping up his access panel. "But we need some information first, information that we think is still in Lewis's head."

You didn't have to spell things out for Integrators; they were deduction personified, able to make stupendous leaps of logic from the simplest of facts. For a moment Handy was silent; then his deep voice rumbled, "You want Integration analysis?"

"You got it," I confirmed, reaching into a flat drawer beneath the access panel.

"I can't do that, Jo," Handy responded.

I was so astonished, I nearly dropped the set of cerebral leads that I had extracted from the drawer. I just sat there for a few seconds, staring dumbly at the soft flutter of Handy's panel lights. "You *what*?" I finally exclaimed.

"I can't do that, Jo," the Integrator repeated calmly. "That isn't a legitimate function of my systems."

My shock left me momentarily speechless. Of all people—yes, Handy as much as anyone: *people*—he was the last one I had expected trouble from. His flourishing personality as much as his incredible abilities had always demanded that I treat him as an equal, not as a device. His refusal was like a betrayal, like denial from a beloved friend. " 'Legitimate'?" I retorted. "Since when are you so joining concerned with *legitimate*?"

"Integration analysis is not a legitimate function of my systems," Handy repeated implacably.

"And I suppose cracking into every cod-swabbing MA Integrator access in the galaxy *is* a legitimate function of your joining systems!" I snapped back, not needing to add that I not only had always tolerated but even had aided and abetted his highly illegal form of informational kleptomania. "Damn it, Handy, don't give me any trouble now—I've had enough!"

From the chair beside me, Lewis suddenly stirred. To my surprise, he reached out with one trembling hand and touched his palm to the curved surface of Handy's access. Handy's lights fluttered. "Please," Lewis said, his voice scarcely audible.

I was about to lean forward and take Lewis by the arm, to tell him that what he was attempting was useless, since Handy was coded to respond to demands from only Raydor and me. But something in the quickening pulse of Handy's panel lights stopped me from intervening.

"Please," Lewis repeated in a whisper.

In the silence I could almost see Handy thinking—weighing, deciding. Suddenly I wondered what he might know, what his egresses into MA on both New Cuba and Heinlein might have gained him, what even the touch of Lewis's hand might be telling him right now.

"There are risks," the Integrator rumbled reluctantly.

"I know," Lewis replied huskily.

Handy was silent again. The bluish flow of his panel lights flickered eerily across our faces. Lewis's expression was frozen in entreaty. "You might find out more than you wish to know," Handy finally observed.

"I know," Lewis repeated, his voice a raw whisper. For the space of several heartbeats he was silent. Then he said hoarsely, "It's all I have."

"All right," Handy suddenly capitulated. "It's dangerous, but it can be done."

Quickly, before the Integrator could add any conditions to that acquiescence, before I could more closely examine my own reasons for not going on, I turned to Lewis. I held out the cerebral leads. "Have you ever used these?" I asked him quietly.

He shook his head. "No." Then he qualified his answer. "Not that I remember, anyway."

"It's simple," I told him, holding up the three silver disk-shaped leads. "Two go here," I explained, fitting their adhesive pads against both of his temples. "And the third." I reached delicately behind him, beneath the collar of his flightsuit. "It varies," I went on, moving the disk up the back of his neck. Lewis shivered. The third lead gave off a muted beep, and I pressed it there, at the base of his skull.

"What—what do you usually use these for?" Lewis asked me, gingerly touching the dangling wires.

"Fast assimilation," I replied. Sometimes there were big, unwieldly chunks of complex data that I had to absorb, usually technical material for which I had no aptitude. Handy would Integrate it and feed it to me through the leads. I hated it; it always gave me one hell of a headache afterward.

"But you've never tried to—"

"Extract data?" I shook my head. "No," I said simply. "All I've ever done is try to cram the stuff in. It's been done, though."

"By MA," Lewis added.

I just nodded, gazing helplessly at him. Powers! How I wished he would just say *no*. Just get up and say, "This is too damned dangerous for me—forget it!" But I knew that he wouldn't do that, couldn't do it.

His face was lit by a sudden shy smile. "Who knows?" he said unexpectedly. "Maybe they've already used it on me."

Surprised, I had to laugh. I reached out and squeezed his arm. "If they did, let's hope they got more than they bargained for," I told him fervently.

"I have correct lead triangulation," Handy interrupted.

I turned back to him, leaning over the console. "You know what we're after, Handy," I said quietly. "We think there's still information about the subterranean part of the complex's layout in Lewis's subconscious memory."

"Along with a lot of other data," Handy reminded me needlessly.

I nodded. "Along with Suns know what," I agreed evenly. "There are two things I want you to do: give us a chip of the relevant data and give us a separate chip with all of it."

"Conscious recall?" Handy inquired neutrally.

I glanced sideways at Lewis, who was poised so tensely beside me, the silver leads on his temples reflecting the panel lights. "The relevant data only," I decided quietly.

Lewis's eyes lifted, seeking mine. Impulsively, I

reached out and grasped one of his hands in both of mine. "Unless—you want the rest?" I began softly.

But Lewis shook his head, shuddering. His fingers tightened on mine. And in that moment I realized that perhaps there could be something worse than not knowing who you were, and that something was finding out exactly who you were.

"Relevant data only, Handy," I repeated. "And code the chips—Lewis's access only."

Lewis's brows lifted. I squeezed his hand again. "It belongs to you," I told him firmly. No one was ever going to take it away from him again.

"Are we ready?" Handy interrupted.

Lewis shifted uncomfortably in his chair. A dappling of perspiration had already dampened his forehead. I squeezed his hand one last time, then released it. Disconcerted, he reached for me again, but I shook my head. "I'm sorry," I said, "but I can't be touching you." I shrugged. "It screws up the leads somehow."

Lewis nodded his understanding, his gaze falling. He leaned back in the padded chair, his forearms aligned on the armrests. "I'm ready," he said quietly.

More ready than I was, I was sure. I had never seen the leads used that way, so I had no way to know what to expect. What I had always regarded as a useful if somewhat noxious function was taking on some deeply ominous possibilities, inverted like that. Apprehensively, I glanced from Handy's panel to Lewis's frozen face.

Initially Lewis just sat there, rigid with expectation, his eyes half-closed. Then, gradually, the small muscles in his face began to jump and twitch. His hands, hanging over the edges of the armrests, clenched into tight claws. Perspiration beaded on his forehead and upper lip.

Automatically, I inclined toward Lewis, alarmed by the grimace that contorted his face. His hands began to tremble convulsively; behind his closed lids, his eyes jumped spasmodically.

"Handy?" I called out anxiously. I had to force myself to hold back and not touch Lewis.

But Handy's only response was a measured, "Function in progress."

No shit—I could see that for myself. I stared apprehensively at Lewis as the intensity of his reaction continued to increase. My pulse began to race, and I felt my mouth go dry with fear. What if the cerebrum of a Class Ten was so intrinsically altered that Integration analysis would irreparably damage it? What if Lewis's Talent was like some delicate vessel, easily breached? We might get the data, but at a far greater cost than we had any right to ask him to pay.

Lewis's body rose in the chair, jerking in an unnatural arc. A low moan escaped from between his clenched teeth. His lips pulled back into a feral snarl, an involuntary rictus that revealed the hard white edge of his teeth. Sweat poured across his face and down his throat, pooling into the neck of his flightsuit.

"Handy?" I tried again, more frantically, my hands hovering helplessly near Lewis's arm. "Handy, how long will—"

But before I could finish speaking, Lewis's body suddenly slumped in the chair. He groaned. His head lolled limply against the padded headrest, dislodging the third lead. It fell to the floor with a soft *ping*.

"Function complete," Handy intoned solemnly.

I leapt to my feet and bent over Lewis's collapsed body, hastily popping the temporal leads from his sweat-slicked forehead. "Lewis?" I asked anxiously, supporting his chin in my hands. "Lewis, are you all right?"

His eyes rolled back distressingly in their sockets, but his head lifted slightly, and he seemed aware of my presence. He tried to stir, but his numb arms tumbled clumsily from the armrests into his lap, and his fingers curled limply.

I brushed back the sweat-soaked forelock of his dark hair from his clammy forehead and tilted his face up toward mine. "Are you all right?" I repeated more softly.

Lewis's eyes fluttered open, and their focus wavered, then settled on me. His pupils were dilated like deep black pools. "Done?" he croaked.

Weak with relief, I dropped down onto my knees and embraced him in a quick but fervent hug. "Yes, *done*," I assured him with a crooked smile. "How do you feel?"

Lewis struggled to sit up straighter. Awkwardly, he brushed one hand across his wet forehead. "My head hurts," he admitted somewhat ruefully.

There was no longer any need for circumspection—least of all there, with only Handy in attendance. A spontaneous snort of laughter escaped me, and I put my arms around him, pulling him into a fierce embrace. "I'll bet it does," I agreed, my head burrowing against his belly.

I felt Lewis's arms come about me, his fingers combing gently through my hair. The thudding cadence of his pulse beat against my forehead, and I snuggled deeper against him, overcome with a giddy sense of relief. I also became aware of something else then, something that I had not expected to find: the undeniable evidence of Lewis's arousal pressed against my chest.

I lifted my face. Lewis met my gaze, his wide blue eyes aswim with an emotion he did not know how to conceal. I don't know just what my own expression revealed, but the color began to rise up Lewis's neck from his damp collar. Then, to my delighted surprise, he flashed a sudden shy smile and announced impishly, "That Lillard!"

Emphatically, I hugged him again. He gathered me up into his lap and held me awkwardly but tenderly in his arms. I nestled my head against his shoulder. Although we were nearly of a size, I felt curiously childlike in his embrace. Lewis began to speak—I could feel the vibration in his throat—but I kept him from starting by pressing my mouth against his.

I don't know what it all was: some pounding mixture of exhilaration and fear, relief and despair. I don't even know if it mattered exactly what it was, just that it existed.

Lewis squirmed beneath me. "Jo," he breathed, encompassing both joy and longing in that single syllable. His hands fumbled at the seam of my flightsuit. I shifted, eager to accommodate him, as he parted the lower end of the fastening. Then I reached for his clothing.

Quickly, desperately, we were coupled, with me straddling him there on the padded chair, riding him while he thrust furiously beneath me, into me.

Words escaped me that time, unwilling words but no less true for that reluctance to voice them. I had no defenses left against him then. Lewis owned those words. He had everything.

I sat alone in Integration, my rumpled flightsuit hastily pulled back together, my upper body leaning over Handy's access. I had sent Lewis on ahead to my cabin to shower, telling him I would wait for Handy to finish the coded chips. I felt somehow insubstantial, almost weightless, stretched out on some balancing point between pure elation and crushing hopelessness.

A soft humming sound came from the panel beneath my forearms. Next to my elbow, Handy neatly disgorged the two small chips we had requested of him. I slipped them both into my pocket. Gently, I ran one hand over the smooth curve of the Integrator's access. It had occurred to me—comfortingly, somehow—that Handy knew everything now.

When I spoke, my voice was so low that it was just a hoarse whisper. "No matter what happens to us—if something goes wrong—just do what you have to do, huh? Just take care of this ship."

Handy was silent.

CHAPTER
ELEVEN

The red hangar was halfway across the sprawling Nethersedge compound from the berth where *Raptor* was housed, a distance that made me grateful for the ground car our Tachs escorts had provided. As we drove over the crumbling tarmac and wound circuitously between the ugly hulks of dilapidated buildings, I stared pensively at the backs of the two Tachs' hairless heads. I still didn't know which one of them was which. I wasn't even sure what time it was anymore except that it was surely later than ten-hundred, since the Camelot sun was high overhead. Beside me, in the car's backseat, Lewis peered out the windows at the grim structures we drove past. His hand rested gently on my knee.

I cleared my throat. One of the Tachs, the one not driving, turned fractionally in acknowledgment. "Are you Ennis or are you Manto?" I asked impulsively.

What could have been a smile on a normal face tugged at his wrinkled mouth. "Which do you think?" he responded wryly.

In the spirit of his smile I shrugged and guessed, "Ennis."

I knew I was right by the subtle shift of expression on his creped face. "What time is it?" I asked him.

"Nearly noon," he replied placidly without checking a chronometer.

Giving a soft grunt, I leaned back against Lewis in companionable silence.

The hangar was massive, one of the largest buildings I'd seen in the whole compound. Inside, beyond the inevitable clutter of decrepit and cannibalized hulks, sat a pair of sleek and spotless MA transatmospheric shuttlecraft. On the grease-spotted pavement before them, Alexandria stood with a group of people: Raydor, Redding, Tachs, and *Nimbus* crew members. As Lewis and I disembarked from the ground car, the group's collective attention turned to our arrival. Our *tardy* arrival, I reminded myself ruefully as we approached them. Only Raydor appeared visibly relieved to see us both intact.

I nodded curtly to Alexandria, then glanced around the assembly. "Did we miss the briefing?" I asked, blinking innocently.

Alexandria surprised me with a sudden gust of braying laughter. Her stern expression had vanished; she winked at me and clapped me on the arm. "Honey," she told me wryly, "in this little venture, you two *are* the briefing!"

I reached into the breast pocket of my flightsuit and produced one of the small coded chips Handy had manufactured from his analysis of Lewis's memories. "I think this is what you've been waiting for," I remarked evenly, dropping it into Alexandria's hand.

"Have you seen it?" she asked me.

I nodded. "Yeah, it's all there." Before leaving the ship Lewis and I had gone through the data in the chip several times on the Integrator screen in my cabin. There was nothing I could add to it. Handy had taken the information he had miraculously extracted from the fathomless depths of Lewis's subconscious memory and had fashioned from it a startling vidchip account of the secret underground complex. He had even extrapolated floor plans, personnel charts, and security patterns from Lewis's subliminal knowledge. It was like a textbook primer on the subterranean area of the facility. It had also made me shudder to imagine, given the resources it revealed, just what might be going on down there.

Redding stepped forward, and Alexandria handed him

the chip. "Run it through for everyone in the team," she told him briskly. "Use the access screen in the old ready room; that should be big enough for everyone to be able to see it. Lewis can key it into that access."

Redding merely grunted his assent, lifting an expectant brow at Lewis. But I interrupted their plans with some questions of my own.

"This is all very helpful," I said, gesturing at the chip in Redding's hand, "but the real problem still is how the hell we get into that complex in the first place."

"We'll get in," Redding replied confidently, clutching the chip more tightly.

Self-satisfied jerk! "Oh?" I commented. "And I suppose we're all going to just walk on in there like some damned Volunteers' tour group?"

Alexandria was smiling indulgently. "Not quite, Jo, but that's not a half-bad idea, either," she remarked. Then her voice lowered companionably. "We really do have a plan, and you're part of it."

My brows rose, and I exchanged a quick but blatantly skeptical look with both Raydor and Lewis. "Then I guess maybe we'd better hear it—or did you think it'd make a fun surprise?" I said.

Alexandria's expression was still mildly amused. "MA had tried to plant an agent in Nethersedge," she told me.

No surprise; MA had agents everywhere, especially unregulated areas. Their brand of scum ought to have fit in very nicely with this bunch of thieves. I gazed stolidly at Alexandria, waiting for some real information.

"A good agent," she continued, her mouth crinkling, "but we eliminated her." The implication was that Alexandria was "good," too. "But we've seen to it that her regular 'secret' reports have continued going back to their headquarters." She grinned openly. "She's been a very busy agent these days. She's just informed the head of Security at the research complex that she's captured some fugitives from MA justice."

I glanced sideways at Lewis, then confronted Alexandria with my suspicion. "Why do I get the feeling that *we're* the fugitives she's captured?'' I asked her.

"It's going to allow us to walk right in there," Redding remarked evenly, fingering the vidchip impatiently.

"No, it's going to allow *us* to walk right in there," I reminded him sourly. I rounded on Alexandria. "I trust you've got a plan for getting *out* again?"

Alexandria laughed. "Don't worry, Jo, this is better organized than you realize. We'll explain it all to you. We've got lots of people inside the research complex. And now, thanks to you and Lewis, we've got a way to get into that illicit facility, too." Her dark eyes hardened. "And that's the crucial thing."

We were all silent a moment, Redding and I still poised like adversaries. Then I shrugged dismissively. "So who's this 'agent'?" I inquired levelly.

"Martz," Alexandria replied.

For the first time I noticed that one of Redding's crew members in the hangar was the red-haired security officer, except she wasn't red-haired anymore. Her hair had been closely cropped and dyed a deep auburn color. The woman caught my eye and nodded slightly at me, her calm face inscrutable.

"Physically, Martz is pretty close in appearance to the dead agent," Alexandria continued. "Close enough to fool MA for a while, anyway. Besides, I expect the complex's security head is going to be more interested in the three of you than in what she looks like."

Redding juggled the chip restively. "Can we get on with this?" he asked.

Automatically, I met Lewis's clear cerulean eyes. and for a moment something passed between us—something so visceral, so intense, that I nearly grinned foolishly at him out of the sheer pleasure of it. But I managed to keep a neutral expression on my face and a bland tone to my voice as I said, "Can you give them a hand, Mr. Lewis?"

"Of course, Captain," he responded just as calmly.

Standing there, I had the sudden feeling we were the only two people in the hangar, maybe the only two peo-

ple on the whole damned planet. I could still feel the
strong pounding of Lewis's heart, the coiled power of his
sinewy body, and could recall with an actual physical
rush the way our hands had felt on each other in the
shower stall in my cabin and hear our laughter as we'd
mopped the telltale stains off our flightsuits. What heady
confidence I had felt then, stepping off *Raptor*'s ramp
with him at my side and out of the building, into the
stinging Camelot sunlight.

He was an incredible person to me; he had been de-
prived of everything that had once made up his life, yet
there was no limit to what he could give. I was so
damned proud of him, I wanted to shout it out loud.
But instead I just watched him as he docilely followed
Redding, the Tachs, and the *Nimbus* crew members off
the hangar floor. And then I turned to Alexandria to
inquire, with an indifferent wave, "Where the hell'd
you get the shuttles?"

Her dark eyes glittered raffishly. "Like 'em?" she
teased. "Part of Redding's latest cargo."

Damn the man! Was there nothing in the whole holy
galaxy he didn't have a finger in?

Alexandria took me by the arm. "Come on, Jo. I want
to get something to eat." Her chin jerked in the direction
of the group that was just disappearing into the hangar's
old ready room. "I can catch up on that later. Right now,
I want to talk to you."

Normally that prospect would have made me apprehen-
sive; now it barely penetrated the unwarranted sense of
confidence I felt. Was it something about Class Tens—
something in their very essence that could be absorbed
into the bodies of mere mortals like a transfusion of courage? I shrugged agreeably at Alexandria and said with a
nonchalance that was only partially feigned, "Sure, why
not?"

Ennis and Manto, appearing almost magically from the
shadows between the two sleek shuttles, dogged our steps
as Alexandria led me across the huge hangar. I could see
that despite its current state of decay, the cavernous
structure had once been a regular showplace. Its vast

floor was littered with useless junk, and its mobile gantries hung empty, cannibalized of all usable fittings by one gang of pirates or another. We wound through the maze of abandoned wrecks and followed a narrow aisle along one wall to what once had been the technicians' commissary. The two burly Tachs automatically bracketed the doorway as Alexandria and I entered.

Nearly everything of even the remotest value had been stripped from that room as well. The walls and floor were still checkered with the shadowy outlines of old equipment long gone. But Alexandria's pirates had installed a sparse fitting of new equipment: a food dispenser, two tables, a few chairs—all of them liberally bolted to the floor.

Alexandria dropped heavily into one of the chairs and began to punch up something rapidly on the dispenser's keyboard. She shot me an inquiring glance. "Hungry?"

Dropping into a chair across the table from her, I made a vague gesture. "Only if you've got some real meat in this dump," I retorted.

Her mouth quirked into a passable smirk, and her black eyes fixed me with a piercing look. "That's one thing this 'dump' doesn't have," she replied.

My response was considerably less indifferent than I would have liked. "Just coffee, then, if you've got that."

Her formidable gaze released me, and her attention returned to the food dispenser. She punched a second code into the keyboard. She didn't speak again or even glance up at me until the unit had disgorged her order. Then, shoving the steaming cup of coffee across the table to me, she said levelly, "I was sorry to hear about your mother's death, Jo."

Totally unexpected, her words were like a hot knife plunged into my belly. Burning tears sprang into my eyes. Choking on my coffee, I retorted, "Yeah, well, in her case the stories were true."

She just stared calmly at me, too blunt to leave me any dignity in my sudden grief. Automatically, almost casually, she passed me a paper napkin from the table holder.

"Did you cry when you heard that I was dead?" she inquired, not unkindly.

I wiped at my eyes with the napkin and glared across the table at her. Damn her! Why was she doing this to me? She had always been able to disarm me, to reduce me to my weakest link. "I don't remember!" I snapped back.

Alexandria settled back into her chair, its metal joints screeching in protest, and tugged at the plate of amorphous, steaming gloop that passed for some kind of hash in that place. If ever there was a cause for regret in our time, then I hoped that mankind would mourn the passing of the sandwich as a food form; food processors just couldn't cope with it. Her dark eyes peered up at me from under hooded brows, and her tone was mildly bemused as she remarked, "Well, I hope you will cry the next time you hear it—when it's true."

I swallowed back a response and took a sip of scalding coffee that brought tears of another kind to my eyes. I watched balefully as Alexandria began scooping up forkfuls of her meal and eating it rapidly, barely bothering to chew—not that there was anything to chew in that pulverized mass. Broodingly, I stared down into my coffee cup until she had finished. When she started on her own cup of coffee, she was ready to resume the conversation.

"What do you know about Lewis?" she asked me with a characteristic lack of tact. But I was suddenly able to see it in another light. She needed our cooperation just as much as we needed hers. And for some reason she wanted into that secret facility just as badly as we did.

"What do you know about Redding?" I countered adroitly, fingering the rim of my cup.

Alexandria's large, even teeth bared in a spontaneous grin of appreciation. She shrugged good-naturedly. "That he can be trusted," she replied evenly.

"Trusted?" I snorted, not bothering to conceal my skepticism. "He's a joining *mercenary*!"

Her long, mobile face sobered with an expression of rueful thoughtfulness. "We're all mercenaries, Jo," she reminded me. "It's just a question of what we take for pay."

I stared morosely at her, my earlier armor of self-confidence fast crumbling. She was right. My own motives were hardly above reproach.

Alexandria was still staring at me calmly and reflectively. "Be careful with Lewis, Jo," she told me, suddenly gentle.

I wasn't sure at first if her concern was for me or for Lewis, and so I hesitated, not replying, and she went on. "There are a lot of things you don't know about him." She paused. "There are still a lot of things he doesn't even know about himself."

I looked across the table into those glittering black eyes, depthless and velvet-dark, like the void of space itself: I saw Lewis's secrets there. She knew, even if we did not.

I leaned forward toward her, my voice taut with urgency. "What's happening to him—how can he be dreaming Lillard's dreams?" I asked her. "And how is he being pulled back to the complex?"

Her expression was still calm and unruffled, but there was real compassion in her voice as she replied. "I don't know, Jo; I wish I did. Maybe it's part of being a Class Ten or part of his Talent. Maybe it's something they did to him here—we really don't know what happened. He's different." Her hand slid up, warm and rough, to cover mine on the tabletop. "Don't let that take away from what you feel for him," she counseled me, the soft earnestness in her tone revealing that she knew very well just what it was I did feel for him. "But be careful with him."

Too late, I thought, suddenly chilled beyond the reach of mere hot coffee. Too damned late for that now.

By the time Alexandria and I returned to the main floor of the hangar, most of the group of Tachs and *Nimbus* crew members had reassembled in a loose knot near the two MA shuttles. Automatically, anxiously, I searched for the bright blue and silver of Lewis and Raydor's flightsuits. The two of them were at the edge of the gathering, standing companionably close. Both looked up as I approached them. Raydor's face was typically impassive, but Lewis was much less expert at concealing his relief.

"We get what we need?" Alexandria asked Redding bluntly.

Redding detached himself from his crew mates and met Alexandria. He nodded tersely. "Yeah, it's all there."

Redding spared an indifferent glance for me and Lewis, but I stubbornly ignored him. Instead, I touched Lewis's arm and said in a near whisper, "You okay?"

Lewis was equally inept at concealing the emotions he read off me. He stared in distress at my reddened and puffy eyes. Without thought, he began to reach out to touch my face; only a necessarily sharp look from me aborted the automatic motion. Lewis stared a moment longer, the concern for me so plain in his guileless eyes that I felt the tears nearly begin again.

At last Lewis nodded. "I'm fine," he offered quietly.

"Then let's get them up," Alexandria boomed, waving inclusively at the people clustered on the hangar floor.

Surprised, I looked to her. "We're lifting?" I echoed stupidly. "Already?"

"Afraid so," she replied with a toothy grin. "You should have had something to eat when I offered, Jo."

I shook my head. "But it's barely past midday. I thought—"

"We've got a three- or four-hour ride, even in these babies," Redding interrupted me, jabbing a forefinger at the nearer of the two shuttles. "And the work shift at the complex changes in less than five hours."

I darted a bewildered glance at Raydor's calm face; then I looked back to Alexandria. "What difference does it make when—"

But it was, of course, Redding who responded again, interrupting my question, answering impatiently. "Our Tachs go in on the maintenance shift." He grinned shortly. "Can't have our boys being late for work."

Still confused, I looked one last time to Alexandria. At least her expression was sympathetic, even if she wasn't being particularly helpful. "Go on, Jo," she said. "We'll have to explain on the way. There really isn't any time to waste now." She gestured toward one of the shuttles, where a *Nimbus* crewman was already lowering the boarding ramp.

I moved with Lewis and Raydor to the waiting shuttle. The main group of Alexandria's Tachs, now in full face wraps and suited in the drab gray of the Authorities' custodial coveralls, were boarding the second shuttle. The soft whine of the revving turbos began to vibrate across the hangar floor. I reached the rail of the boarding ramp and then paused, glancing out over the pitted pavement.

Alexandria, standing at the belly of the second shuttle, gave me a cheery little salute. Then she disappeared into the line of Tachs boarding the vessel. It appeared that Redding was coming on our shuttle. Initially I had thought that perhaps he and the red-haired woman, Martz, had some sort of relationship, old joiners if nothing else. But I rethought the concept. I saw Martz hurrying across the hangar floor to give a hasty but fervent embrace to one of the remaining *Nimbus* crewmen, a thin, dark-haired man with a narrow strip of mustache. Somehow their emotional farewell in the dingy building only served to fuel my own growing sense of melancholy.

Redding had come up behind me. "Let's go," he said brusquely, gesturing at the ramp. There was no resistance in me this time. I just nodded to Raydor and Lewis, and the three of us preceded Redding up the ramp into the vessel.

Transatmospheric shuttles were a reasonably quick and smooth way to hop from one side of a planet to another, but they were hardly built for luxury. The military version in particular seemed claustrophobically cramped. The Control area had seats for a pilot and copilot/navigator, but the passenger area had seating couches for a half dozen people at best. I couldn't imagine how Alexandria had managed to stuff all those Tachs—there must have been a dozen of them at least—into that other shuttle. But I realized we couldn't go blasting onto the complex's landing field with five or six unexplained ships, and in fact, I was beginning to wonder how the hell we were going to get in with just two of the damned things.

Redding went forward immediately. When Martz boarded, she joined him in Control. Lewis, Raydor, and I stayed in the passenger bay, along with five *Nimbus* crew members clad in their dusty-green flightsuits. They stoically scrunched themselves into the remaining seating, doubling up when necessary, without complaint, to leave the three of us with our own couches. I sank down onto the padded seat and looked across at Raydor. "You going to tell me what's going on?" I asked him wearily.

The shuttle's hovers began to maneuver the ship out of the massive hangar. As the craft rotated sideways, Raydor ran one big hand over his smooth and hairless head and then began to explain what he knew.

Over the past months Alexandria had managed to infiltrate the research complex's maintenance crews with her own Tachs. It had actually presented very little problem, since custodial personnel tended to come and go frequently anyway, like most people in low-paying jobs. And in coveralls and face wraps, one Tachs looked pretty much like another, especially to MA. In fact, Alexandria had eventually arranged to have four or five different Tachs, in sequence, working each custodian's job, and MA had never noticed the difference. In addition to the information the Tachs had been able to glean for her, they now gave her a perfect way to literally just walk her own men right into the complex when she needed them.

I already knew how Alexandria planned to walk the three of us in: at the point of a beam rifle. But as Raydor elaborated the rest of the plan to me, I had to admit grudgingly that not only was it far more feasible than anything I could have devised on my own, it actually might even work. And we had asked her help to get us in, I reminded myself grimly.

"What about Bertram, the guy MA 'eliminated'?" I inquired skeptically. "Doesn't she think MA's going to be on the lookout for trouble now?"

The shuttle nosed up; we were already on the tarmac, accelerating for our takeoff into suborbit. The launch itself was so smoothly executed that in my preoccupied state I barely noticed it.

Raydor just grunted in reply to my doubts. "Could be a problem," he admitted. "But we can't take the risk of waiting any longer. Like she said, time's running out for the other Class Tens. If whoever is doing this research is suspicious now, the whole secret project might just be sealed off—terminated."

I felt rather than saw the little jerk of alarm that jolted Lewis's body. He was reclining on the couch directly across the aisle from me, but his whole frame was tense, as if the padded upholstery beneath him had suddenly turned uncomfortably hot.

"What kind of security have they got?" I continued, trying to bend down the sharp edge of panic that threatened to wedge itself in between my ribs.

Raydor shrugged, shifting his big body on the too-small couch. "Supposedly, it's a scientific complex," he responded. "So officially they've got nothing military but their security guards. *Unofficially*—" He made a little snorting sound, as if the answer was probably self-evident. "*—unofficially*, they might have almost anything in there."

I glanced sideways at Lewis. His arms were folded stiffly across his body. I caught his eye, gave him a determined little grin, and was rewarded by one of his shy and dazzling smiles in return. I reached across the aisle and, not feeling self-conscious at all, took hold of his hand. Then I said to Raydor, "Now, maybe you can explain to me just how our part in this little ruse is supposed to work."

To my surprise, after two or three hours of flight I

found that I was actually becoming bored. Anxiety, even fear, I had anticipated, but not boredom! The *Nimbus* crew members were all lumped silently together. Some were occupied with vidtapes; others seemed to be dozing—or suffocating, I thought ruefully, considering the way they were packed in together. Raydor had put back the top of his couch and had fallen soundly asleep, complete with gentle snoring; I envied him his congenital sense of sangfroid. Lewis was still awake, but he had discovered the vidtape collection above his seat and, at my urging, was fairly well-absorbed in some popular entertainment vid. Depending on how long ago Redding had lifted those shuttles, the vids were probably even reasonably current.

I finally stood up, stretching my stiff legs and back. Then I hobbled toward the forward compartment. I was so restless that even confinement with Redding's company seemed preferable to continued confinement with my own obsessively gnawing thoughts. Martz looked up from the copilot's chair as I came through the hatch. She smiled at me. Redding, in the pilot's seat, didn't even turn.

"How long?" I asked.

"Only another hour or so," Martz assured me. She looked me over sympathetically. "Waiting sucks," she commented succinctly.

I half smiled back at her, suddenly wondering just what her stake was in all this. If she wasn't joining with Redding, what had motivated her to take this kind of risk? For that matter, it seemed above and beyond the call of duty for any of the *Nimbus* crew members. Maybe Redding paid really well.

I must have been staring, because Martz gave me a funny, quizzical sort of look. Then she got to her feet and stretched elaborately. "You leave an empty couch back there?" she asked me. When I nodded, she said, "Good!" and moved past me and out the hatch before I could even protest her untimely defection.

Alone in Control with Redding, I gazed straight ahead, out the streamlined bubble of the shuttle's aft viewport.

The enormous dun-colored curve of Camelot rolled beneath us, speckled with the dirty blue patches of her small bodies of water. Above stretched the midnight-blue of space. And between the two, where we soared, an incandescent corona of sparkling particles glittered in the light of Camelot's primary. The particles flew away from the viewport like luminescent confetti in an endless, dazzling spray: a churning spume of planetary debris, trapped forever at the edge of the planet's atmosphere.

After a few moments of my silent gaping Redding suddenly turned from the console. Seeing the expression on my face, he lifted his lip slightly. He gestured at Martz's empty chair. I hesitated, then sat.

"Pretty, huh?" he commented, glancing down at his board.

I gazed straight ahead at the effervescent light show. "Yeah," I agreed, quite frankly impressed by the phenomenon. I darted a brief sideways look at Redding. "What the hell causes that effect?" I asked him curiously.

Touching a switch at his console, Redding gave a little shrug. "Damned if I know," he replied indifferently. A steady stream of figures moved across the Integrator screen; the greenish light reflected eerily off his placid face. "Pretty, though," he added.

I stared out the viewport again, then glanced over at him. "Don't you ever wonder?" I persisted, temporarily forgetting my antipathy for the man.

Redding leaned back in the pilot's chair, stretching his arms up over his head in a feline arc as he studied the particle display. "Yeah," he finally conceded. "I guess sometimes I do wonder a little."

We both were silent for the space of several minutes, each lost in something unfamiliar. Then Redding looked over at me and gestured at his board. "Want to take her for a while?" he offered.

Surprised, I quickly shook my head. "No, I'm not much of a pilot." That admission surprised me even more than his offer, especially since I had made it to him.

But Redding just grinned that crooked, tooth-revealing

grin of his and quipped, "Neither am I! Integrators do the real work, anyway,"

"What about Martz?" I asked him.

Redding cocked a brow. "She's ship's Security—no pilot."

"Then why did she volunteer for this business?" I asked bluntly, choosing my term for the little venture with deliberation.

But Redding wasn't so easily baited. "Guess she has her reasons," he offered mildly. A slight motion of his head indicated the passenger compartment. "Guess we all do, huh?"

An old irritation stirred in me, but this time it failed to kindle or hold any heat. "Lewis doesn't have any choice," I reminded him quietly, gazing ahead at the fiery swirl in the viewport.

But I could feel that Redding's eyes were still on me. "Neither do you, then, since you're in love with him," he completed, no trace of the old sarcasm in his voice.

I stared suddenly at him, considering a response. There were a hundred things I could have said if only Redding had played fair and stuck to his cool quips, his sardonic wit. But when he was like this, I had no ready defense. "Yeah," I said at last, my voice scarcely more than a whisper. "Then neither do I."

There were two things about the research complex that immediately surprised me as our shuttle soared over it on an identification flyby in the spectacular red blaze of Camelot's sunset. One thing was that the building itself was actually architecturally and aesthetically pleasing, a sprawling structure of rough native stone and gleaming panes of glass set on several acres of verdant landscaping. Then again, two things Camelot had plenty of were rocks and sand, but the greenery must have required some effort to maintain. The complex looked more like the corporate headquarters of some successful intersystem trading company than an MA facility. The second surprising thing was how much air traffic was casually buzz-

ing around the well-laid-out landing field and how much
of it appeared to be civilian in origin.

The research complex was set like a bull's-eye in the
center of a target, that target being its attendant colony.
Unlike Nethersedge, Camelot's other settlement, the
"satellite community" of the complex was precisely laid
out, immaculately maintained, and absolutely conformist
in appearance. As was true on many planets sponsored
and colonized by MA, the settlement existed solely to
serve the needs of the complex, and MA constituted the
total means of support for its inhabitants. Although most
of them were civilians, many of them scientists employed
by MA in a nonmilitary capacity, they all lived like re-
cruits in a barrackslike stone and steel ghetto. Looking
down at the dreary ring of monotonously identical housing units radiating out from the complex, relieved only
by the occasional MA-run shop or entertainment outlet,
I found myself wondering what sort of person could be
attracted to that kind of existence. In a way I could understand the common presence of Tachs; their low Class
and social status often made it necessary for them to accept manual work on remote worlds. And I knew that the
scientists could be an eccentric lot, easily swayed by the
technological opportunities and superior facilities MA offered. But it did not seem tenable that any other civilians
would choose to live that way.

To my extreme relief, our arrival was hardly notewor-
thy in all the confusion on the busy field. Our shuttle had
taken a somewhat roundabout course so that we would
reach the complex in a comfortable interval after, and
from a different direction than, the ship containing Alexandria and the Tachs. The Tachs working at the complex maintained a separate settlement on the outskirts of
the main compound, and they were frequently shuttled
in. With Redding safely out of sight in the passenger
compartment, Martz brought our shuttle in. She com-
municated briefly with Port, using the dead agent's code
and landing coordinates.

As soon as the ship's systems were shut down, Martz
came back through the hatch into the rear compartment.

She held up a trio of wrist cuffs. "My prisoners ready?" she inquired cheerfully.

It was hard not to smile at her. Lewis, Raydor, and I each fastened our own cuffs, and Martz demonstrated how to release them.

"Don't make a move until you get the signal," Redding cautioned us as Martz herded us toward the rear hatch.

I looked over my shoulder at him. "What signal?" I protested. "From who?"

"Just wait," he insisted. "You'll know."

By then Raydor and Lewis were moving obediently down the ramp, and I was forced to follow, a little kick of adrenaline flaring uselessly in my veins.

On the landing field tarmac, Martz quickly reconnoitered the immediate area. The nearest buildings, a row of low, single-story shedlike structures, were several hundred meters from our berth on the field. Dozens of other craft, mostly small hover cars, dotted the area between our shuttle and the buildings. There was a smattering of other pedestrian traffic on the tarmac. Then she waved a perfectly functional looking beam rifle at us and snarled menacingly, "Come on, let's go!"

The transformation of her familiar face was so swift, so complete, and so dramatic that for a moment I hesitated, stumbling, while another unbidden rush of fear lurched through me, compelling Martz to prod me roughly with the barrel of her weapon. "Now!" she snapped convincingly.

Raydor led the way across the paved field, followed by Lewis and with me bringing up the rear. Recovering from my initial stab of panic, I still felt a relentless loss of control over the situation. It was a position that I had always tried desperately to avoid, and I had been instrumental in putting all three of us into it. I glanced back helplessly at Martz, but it was too late for any final reassurances. Her face was grimly set.

We followed a broad walkway from the edge of the landing field to the complex's entrance. It was a short distance, a quarter kilometer at most, but at least two dozen people must have passed us, some sidestepping onto the lush turf to avoid us. Most of them looked like the typical MA civilian lackeys: middle-aged Normals, both men and women, nearly indistinguishable in their conservative cream and maroon jumpsuits, carrying nearly identical papers cases or equipment grips. None of them were walking in pairs or groups, and there was no conversation. None of them seemed particularly interested in us, except to stay out of our way. Apparently MA's military presence was strongly enough expressed in the area that even Martz's openly displayed beam rifle and our wrist cuffs aroused no comment. I just kept my head down and concentrated on the band of silver piping on the waist of Lewis's flightsuit ahead of me.

At the entrance to the massive building Martz confidently thrust her acquired ID into the Integrator slot that governed the door mechanism. There were no human guards in attendance. After a brief interval the gleaming glass doors cycled open with a *whoosh* of escaping filtered air.

''*In!*'' Martz barked at us.

I noticed that the workers who were leaving the complex, of whom there seemed to be a fairly steady stream, used specially marked exit doors that appeared to require no ID verification. That observation caught my attention just long enough to make me fall a half step behind. Suddenly I felt the barrel of Martz's rifle jammed into the small of my back.

''Move!'' she snapped curtly. She pushed me so hard that I staggered forward, my back aching, and nearly collided with Lewis. He began to turn with a look of untempered alarm on his face, but I bumped fiercely into him, hissing inarticulately to prevent him from trying to intervene. Several workers crossing the lobby had witnessed the little scuffle, but all of them had determinedly averted their eyes and continued on their way, pretending—much as people everywhere do—that nothing had happened and that, most important, they definitely were not involved. No one there wanted to be part of any trouble.

The lobby was huge and airy, with a high, lofted cathedral ceiling and lots of chrome and glass. We crossed the polished poured-stone floor to a gigantic bank of Integrator accesses, a bewildering array of fluttering lights and waiting slots. But Martz whipped out the ID again and, with a nonchalance that bordered on impatience, thrust the card into one of the seemingly endless aperatures. The woman certainly had done her homework.

Martz scowled effectively at us, her rifle leveled at ready, as she waited for clearance. I just stared fixedly at the gleaming floor, afraid to risk catching Lewis's or Raydor's eye. After an agonizing interval—probably two or three minutes but stretched out to infinity by my interminable anxiety—the Integrator disgorged Martz's ID and announced, "Level three, block twelve. Please use a secure lift."

"Secure" lifts were those equipped with surveillance devices. At the bank of shiny steel lifts Martz herded us into one of the little cubicles. As she entered, she briefly wedged her back between us and the blank eye of the monitor camera, flashed us a most un-MA-like grin, and then stepped aside again. I think she must have realized by then how close to the edge of panic I was; at any rate, I blessed her ancestors for her momentary kindness.

On the third level, the wide corridors appeared deserted, the endless steel doors all closed. With the end of the last day shift, the building apparently operated with only a skeleton crew. Only the wandering eyes of the monitor cameras dotted the passageways. Block 12 was only a short distance from the lift shafts. Once again I was impressed by Martz's familiarity with the complex's layout. It was obvious that she had studied all the information provided by Alexandria's Tachs and that she took her role very seriously. We paused before a set of wide double doors of opaqued plasteel labeled SECURITY ONLY. As before, Martz's ID inserted in the access slot gained us entrance.

The room we entered was large but nearly empty. Three of the walls were covered with the flat, monochromatic screens of the feed-ins for the complex's surveillance cameras. The fourth wall, the one opposite the door, was all glass and overlooked the landing field, which was awash in the glare of the field lights. Against that backdrop was a long, simple desk, nearly barren of any personal accoutrements; behind that desk sat a single uniformed security man. He was thoroughly unremarkable in the manner of far too many Normals, in his late fifties, I guessed, with closely cropped salt and pepper hair and blandly regular features. Only the insignia on the collar tabs of his cream and maroon jumpsuit indicated his rank as chief of Security. As we came through the doorway, he stood.

Martz halted, executed a very passable MA salute, and said stiffly, "Petersen reporting, sir!"

The chief's salute was sloppy, a throwaway gesture. His eyes were already greedily on the three of us, no doubt anticipating the hefty kickback he was likely to receive under some table for facilitating our capture. "Good work, Petersen," he said automatically.

Raydor was behind me, and so I heard rather than saw the side step that put the bulk of his big body against the door frame and over the swiveling lens of the monitor camera that was silently sweeping the room. His unexpected motion drew just enough of my attention that for a second I wasn't sure if I was actually seeing what was happening in front of me or if it was instead some weird sort of peripheral visual hallucination. In one smooth arc Martz brought up the barrel of her beam rifle and fired. A large charred cavity immediately appeared in the center of the Security chief's chest, spattering the front of his jumpsuit and the desk with gobbets of fried flesh and blood and sending a boomlet of foul black smoke up into the air. There was a totally bewildered look on his face, as though what had just happened was as incomprehensible to him as it was to me. Then, wordlessly, he crumpled backward into his chair. As he landed, the chair overturned, sending his body crashing into the window behind him. By then Martz was lunging around the desk. She jerked his body sideways and fell to the floor on top of him.

CHAPTER
TWELVE

Stunned, I stared dumbly at Martz as she pushed herself to her feet again. "Here!" she commanded briskly, tossing the beam rifle at me. Awkwardly but reflexively, I made a grab for the weapon and caught it by the stock, the wrist cuffs biting painfully into my skin. But Martz was already punching at the room controls panel behind the desk. In a moment the heavy drapes glided shut over the big windows, not only concealing the dead Security chief's body from outside detection but also signaling our companions outside the complex to be ready to move.

"Shit! They keep changing the code arrangements on these things!" Martz muttered vehemently, working over the Security panel itself. She searched for the code to release the access to the front entrance. In about thirty seconds Alexandria, Redding, and five *Nimbus* crew members would be walking casually among the remnants of the last shift's departing workers, up to the main doors of the complex, where they would pantomime legitimate ID card access. If Martz failed to override the lock mechanism, not only were they not going to be able to get in, they were also quickly going to begin to look fairly suspicious. And one thing we didn't need was unwanted attention.

Beside me, Lewis moved closer. I shuddered slightly, still staring at the body of the slain MA officer. I don't know why his death affected me that much; Powers knew, I had fried some MA men recently, too—plenty of them, in fact, on *Argent* and *Corona*. But those had been safely

214

remote deaths, executed at long distance. The image of the calm expression on Martz's face as she had brought up the beam rifle still unnerved me.

A little whoop of triumph punctuated Martz's success with the Security panel. "We'll give it sixty seconds," she announced, her gaze sweeping rapidly over the rest of the console. "Then we've got to get the hell out of here before anyone discovers anything's wrong."

Raydor's back still blocked the diligently swiveling monitor camera. I sincerely hoped that surveillance for the Security headquarters itself was not a very high-priority item, especially this time of the day, and that no other Security station anywhere else in the building would notice a brief blackout in the system. With the dead chief's body concealed behind his desk, once we left the office the room would merely appear deserted. But if we were to be caught there, I knew the others would still attempt to proceed without us. The four of us—even Lewis, ultimately—were expendable in the larger scheme of things. Somehow that thought failed to provide me with any consolation as we tensely waited.

"Okay, that's it," Martz decided firmly, coming around the desk again and reaching to reclaim her rifle. "Let's go! We've got to get down to the ground level again."

Our cover as an MA agent and her three prisoners still could serve us, although the only attention we appeared to attract as we left the Security office was from the ever-present cameras in the corridor. Martz directed us into one of the secure lifts, and we exited on the main floor again. I was unreasonably reassured to see Redding and his dusty-green-clad crew members casually perusing the schematic directory in the huge lobby. They crossed not ten feet from us and headed up a side corridor, talking among themselves. Martz scowled convincingly at them as they passed and then waved the barrel of the rifle at us. "Go!" she demanded, pointing us toward the same corridor.

My pulse was thudding painfully, and perspiration had fused my suit liner to my skin on my back and belly.

When I tried to swallow, I nearly choked on my dry tongue. By then my anxiety about getting into the complex had been superseded by my anxiety about being in the complex. I tried to concentrate on Lewis's and Raydor's backs ahead of me. After having seen Martz's facility with the beam rifle in the Security office, I was less than happy to have that same weapon directed at my back.

I knew from what Lewis had recalled that the entrance to the hidden research facility was accessible only from the complex's maintenance area, one level below the ground floor. I wasn't sure just how plausible it would look for an MA agent to be herding three prisoners down to maintainence, but at that time of day we were unlikely to encounter anyone whose authority would entitle him to an explanation. The corridor was empty. After we rode the slowly gliding escalator ramp down to the subterranean level, even the omnipresent monitor cameras began to thin out. We began to occasionally pass a Tachs in gray coveralls—Alexandria's or not, I wasn't sure. Then, at last, I saw Raydor nod minutely to one of them as we passed, and I realized that all of them had probably been hers.

The decor down there was considerably less polished and more starkly functional than that of the upper levels. The walls of the corridors were painted formblock, and the lighting was provided by ugly suspended bars of bare tubing. Exposed ducts and conduits crossed the ceiling, and the air was faintly scented with floor cleaner and the floral tang of the recycling agent. A gray-clad Tachs, bent over an industrial-sized automop, glanced up as we passed. I had to fight down a totally inappropriate smile.

The corridor we were following came to a dead end. To our left a short hall led to a stout, windowless metal-faced door with the legend DANGER—POWER STATION—NO ADMITTANCE stenciled on its neutral beige surface. Flanking the door, their backs to the walls, Redding waited with his crew members. His brows rose as we approached. "You got it?" He asked Martz.

She nodded, reaching into the breast pocket of her MA jumpsuit and producing a small plastic key card. Deftly, she inserted it in the narrow slot beside the massive lock on the door's featureless face. The door cycled open. Then the three of us—Lewis, Raydor, and I—were thrust ahead of her and into the room beyond.

I guess after everything we'd been through to get to that point I'd expected something a little more exotic for the gateway to the clandestine facility. The entrance was absolutely prosaic. The room into which we were thrust was claustrophobically small and ascetically barren. Against the far wall stood a slanted console desk, standard MA office issue, and beyond it, set deeply into the wall itself, was a gleaming stainless-steel vault door. Behind the desk, a dark-haired woman in MA's cream and maroon literally leapt to her feet as we entered. Her caster-legged chair skittered away from her like a panicked horse and crashed into the steel door. She gaped at us, her mouth working soundlessly. Then I realized that it was less the intrusion that had astonished her than the identity of the intruders. It was Lewis she was staring at and her shock was the shock of recognition.

For a moment we regarded each other in frozen silence. Then, suddenly galvanized into action, the woman lunged across her console, reaching for the alarm switch. From behind us someone fired a beam pistol. I actually felt the heat of it sizzle past my ear. The woman crumpled across her desk, smoke curling from the scorched and fused fabric of her jumpsuit.

"Great," Redding exclaimed darkly, pushing past me and grasping the guard by the shoulders. He glared from her lifeless form to one of his crew members behind me, an olive-skinned man with taupe-colored eyes and sleek black hair gathered back in a single short pigtail. "Couldn't you just've *winged* her, for Light's sake?"

"And have her set off every joining alarm in this whole place?" Martz responded heatedly, springing to the defense of her fellow crew mate. She still clutched the beam rifle in one hand. With her free arm she helped Redding pull the dead woman off the console and drag her over against one of the walls. For the first time, I think, I began to realize the stress Martz was under. Her hands were shaking, although she was pushing herself fiercely to conceal the fact.

That death upset me less than the last, but I still felt inexplicably queasy. I glanced toward Lewis, suspecting the source of my unease. Raydor had removed his own cuffs and was now working on freeing Lewis's. I fumbled out of my cuffs, and Raydor took them from me. I glanced over at the five *Nimbus* crew members, the two women and three men, but none of us spoke.

Redding and Martz were already huddled over the console. The unit had the sophisticated complexity of a Port air control board. Muttering in frustration, Martz tried several of the different purloined plastic key cards from her pockets in the console's input slot. But to her and Redding's continued mutual dismay, nothing was happening.

Then the armored beige door swung open again and several more people crowded into the already cramped room. I was relieved to see Alexandria with two of her Tachs. Her commanding gaze swept from the obviously dead woman guard to the control console, and then she shouldered forward into the room. "What the hell's the problem?" she asked gruffly.

"Aw, they got some kind of damned code keyed in," Martz responded, jiggling one of the many useless plastic key cards in helpless exasperation.

Redding met Alexandria's eyes. "Maybe they've upped security," he suggested blandly.

Alexandria shrugged, glancing over at the dead guard. "Well, it's a cinch we're not going to find out anything from *her*," she noted acerbically. She stared thoughtfully at the console. "What do you think?" she asked Martz. "Some kind of numerical sequence?"

Martz looked up, her mouth pulled into a straight line. I could easily read the sense of frustration in those ginger-colored eyes. "Yeah, probably," she muttered. "One thing's for sure, it's bound to be randomly assigned."

My attention had been on the trio at the console; I didn't notice that Lewis had moved until he nearly bumped into me. He crossed to the front edge of the desk, angling in between Redding and Alexandria, and leaned across the console. There was a strangely detached look on his face; I hadn't seen an expression like it from him since New Cuba, when he had been heavily drugged. Eyeing him, Martz took an automatic half step backward, out of his way. She traded a puzzled glance over Lewis's shoulder with Alexandria and Redding, but nobody moved to stop him.

Lewis hesitated a moment, scanning the bewildering array of components on the console. His right hand hovered over the keyboard, his slender fingers circumscribing a kind of restless dance in the air above it. Then, without even looking down at the board, as if without conscious thought, Lewis punched a dizzyingly rapid sequence of numbers into the input. For a moment nothing happened. Behind him the huge metal vault door gave a gentle hiss, then it cycled open.

"Sweet stars!" someone behind me softly exclaimed—one of the *Nimbus* crew members.

I took the necessary two steps forward to where I could reach across the Security panel and catch hold of Lewis's arm. He was looking in utter confusion from the gaping doorway to the faces of the people in the room. There was a moment of stunned silence. Then Alexandria made a small gesture at the console keyboard.

"How did you do that?" she asked Lewis gently.

Somehow troubled, Lewis shook his head, as if the answer to that question had eluded him as well. Now that I was actually touching him again, I could feel his almost overwhelming anxiety; it was a distressing thing, beating with a throbbing pulse, like a bad tooth. "I don't know," he whispered helplessly.

I squeezed his arm, and his eyes finally jumped to my face. "I don't know," he repeated softly to me.

It was Redding who broke the moment, as it had to be broken. "Come on," he said abruptly, "we don't have time to discuss this."

Alexandria nodded in agreement, motioning to her two Tachs. They took hold of the body of the dead MA guard by her arms and dragged her through the armored doorway into the corridor beyond. The *Nimbus* crew members followed them, trailed by Raydor. Martz had seated herself in the dead woman's chair, wheeling it up close to the desk again, with her beam rifle resting across her knees. She watched impassively as the rest of us filed through the steel door.

I was still clutching Lewis's arm, reluctant to release him. I had the sharp, aching premonition that once I let go of him, they would take him away from me—as Redding had said they must—and that I might never see him again. I finally had a name for the thing I feared most: the pain of loss. Lewis's own fear, a palpable thing in that place, washed through me in a cold, shimmering wave. My knees felt like jelly; only my grip on Lewis's arm kept me from actually swaying as we moved to join the others in the entry hall of the secret facility.

In confusion and desperation I looked at Alexandria, but her gaze was sweeping the assembly. She raised a hand for everyone's attention. "This is where we split up," she announced. In the brilliant, diffused glow of the corridor's lighting, she looked weirdly out of place: a creature of bone and blood and earth in that relentlessly sterile passageway. Her wild gray hair framed her strongly featured face like a frenzied corona, but her voice was stern and calm. "We think that there were once six Class Tens imprisoned here. Now, as far as we know, there are still five of them."

Beside me, Lewis shifted. His arm was trembling in my grasp. I fought the urge to reach up and take hold of him with both hands. His anxiety was wrenching me, bringing up the bile in my throat. I had to swallow twice in rapid succession to choke down the sour taste of it.

"Just remember," Alexandria was continuing, "this security door is the only way in here—and it's the only way out again." She gestured beyond the steel door to the little antechamber where Martz sat implacably with her beam rifle. "We'll hold that corridor as long as we can, but obviously it's going to be a hell of a lot easier to get out of here again if we don't attract any attention to ourselves while we're in here." Was it my imagination, or was Alexandria sparing a particularly long look for the *Nimbus* crew members? "No offensive action," she dictated crisply, "no matter what happens. Stealth and surprise are the only advantages we have." Her gaze swung now, panning over all of us, those black eyes piercingly direct. "We'll get out everyone we can, but whoever we can't get to . . ."

As her voice trailed off, Lewis's spurt of adrenaline hit me like a staggering blow, and a part of me was surprised that I could actually feel it with such intensity. Alexandria's eyes were on Lewis, traveling right through him. "Whoever we can't get to can't be left alive," she concluded softly.

Then, abruptly, she swung away, gesturing down the corridor. "You all know the floor plans and the specs. Stay in pairs, if you can, and keep your asses covered. I want you all back here in twenty minutes; that's all the time we've got before the next Security sweep upstairs."

Alexandria reached for Lewis's other arm. Automatically, he shied away from her, his eyes rolling in alarm. Then he steadied himself and allowed her to grasp his wrist.

"You think you can find Lillard?" she asked him bluntly.

Lewis nodded, swallowing dryly.

I still held his arm, refusing to let go. Alexandria determinedly caught my eye. "Go ahead, Jo," she told me, not unkindly. "Stick with Raydor. I'll take care of him for you."

I don't think that she could have made me let go of Lewis—not unless she had coldcocked me on the spot. But Lewis could make me. His eyes, wide with fear and dilated with emotion, locked on to mine. He hesitated, then fumbled awkwardly but briefly with his free hand in one of the breast pockets of his flightsuit. He pressed something into my hand, squeezing my limp fingers tightly around it. As my hold on his arm loosened, his face was just inches from mine. "Just in case," he whispered in my ear. Then I felt his lips brush the side of my cheek, and he pulled away.

The two Tachs had already started moving up the hallway; Redding's crew members were close behind them. Alexandria began to lead Lewis briskly away, and with him went some of the immediacy of the visceral sense of alarm that churned in me. I looked suddenly to Raydor, desperately catching his eye.

"Want me to go with them?" he asked me, his voice a soft growl.

I was horrified by how close to tears I was then; they nearly sprang helplessly from my eyes as I spoke. "Yes!" I said hoarsely, nodding to add the emphasis that I couldn't seem to force into my panicked voice.

But Redding—whom I had temporarily forgotten—stepped forward and held up one hand. "No," he countermanded. Seeing the open rebellion on my face, he made a chopping motion with his hand and repeated with even more vehemence, "*No!* You can't help him that way."

Raydor's eyes were on me but I shook my head in utter capitulation. Redding was right. Damn the man! He was right.

Redding gestured brusquely. "Come on, we don't have much time." And when he moved out, the two of us followed him. I was a good way down the curved and gleaming corridor before I transferred the object I held clutched in my hand to one of my flightsuit pockets. It was the little coded chip of Lewis's total Integration analysis that Handy had made for him.

The labyrinth's hallways were laid out in concentric rings; it seemed both senseless and baffling. The corridors looked like the sterile passages in a med center: uniformly white, featureless, and dazzlingly empty. The indirect lighting in the ceiling was diffuse but stingingly brilliant. Because of the perpetual curve in the corridors, one could never see very far ahead or behind, and because everything looked exactly the same anyway, there was a surrealistic sense of infinity to the hallways. Lewis's terror, blunted somewhat by the distance between us but still palpable, pressed delicately against my adrenals,

keeping my nerves on a hair trigger and my head throbbing in time to my pulse.

The three of us passed several side corridors without
pausing, but at one of the intersections Raydor suddenly
halted—so abruptly that I bumped into him. His big head
was cocked, a curiously intricate gesture in a man his
size. He held up oné hand, ignoring Redding's skeptical
expression. "I hear something," he said quietly.

"I'll check it out," Redding announced automatically,
starting to turn. But Raydor reached out and blocked his
way with one beefy forearm. Wordlessly, the Tachs shook
his head, gesturing for us to stay put. Then he was off,
creeping with surprising stealth down the side corridor.

Even before the arc of the corridor hid Raydor from
our view, Redding turned on me with a look of unconcealed irritation. "I thought he was supposed to stick
with you," he said. I hissed at him to be quiet, my every
faculty straining to listen down the empty corridor. All I
could hear was the faint mechanical hum of the air-
circulating system and the persistent thud of my own
pulse in my ears. Then I heard the sound of footsteps.

I stepped abruptly backward, forcing Redding to retreat around the corner behind me. We were neatly caught
in the open there; there wasn't a doorway near enough
to provide us with any cover in the few remaining seconds we had left. And unless the person approaching us
was blind, he was hardly going to just walk right past us.
Unarmed, I felt numbingly helpless. And even though I
suspected Redding was carrying at least one concealed
weapon, I didn't know how he could have used it there
without attracting even more attention to our presence.

The man coming up the corridor rounded the corner
and nearly collided with me. He was a slightly built Normal, a head shorter than me at least, and was dressed in
a shapeless white tech's smock. Only his eyes seemed
immediately real to me, registering shock at finding me
and Redding there where no one should have been. The
tech stumbled backward, his hands coming automatically
up. One more step and he would have bumped into Raydor, who was right behind him, impossibly silent. With

one hammerlike blow to the back of the man's head, Raydor brought him down. The stunned man crumpled to the floor.

I let out the breath I had been holding. My throat ached.

"Told you I heard something," Raydor said, already hefting the unconscious body over his shoulder. "We better dump him somewhere where he won't attract any attention for a while," he added matter-of-factly. He started down the side corridor. "Lots of doors here; good place to start looking."

Redding merely nodded, nonplussed, and said nothing.

Raydor paused before the first rectangular hatch we encountered that was marked with the maintainence system's logo. Unceremoniously, he stuffed the unresisting body of the tech down the chute. "Hope it doesn't go to the incinerator," he remarked mildly. And I grinned up gratefully at him.

Redding was already a few meters ahead of us, trying a door. It was sealed, as I expected most of them to be. But Redding seemed undeterred. He withdrew a small cylindrical object from one of his pockets and manipulated it briefly against the lock panel. The door cycled open.

Redding turned to us. "Either of you know how to use one of these?" he asked, waving the device at us. Raydor grunted affirmatively. That rather surprised me, though Powers knew, it shouldn't have; I should have been beyond surprise. Redding then produced a second cylindrical device for him. "Take that side of the hall," he directed briskly. He motioned to me. "You come with me."

My eyes narrowed, and I exchanged a quick glance with Raydor. "Why?" I asked Redding suspiciously.

"Because I've got a gun," Redding replied simply.

After a moment of silence Raydor waved the lock-breaking device at me in a little salute. "Go," he agreed gruffly.

The first room Redding and I checked out was some

kind of data storage area. The walls were covered with built-in cabinets from floor to ceiling, and the shelves were filled with cases of filed vidchips. The next two rooms on our side of the corridor were pretty much the same, and I was beginning to suspect that maybe that whole area of the facility was just some kind of warehouse or library. The information contained in all those rooms was no doubt unduplicated and possibly quite crucial to the illicit research, but it wasn't helping us find Lillard and the others. I did have the fleeting thought, however, that Handy would probably have been willing to trade his master circuits to be able to tap into even a fraction of what was hidden there.

The fourth room we tried was unsealed. Redding entered first, shouldering cautiously through the doorway into the darkened room. I palmed the wall panel, and illumination filled the room. It looked like some kind of small med center: examination table, cabinets, sink, and a desk with an Integrator access. We exchanged a quizzical look as I stepped into the room, closing the door behind me.

Inside, we each made a half circuit of the room, meeting at the desk. Redding's brows were drawn up in a puzzled frown, and he gestured at something on the Integrator access panel. "Here," he began. "What the hell do you make of this?"

But I cut him off, gripping his forearm in a sudden clutch. "*Shh!*" I hissed. Listening carefully and trying to ignore my heart pounding in my chest, I could hear footsteps in the corridor outside the room; it was more than one person, too. "Shit!" I whispered. I jerked on Redding's arm, catching him enough by surprise that I nearly pulled him off his feet. "In here!"

Beside the exam table there was a tall, narrow steel cabinet across from the desk. The doors were solid, and mercifully, it was nearly empty. There was just enough room inside for the two of us if we didn't expect to be able to stand up or both take a deep breath at the same time. I jiggled the latch shut with a soft click just as I heard the door cycle open. I wondered somewhat belatedly if it was possible to reopen the cabinet from the inside.

We had left the room's lights on; if that registered as something alarming to whoever was coming in, I figured we'd know about it soon enough. But when I heard the footsteps entering the room, there was no suggestion of anything amiss. I could see a narrow bar of light shining through at the juncture where the cabinet's two steel doors met. I was half squatting, half sitting on the floor of the cabinet, with Redding crouched in an equally awkward position in the darkness above me. There was something hard and angular beneath my bent legs: cassette cases, perhaps, or some piece of equipment. I could only hope it wasn't whatever the people in the room had come looking for. I could hear the murmur of their voices, but I couldn't make out what they were saying or even how many of them there were. At least it sounded like casual conversation, not like they were on any kind of alert.

It took only about sixty seconds for me to realize that I couldn't hold that cramped position much longer. My bent legs ached stupendously. Reaching up with one hand in the darkness, I encountered the front of one of Redding's thighs. I tapped it gently to be sure I had his attention; then, grasping the fabric of his coveralls leg, I pulled myself up a few inches out of my squat. When I was able to straighten my legs out a little, I sank back down again without quite the same stabbing pain in my knees. At least that position was bearable. It also had placed my face about two inches from the crotch of Redding's coveralls, but we were hardly in a situation to be able to observe all the social proprieties.

Above me, I could feel Redding shift his body. I was sure he wasn't exactly wildly happy with his position, either. I heard the soft *sisss* of something moving against the fabric of his coveralls and felt his arm move across the top of my shoulders. Then I realized that he was withdrawing some kind of weapon, probably a small beam pistol, from inside his clothing. I was abruptly reminded that that little evasive maneuver wasn't just a mere minor inconvenience: There were people out there who were the enemy, even if they weren't armed. And maybe they were armed. If they discovered us there, we might very well have to kill them to protect ourselves.

Their droning conversation seemed endless rather than reassuringly normal. What if they were techs, starting some kind of work shift in the lab? Sweat had begun to trickle down my face from my hairline and to soak my suit liner under my arms and beneath my breasts. I longed to shift again any way I could, but there really was nowhere to go. I was acutely aware of even the most minute and unavoidable motions caused by my breathing and of the gentle bumping of Redding's body against mine. And I could smell myself: the concentrated essence of my damp hair, the soap I'd used that morning in the shower with Lewis, and the wet-fabric smell of my liner. I could smell Redding, too, but it was all less familiar to me: the faint lube smell of his coveralls, the musky scent of his skin, and something warm and almost spicy.

Once, Redding turned slightly, his ear against the cabinet's steel door. In the tiny shaft of light that breached the crack in the doors I could see the quick glint of something metallic in his hand: his pistol. The conversation outside in the room had stopped. Footsteps moved across the floor. I held my breath then, willing whoever it was to stay away from the cabinet. *Let them go away!* I thought furiously, my legs throbbing. Then something broke the line of light in the crack in the doors, and I realized that someone was standing right outside the cabinet.

For an instant I felt as though my heart had stopped beating. I know I had stopped breathing; my chest ached, and my head swam from lack of oxygen. Then my pulse kicked in, driven by a frantic burst of adrenaline, and I felt my heart hammer wildly. Just as I was forced to gasp for air, a voice spoke right outside the steel doors, startling me with its unexpected clarity.

"In that case, she's the one we should be talking to," the disembodied voice said, just inches from us. The response, coming from the other side of the room, was nearly inaudible.

"Well, it's not *our* responsibility," the voice near us noted tersely.

The irony of his words was not lost on me, despite my racing pulse, my sweating palms, and my dry mouth. Not ours, either, I thought ruefully, but there we were, just the same.

Suddenly the man by the cabinet moved away, and the bar of light between the doors was complete again. The conversation continued on the other side of the room. Gulping another breath of air, I slumped even farther down on the cabinet floor. I felt Redding's hand land gently on the top of my head and for the first time on that damned planet I was profoundly grateful for his presence.

Across the room the conversation died out. For a few moments I could hear nothing; then I heard the muffled thump of footsteps across the floor toward the doorway. One of the men? Both? All of them? Suddenly aware of a cloying sense of claustrophobia I had never known before, I realized that it hardly mattered anymore. I was getting out of the cabinet, no matter what!

I started to shift, trying to push myself upward with my fingers fumbling in the stultifying darkness for the catch to the door lock. "No!" Redding's voice rasped above me, soft but urgent. His free hand, the one without the pistol, closed over mine. I huddled there, panting, my heart racing. I didn't smell very good anymore, either; I smelled like fear.

For the space of a few carefully drawn breaths we both just hung there in silence. Then Redding slowly released my hand and straightened up slightly. "I think they're gone," he whispered so quietly that had it not been for our crushing proximity, I never would have been able to hear him. "Don't move yet; I'm going to see if I can crack the doors."

The latch released with a tiny click. All that kept us both from tumbling right out into the room was Redding's tight grip on the lock. Through the narrow slot between the steel doors, he scanned the room. It was empty, but the lights were still on. Were the techs gone for good? And if not, how quickly might they come back?

Bound by the same questions, Redding whispered, a fraction louder than before, "We'd better wait a minute, just to be sure." He eased one of the doors open a few more inches and set his foot down outside the cabinet, levering his body sideways so that he could finally stand upright. He looked down at me, squinting in the sudden brightness of the room. "Can you get up?" he asked.

"I'm not sure," I admitted. I tried to rise, but my legs had gone numb from the knees down. Redding chucked his pistol into his waistband and reached down to help me up; I swayed distressingly, nearly falling. His arm caught me around the waist, and I lurched forward, bumping into him, our chins nearly colliding. I felt my teeth click together with an audible snap. Then I felt the tears—sudden, hot, inexplicable—begin to form in my eyes.

Redding embraced me, stumbling to keep his balance where he stood, half in and half out of the cabinet. I buried my face against the rough fabric of the shoulder of his dusty-green coveralls, sobbing convulsively. I didn't know what the hell was the matter with me; I felt vaguely angry with myself and horrified at my lack of control. And in some remote part of my mind I realized that if anyone had decided to enter the room right then, I would have gladly shot him outright rather than cram myself back into that steel cabinet again.

Redding held me tightly in his arms with a surprising tenderness I had ever expected from him—or had I? His hand gently swept the hair back from my wet cheek. He murmured to me in a soft voice, something senseless but comforting. The steady drumming of my pulse strengthened, sending a radiant flush of heat through my body, igniting something I had not anticipated with him. My fingers, clutching his coveralls, were trembling violently. I had to force myself to pull my head back, to meet his eyes. Blinking, I stared into that familiar face, astounded by what I felt for him. Lust or adrenaline: sometimes it's hard to tell them apart, they feel so much alike. I started to lift my mouth to his.

But Redding's hand came up, his fingers touching my lips in a soft gesture, much like a plea for silence. He made a funny sound deep in his throat, almost like a groan of pain. There was nothing cool about those gun-metal gray eyes now, nothing remote about him at all.

I wondered when I had so completely stopped under-standing myself, when I had become this total stranger. I gazed in amazement into Redding's eyes, the salt taste of my tears burning across my tongue. "Who—who are you?" I asked him quietly.

Redding swallowed; in his arms, I felt the movement as much as saw it. His hand dropped from my face. "I think," he said, "that I might be your father."

CHAPTER THIRTEEN

To disbelieve Redding never occurred to me, but to question the validity of his belief was automatic. "Why?" I asked him, my voice surprisingly level.

Redding's eyes dropped from mine; it was the first time he had ever backed down first with me. He slowly released his arm from around my waist, and I was grateful to find that I could stand unaided. He cleared his throat. "I shipped with your mother," he told me, his voice barely above a hoarse whisper. "We were lovers."

His choice of that archaic term over the ubiquitous "joiners" was curiously touching. I stared calmly at him. "But you're not sure," I reiterated evenly.

Redding cleared his throat again, softly. I had never seen him ill at ease before, and it affected me profoundly. He finally met my eyes again. He shook his head. "No. I—I don't know how to say this so it won't sound like I'm putting her down, but no, I'm not sure. I think that I was the only one, then, but—"

He broke off helplessly. And I looked into those clear gray eyes, eyes that were swimming with the memories of something so enormous that I wasn't sure how to take it all in. How had those eyes ever seemed so cool, so self-possessed to me? They were warm, like ash. They were the eyes my mother had once gazed into, her heart laid open to him—

"Jo—" Redding began, reaching for my arm. But I squirmed past him, pushing myself out of the cabinet and into the room.

"Let's go," I said calmly, rapidly scanning the empty room. "They're gone. And we don't have much time left."

Quite honestly, I had lost all track of time. But I was certain that most of Alexandria's twenty minutes was already gone, and we still hadn't found what we had come for. I started toward the door, forcing Redding to follow me. As I stepped through the threshold, the folly of my rashness became all too apparent when I rudely collided with two white-smocked techs.

The impact startled them as much as me and knocked all three of us apart. Behind me, Redding already had his beam pistol up. "In here!" he snapped to the techs, jerking his head back toward the room.

"What the hell are you—" one of them began, but Redding leveled the pistol in a businesslike manner, truncating the man's indignant question. The two techs stumbled into the room.

"No heroics and there'll be no mess," Redding assured them evenly, waving them toward the exam table. "All we want is a little information."

"How the hell did you get in here?" the more vocal of the pair persisted, obviously amazed that their security had been breached. I recognized his voice as that of the man who had stood right outside the steel cabinet only minutes earlier. He was tall and thin, a Normal with an imperfectly Restructured nose that was about a centimeter too long for his unassuming face.

"Magic," Redding replied, grinning mirthlessly. "Where are Lillard and the other Class Tens?"

At the mention of Lillard's name the two techs exchanged a quick, involuntary look of alarm. The second man, shorter and almost potbellied, with pale thinning hair, made a sudden leap sideways. He wasn't going for Redding—even MA techs aren't stupid enough to tackle an armed man—but toward the wall intercom panel. He never made it. Redding's shot caught him right behind the ear, spinning him around. Beam weapons are unnervingly quiet; the only sound was the soft *shuss* of vaporizing tissue. The tech crumpled to the floor, striking the edge of the exam table as he fell and trailing a thin streamer of fetid smoke.

"No heroics," Redding reiterated calmly to the remaining, horrified tech. There was a dull gleam in Redding's eyes: steel again, not ash. "Now, where are they?"

I had to reach out and grip the door frame to steady myself. My knees still felt disappointingly weak. I forced myself to keep my attention on the long-nosed tech and not on his dead companion on the floor. Then I sensed a familiar presence behind me. I didn't have to turn to know that the big hand that landed silently on my shoulder was Raydor's. I was desperately relieved that he was there.

Whether it was the sudden appearance of the new intruder, a hulking Tachs, or the unceremonious demise of his companion, the remaining tech was suddenly quite willing to speak. "L-Lillard is in the central Integration lab," he stammered. "It's on the third sublevel, north wing." He hesitated, then blurted out, "B-but you can't get in there—not without clearance."

"Yeah?" Redding drawled, his lip curling crookedly as he tipped up the barrel of the beam pistol. "We've got 'clearance,' right here."

I was terrified—quite suddenly and probably with nearly the same intensity as the tech himself—that now that he had what he wanted from the man, Redding would shoot him as well. But as I took an involuntary step forward, out from under Raydor's protective hand, and while the hapless tech scrunched up his face in a closed-eye grimace of anticipatory dread, Redding merely raised his gun hand and brought the butt of the pistol down in one sharp chop to the tech's temple. Knocked unconscious, the long-nosed man folded quietly to the floor. Then Redding turned to Raydor and remarked with casual irritation, "What the hell took you so long?"

Since Raydor's usual countenance was relatively expressionless, I'm not sure just what response that comment would have provoked under more normal circumstances. As it was, Raydor and Redding each just took one of the techs' bodies, wedged them into the steel cabinet, and locked it. Then Redding strode out into the corridor, leaving me and Raydor to catch up.

"Our time's running out," Redding announced, probably as much to himself as to us. "If this central Integration thing doesn't pan out, we've got to get the hell out of here."

"Before either of those techs are scheduled to report in again," Raydor added blandly.

I half choked at the veiled barb, but Redding ignored the comment. At the main corridor we found a lift and rode in silence down to the third sublevel. I stubbornly focused my thoughts on Lewis, Alexandria, and Lillard. Thinking about Redding would have been inappropriate and quite possibly dangerous.

The third-level corridor where we exited the lift was deserted. The curved hallways appeared identical to those of the first level. None of the doors appeared to be marked in any way, so the designation the tech had given us turned out to be pretty useless. But it really didn't matter, for I found, alarmingly and inexorably, that I knew which way to go. Lewis's pain was with me again, more strongly than ever, his terror like a throbbing beacon behind my eyes. I must have looked dazed—I know that I staggered slightly, nearly bumping into the blindingly white wall—because Raydor reached protectively for me.

"Jo?" he asked gruffly. "You all right?"

"This way—I can feel him," I murmured, lurching forward, pulling Raydor with me. Redding, the beam pistol still leveled in his hand, brought up the rear.

The barren, glaring corridors were bizarrely empty, disorientingly identical. But the closer we drew to our goal, the stronger the pulsing fear in me grew. Rather than repel me or turn me away, it only intensified the powerful compulsion I felt. *Lewis!* Oh, Light! It was like his heart was driving the blood through my veins, like his brain was ruling my dancing nerves, like his voice was crying the silent scream that was rapidly building inside my head. I was nearly running then, heedless of discovery.

The door to the central Integration lab was closed but

not sealed. Panting breathlessly, I slammed my palm against the lock panel, and the door cycled open. I half fell into the room. "Lewis!" I cried.

The lab was huge, nothing like the sterile little warrens we had explored on the upper level—a towering cathedral of light, a glittering, blinking maze of biomechanical components. The entire room was like one massive conglomerate Integrator, awash in the cruelly brilliant glare of high-intensity lights. The only reference scale, the only thing adding any sense of perspective—if not any sense of reality—to the nearly incomprehensible size of the thing was the two human figures: Lewis, slumped over the console board of what appeared to be the largest Integrator access panel I had ever seen, and Alexandria, standing behind him, her hand clutching his arm.

At the sound of my cry Lewis pulled himself up. He staggered when he tried to stand. I crossed the space between us in one frantic lurch and flung my arms around him, seizing him in a crushing embrace, while his tremendous pain broke over me like a tidal wave.

"Oh, God," I whispered: a nondenominational plea to all deities.

The back of Lewis's flightsuit was soaked through with sweat, and his body was trembling wildly in my arms. When I pulled back my head, I could see that his face was wet with tears. I held his shoulders tightly, but my voice still cracked. "What is it?" I whispered, feeling the sour whine of spent adrenaline burning in my veins.

Lewis's face was contorted with grief; it was somehow the most frightening expression I had ever seen on his face. Those brilliant blue eyes, overly intense, were like circuits on the verge of overload. "Lillard," he whispered thinly.

"What?" I repeated urgently, my fingers biting into his shoulders. I shook him gently as if to jar the answer free but no more words came. My eyes flew to Alexandria. Her broad, powerful face was frozen into stonelike stolidness. "What is it?" I asked her, nearly pleading.

"Lillard," she responded, infuriatingly obtuse. Damn

her! Maybe the sudden flash of anger in my eyes made her go on then, pushing her reluctantly forward.

"The Integrator," she began, gesturing at the monumental creation, "is Lillard." She blinked and her black eyes, glittering with tears, began to assume some animation again. "*Was* Lillard," she automatically corrected herself.

The enormity of what she had just proposed made me feel suddenly and overwhelmingly the consequences of everything else I had already been through on that bizarre and seemingly endless night. My hands slipped nervelessly from Lewis's shoulders, and I had to grip the edge of the console for support. I stared stupidly into Alexandria's heavily lined face. "They—*integrated* him?" I echoed hollowly. "A Class Ten—a *living* man?"

Had Alexandria somehow aged twenty years in the time since I had last seen her at the subterranean facility's entrance? She looked as though time had eaten greedily at her. Only those formidable eyes still seemed right: gleaming darkly, full of the old outrage.

"Yes, a Class Ten—a living man," she replied quietly, glancing up at the monstrous construct that filled the room around us. Gently, she rested one broad, callused hand on the gleaming surface of the console; the gesture was almost a caress. "They tried it on the other Class Tens first, one by one," she continued, her voice a soft growl. "But none of them survived the process. Something about them—a Class Ten's neurological biochemistry—they couldn't be integrated without going mad and destroying themselves." Her eyes, hardening, came back abruptly to my face. "With Lillard, they finally found a way to succeed."

Suddenly, emphatically, I didn't want to know any more of it. Lewis's terror bloomed in me anew, like a wash of acid through my veins. I just wanted to get out of that dreadful place and the horrifying spectacle it held. I slipped my arms around Lewis's waist, hugging his wiry body to mine; I held him fiercely, defiantly, protectively. But still Alexandria went on.

Her gaze swept almost fondly over the massive Integrator—the biomechanical construct that had once been a man. "They were able to prevent Lillard from terminating himself by implanting his biomatrix with a template made from a nest of neurons taken from one of his companions." She was looking at the Integrator, not at us. There was no need to look at us, because it was all so clear. "That companion was the last of the Class Tens they held: It was Lewis."

Fresh tears streamed across Lewis's face, soaking the shoulder of my flightsuit. He had found what he had been obsessed to seek; he had been searching for his soul and had found it enmeshed in the artificial brain of a machine.

"That's why he felt the compulsion to return here, even though he was terrified of it," Alexandria continued, needlessly now, her voice gone flat, totally without inflection. "Because a part of him is still here, in Lillard."

"You *knew*, didn't you?" I accused her, my voice a bitter rasp. "You *knew* they were doing this!" How else could she have gotten involved?

But Redding cut into our painful dialogue, announcing tersely, "Come on, we've got to get out of here."

Alexandria answered him, an abrupt swing of her head sending the frothy halo of her frizzy hair bouncing. Her hands spread possessively on the console. "No!" Her voice dropped a notch. "No," she repeated more calmly. "We can't just leave him here like this."

"Him?" Redding's expression was a classic mixture of concern and exasperation. He waved his beam pistol in an all-inclusive arc about the room. "You mean all this? Alexandria, there's no way in hell we can—"

But she interrupted him, her hand falling in a sharp chopping motion to the surface of the access panel. "We *can't* leave him," she repeated, her voice as taut as steel wire.

Redding's voice had leveled out, too, stretched as flat and toneless as the lab's gray poured-stone floor. "What do you mean, destroy it? If this thing goes prime, it'll take the whole complex out with it!"

"And I'm afraid I couldn't permit you to do that."

For one wildly disarticulated moment I had the weird impression that the low, neutral voice had come from the huge Integrator itself. But the speaker was a human being, and when she stepped out from behind one wing of the towering access console, I could see that she was a very real, corporeal woman, dressed in MA's cream and maroon, with an equally real beam pistol held aimed at Alexandria's head.

Across the room Redding froze, his weapon jerking slightly in his hand. The woman moved almost casually to Alexandria's side, her gaze taking in the rest of us with an ugly, feral grin.

"Hanlon!" Alexandria snarled, making the name an epithet.

The woman acknowledged Alexandria's expression of rage with a smug little nod. "So," she remarked sardonically, "it was you after all, Alexandria; I should have known it when our Mr. Lewis so mysteriously disappeared."

Hanlon was moving past middle age, gray-haired but probably cosmetically Restructured beyond any detectable chronology. Next to Alexandria's bulk she appeared almost diminutive, although she actually was nearly my height and decidedly plump. She was also normal, I thought, even despite the surgical conservations that had been performed on her. MA's surgeons never would have left her with that low forehead or that receding chin had she been Normalized. Her small eyes, the color of pale amber, were incongruously cold in that full and motherly face. And those reptilian eyes fixed Alexandria with contemptuous delight.

"I wanted my laboratory rat back," she smirked, "but I didn't expect to catch the poacher, too. I should have known I'd find you mixed up in all this, Alexandria." Briskly, she gestured with the pistol for Alexandria to move back from the console.

But Alexandria refused to be moved. Her broad hand still rested on the access panel. "You slime-joined *murderer*," she hissed, her black eyes as hard as obsidian. "You've *killed* him!"

Hanlon's gray brows rose in mock offense. "Murderer?" she echoed, her lips curling in a sneer. "How touching. Still coming to the defense of your old joiner, Alexandria? I haven't 'killed' him." She waved her free hand in an expansive arc, encompassing the entirety of the room. "He isn't dead—he's *evolved*!"

But Alexandria refused to be baited in that fashion; she just flared at the woman who had once been her teammate. "The private censure didn't affect you much, did it, Hanlon?" she prodded deftly. "Or did the Ethics Review Board just drive you underground?"

The gray-haired woman stiffened, the beam pistol jerking in her hand. So, she was vulnerable, after all. "Idealistic idiots!" she spit. "And you were as bad as any of them, Alexandria. You quit IRD just when together we could have made a tremendous breakthrough!"

"And what would that have been?" Alexandria taunted her. "Integrating living people—Citizens? *Class Tens*, for God's sake?"

Hanlon's predatory face tightened, her mouth twisting into a triumphant leer. "It worked, didn't it?" She waved her free hand again at the huge Integrator around us. "Damn it, Alexandria—it *worked*!"

"After you *murdered* five people," Alexandria retorted, "and tried to murder the sixth."

Hanlon's glance shifted briefly to Lewis and me. "That wouldn't have been necessary if you hadn't stolen him, Alexandria." She gave a short, mirthless laugh. "But you can see now that you were wasting your time with him. He *had* to come back here, anyway; we saw to that."

Alexandria's rage flared again, untempered, her head tossing, the manic hair whipping. "And how much more would you have been willing to do to Lillard to get Lewis back, Hanlon? Torturing him by shutting down his service cores one by one, driving him to the brink of madness by making him think you were ready to destroy him—"

Hanlon's face hardened into a snarl, and she gestured

emphatically, this time with the pistol. "Shut up! Just shut up. It's over, Alexandria. Move!"

It was Lewis who warned me. In his embrace, I felt the sudden jolt of adrenaline sailing into his veins as he sensed what Alexandria was going to do. I released him, spinning around, the cry half out of my mouth as I turned toward Alexandria.

"No!"

But it was too late. As Alexandria swung on her tormentor, amazingly agile for a person her size, she crossed her massive forearms like a bludgeon and launched herself at Hanlon. The soft whine of Hanlon's beam pistol was nearly lost in the loud *whump*! of their two bodies colliding. Hanlon hit the floor beneath Alexandria's plummeting mass. Her head made a cracking noise like a weak strut giving way, and her pistol skittered off across the lab's polished floor.

Redding had moved nearly as quickly as Alexandria had. He plunged to his knees as the two women fell. Not to my surprise, he had his beam pistol to Hanlon's head; again not to my surprise, he fired, point-blank. The back of Hanlon's skull vaporized, leaving a blackened and smoking shell.

"Alexandria!"

The actual cry came from Raydor; it could have come from any of us in the room. As we rushed around her, Redding gripped the big woman's shoulders. Quickly, but as gently as he could, he pulled her over and off her antagonist's body. The familiar broad face was convulsed in pain; blood was running from her nostrils and from the corner of her mouth. There was a big scorched mark in the center of her tunic, just below her breastbone. And in the middle of that scorched mark there was a charred, fist-sized hole.

Redding's head jerked up. There was a wild, agonized look on his face; tears streamed from his eyes. It frightened me to see him so uncharacteristically out of control. But his eyes didn't seek mine; they locked urgently and automatically with Lewis's.

"No!" I cried, wheeling around to grab for Lewis's arm.

But Lewis evaded me, already dropping to his knees beside Alexandria. With absolutely no hesitation and no more preparation than just tightly closing his eyes, Lewis plunged both of his hands into that smoking wound.

"No!" I repeated frantically, lunging forward to try to pull Lewis away from her. But Raydor seized me from behind, his huge arms grasping me in an unbreakable bear hug. "No, no, *no*!" I chanted, struggling desperately. "It'll kill him—Powers! Can't you see? It'll *kill* him!"

A rush of nausea went through me, a stunning visceral twist. I hung limply in Raydor's embrace. On the floor Lewis slumped and fell back from Alexandria with a groan. Blood trickled from his nostrils. Although there wasn't even a mark on the front of his flightsuit, the fabric was soaked in a large circle with blood. And although Alexandria's tunic was still dramatically ruptured, all that remained of her gaping wound was a slight, shiny dimple in her flesh.

Raydor released me—carefully, since I was still swaying unsteadily. I crouched on the floor, pulling Lewis into my arms, sobbing his name. Damn Alexandria! Her life wasn't worth his. How could he risk himself to—

But Lewis's eyes flew open, overly bright but lucid, and focused on my face. He pulled back from me, touching my wet cheek in a shaky gesture of reassurance. "I'm all right," he panted, trying to wipe his bloody nose with one sleeve. "Jo, I'm all right."

Stunned, I could only stare speechlessly at him: a Midas who had touched certain death and turned it into life again. Relief and astonishment rolled through me like a wave. Then, beside us, Alexandria groaned. Raydor and Redding were immediately attending her, helping her to her feet. She swayed uneasily for a moment; then she extended a trembling hand to Lewis.

"Now we've *really* got to get the hell out of here!" Redding proclaimed with some of his old asperity.

But Alexandria, still grasping Lewis's hand, helped me pull him slowly to his feet. Her dilated eyes locked with his. "Please," she beseeched him, her voice a hoarse whisper. "Do it, Lewis—tell him we *have* to do it!"

Redding and Raydor exchanged telling glances. I was certain Redding was on the brink of another protest, but neither of them could feel the bolt of pain that lanced through Lewis's heart. Only I could feel that.

"We don't have—" Redding began but I interrupted him vehemently, confronting Alexandria, literally shaking with anger.

"What are you going to make him do?" I demanded, my face flushed. "Destroy Lillard?"

Alexandria, no less stubborn for her flirtation with eternity, faced me squarely. "He's the only one who can do it, Jo," she told me firmly.

"No!" I protested. "If this thing has a part of Lewis— a template made from his cells—then how do you know that destroying it won't destroy him, too?"

With a certain grim sense of satisfaction I could see that that possibility hadn't occurred to Alexandria. But I suspect it had occurred to Lewis, because his response was swift and unnaturally composed.

"I'll go into the system," he told us quietly. "Use the cerebral leads—sever the connection."

I shook my head, belligerent even with him. "No," I repeated: my word of choice that night, it seemed. "It's too dangerous. What if you get trapped in there? There's no way in hell we could get you out again."

Lewis's hand squeezed my arm. "Jo, it's the only way," he said softly. "If we leave Lillard here, like this, I'm as good as dead, anyway. They'll continue to use him, and they'll always have control over me through him."

Void curse it! I could feel the tears, fresh and relentlessly close, pressing at my lids again. He was right, of course. There was—as always—no other way.

Nothing if not expeditious, Redding was already rifling through one of the access console's drawers for a set of leads. Hanlon and her cohorts must have been very busy with Lillard: There were at least a dozen sets of leads in the drawer. As I stood helplessly by, Redding and Raydor helped Lewis adjust the leads. While they hooked him to the access input plug, Lewis threw me one last, tenaciously reassuring look.

Jo . . .

Then, quite suddenly, Lewis's face went slack and expressionless. He slowly bent over the Integrator access panel, bracing his slumping body by draping himself across the console's surface. Every muscle in his body seemed to lose its strength simultaneously; he was boneless, nerveless, without form. It took me a few baffling moments to realize what was absent at last from my own brain and body: Lewis's terror, Lewis's pain. For the first time in days my consciousness was entirely, frighteningly my own.

Instead of being reassured and relieved by the radical contrast between Lewis's interaction with Handy at Nethersedge and this episode, I was abruptly alarmed. I glanced quickly at Alexandria's taut face, but she had no way to judge what was really happening to Lewis. All she or Redding or Raydor could see was that he was completely relaxed, sprawled tranquilly over the huge Integrator's access. Only I could feel that Lewis was already—*gone*.

Panicked beyond caution, I lunged forward and seized Lewis by his slackened shoulders. All three of the others leapt after me, shouting inarticulate cries of warning, but I clung to Lewis like a bulldog. After that I wasn't even aware of their less than gentle efforts to dislodge me; I couldn't feel them at all. Because from the moment I fused my body with Lewis's, I was propelled violently with him into Lillard's state of awareness, and everything that I could perceive was shockingly, wildly distorted.

Imagine falling: falling fast, the air rushing furiously, speed helplessly accelerating—

But never having to land.

Euphoria. Pleasure so intense that it's nearly painful.

The falling: like an orgasm that has no resolution; the closeness: like one flesh.

Knowing everything. Understanding everything—finally understanding everything:

Lillard is a big man, black-haired, like a good-humored bear, and he has the Talent of telekinesis, and he is Alexandria's lover, and I see them together, laughing at how funny the joining is, and Alexandria is a young woman, and he loves her and he loves her and he loves her—

And Lewis loves me.

Brilliant, like a flash of lightning, breaking over me in a great electric wave: Lewis loves me. It is an absolute thing, a verity so stunningly simple that it blinds me, terrifies me, fills me with its awesome light—

And I am falling and falling—

Suns! I landed hard. It took all three of them to pry me off Lewis, to wrestle me to the lab floor. My head cracked against the side of the console, jarring me back to non-Lillard reality, and I cried out spontaneously in pain and disappointment.

"By the Arm!" Redding was cursing, still pinning me to the floor even though I had ceased to struggle. "Are you trying to get yourself *killed*?"

"He's trapped," I panted, surprised to find that I had bitten my tongue. I nearly gagged on the sudden taste of blood.

"The template—" Alexandria began, finally comprehending the reason for my hysteria.

"He's fusing with Lillard," I elaborated, my voice cracking. I couldn't explain the rest of it: the sense of ecstasy, the oneness in the Integration, why Lewis couldn't return.

As the enormity of what was happening broke over them, Raydor, Redding, and Alexandria all bent over me, helping me to my feet. Lewis was still flopped limply across the console, his arms dangling jointlessly. He was as frighteningly lifeless as he had been when he had slumped in his chair on *Raptor*, after the Integration analysis, when Handy had—

"Great Light!" I exclaimed softly. "The chip."

My three companions were staring at me in baffled alarm; I must have looked more than a little crazy. My fingers clumsy with the urgency of adrenaline, I fumbled frantically in my flightsuit pocket for Lewis's last gift to me: the chip Handy had made of Lewis's total subconscious recall. Now it was a lifeline, a capsule of everything that Lewis was—and it just might be the only thing that could bring Lewis back. Struggling to align the little bit of plastic, I thrust the chip into the massive Integrator's input slot.

An Integrator's hypertrophied neurons reacted at a speed too great for the unaltered human brain to comprehend. A literal lifetime—Lewis's lifetime—careened through the huge construct in the space of seconds. I had barely inserted the chip before Lewis's body jerked back to life. He arced, his face contorted with a sudden effort of will. His hands, slick with perspiration, spread on the console's gleaming surface, and his body began to sway.

"Lewis?" I whispered, forcing myself not to touch him.

I was the only one close enough to hear the murmured fragments of Lewis's final contact with the monumental thing that he had once, however unwittingly, been a part of. "I'm sorry," he whispered, his shoulders shaking, the tears leaking from his closed lids. "So sorry . . . so sorry . . ."

And I wasn't sure if he was speaking for himself or for Lillard.

Then, abruptly, Lewis straightened. He swept the cerebral leads from his head with one absent wave of his hand. His eyes were clear, almost preternaturally lucid, and his mouth quickly assembled itself into a firm line. "We have to go now," he said with amazing calmness. "Lillard is going Prime Destruct; there's very little time left."

As we poured from the lab, Redding, his pistol at the ready, took the lead. "We're long overdue at the rendezvous point," he flung back at us, nearly jogging up the corridor. "They'll have had to go on without us."

"They damn well *better* have gone on without us,"

Alexandria retorted, surprising me with the intensity of the old fire in her voice. "If those idiots can't follow orders any better than that—"

I clung to Lewis's arm, letting him pull me along as we fled back toward the lifts. In spite of everything that had happened, he seemed to have twice the energy that I did. That strange rapport we had, that palpable emotional bond, was back and I could feel a strange new force throbbing in him—and me—a tautness that was not entirely unpleasant, a tension both aching and imperative. It was as though he had finally come back into his own. And as I stumbled after him down that empty, brilliantly lit corridor, I realized that in a way all of us had come into our own that night.

The lift carried us back up to the first sublevel. The five of us huddled wordlessly in the barren car. I meshed fingers with Lewis, squeezing tightly, more for my own comfort than for his. He kept glancing over at me, an incongruous mixture of fear and confidence in his eyes. He stood so close that our hips and shoulders touched.

We were a hundred meters back up the main corridor, headed toward the security door, when the sound of running footfalls reached us. No alarm had sounded, but reflexively we assumed the worst. As we flattened ourselves wedgelike against the curving wall, with Redding and his pistol at point, Martz burst into view. She was sprinting full out, the beam rifle held aloft like the standard of a flag. She slid to a halt, her eyes wide with alarm.

"Forget it," she panted, jerking her chin to indicate the direction from which she'd just come. "We've been breached!"

"What about the others?" Alexandria asked her.

Martz shook her head, her eyes darting over the front of Alexandria's conspicuously damaged tunic, her auburn brows arching. "I don't know," she gasped. "They got through by my station, but they may not be involved in the ruckus up there." She had to pause to catch her breath. "But one thing's for sure—we can't get back out that way. I had to seal the security door and fuse the lock from the inside.''

''Terrific,'' Redding snorted. ''That was the only way out of here.''

Martz glared at him, still puffing for breath. Her brows rose archly. ''I suppose you'd rather have a squadron of MA goons coming through?'' she retorted hotly.

Alexandria held up her hand, silencing their acerbic exchange. ''But our people got through?'' she reiterated.

Martz nodded. ''They should have gotten out of the building; they went past me a good ten minutes before those goons showed up.''

Alexandria touched Martz's arm in an almost motherly fashion; her expression was curiously serene. ''Then we've done all that we can,'' she said quietly, as if to herself.

But Redding shook his head, his hand with the beam pistol tightening into a white-knuckled fist. ''Uh-uh!'' he contradicted emphatically, waving the weapon toward the still-empty corridor. ''In about ten seconds that Prime Destruct intent is going to hit their main Integration system—and this whole joining place is going to go to general alert! We'll be stuck here like targets in a bombing range. We're not done until we get the hell *out* of here. There's *got* to be another way out.''

Redding reached for my arm and pulled me hard; I was stretched out between him and Lewis. But it was not the half-formed protest that sprang to my astonished lips that stopped Redding. It was Lewis.

''Wait,'' he said, his voice calm but absolutely firm. ''There might be another way out of here.''

We all were staring at him with varying degrees of hope and confusion.

''But in your analysis—'' Alexandria began.

''Another way,'' Lewis repeated, tightening his grip on my hand, ''a way I didn't know about. Lillard told me. But we have to hurry.''

''I'm all in favor of that,'' Redding muttered, releasing me.

Lewis had already spun around and started back up the

corridor, the way we had come, pulling me with him. We had gone only about fifty meters when the general alert Klaxons began to shriek.

CHAPTER
FOURTEEN

Having to go back into that brilliantly lit labyrinth of curved and featureless corridors was like having to reenter a nightmare fully awake. But Lewis set a relentless pace; with the single-mindedness of the possessed, his bone-wrenching grip on my fingers never slackened. Within a few minutes I was panting for breath as I stumbled after him at a near run.

The noise of the alert Klaxons was so loud that I couldn't even hear the others behind us, although I knew they were there, struggling to follow Lewis's lead. Raydor had one arm around Alexandria's waist, pulling her along despite her vehement insistence that, once again, she wasn't dead yet. I quickly lost all sense of where we were in the subterranean facility. For all I knew, we could have been going around in circles, and for some bizarre reason that thought almost seemed more amusing than alarming.

Still deafened by the Klaxons, I saw the beam fire before I heard it. Bright explosions of light erupted along the line of my peripheral vision: beam-weapon fire splattering off the gleaming white walls of the curved corridor. I spun around, causing Lewis to whip around so abruptly that he nearly fell. Behind us Martz had dropped to one knee, her beam rifle braced. Redding flung himself against the wall on the inside arc of the curve, his pistol leveled. Raydor pulled Alexandria past us, shouting, "Go, *go!*"

I knew it was stupid for me to stop, to try to stay and

fight. Lewis and I were nothing but unarmed targets. These were very real Security guards, not stunned and defenseless techs; they would be shooting to kill. But still I froze, reluctant to leave Redding and Martz to stand alone.

"Go on!" Redding bellowed, seeing my hesitation. He squeezed off an answering shot as he caught the flash of a cream and maroon uniform around the curve in the hallway. More beam fire bloomed, fusing long score marks on the walls into blackened slag. Foul smoke began to swirl around us.

With a superhuman lurch, Lewis jerked me forward again. From the corner of my eye I could see two guards, their beam rifles on full fire, rounding the curve. Redding took the first of them out; Martz's shot hit the second. Their bodies fell, rolling, but they had been dead on their feet. Martz had to leap over one of the fallen men to catch up with us. Then we all were running again.

"Where the hell is this exit?" Redding panted behind us.

"This way!" Lewis shouted, making a sudden turn down a side corridor. I flew helplessly after him, my arm nearly wrenched from its socket. I fervently hoped it wasn't too far; I just didn't have too much run left in me.

We literally collided with the second pair of MA guards at the end of the corridor. They stepped out from a doorway just as we were dashing past, and Raydor and Lewis ran right into them. All four of the men—and me, by extension—went sprawling on the floor. Even though Redding and Martz were right behind us, their weapons were at first of limited usefulness in the close tangle of bodies. I saw Raydor rear up, using his fists like a bludgeon on the guard beneath him. Beneath Lewis, the second guard struggled to raise his rifle, cursing impotently as he squirmed.

Several shots were fired at once. Although I had no way of seeing them coming, another pair of guards had just appeared in the hallway behind us. I twisted frantically on the floor, trying to get to my feet amid the flailing limbs, just as Redding opened fire on the second pair. One of the advancing guards went down. The other spun as if to retreat, but as he turned, he fired back at us. Redding bellowed in pain, smoke fuming up from the leg of his coveralls. Then Redding fired, taking down his fleeing assailant.

Martz and Alexandria had joined Raydor's cause, disarming the downed Security guard, but their heads all jerked up when they heard Redding cry out. And Lewis, reacting without volition to the sound of another human being in distress, suddenly stopped struggling with the man he had pinned on the floor. In that instant of inattention the guard beneath Lewis seized the advantage; he twisted the barrel of his rifle up between his and Lewis's bodies and fired.

Lewis gasped. Then he pulled back, a look of shock and rage on his pale face. A blackened hole had been burned in the chest of his flightsuit, and beneath that hole gaped a hideously mortal wound. Lewis went wild with pain. I had never seen such a look of pure and utter hatred on the face of another human being. Howling like a wounded animal, Lewis locked his hands around the guard's neck, sending the beam rifle clattering across the floor. Almost instantaneously, the smoking wound began to disappear from Lewis's chest, to reappear on the guard's neck, searing through the major vessels, leaving a grisly wound of fried blood and scorched tissue.

Martz grabbed Lewis by the collar of his flightsuit and practically lifted him to his feet. "That's enough!" she shouted. "Lewis! He's *dead*!"

I scrambled up, still stunned, and took hold of Lewis's arm. Lewis, obviously dazed, had to stagger to keep his balance.

"Holy Powers," I gasped, gaping at the mutilated body. "I—I didn't know you could do *that*!"

Lewis's eyes had regained their focus. Almost sheepishly, he tried to wipe his bloody hands on the front of his flightsuit. He shook his head in shocked commiseration. "I didn't know that I could, either," he admitted ruefully.

"Let's go," Redding interrupted, gathering up the

scattered beam weapons from the floor. "How much farther?"

"We're almost there," Lewis assured him, stumbling
forward again. Then he paused, hesitating, swinging
around like a hound catching scent. He noticed Redding's maimed leg. "You're hurt," he said accusingly.
And before Redding could protest or push past him,
Lewis dropped down on his knees beside him and touched
the wound.

Redding made an inarticulate little sound like a grunt
of dissent, but it was too late. Already the beam wound
had vanished from Redding's thigh and was fading with
amazing speed from its temporary position on Lewis's
leg. Then Lewis leapt to his feet and started rapidly up
the corridor again.

The hallway reached a dead end at a steel-faced door
locked with a complicated-looking coded access key system. Lewis slid to a halt, quickly scanning the code
board. Martz peered over his shoulder, but she shook her
head. "It's not the same!" Lewis exclaimed in frustration.

"Stand away," Raydor announced calmly. As we all
moved back, he raised the MA guard's beam rifle and
obliterated the entire panel. Then he nonchalantly kicked
the scorched door open.

Beyond the door there was another door. It wasn't the
kind of door that was amenable to beam fire, either. Like
the original steel vault door we had used to enter the
subterranean facility, it was a huge stainless-steel mono-
lith, set up into the wall at a forty-five-degree angle and
flanked by an impressive lock panel console.

"I'll be damned," Alexandria said in wonder. "Where
the hell did this come from?"

"It was the secret entrance they used when the underground facility was being constructed," Lewis explained
distractedly, examining the panel lock system. "But it's
been sealed ever since." Obviously, it wouldn't have done
for everyone on the upper levels to have seen some of the
things—and some of the people—that had been brought
in there.

Martz nodded toward the door, her brows arched skeptically. "You know how to open that?" she asked Lewis.

Lewis half shrugged, a boyish gesture that was so profoundly self-effacing for a man who had already performed miracles that I almost had to laugh out loud. "Lillard knows how to open it," Lewis said quietly. Silently, he surveyed the panel for a moment. His slender fingers spread gently over the buttons as if invoking some power that he could pull right out of thin air. Then he punched in a rapid sequence of numbers, and the gigantic doorway cycled open.

We all were nearly buried in a small avalanche of dirt, rocks, and assorted ornamental shrubbery that rained down through the gap left by the opened door. The slanted outer surface of the massive panels must have been buried under at least two meters of the research complex's ornate landscaping. Undaunted by the organic deluge, Lewis seized my hand and started scrambling up over the pile of rubble.

Outside, the cool air hit me like a balm. But the night sky was strangely awash with light. Twisting around against the pull of Lewis's grasp, I tried to orient myself in the darkness. We were nearly fifty meters from the aboveground portion of the complex, but I had no way of telling which side of the building we were on. Since I couldn't see the lights of the landing field and tower, I assumed we were on the far side of the complex, farthest from the port facility. But over the top of the huge building the sky pulsed with a weird orange glow.

No matter where we were, our only hope was to get away from the complex before Lillard went prime and took it out. When Lewis pulled me along, I stumbled after him, the manicured grass of the complex's plush lawn slick beneath my scrambling feet. In the darkness we tripped over low shrubbery and even a few pieces of abstract sculpture, but Lewis's pace never slackened. Then, as we rounded the corner of the complex, I felt what little remained of my breath leave me in one helpless gasp.

The entire landing field was afire, littered with the

blazing husks of incinerating ships. The explosive flames leapt into the night sky, coloring it a garish hue, their reflections dancing wildly off the thousands of glittering glass panes of the complex's windows. Black smoke roiled up in huge billowing clouds. The heat, even at that distance, was considerable. There was nothing skyworthy left on the whole field—hell, there was nothing even left in one piece on the whole field.

Considering that we'd left a rather obvious trail of bodies behind us, it wouldn't take MA Security long to figure out where we'd gone. Even if the existence of the abandoned underground entrance had been a secret till that time, its location would be rather apparent now. It looked like we were caught on the ground in MA's territory: definitely not the way I had planned on ending it. I clung tightly to Lewis's hand, my heart racing and my legs trembling with fatigue, watching the flames roll across the blazing field.

"Sweet Suns!" Redding exclaimed from behind us. "What the hell—the whole damned field has gone up!"

"I hope they got out," Alexandria said quietly. No one had to ask who she was referring to.

"Yeah," Martz echoed, staring into the voracious flames. "Now if *we* could just get the hell out."

"Shouldn't be a problem," Raydor remarked laconically.

I spun around to face him, amazed that Raydor would indulge in the nearest thing to humor a Tachs would permit himself in a situation as grave as ours. That's when I saw her, too: *Raptor*, hovering almost silently behind us like a glittering bird in the flame-seared sky.

For a moment no one spoke. I was the only one who understood; she was my ship. "Handy," I breathed softly, stirring my exhausted limbs into action. "Come on, let's go!"

I began to sprint across the slippery grass, leaving even Lewis behind as I raced toward my gently descending bird of prey. One of Handy's better landings! I thought gleefully, nearly giddy with relief, as the ship gracefully settled herself onto the complex's grounds. The heat of her belly sent streamers of steam roiling up from the damp turf. The boarding ramp arced daintily down. I half tripped over the sod, nearly braining myself on a hull strut, and slammed my palm against the access latch lock. The whir of that hatch opening was one of the sweetest sounds I had ever heard.

I galloped up the ramp, leaving the others behind, not even looking to see that they were following. Inside, I went directly to Control. Flinging myself across the Integrator access panel, I spread my grimy palm over the pristine sheen of Handy's curved input.

"You call this taking care of the ship?" I panted without preamble.

"I'm glad you're okay," Handy rumbled implacably, his deep voice maddeningly even. "It seems there's been a lot of damage done on the landing field, and someone is going to have to answer all these inquiries coming in from Port Security."

"You were supposed to take care of the ship," I repeated, my voice rising sharply.

Handy heaved an Integrator's equivalent of a sigh. "Well, she's not much of a ship without a crew," he offered calmly by way of explanation, not defense. "I'm programmed to protect you, Jo, remember?"

His logic was indefeasible, and I had been manipulated so many times that night that there was no capacity for argument left in me. I was aware that the others were crowding into Control behind me, but my focus was still totally on the fluttering lights of Handy's panel.

"This wasn't exactly what I had in mind," I told him dryly.

"Well, how was I supposed to know that?" Handy responded patiently. "You told me to do what I had to do."

I felt as though everything I had always known, everything I had held as true, had been routed out of me that night—carved out of my heart and mind, rearranged in some bizarre new pattern, and then poured back into me in one big shocking *glug*. Still physically dizzied, I swayed over the Integrator access. "Well, I'm liking your idea more and more all the time," I assured him.

"It kind of grows on you," Handy agreed placidly. "I just wish you hadn't made me cut the timing so close."

"*You* fried the field," Raydor said from over my shoulder, his voice filled with a pleased, admiring comprehension.

"Of course," Handy said. "You didn't want anyone from this place to be able to follow us back, did you?" His panel lights flickered almost capriciously. "And I waited until our other shuttle got clear, of course."

I could imagine *Raptor*'s high-intensity beam cannon driving across that complacent landing field, splattering the tarmac in a hail of liquid fire: Handy doing what he had to do.

From the hatchway to Control, Redding's stunned voice demanded indignantly, "How the hell did you know we weren't out here already? You could have fried *us*!"

But I knew the answer to that already. I dug into my flightsuit pocket, triumphantly producing my discarded detention cuff. Behind me, Raydor grinned broadly. "The transmitter," he explained. "He could keep track of where you and Lewis were by your cuffs."

"Of course," Handy repeated. "But now I suggest we lift—unless you want more boarders."

On the view screen I could see a disorganized smattering of Security personnel spilling out from one of the complex's main entrances. Apparently a few of them had also discovered our recent rudely excavated exit as well, for more guards were sprinting across the grassy verge behind the complex, too.

"Get her up, Handy," I said evenly, engaging his flight sequence.

Raydor dropped into his copilot's chair beside me. Behind us I heard the others scrambling to find a place to strap in. I fumbled with my harness, my fingers gone weak and clumsy from the sudden rush of relief I felt. Raydor finally had to lean across from his chair and help me fasten the catches.

Raptor lifted, spurning the tiny splats of beam fire di-

rected at us by the Security teams' rifles. All the ground
artillery had been taken out with the port facility. The
ground dropped away from below us in a dizzying spiral.
I clung to the arms of my chair, my eyes glued to the
view screen despite the sense of vertigo that view produced.

And when the end came, it was almost an anticlimax.
I heard a soft plopping sound, barely audible above the
whine of our lifters, then a series of staccato pops. The
center of the glass and stone monstrosity below us glowed
a brilliant gold, like the gleam of Camelot's sun. Then
the entire structure exploded in a fusillade of glistening
shards.

Good-bye, Lillard . . .

I squeezed my lids tightly shut against a sudden push
of tears. But I felt something else inside of me: something new, irrepressible, forged in triumph. And I
dropped back into my padded chair and let myself go as
the accelerating pull of our ascent took me.

CHAPTER
FIFTEEN

It was nearly dawn. A listless gray fog floated over the broken, greasy tarmac of the landing field at Nethersedge. The air was equally lifeless, depressingly muggy and promising to become hot. I stood with Redding near the boarding ramp of a *Nimbus* shuttle, the craft sitting just a wing's breadth from *Raptor*.

Raydor and Lewis were off with Alexandria, helping her to hastily salvage what she could of her personal belongings from her quarters. A group of Alexandria's Tachs and *Nimbus* crew members were loading the most valuable and easily portable items from the compound onto a second *Nimbus* shuttle nearby. It wouldn't take the MA forces at the research complex long to regroup and figure out what happened; it certainly wouldn't take them long to figure out who had been responsible for it, either. Nethersedge was no longer a safe port for all the scum of the galaxy, or for us.

A sweating crewman, hurriedly transcribing code numbers off a sled piled full of cargo containers, shouted something to Redding. "If you can," Redding called back in response. "But only if you can move it *fast*!"

At the second shuttle's ramp a wildly gesticulating Martz was trying to convince another dusty-green-clad worker that the bulky equipment he was struggling so valiantly to load would not be worth the cargo space. I smiled at her automatic assumption of authority.

I realized that Redding was looking at me. In spite of everything we had been through together, I acutely felt the awkwardness of the moment. I felt like I knew less than ever just what to expect from the man. Quickly, I filled the clumsy and obvious silence with the first comment that came to mind. Nodding toward Martz, I remarked, "I don't know why she did it, but I'm sure glad she came with us."

Redding snorted in agreement. "Yeah," he replied, glancing toward his once-again red-haired crew member. "Guess I'll have to promote her—that is, if I don't have to space her for insubordination first."

"You said she had her reasons," I continued, frankly curious now as well as trying to make conversation.

"Yeah," Redding responded. He tugged unconsciously at the tattered leg of his coveralls, where the fused fabric around the edges of the burn hole still stuck to his unmarked skin. "You remember Bertram, the guy we had who infiltrated the complex?"

I nodded, still puzzled.

Redding glanced down at his coveralls leg as if discovering for the first time the scorched hole in the material. "Well, Martz and Bertram were—" He shrugged. "They'd been real close for a long time," he completed.

My brows rose as I remembered the passionate farewell scene I'd witnessed between Martz and the mustached crew member in the red hangar. "But right before we left yesterday, I saw her, and—"

Redding looked over at me, making a dismissive gesture with his hand. "Hell, that was her brother," he explained with a hint of his old quirky smile on his lips.

Martz and Bertram. Somehow it all made more sense, especially when I recalled the chilling sight of the red-headed woman calmly gunning down the Security chief in the research complex.

Redding and I both began to speak at the same time. Then we both stopped, each staring expectantly at the other. "You first," he insisted.

"You're taking Alexandria off here," I said. "Where will you take her?"

Redding shrugged, a trace of the old guardedness returning to his expression. "Wherever she wants to go," he replied too easily. "It's a big galaxy."

"Would you do something for me?" I asked him quietly.

His gray eyes narrowed. I could see the emotions warring there: curiosity, doubt, hope, apprehension. "What?" he asked warily.

"Lewis," I replied. "Will you take him off with you?"

Redding's expression was one of unconcealed surprise. "You're not taking him with you?" he asked me, obviously puzzled.

I shook my head. "No, it's too dangerous. He wouldn't be safe with me right now." I glanced down at the cracked tarmac for a moment before I went on. "I want to give the situation a little time to cool off."

Redding scrutinized me with his old familiar bluntness, forcing my gaze to lift to meet his. "The situation with MA or the situation with Lewis?" he asked me wryly. But when I failed to respond to that, he let it go and picked up on the first part of my comment. "Just where the hell do you think he *would* be safe?"

"Heinlein."

Redding gave a skeptical snort. "You sure you want him there?"

I just smiled a small, tight smile. "Oh, I'm sure that by now Mahta has booted MA's collective ass off-planet. She's not exactly known for her goodwill where the A's are concerned." I met his eyes more easily. "Besides, this whole thing is going to blow wide open very quickly; there'll be a big shake-up in MA. I don't think anyone's going to bother to look for Lewis now—not there, anyway, and not if I don't bring him in."

Redding just shrugged casually, as if it was of no concern to him. "Sure, I'll take him for you."

I looked steadily into those calm gray eyes. "There's something else, too, as long as you're going to Heinlein."

To his credit, Redding did not bother to feign mild curiosity this time. I think my expression told him what he needed to know.

"The Registry of Genetic Profiles," I went on quickly. "My mother and I both have chromosomal indices filed there." I paused, feeling a sudden chilling stab of doubt. "If you really want to know," I rushed on awkwardly.

Redding reached out, gripping both my arms. "Of course I want to know," he whispered roughly, his voice catching thickly in his throat.

I could have embraced him then. I could even have given him the chance to embrace me. But I wasn't capable of either capitulation yet. "I'll meet you there, then," I said levelly, stepping back from him, forcing him to release me. "Once all this blows over."

A ground car was speeding toward us across the foggy field, sending a wake of oily mist shooting around it. I recognized Raydor's style of driving. He, Lewis, and Alexandria stepped out from the car. Several of the Tachs left the task of loading the *Nimbus* shuttle to attend to the transfer of Alexandria's personal effects. Raydor, carrying a small cargo crate, nodded to me as he headed for *Raptor*'s hatch.

"Stars, Alexandria," Redding complained elaborately as she and Lewis approached us. "What the hell do you have there, half the damned compound?"

Alexandria just snorted. Her dark eyes had regained most of their old luster. "This is nothing," she asserted. "I'll have to leave almost everything behind."

"I'm sorry," I said with genuine regret.

But Alexandria just pounded my shoulder good-naturedly and shrugged her all-purpose shrug. "Got to leave something for the next Queen of the Pirates," she explained philosophically.

Lewis had come up beside me; he was within touching distance, but we did not touch. Even at that, his nearness reverberated in me, making everything to the very tips of my fingers ache.

"So," Alexandria went on, "where are you off to now, Jo?" She spoke matter-of-factly, almost cheerily, as if we were all going off on some lark and not running for our lives.

I avoided Lewis's eyes. "We're going to have to lay

low for a while," I told her, my voice carefully neutral. "For now I just want to get out-system. Then, eventually, probably Heinlein."

"Heinlein?" Alexandria laughed, the sound encouragingly raucous. "Hell, I may drop in on Mahta myself. She'll be thrilled to see me, I'm sure." She punched Redding's arm. "What do you say, Captain?" she teased him.

Redding's expression remained perfectly bland. "Anywhere you want to go, Alexandria," he told her.

Quickly then, before I lost my desperate resolve, I turned to face Lewis. I had wished for some kind of private good-bye, something more than our last hasty embrace when we had touched down again at Nethersedge. But I knew that if I were to confront him in private, there might very well be no good-bye at all. If I even allowed myself to touch him—hold him, feel his lips—well, there was just no way I would have been able to do what I had to do. And so I looked evenly into those brilliant cerulean eyes, eyes that had trapped me forever, and said, "I want you to go with Alexandria and Redding to Heinlein."

The enormous pain in those stunning blue eyes never reached Lewis's voice, which was so tightly controlled that he had to force out each word in separate syllables. "What about you?" he asked me tersely.

The only way I could possibly go through with it was to try to stare right through him, right past those anguished, betrayed eyes and into some imaginary place deep within, a place where I had to believe that he would understand why I had to do it to him, to us. "I'll meet you there later, when it's safe," I replied.

Lewis was silent a moment, unblinking, motionless. He was his own man now; he could have gone anywhere he pleased. But he wanted to go with me. His longing throbbed in me—his anxiety, his despair, his tremendous desire. He had taken me over, *become* me. As surely as he had once been a part of that monstrous creation Lillard had become, Lewis was a part of me. And I didn't know what would happen to either one of us without the other.

At last his head dipped in an abrupt nod: the final acquiescence. "All right," he said quietly.

I had never wanted more to touch him, even just to feel his fingers on mine. It was almost physically impossible for me to step back from him then, to just turn away.

But I did.

I nodded a silent farewell to Redding and Alexandria and then forced myself to move away across the cracked and pitted tarmac toward my ship.

"See you on Heinlein," Alexandria called after me. "We'll save you some real meat."

But I didn't look back. I felt those perfect blue eyes, swimming with tears, on my back as I climbed *Raptor*'s boarding ramp. I was shaking then, and my hands fumbled a moment with the mechanism to raise the ramp. But I didn't turn. I couldn't.

Because if I had turned, I never would have gone.

ABOUT THE AUTHOR

KAREN RIPLEY, a Wisconsin native, was "born with the soul of a farmer in postagricultural America" and was an inveterate storyteller as a child. She learned to write at the age of four and, after discovering science fiction and fantasy in high school, had her first short story published in *Worlds of If* at the age of eighteen.

After graduating from the University of Minnesota in 1973 as a doctor of veterinary medicine, she went into private practice in her hometown. Her long-neglected interest in science fiction and fantasy was rekindled in 1983 when she discovered the world of organized fandom and SF conventions.

Besides reading and writing, her interests include "recreational bicycling, the Old West, and growing things." She still lives in Wisconsin, where she is the "sole support of several Arabian horses, a quartet of peacocks, and two large and otherwise useless dogs."

Prisoner of Dreams is her first novel.